PUFFIN BOOKS

The Truth about Forever

Hi there,

Here's a confession for you: I've always been a bit of a perfectionist. I know, I know, there's no such thing as truly perfect, but that's never stopped me from trying anyway. Which is why I can relate so much to Macy, the narrator of *The Truth about Forever*. When her entire life falls apart, the only way she can think of to make things feel okay again is to do everything in her life *exactly* right. But I know I've discovered – and I'm sure you have too – that perfection isn't the answer to everything. Sometimes we just need a little help from our friends to see things differently.

The Truth about Forever is a book about loss, but also all we have to gain: new friendships, new chances and the realization that, sometimes, the unpredictability of the world around us is exactly what we need to learn to live. Writing this book made me feel a little better about my own imperfections. I hope that maybe you'll feel the same way.

Let me know by dropping me a line through my website, *sarahdessen.com*, where you'll also find links to my MySpace page, info about my other novels and my blog.

Happy reading!

Sarah Dessen

Books by Sarah Dessen

JUST LISTEN

THE TRUTH ABOUT FOREVER

sarahdessen.com

The Truth about Forever

Sarah Dessen

PUFFIN BOOKS

Published by the Penguin Group
Penguin Books Ltd, 80 Strand, London WC2R 0RL, England
Penguin Group (USA) Inc., 375 Hudson Street, New York, New York 10014, USA
Penguin Group (Canada), 90 Eglinton Avenue East, Suite 700, Toronto, Ontario, Canada M4P 2Y3
(a division of Pearson Penguin Canada Inc.)
Penguin Ireland, 25 St Stephen's Green, Dublin 2, Ireland (a division of Penguin Books Ltd)
Penguin Group (Australia), 250 Camberwell Road, Camberwell, Victoria 3124, Australia
(a division of Pearson Australia Group Pty Ltd)
Penguin Books India Pvt Ltd, 11 Community Centre, Panchsheel Park, New Delhi – 110 017, India
Penguin Group (NZ), 67 Apollo Drive, Rosedale, North Shore 0632, New Zealand
(a division of Pearson New Zealand Ltd)
Penguin Books (South Africa) (Pty) Ltd, 24 Sturdee Avenue, Rosebank,
Johannesburg 2196, South Africa

Penguin Books Ltd, Registered Offices: 80 Strand, London WC2R 0RL, England

puffinbooks.com

First published in the USA by Viking, a member of Penguin Group (USA), Inc. 2004
First published in Great Britain by Penguin Books 2008
12

Set in ITC Century Book
Made and printed in England by Clays Ltd, St Ives plc

British Library Cataloguing in Publication Data
A CIP catalogue record for this book is available from the British Library

ISBN: 978-0-141-32292-6

www.greenpenguin.co.uk

Penguin Books is committed to a sustainable future for our business, our readers and our planet. The book in your hands is made from paper certified by the Forest Stewardship Council.

For Jay, as ever, and for my cousins

who, like me, know by heart the view
of the river and the bay,
the complex rules of Beckon,
and all the ways you Can't Get to Heaven

to name you all would be a book in itself:
you know who you are.

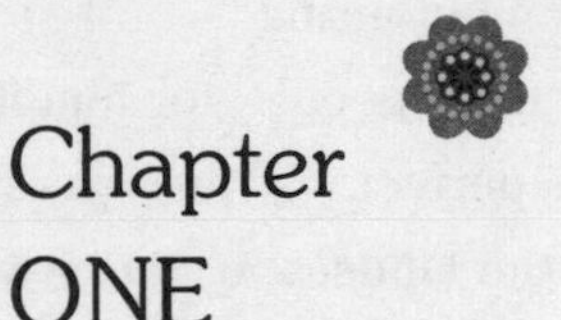

Chapter ONE

Jason was going to Brain Camp. It had another name, a real name, but that's what everyone called it.

'Okay,' he said, wedging a final pair of socks along the edge of his suitcase. 'The list. One more time.'

I picked up the piece of paper beside me. 'Pens,' I said. 'Notebooks. Phone card. Camera battery. Vitamins.'

His fingers moved across the contents of the bag, finding and identifying each item. Check and double-check. With Jason, it was always about being sure.

'Calculator.' I continued, 'Laptop . . .'

'Stop,' he said, putting up his hand. He walked over to his desk, unzipping the slim black bag there, then nodded at me. 'Skip down to list number two.'

I scanned down the page, found the words LAPTOP (CASE) and cleared my throat. 'Blank CDs,' I said. 'Surge protector. Headphones . . .'

By the time we'd covered that, then finished the main list – stopping to cover two other sub-headings, TOILETRIES and MISCELLANEOUS – Jason seemed pretty much convinced he had everything. Which did not, however, stop him from continuing to circle the room, mumbling to himself. It took a lot of work to be perfect. If you didn't want to break into a sweat, there was no point in even bothering.

Jason knew perfect. Unlike most people, for him it wasn't some distant horizon. For Jason, perfect was just over the next hill, close enough to make out the landscape. And it wasn't a place he would just visit. He was going to live there.

He was the all-state maths champ, head of the debate team, holder of the highest GPA in the history of our high school (he'd been taking AP classes since seventh grade, college sections since tenth), student council president two years running, responsible for an innovative school recycling programme now implemented in districts around the country, fluent in Spanish and French. But it wasn't just about academics. Jason was also a vegan and had spent the past summer building houses for Habitat for Humanity. He practised yoga, visited his grandmother in her rest home every other Sunday and had a pen pal from Nigeria he'd been corresponding with since he was eight years old. Anything he did, he did well.

A lot of people might find this annoying, even loathsome. But not me. He was just what I needed.

I had known this from the first day we met, in English class, second year of high school. We'd been put into groups to do an assignment on *Macbeth*, me and Jason and a girl named Amy Richmond who, after we pulled our desks together, promptly announced she was 'no good at this Shakespeare crap' and put her head down on her backpack. A second later, she was sound asleep.

Jason just looked at her. 'Well,' he said, opening his textbook, 'I guess we should get started.'

This was right after everything happened, and I was in a silent phase. Words weren't coming to me well; in fact I had trouble even recognizing them sometimes, entire sentences seeming like they were another language, or backwards, as my eyes moved across them. Just printing my own name on the top of a page a few days previously, I'd second-guessed the letters and their order, not even sure of that any more.

So of course *Macbeth* had totally mystified me. I'd spent the entire weekend struggling with the antiquated language and weird names of the characters, unable to even figure out the most basic aspects of the story. I opened my book, staring down at the lines of dialogue: *Had I but died an hour before this chance/I had liv'd a blessed time; for, from this instant,/ There's nothing serious in mortality,/All is but toys.*

Nope, I thought. *Nothing*.

Luckily for me, Jason, who was not about to leave his grade in someone else's hands, was used to taking control of group work. So he opened his notebook to a clean page, pulled out a pen and uncapped it. 'First,' he said to me, 'let's just get down the basic themes of the play. Then we can figure out what to write about.'

I nodded. All around us I could hear our classmates chattering, the tired voice of our English teacher, Mr Sonnenberg, telling us again to please settle down.

Jason skipped down a few lines on his page. *Murder*, I watched him write. His handwriting was clean, block-style, and he moved across the page quickly. *Power. Marriage. Revenge.*

Prophecy. Politics. It seemed like he could go on forever, but then he stopped and looked at me. 'What else?' he asked.

I glanced back down at my book, as if somehow the words there would suddenly form together into something coherent. I could feel Jason looking at me, not unkindly, just waiting for me to contribute.

'I don't . . .' I said finally, then stopped, the words sticking. I swallowed, then started over. 'I don't understand it. Actually.'

I was sure, hearing this, he'd shoot me the same look he'd given Amy Richmond. But Jason surprised me, putting down his pen. 'Which part?'

'Any of it,' I said, and when he didn't roll his eyes as I'd been expecting, I added, 'I mean, I know there's a murder plot and I know there's an invasion but the rest . . . I don't know. It's totally confusing.'

'Look,' he said, picking up his pen again. 'It's not as complicated as you think. The key to really understanding is to start with the prophecy about what's going to happen . . . see, here . . .' He started flipping pages in his book, still talking, and pointed out a passage to me. Then he read it aloud, and as his finger moved across the words it was like he changed them, magic, and suddenly they made sense.

And I felt comfort. Finally. All I'd wanted for so long was for someone to explain everything that had happened to me in this same way. To label it neatly on a page: this leads to this leads to this. I knew, deep down, it was more complicated than that, but, watching Jason, I was hopeful. He took the mess that was *Macbeth* and fixed it, and I had to wonder if he might, in some small way, be able to do the same for me. So I moved myself closer to him, and I'd been there ever since.

Now, he zipped up his laptop case and put it on the bed with the rest of his stuff. 'Okay,' he said, taking one last glance around the room. 'Let's go.'

His mom and dad were already in their Volvo when we came outside. Mr Talbot got out, opened the trunk and he and Jason took a few minutes getting everything situated. As I got in the back seat and put on my seat belt, Mrs Talbot turned round and smiled at me. She was a botanist, her husband a chemist, both of them professors. They were so scholarly that every time I saw either of them without a book in their hands they looked weird to me, as if they were missing their noses, or their elbows.

I tried not to think about this as she said, 'So, Macy. What are you going to do until August without Jason?'

'I don't know,' I said. I was working at the library, taking over Jason's job at the information desk, but other than that, the next eight weeks were just looming ahead, empty. While I had a few friends from student council, most had gone away for the summer themselves, to Europe or camp. To be honest, Jason's and my relationship was pretty time consuming: between yoga classes and student government stuff, not to mention all the causes we dealt with, there just hadn't been much time for anyone else. Besides, Jason got easily frustrated with people, so I'd been hesitant to invite new people out with us. If they were slow, or lazy in any way, he lost patience fast, and it was just easier to hang out with him, or with his friends, who could keep up with him. I'd never really thought about this as a bad thing, actually. It was just how we were.

On the way to the airport, Jason and his dad discussed some elections that had just happened in Europe, his mom fretted about construction traffic and I sat there, looking at the inch between Jason's knee and mine and wondering why I didn't try to move closer to him. This wasn't new. He hadn't even kissed me until our third date, and now, after a year and a half, we still hadn't discussed going all the way. At the time we met, someone just hugging me still felt like too much to bear. I didn't want anyone to get too close. So this had been all I wanted, a boy who understood how I felt. Now, though, I sometimes wished for more.

At the airport, we said goodbye at the gate. His parents hugged him, then discreetly walked across the waiting room to stand at the window there, looking out at the runway and the big stretch of blue sky that hung over it. I put my arms round Jason, breathing in his smell – sport stick deodorant and acne cleanser – deeply, so I'd get enough to last me a while.

'I'm going to miss you,' I told him. 'So much.'

'It's only eight weeks,' he said.

He kissed me on the forehead. Then, quickly, so quickly I didn't even have time to react, on the lips. He leaned back and looked at me, tightening his arms round my waist.

'I'll email you,' he said, and kissed me on the forehead again. As they called his flight and he disappeared down the hallway to the plane, I stood with the Talbots and watched him go, feeling a tug in my chest. It was going to be a long summer.

I'd wanted a real kiss, something to remember, but I'd long ago learned not to be picky in farewells. They weren't guaranteed or promised. You were lucky, more than blessed, if you got a goodbye at all.

My dad died. And I was there.

This was how people knew me. Not as Macy Queen, daughter of Deborah, who built pretty houses in brand new cul-de-sacs. Or as sister of Caroline, who'd had just about the most beautiful wedding anyone had ever seen at the Lakeview Inn the previous summer. Not even as the one-time holder of the record for the fifty-yard dash, middle-school division. Nope. I was Macy Queen, who'd woken up the day after Christmas and gone outside to see her father splayed out at the end of the road, a stranger pumping away at his broad chest. I saw my dad die. That was who I was now.

When people first heard this, or saw me and remembered it, they always made that face. The one with the sad look, accompanied by the cock of the head to the side and the softening of the chin – *oh my goodness, you poor thing.* While it was usually well intentioned, to me it was just a reaction of muscles and tendons that meant nothing. Nothing at all. I hated that face. I saw it everywhere.

The first time was at the hospital. I was sitting in a plastic chair by the drink machine when my mother walked out of the small waiting room, the one off the main one. I already knew this was where they took people to tell them the really bad news: that their wait was over, their person was dead. In fact, I'd just watched another family make this progression, the ten or so steps and the turn of a corner, crossing over from hopeful to hopeless. As my mother – now the latter – came towards me, I knew. And behind her there was this plump nurse holding a chart, and she saw me standing there in my sweatpants and baggy sweatshirt, my old smelly running shoes, and she made the face. *Oh, poor dear.* Then, though, I had no idea how it would follow me.

I saw The Face at the funeral, everywhere. It was the common mask on the people clumped on the steps, sitting quietly murmuring in the pews, shooting me sideways looks that I could feel, even as I kept my head down, my eyes on the solid black of my tights, the scuffs on my shoes. Beside me, my sister, Caroline, sobbed: through the service, as we walked down the aisle, in the limo, at the cemetery, at the reception afterwards. She cried so much it seemed wrong for me to, even if I could have. For anyone else to join in was just overkill.

I hated that I was in this situation, I hated that my dad was gone, I hated that I'd been lazy and sleepy and had waved him off when he'd come into my room that morning, wearing his smelly Waccamaw 5K shirt, leaning down to my ear to whisper, *Macy, wake up. I'll give you a head start. Come on, you know the first few steps are the hardest part.* I hated that it had been not two or three but five minutes later that I changed my mind, getting up to dig out my sweatpants and lace my shoes. I hated that I wasn't faster on those three-tenths of a mile, that by the time I got to him he was already gone, unable to hear my voice, see my face, so that I could say all the things I wanted to. I might have been the girl whose dad died, the girl who was there, and everyone might have known it. Like so much else, I could not control that. But the fact that I was angry and scared, that was my secret to keep. They didn't get to have that too. It was all mine.

When I got home from the Talbots', there was a box on the porch. As soon as I leaned over and saw the return address, I knew what it was.

'Mom?' My voice bounced down the empty front hall as I came inside, bumping the door shut behind me. In the dining room, I could see fliers stacked around several floral arrangements, everything all set for the cocktail reception my mother was hosting that night. The newest phase of her neighbourhood, luxury townhouses, was just starting construction, and she had sales to make. Which meant she was in full-out schmooze mode, a fact made clear by the sign over the mantel featuring her smiling face and her slogan: *Queen Homes – Let Us Build Your Castle.*

I put the box on the kitchen island, right in the centre, then walked to the fridge and poured myself a glass of orange juice. I drank all of it down, rinsed the cup and put it in the dishwasher. But it didn't matter how I busied myself. The entire time, I was aware of the box perched there waiting for me. There was nothing to do but just get it over with.

I pulled a pair of scissors out of the island drawer, then drew them across the top of the box, splitting the line of tight brown packing tape. The return address, like all the others, was Waterville, Maine.

Dear Mr Queen,

As one of our most valued EZ Products customers, please find enclosed our latest innovation for your perusal. We feel assured that you'll find it will become as important and time-saving a part of your daily life as the many other products you've purchased from us over the years. If, however, for some reason you're not completely satisfied, return it within thirty days and your account will not be charged.

Thank you again for your patronage. If you have any questions, please feel free to contact our friendly customer service staff at the number below. It's for people like you that we work to make daily life better, more productive and, most of all, easy. It's not just a name: it's a promise.

Most cordially,

Walter F. Tempest
President, EZ Products

I scooped out Styrofoam peanuts, piling them neatly next to the box, until I found the package inside. It had two pictures on the front. In the first one, a woman was standing at a kitchen counter with about twenty rolls of tinfoil and waxed paper stacked up in front of her. She had a frustrated expression on her face, like she was about two breaths away from some sort of breakdown. In the picture beside it, the woman was at the same counter. Gone were the boxes, replaced instead by a plastic console, which was attached to the wall. From it, she was pulling some plastic wrap, now sporting the beatific look usually associated with madonnas or people on heavy medication.

Are you tired of dealing with the mess of so many kinds of foil and wrap? Sick of fumbling through messy drawers or cabinets? Get the Neat Wrap and you'll have what you need within easy reach. With convenient slots for sandwich and freezer bags, tinfoil and waxed paper, you'll never have to dig through a drawer again. It's all there, right at your fingertips!

I put the box down, running my finger over the edge. It's funny what it takes to miss someone. A packed funeral, endless sympathy cards, a reception full of murmuring voices, I could handle. But every time a box came from Maine, it broke my heart.

My dad loved this stuff: he was a sucker for anything that claimed to make life simpler. This, mixed with a tendency to insomnia, was a lethal combination. He'd be downstairs, going over contracts or firing off emails late into the night, with the TV on in the background, and then an infomercial would come on. He'd be sucked in immediately, first by the happy, forced banter between the host and the gadget designer, then by the demonstration, followed by the bonus gifts, just for ordering Right Now, by which point he was already digging out his credit card with one hand as he dialled with the other.

'I'm telling you,' he'd say to me, all jazzed up with that prepurchase enthusiasm, 'that's what I call an *innovation*!'

And to him, it was: the Jumbo Holiday Greeting Card Pack he bought for my mother (which covered every holiday from

Kwanzaa to Solstice, with not a single Christmas card), and the plastic contraption that looked like a small bear trap and promised the perfect French twist, which we later had to cut out of my hair. Never mind that the rest of us had long ago soured on EZ Products: my father was not dissuaded by our cynicism. He loved the *potential*, the possibility that there, in his eager hands, was the answer to one of life's questions. Not 'Why are we here?' or 'Is there a God?' These were queries people had been circling for aeons. But if the question was, 'Does there exist a toothbrush that also functions as a mouthwash dispenser?' the answer was clear: yes. Oh, yes.

'Come look at this!' he'd say, with an enthusiasm that, while not exactly contagious, was totally endearing. That was the thing about my dad. He could make anything seem like a good time. 'See,' he'd explain, putting the coasters cut from sponges/talking pocket memo recorder/coffeemaker with remote-control on-off switch in front of you, 'this is a great idea. I mean, most people wouldn't even think you could come up with something like this!'

Out of necessity, if nothing else, I'd perfected my reaction – a wow-look-at-that face, paired with an enthusiastic nod – at a young age. My sister, the drama queen, could not even work up a good fake smile, instead just shaking her head and saying, 'Oh, Dad, why do you buy all that crap, anyway?' As for my mother, she tried to be a good sport, putting away her top-end coffeemaker for the new remote-controlled one, at least until we realized – after waking up to the smell of coffee at 3 a.m. – that it was getting interference from the baby monitor next door and brewing spontaneously. She even tolerated the tissue dispenser he installed on the visor of her BMW (*Never risk an accident reaching for a Kleenex again!*), even when it dislodged while she was on the highway, bonking her on the forehead and almost hurling her into oncoming traffic.

When my dad died, we all reacted in different ways. My sister seemed to take on our cumulative emotional reaction: she cried so much she seemed to be shrivelling right in front of our eyes. I sat quiet, silent, angry, refusing to grieve, because it seemed like to do so would be giving everyone what they wanted. My mother began to organize.

Two days after the funeral, she was moving through the house with a buzzing intensity, the energy coming off her palpable enough to set your teeth chattering. I stood in my bedroom door, watching as she ripped through our linen closet, tossing out all the nubby washcloths and old twin sheets that fitted beds we'd long ago given away. In the kitchen, anything that didn't have a match – the lone jelly glass, one freebie plate commemorating Christmas at Cracker Barrel – was tossed, clanking and breaking its way into the trash bag she dragged behind her from room to room, until it was too full to budge. Nothing was safe. I came home from school one day to find that my closet had been organized, rifled through, clothes I hadn't worn in a while just gone. It was becoming clear to me that I shouldn't bother to get too attached to anything. Turn your back and you lose it. Just like that.

The EZ stuff was among the last to go. On a Saturday morning, about a week after the funeral, she was up at 6 a.m., piling things in the driveway for Goodwill. By nine, she'd emptied out most of the garage: the old treadmill, lawn chairs and boxes of never-used Christmas ornaments. As much as I'd been worried about her as she went on this rampage, I was even more concerned about what would happen when she was all done, and the only mess left was us.

I walked across the grass to the driveway, sidestepping a stack of unopened paint cans. 'All of this is going?' I asked as she bent down over a box of stuffed animals.

'Yes,' she said. 'If you want to claim anything, better do it now.'

I looked across these various artefacts of my childhood. A pink bike with a white seat, a broken plastic sled, some life jackets from the boat we'd sold years ago. None of it meant anything, and all of it was important. I had no idea what to take.

Then I saw the EZ box. At the top, balled up and stuffed in the corner, was the self-heating hand towel my dad had considered a Miracle of Science only a few weeks earlier. I picked it up carefully, squeezing the thin fabric between my fingers.

'Oh, Macy.' My mother, the stuffed-animal box in her arms, frowned at me. A giraffe I vaguely remembered as belonging to my sister was poking out the top. 'You don't want that stuff, honey. It's junk.'

'I know,' I said, looking down at the towel.

The Goodwill guys showed up then, beeping the horn as they pulled into the driveway. My mother waved them in, then walked over to point out the various piles. As they conferred, I wondered how many times a day they went to people's houses to take things away – if it was different when it was after a death, or if junk was junk, and they couldn't even tell.

'Make sure you get it all,' my mother called over her shoulder as she started across the grass. The two guys went over to the treadmill, each of them picking up an end. 'I have a donation . . . just let me get my chequebook.'

As she went inside I stood there for a second, the guys loading up things from all around me. They were making a last trip for the Christmas tree when one of them, a shorter guy with red hair, nodded towards the box at my feet.

'That too?' he asked.

I was about to tell him yes. Then I looked down at the towel and the box with all the other crap in it, and remembered how excited my dad was when each of them arrived, how I could always hear him coming down the hallway, pausing by the dining room, the den, the kitchen, just looking for someone to share his new discovery with. I was always so happy when it was me.

'No,' I said as I leaned over and picked up the box. 'This one's mine.'

I took it up to my room, then dragged the desk chair over to my closet and climbed up. There was a panel above the top shelf that opened up into the attic, and I slid it open and pushed the box into the darkness.

With my dad gone, we had assumed our relationship with EZ Products was over. But then, about a month after the funeral, another package showed up, a combination pen/pocket stapler. We figured he'd ordered it right before the heart attack, his final purchase – until the next month, when a decorative rock/sprinkler arrived. When my mother called to complain, the customer service person apologized profusely. Because of my father's high buying volume, she explained, he had been bumped up to Gold Circle level, which meant that he received a new product every month to peruse, no obligation to buy. They'd take him off the list, absolutely, no problem.

But still the stuff kept coming, every month, just like clockwork, even after we cancelled the credit card they had on file. I had my own theory on this, one I shared, like so much else, with no one. My dad had died the day after Christmas, when all the gifts had already been put into use or away. He'd given my mom a diamond bracelet, my sister a mountain bike, but when it was my turn, he'd given me a sweater, a couple of CDs and an I.O.U. written on gold paper in his messy scrawl. *More to come*, it had said, and he'd nodded as I read the words, reassuring me. *Soon.* 'It's late, but it's special,' he'd said to me. 'You'll love it.'

I knew this was true. I would love it, because my dad just *knew* me, knew what made me happy. My mother claimed that when I was little I cried any time my dad was out of my sight, that I was often inconsolable if anyone but he made my favourite meal, the bright orange macaroni-and-cheese mix they sold at the grocery store three for a dollar. But it was more than just emotional stuff. Sometimes, I swear, it was like we were on the same wavelength. Even that last day, when he'd given up trying to rouse me from bed, I'd sat up those five minutes later as if something had summoned me. Maybe, by then, his chest was already hurting. I'd never know.

In those first few days after he was gone, I kept thinking

back to that I.O.U., wondering what it was he'd picked out for me. And even though I was pretty sure it wasn't an EZ Product, it felt strangely soothing when the things from Waterville, Maine, kept arriving, as though some part of him was still reaching out to me, keeping his promise.

So each time my mother tossed the boxes, I'd fish them out and bring them upstairs to add to my collection. I never used any of the products, choosing instead to just believe the breathless claims on the boxes. There were a lot of ways to remember my dad. But I thought he would have especially liked that.

Chapter TWO

My mother had called me once ('Macy, honey, people are starting to arrive.') and then twice ('Macy? Honey?') but still I was in front of the mirror, parting and reparting my hair. No matter how many times I swiped at it with my comb, it still didn't look right.

Once, I didn't care so much about appearances. I knew the basics: that I was somewhat short for my age, with a round face, brown eyes and faint freckles across my nose that had been prominent, but now you had to lean in close to see. I had blonde hair that got lighter in the summertime, slightly green if I swam too much, which didn't bother me since I was a total track rat, the kind of girl to whom the word *hairstyle* was defined as always having a ponytail elastic on her wrist. I'd never cared about how my body or I looked – what mattered was what it could do and how fast it could go. But part of my new perfect act was my appearance. If I wanted people to see me as calm and collected, together, I had to look the part.

It took work. Now, my hair had to be just right, lying flat in all the right places. If my skin was not cooperating, I bargained with it, applying concealer and a slight layer of foundation, smoothing out all the red marks and dark circles. I could spend a full half hour getting the shadowing just right on my eyes, curling and recurling my eyelashes, making sure each was lifted and separated as the mascara wand moved over them, darkening, thickening. I moisturized. I flossed. I stood up straight. I was fine.

'Macy?' My mother's voice, firm and cheery, floated up the stairs. I pulled the comb through my hair, then stepped back from the mirror, letting it fall into the part again. Finally: perfect. And just in time.

When I came downstairs, my mother was standing by the door, greeting a couple who was just coming in with her selling smile: confident but not off-putting, welcoming but not kiss-ass. Like me, my mother put great stock in her appearance. In real estate, as in high school, it could make or break you.

'There you are,' she said, turning round as I came down the stairs. 'I was getting worried.'

'Hair issues,' I told her, as another couple came up the front walk. 'What can I do?'

She glanced into the living room, where a group of people were peering at a design of the new townhouses that was tacked up on the wall. My mother always had these cocktail parties when she needed to sell, believing the best way to assure people she could build their dream house was to show off her own. It was a good gimmick, even if it did mean having strangers traipsing through our downstairs.

'If you make sure the caterers have what they need,' she said to me now, 'that would be great. And if it looks like we're running low on brochures, go out and get another box from the garage.' She paused to smile at a couple as they crossed the foyer. 'Oh,' she said, 'and if anyone looks like they're looking for a bathroom –'

'Point them towards it graciously and with the utmost subtlety,' I finished. Bathroom detail/directions were, in fact, my speciality.

'Good girl,' she said as a woman in a trouser suit came up the walk. 'Welcome!' my mother called out, pushing the door open wider. 'I'm Deborah Queen. Please come in. I'm so glad you could make it!'

My mother didn't know this person, of course. But part of selling was treating everyone like a familiar face.

'Well, I just love the neighbourhood,' the woman said as she stepped over the threshold. 'I noticed you were putting up some new townhouses, so I thought I'd . . .'

'Let me show you a floor plan. Did you see that all the units come with two-car garages? You know, a lot of people don't even realize how much difference a heated garage can make.'

And with that, my mother was off and running. Hard to believe that once schmoozing was as painful to her as multiple root canals. But when you had to do something, you had to do it. And eventually, if you were lucky, you did it well.

Queen Homes, which my dad had started right out of college as a one-man trim carpenter operation, already had a good business reputation when he met my mother. Actually, he hired her. She was fresh out of college with an accounting degree, and his finances were a shambles. She'd come in, waded through his paperwork and receipts (many of which were on bar napkins and matchbooks), handled a close call with the IRS (he'd 'forgotten' about his taxes a few years earlier) and got him into the black again. Somewhere in the midst of all of it they fell in love. They were the perfect business team: he was all charm and fun and everyone's favourite guy to buy a beer. My mother was happy busying herself with file folders and The Bigger Picture. Together, they were unstoppable.

Wildflower Ridge, our neighbourhood, had been my mother's vision. They'd done small subdivisions and spec houses, but this would be an entire neighbourhood, with houses and townhouses and apartments, a little business district, everything all enclosed and fitted round a common green space. A return to communities, my mother had said. The wave of the future.

My dad wasn't sold at first. But he was getting older, and his body was tired. This way he could move into a supervisory position and let someone else swing the hammers. So he agreed. Two months later, they were breaking ground on the first house: ours.

They worked in tandem, my parents, meeting potential clients at the model home. My dad would run through the basic spiel, tweaking it depending on what sort of people they were: he played up his Southern charm for Northerners, talked NASCAR and barbecue with locals. He was knowledgeable, trustworthy. Of course you wanted him to build your house. Hell, you wanted him to be your best friend. Then, the hard selling done, my mom would move in with the technical stuff like covenants, specifications and prices. The houses sold like crazy. It was everything my mother said it would be. Until it wasn't.

I knew she blamed herself for his death, thought that maybe it was the added stress of Wildflower Ridge that taxed my dad's heart, and if she hadn't pushed him to expand so much everything would have been different. This was our common ground, the secret we shared but never spoke aloud. I should have been with him; she should have left him alone. Shoulda, coulda, woulda. It's so easy in the past tense.

But here in the present, my mother and I had no choice but to move ahead. We worked hard, me at school, her at outselling all the other builders. We parted our hair cleanly and stood up straight, greeting company – and the world – with the smiles we practised in the quiet of our now-too-big dream house full of mirrors that showed the smiles back. But under it all, our grief remained. Sometimes she took more of it, sometimes I did. But, always, it was there.

I'd just finished directing an irate woman with a red-wine stain on her shirt to the powder room – one of the catering staff had apparently bumped into her, splashing her Cabernet across her outfit – when I noticed the stack of fliers on the foyer table was looking a bit low. Grateful for any excuse to escape, I slipped outside.

I went down the front walk, cutting round the caterer's van in the driveway. The sun had just gone down, the sky pink and orange behind the line of trees that separated us from the apartments one phase over. Summer was just starting. Once that had meant early track practice and long afternoons at the pool perfecting my backflip. This summer, though, I was working.

Jason had been at the library information desk since he

was fifteen, long enough to secure a reputation as the Guy Who Knew Everything. Patrons of the Lakeview Branch had become accustomed to him doing everything from finding that obscure book on Catherine the Great to fixing the library computers when they crashed. They loved him for the same reason I did: he had all the answers. He also had a cult following, particularly among his co-workers, who were both girls and both brilliant. They'd never taken kindly to me as Jason's girlfriend, seeing as how, in their eyes, I wasn't even close to their intellectual level, much less his. I'd had a feeling that their acceptance of me as a sudden co-worker wouldn't be much warmer, and I was right.

During my training, they snickered as he taught me the intricate ins and outs of the library search system, rolled their eyes in tandem when I asked a question about the card catalogue. Jason had hardly noticed and, when I pointed it out to him, he got impatient, as if I were wasting his time. That's not what you should be worrying about, he said. Not knowing how to reference the tri-county library database quickly in the event of a system crash: now *that* would be a problem.

He was right, of course. He was always right. But I still wasn't looking forward to it.

Once I got to the garage, I went to the shelves where my mom kept her work stuff, moving a stack of FOR SALE and MODEL OPEN signs aside to pull out another box of fliers. The front door of the house was open, and I could hear voices drifting over, party sounds, laughing and glasses clinking. I hoisted up the box and cut off the overhead light. Then I headed back to the party and bathroom duty.

I was passing the garbage cans when someone jumped out at me from the bushes.

'Gotcha!'

I shrieked and dropped the box, which hit the ground with a thunk, spilling fliers sideways down the driveway. Say what you will, but you're never prepared for the surprise attack. It defines the very meaning of taking your breath away: I was gasping.

For a second, it was very quiet. A car drove by.

'Bert?' A voice came from down the driveway, by the catering van. 'What are you doing?'

Beside me, a bush rustled. 'I'm . . .' a voice said hesitantly – and much more quietly – from somewhere within it, 'I'm scaring *you*. Aren't I?'

I heard footsteps, and a second later could make out a guy in a white shirt and black trousers walking towards me up the driveway. He had a serving platter tucked under his arm. As he got closer he squinted, making me out in the semi-dark.

'Nope. Not me,' he said. Now that he was right in front of me, I could see that he was tall and had brown hair that was a little bit too long. He was also strikingly handsome, with the sort of sculpted cheekbones and angular features that you couldn't help but notice, even if you did have a boyfriend. To me he said, 'You okay?'

I nodded. My heart was still racing, but I was recovering.

He stood there, studying the bush, then stuck his hand right into its centre. A second later, he pulled another guy, this one shorter and chunkier but dressed identically, out through the foliage. He had the same dark eyes and hair, but looked younger. His face was bright red.

'Bert,' the older guy said, sighing, as he let his hand drop. 'Honestly.'

'You have to understand,' this Bert said to me, solemnly, 'I'm down in a big way.'

'Just apologize,' the older guy said.

'I'm very sorry,' Bert said. He reached up and picked a pine needle out of his hair. 'I, um, thought you were someone else.'

'It's okay,' I told him.

The older guy nudged him, then nodded towards the fliers. 'Oh, right,' Bert said, dropping down to his knees. He started to pick them up, his fingers scratching the pavement, as the other guy walked a bit down the driveway, picking up the ones that had slid there.

'That was a good one too,' Bert was muttering as I squatted down beside him to help. 'Almost had him. Almost.'

The light outside the kitchen door popped on, and suddenly it was very bright. A second later the door swung open.

'What in the world is going on out here?' I turned to see a woman in a red apron, with black curly hair piled on top of her head, standing at the top of the stairs. She was pregnant, and was squinting out into the dark with a curious, although somewhat impatient, expression. 'Where is that platter I asked for?'

'Right here,' the older guy called out as he came back up the driveway, a bunch of my fliers now stacked neatly upon the platter. He handed them to me.

'Thanks,' I said.

'No problem.' Then he took the stairs two at a time,

handing the platter to the woman, as Bert crawled under the deck for the last few fliers that had landed there.

'Marvellous,' she said. 'Now, Wes, get back to the bar, will you? The more they drink, the less they'll notice how long the food is taking.'

'Sure thing,' the guy said, ducking through the doorway and disappearing into the kitchen.

The woman ran her hand over her belly, distracted, then looked back out into the dark. 'Bert?' she called out loudly. 'Where –'

'Right here,' Bert said, from under the deck.

She turned round, then stuck her head over the side of the rail. 'Are you on the ground?'

'Yes.'

'What are you *doing*?'

'Nothing,' Bert mumbled.

'Well,' the woman said, 'when you're done with that, I've got crab cakes cooling with your name on them. So get your butt in here, please, okay?'

'Okay,' he said. 'I'm coming.'

The woman went back inside, and a second later I heard her yelling something about mini crackers. Bert came out from under the deck, organizing the fliers he was holding into a stack, then handed them to me.

'I'm really sorry,' he said. 'It's just this stupid thing.'

'It's fine,' I told him as he picked another leaf out of his hair. 'It was an accident.'

He looked at me, his expression serious. 'There are,' he said, 'no accidents.'

For a second I just stared at him. He had a chubby face and a wide nose, and his hair was thick and too short, like it had been cut at home. He was watching me so intently, as if he wanted to be sure I understood, that it took me a second to look away.

'Bert!' the woman yelled from inside. 'Crab cakes!'

'Right,' he said, snapping out of it. Then he backed up to the stairs and started up them quickly. When he got to the top, he glanced back down at me. 'But I am sorry,' he said, saying the words that I'd heard so much in the last year and a half that they hardly carried meaning any more. Although I had a feeling he meant it. Weird. 'I'm sorry,' he said again. And then he was gone.

When I got inside my mother was deep in some conversation about zoning with a couple of contractors. I refreshed the fliers, then directed a man who was a bit stumbly and holding a glass of wine he probably didn't need to the bathroom. I was scanning the living room for stray empty glasses when there was a loud crash from the kitchen.

Everything in the front of the house stopped. Conversation. Motion. The very air. Or so it felt.

'It's fine!' a voice called out, upbeat and cheerful, from the other side of the door. 'Carry on as you were!'

There was a slight surprised murmur from the assembled crowd, some laughter and then slowly the conversation built again. My mother smiled her way across the room, then put a hand on the small of my back, easing me towards the foyer.

'That's a spill on a client, not enough appetizers and a

crash,' she said, her voice level. 'I'm not happy. Could you go and convey that, please?'

'Right,' I said. 'I'm on it.'

When I came through the kitchen door, the first thing I did was step on something that mushed, in a wet sort of way, under my foot. Then I noticed that the floor was littered with small round objects, some at a standstill, some rolling slowly to the four corners of the room. A little girl in pigtails, who looked to be about two or three, was standing by the sink, fingers in her mouth and wide eyed as several of the marble-like objects moved past her.

'Well.' I looked over to see the pregnant woman standing by the stove, an empty cookie sheet in her hands. She sighed. 'I guess that's it for the meatballs.'

I picked up my foot to examine it, stepping aside just in time to keep from getting hit by the door as it swung open. Bert, now leafless and looking somewhat composed, breezed in carrying a tray filled with wadded-up napkins and empty glasses. 'Delia,' he said to the woman, 'we need more crab cakes.'

'And I need a sedative,' she replied in a tired voice, stretching her back, 'but you can't have everything. Take the cheese puffs and tell them we're traying the crab cakes up right now.'

'Are we?' Bert asked, passing the toddler, who smiled widely, reaching out for him with her spitty fingers. He sidestepped her, heading for the counter, and, unhappy, she plopped down into a sitting position and promptly started wailing.

'Not exactly at this moment, no,' Delia said, crossing the room. 'I'm speaking futuristically.'

'Is that a word?' Bert asked her.

'Just take the cheese puffs,' she said as she picked up the little girl. 'Oh, Lucy, please God okay, just hold back the hysterics for another hour, I'm begging you.' She looked down at her shoe. 'Oh no, I just stepped in a meatball. Where's Monica?'

'Here,' a girl's voice said from the other side of the side door.

Delia made an exasperated face. 'Put out that cigarette and get in here, *now*. Find a broom and get up these meatballs . . . and we need to get some more of these cheese puffs in, and Bert needs . . . what else did you need?'

'Crab cakes,' Bert said. 'Futuristically speaking. And Wes needs ice.'

'In the oven, ready any second,' she said, shooting him a look as she walked over to the broom closet, toddler on her hip, and rummaged around for a second before pulling out a dustpan. 'The crab cakes, not the ice. Lucy, please, don't slobber on Mommy . . . And the ice is . . . oh, shit, I don't know where the ice is. Where did we put the bags we bought?'

'Cooler,' a tall girl said as she came inside, letting the door slam behind her. She had long honey-blonde hair and was slouching as she ambled over to the oven. She pulled it open, a couple of inches at a time, then glanced inside before shutting it again and making her way over to the island, still moving at a snail's pace. 'Done,' she announced.

'Then please *take* them out and *put* them on a tray, Monica,' Delia snapped, shifting the toddler to her other hip. She started scooping up the meatballs into the dustpan as

Monica made her way back to the oven, pausing entirely too long to pick up a pot holder on her way.

'I'll just wait for the crab cakes,' Bert said. 'It's only –'

Delia stood up and glared at him. It was quiet for a second, but something told me this was not my opening. I stayed put, scraping meatball off my shoe.

'Right,' he said quickly. 'Cheese puffs. Here I go. We need more servers, by the way. People are grabbing at me like you wouldn't believe.'

'Monica, get back out there,' Delia said as the tall girl ambled back over, a tray of sizzling crab cakes in her hand. Putting down the dustpan, Delia moved to the island, grabbing a spatula, and began, with one hand, to load crab cakes onto the plate at lightning speed. 'Now.'

'But –'

'I know what I said,' Delia shot back, slapping a stack of napkins onto the edge of the tray, 'but this is an emergency situation, and I have to put you back in, even if it is against my better judgement. Just walk slowly and *look* where you're going, and be careful with liquids, please God I'm begging you, okay?'

This last part, I was already beginning to recognize, was a mantra of sorts for her, as if by stringing all these words together, one of them might stick.

'Okay,' Monica said, tucking her hair behind her ear. She picked up the tray, adjusted it on her hand, and headed off round the corner, taking her time. Delia watched her go, shaking her head, then turned her attention back to the meatballs, scooping the few remaining into the dustpan and chucking them into the garbage can. Her daughter was still sniffling, and she was talking to her, softly, as she walked to a metal cart by the side door, pulling out a tray covered with clingfilm. As she crossed the room she balanced it precariously on her free hand, her walk becoming a slight waddle. I had never seen anyone so in need of help in my life.

'What else, what else,' she said as she reached the island, sliding the tray there. 'What else did we need?' She pressed a hand to her forehead, closing her eyes.

'Ice,' I said, and she turned round and looked at me.

'Ice,' she repeated. Then she smiled. 'Thanks. Who are you?'

'Macy. This is my mom's house.'

Her expression changed, but only slightly. I had a feeling she knew what was coming.

I took a breath. 'She wanted me to come and check that everything's all right. And to convey that she's –'

'Incredibly pissed,' she finished for me, nodding.

'Well, not *pissed*.'

Just then, there was a splashing crash from the next room, followed by another short silence. Delia glanced over at the door, just as the toddler started wailing again.

'Now?' she said to me.

'Well . . . yes,' I said. Actually, I was betting this was an understatement. 'Now, she's probably pissed.'

'Oh, dear.' She put a hand on her face, shaking her head. 'This is a disaster.'

I wasn't sure what to say. I felt nervous enough just watching all this; I couldn't imagine being responsible for it.

'Well,' she said, after a second, 'in a way, it's good. We know where we stand. Now things can only get better. Right?'

I didn't say anything, which probably didn't inspire much confidence. Just then, the oven timer went off with a cheerful *bing!* noise. 'Okay,' she said suddenly, as if this had signalled a call to action. 'Macy. Can you answer a question?'

'Sure,' I said.

'How are you with a spatula?'

This hadn't been what I was expecting. 'Pretty good,' I said finally.

'Wonderful,' she said. 'Come here.'

Fifteen minutes later, I'd figured out the rhythm. It was like baking cookies, but accelerated: lay out cheese puffs/crab cakes on cookie sheet in neat rows, put in oven, remove other pan from oven, pile onto tray, send out. And repeat.

'Perfect,' Delia said, watching me as she laid out mini-toasts at twice my speed and more neatly. 'You could have a bright future in catering, my dear, if such a thing even exists.'

I smiled at this as Monica, the sloth-like girl, eased through the door, carrying a tray laden with napkins. After her second spill she'd been restricted to carrying only solids, a status further amended to just trash and empty glasses once she'd bumped into the banister and sent half a tray of cheese puffs down the front of some man's shirt. You'd think moving slowly would make someone less accident prone. Clearly, Monica was bucking this logic.

'How's it going out there?' Delia asked her, glancing over at her daughter, Lucy, who was now asleep in her car seat on the kitchen table. Frankly, Delia had astounded me. After acknowledging the hopelessness of her situation, she had immediately righted it, putting in two more trays of canapés, getting the ice from the cooler and soothing her daughter to sleep, all in about three minutes. Like her mantra of Oh-please-God-I'm-begging-you-okay, she just did all she could, and eventually something just worked. It was impressive.

'Fine,' Monica reported flatly, shuffling over to the garbage can, where, after pausing for a second, she began to clear off her tray, one item at a time.

Delia rolled her eyes as I slid another tray into the oven. 'We're not always like this,' she told me, opening another package of cheese puffs. 'I swear. We are usually the model of professionalism and efficiency.'

Monica, hearing this, snorted. Delia shot her a look.

'But,' she continued, 'my babysitter flaked on me tonight, and then one of my servers had other plans, and then, well, then the world just turned on me. You know that feeling?'

I nodded. *You have no idea*, I thought. Out loud I said, 'Yeah. I do.'

'Macy! There you are!' I looked up to see my mother standing by the kitchen doorway. 'Is everything okay back here?'

This question, while posed to me, was really for Delia, and I could tell she knew it: she busied herself laying out cheese puffs, now at triple speed. Behind her, Monica had finally cleared her tray and was dragging herself across the room, the tray bumping against her knee.

'Yes,' I said. 'I was just asking Delia about how to make crab cakes.'

As she came towards us, my mother was running a hand through her hair, which meant she was preparing herself for some sort of confrontation. Delia must have sensed this too, as she picked up a dish towel, wiping her hands, and turned to face my mother, a calm expression on her face.

'The food is getting rave reviews,' my mother began in a voice that made it clear a *but* was to follow, 'but –'

'Mrs Queen.' Delia took a deep breath, which she then let out, placing her hand on her chest. 'Please. You don't have to say anything more.'

I opened up another tray of crab cakes, keeping my head down.

'I am so deeply sorry for our disorganized beginning tonight,' Delia continued. 'I found out I was understaffed at the last minute, but that's no excuse. I'd like to forgo your remaining balance in the hopes that you might consider us again for another one of your events.'

The meaningful silence that followed this speech held for a full five seconds, until it was broken by Bert bursting back through the door. 'Need more blinis!' he said. 'They're going like hotcakes!'

'Bert,' Delia said, forcing a smile for my mother's sake, 'you don't have to bellow. We're right here.'

'Sorry,' Bert said.

'Here.' I handed him the tray I'd just finished and took his empty one. 'There should be crab cakes in the next few minutes too.'

'Thanks,' he said. Then he recognized me. 'Hey,' he said. 'You work here now?'

'Um, no.' I put the empty tray down in front of me. 'Not really.'

I glanced over at my mother. Between Delia's heartfelt 'sorry' and my exchange with Bert, I could see she was struggling to keep up. 'Well,' she said finally, turning her attention back to Delia, 'I appreciate your apology, and that seems like fair compensation. The food *is* wonderful.'

'Thank you so much,' Delia said. 'I really appreciate it.'

Just then there was a burst of laughter from the living room, happy party noise, and my mother glanced towards it, as if reassured. 'Well,' she said, 'I suppose I should get back to my guests.' She started out of the room, then paused by the fridge. 'Macy?' she said.

'Yes?'

'When you're done in here, I could use you. Okay?'

'Sure,' I said, grabbing a pot holder and heading over to the oven to check on the crab cakes. 'I'll be there in a sec.'

'She's been wonderful, by the way,' Delia told her. 'I told her if she needs work, I'll hire her in a second.'

'That's so nice of you,' my mother said. 'Macy's actually working at the library this summer.'

'Wow,' Delia said. 'That's great.'

'It's just at the information desk,' I told her, opening the oven door. 'Answering questions and stuff.'

'Ah,' Delia said. 'A girl with all the answers.'

'That's Macy.' My mother smiled. 'She's a very bright girl.'

I didn't know what to say to this – what could you say to this? – so I just reached in for the crab cakes, focusing on that. When my mother left the kitchen, Delia came over, pot holder in hand, and took the tray as I slid it out of the oven. 'You've been a great help,' she said, 'really. But you'd better go out there with your mom.'

'No, it's fine,' I said. 'She won't even notice I'm not there.'

Delia smiled. 'Maybe not. But you should go anyway.'

I stepped back, out of the way, as she carried the tray over to the island. In her car seat, Lucy shifted slightly, mumbling to herself, then fell quiet again.

'So the library, huh?' she said, picking up her spatula. 'That's cool.'

'It's just for the summer,' I told her. 'I'm filling in for someone.'

She started lifting crab cakes off the cookie sheet, arranging them on a tray. 'Well, if it doesn't work out, I'm in the book. I could always use someone who can take directions and walk in a straight line.'

As if to punctuate this, Monica slunk back in, blowing her bangs out of her face.

'Catering is an insane job, though,' Delia said. 'I don't know why you'd want to do it, when you have a peaceful, normal job. But if for some reason you're craving chaos, call me. Okay?'

Bert came back in, breezing between us, his tray now empty. 'Crab cakes!' he bellowed. 'Keep 'em coming!'

'Bert,' Delia said, wincing, 'I'm *right here*.'

I walked back to the door, stepping aside as Monica ambled past me, yawning widely. Bert stood by impatiently, waiting for his tray, while Delia asked Monica to God, please, try and pick up the pace a little, I'm begging you. They'd forgotten about me already, it seemed. But for some reason, I wanted to answer her anyway. 'Yeah,' I said, out loud, hoping she could hear me. 'Okay.'

The last person at the party, a slightly tipsy, very loud man in a golf sweater, left around nine thirty. My mother locked the door behind him, took off her shoes, and, after kissing my forehead and thanking me, headed off to her office to assemble packets for people who had signed the YES! I WANT MORE INFO sheet she'd had on the front hall table. Contacts were everything, I'd learned. You had to get to people fast, or they'd slip away.

Thinking this, I went up to my room and checked my email. Jason had written to me, as promised, but it was mostly about things that he wanted to remind me of concerning the info desk (make sure to keep track of all copier keys, they are *very expensive* to replace) or other things I was handling for him while he was away (remember, on Saturday, to send out the email to the Foreign Culture group about the featured speaker who is coming in to give that talk in August). At the very end, he said he was too tired to write more and he'd be in touch in a couple of days. Then just his name, no 'love'. Not that I'd been expecting it. Jason wasn't the type for displays of affection, either verbal or not. He was disgusted by couples that made out in the hallways between classes, and got annoyed at even the slightest sappy moments in movies. But I knew that he cared about me: he just conveyed it more subtly, as concise with expressing this emotion as he was with everything else. It was in the way he'd put his hand on the small of my back, for instance, or how he'd smile at me when

I said something that surprised him. Once I might have wanted more, but I'd come round to his way of thinking in the time we'd been together. And we were together, all the time. So he didn't have to do anything to prove how he felt about me. Like so much else, I should just know.

But this *was* the first time we were going to be apart for more than a weekend since we'd got together, and I was beginning to realize that the small reassurances I got in person would not transfer over to email. But he loved me, and I knew that. I'd just have to remember it now.

After I logged off, I opened my window and crawled out onto the roof, sitting against one of the shutters with my knees pulled up to my chest. I'd been out there for a little while, looking at the stars, when I heard voices coming up from the driveway. A car door shut, then another. Peering over the edge, I saw a few people moving around the Wish Catering van as they packed up the last of their things.

'. . . this *other* planet, that's moving within the same trajectory as Earth. It's only a matter of time before it hits us. I mean, they don't talk about these things on the news. But that doesn't mean it's not *happening*.'

It was Bert talking. I recognized his voice, a bit high-pitched and anxious, before I made him out, standing by the back of the van. He was talking to someone who was sitting on the bumper smoking a cigarette, the tip of which was bright and red in the murky dark.

'Ummm-hmmm,' the person said slowly. Had to be Monica. 'Really.'

'Bert, give it a rest,' another voice said, and Wes, the older guy, walked up, sliding something into the back of the van. I'd hardly seen him that night, as he'd worked the bar in the den.

'I'm just trying to help her be informed!' Bert said indignantly. 'This is serious stuff, Wes. Just because *you* prefer to stay in the dark –'

'Are we ready to go?' Delia came down the driveway, her voice uneven, Lucy on her hip. She had the car seat dangling from one hand, and Wes walked up and took it from her. From where I was sitting, I could make out the top of his head clearly, the white of his shirt. Then, as if sensing this, he leaned his head back, glancing up. I slid back against the wall.

'Did we get paid?' Bert asked.

'Had to comp half,' she said. 'The price of chaos. Probably should bother me, but frankly I'm too pregnant and exhausted to care. Who has the keys?'

'I do,' Bert said. 'I'll drive.'

The silence that followed was long enough to make me want to peer over the edge of the roof again, but I stopped myself.

'I don't think so,' Delia said finally.

'Don't even,' Monica added.

'What?' Bert said. 'Come on! I've had my permit for a year! I'm taking the test in a week! And I have to have some more practice before I get the Bertmobile.'

'You have,' Wes said, his voice low, 'to stop calling it that.'

'Bert,' Delia said, sighing, 'normally, I would love for you to drive. But it's been a long night and right now I just want to get home, okay? Next time, it's all you. But for now just let your brother drive. Okay?'

Another silence. Someone coughed.

'Fine,' Bert said. 'Just fine.'

I heard a car door slam, then another. I leaned back over to see Wes and Bert still standing at the back of the van. Bert was kicking at the ground, clearly sulking, while Wes stood by impassively.

'It's not a big deal,' he said to Bert after a minute, pulling a hand through his hair. Now I knew for sure that they were brothers. They looked even more alike to me, although the similarities – skin tone, dark hair, dark eyes – were distributed on starkly different builds.

'I never get to drive,' Bert told him. 'Never. Even lazy Monotone got to last week, but never me. Never.'

'You will,' Wes said. 'Next week you'll have your own car, and you can drive whenever you want. But don't push this issue now, man. It's late.'

Bert stuffed his hands in his pockets. 'Whatever,' he said, and started around the van, shuffling his feet. Wes followed him, clapping a hand on his back. 'You know that girl who was in the kitchen tonight, helping Delia?' Bert asked.

I froze.

'Yeah,' Wes answered. 'The one you leaped out at?'

'Anyway,' Bert said loudly, 'don't you know who she is?'

'No.'

Bert pulled open the back door. 'Yeah, you do. Her dad –'

I waited. I knew what was coming, but, still, I had to hear the words that would follow. The ones that defined me, set me apart.

'– was the coach when we used to run in that kids' league,

back in elementary school,' Bert finished. 'The Lakeview Zips. Remember?'

Wes opened the back door for Bert. 'Oh yeah,' he said. 'Coach Joe, right?'

Right, I thought, and felt a pang in my chest.

'Coach Joe,' Bert repeated, as he shut his door. 'He was a nice guy.'

I watched Wes walk to the driver's door and pull it open. He stood there for a second, taking a final look around, before climbing in and shutting the door behind him. I had to admit, I was surprised. I'd become so used to being known as the girl whose dad died, I sometimes forgot that I'd had a life before that.

I moved back into the shadows by my window as the engine started up and the van bumped down the driveway, brake lights flashing as it turned out onto the street. There was a big wishbone painted on the side, thick black paint strokes, and from a distance it looked like a Chinese character, striking even if you didn't know, really, what it meant. I kept my eye on it, following it down through the neighbourhood, over the hill, down to the stop sign, until it was gone.

Chapter THREE

I couldn't sleep.

I was starting my job at the library the next day, and I had that night-before-the-first-day-of-school feeling, all jumpy and nervous. But, then again, I'd never been much of a sleeper. That was the weird thing about that morning when my dad came in to get me. I'd been out. Sound asleep.

Since then, I had almost a fear of sleeping, sure that something bad would happen if I ever allowed myself to be fully unconscious, even for a second. As a result, I only allowed myself to barely doze off. When I did sleep enough to dream, it was always about running.

My dad loved to run. He'd had me and my sister doing it from a young age with the Lakeview Zips, and later he was always dragging us to the 5Ks he ran, signing us up for the kids' division. I remember my first race, when I was six, standing there at the starting line a few rows back, with nothing at my eye level but shoulders and necks. I was short for my age, and Caroline had of course pushed her way to the front, stating clearly that at ten-almost-eleven, she didn't belong at the back with the babies. The starting gun popped and everyone pushed forward, the thumping of sneakers against asphalt suddenly deafening, and at first it was like I was carried along with it, my feet hardly seeming to touch the ground. The people on the sides of the street were a blur, faces blowing by: all I could focus on was the ponytail of the girl in front of me, tied with a blue grosgrain ribbon. Some big boy bumped me hard from the back, passing, and I had a cramp in my side by the second length, but then I heard my dad.

'Macy! Good girl! Keep it up – you're doing great!'

I knew by the time I was eight years old that I was fast, faster than the kids I was running with. I knew even before I started to pass the bigger kids in the first length, even before I won my first race, then every race. When I was really going, the wind whistling in my ears, I was sure that, if I wanted to, it was only another burst of breath, one more push, and I could fly.

By then it was just me running. My sister had lost interest around seventh grade, when she discovered her best event was not, as we'd all thought, the hundred metres, but in fact flirting with the boys' track team afterwards. She still liked to run, but didn't much see the point any more if she didn't have someone chasing after her.

So it was me and my dad who went to meets, who woke up early to do our standard five-mile loop, who compared T-band strains and bad-knee horror stories over icepacks and PowerBars on Saturday mornings. It was the best thing we had in common, the one part of him that was all mine. Which was why, that morning, I should have been with him.

From that morning on, running changed for me. It didn't matter how good my times were, what records I'd planned to break just days before. There was one time I would never beat, so I quit.

By altering the familiar route that took me past the intersection of Willow and McKinley whenever I went out, and looping one extra block instead, I'd been able to avoid the place where everything had happened: it was that easy, really, to never drive past it again. My friends from the track team were a bit harder. They'd stuck close to me, loyal, at the funeral and the days afterwards, and while they were disappointed when the coach told them I'd quit, they were even more hurt when I started to avoid them in the halls. Nobody seemed to understand that the only person I could count on not to bring up my dad, not to feel sorry for me, or make The Face – other than my mother – was me. So I narrowed my world, cutting out everyone who'd known me or who tried to befriend me. It was the only thing I knew to do.

I packed up all my trophies and ribbons, piling them neatly into boxes. It was like that part of my life, my running life, was just gone. It was almost too easy, for something I once thought had meant everything.

So now I only ran in my dreams. In them, there was always something awful about to happen, or there was something I'd forgotten, and my legs felt like jelly, not strong enough to hold me. Whatever else varied, the ending was the same, a finish line I could never reach, no matter how many miles I put behind me.

'Oh, right.' Bethany looked up at me through her slim, wire-framed glasses. 'You're starting today.'

I just stood there, holding my purse, suddenly entirely too aware of the nail I'd broken as I unfastened my seat belt in the parking lot. I'd put so much time into getting dressed for this first day, ironing my shirt, making my hair part perfectly straight, redoing my lipstick twice. Now, though, my nail, ripped across the top, jagged, seemed to defeat everything, even as I tucked it into my palm, hiding it.

Bethany pushed back her chair and stood up. 'You can sit on the end, I guess,' she said, reaching over to unlatch the knee-high door between us and holding it open as I stepped through. 'Not in the red chair, that's Amanda's. The one next to it.'

'Thanks,' I said. I walked over, pulling the chair from the desk, then sat down, stowing my purse at my feet. A second later I heard the door squeak open again and Amanda, Bethany's best friend and the student council secretary, came in. She was a tall girl with long hair she always wore in a neat braid that hung halfway down her back. It looked so perfect that during long meetings, when my mind wandered from the official agenda, I'd sometimes wondered if she slept in it, or if it was like a clip-on tie, easily removed at the end of the day.

'Hello, Macy,' she said coolly, taking a seat in her red chair. She had perfect posture, shoulders back, chin up. Maybe the braid helped, I thought. 'I forgot you were starting today.'

'Um, yeah,' I said. They both looked at me, and I was distinctly aware of that *um*, so base, hanging in the air between us. I said, more clearly, 'Yes.'

If I were working towards perfect – working being the operative word – these girls had already reached it and made maintaining it look effortless. Bethany was a redhead with short hair she wore tucked behind her ears, and had small freckled hands with the nails cut straight across. I'd sat beside her in English, and had always been transfixed when I saw her taking notes: her print was like a typewriter, each letter exact. She was quiet and always composed, while Amanda was more talkative, with a cultured accent she'd picked up from her early years in Paris, where her family had lived while her father did graduate work at the Sorbonne. I'd never seen either of them sporting a shirt with a stain on it, or even a wrinkle. They never used anything but proper English. They were the female Jasons.

'Well, it's been really slow so far this summer,' Amanda said to me now, smoothing her hands over her skirt. She had long, pale white legs. 'I hope there's enough for you to do.'

I didn't know what to say to that, so I just smiled my fine-just-fine smile again and turned back to the wall that my desk area faced. Behind me, I could hear them start talking, their voices low and soothing. They were saying something about an art exhibit. I looked at the clock. It was 9:05. Five hours, fifty-five minutes to go.

By noon, I'd answered only one question, and it concerned the location of the bathroom. (So it wasn't just in my house. Anywhere, I looked like I knew about the toilet, if nothing else.) There'd been a fair amount of activity at the desk: a problem with the copy machine, some enquiries into an obscure periodical, even someone with a question about the online encyclopedia that Jason had specifically trained me to handle. But even if Amanda or Bethany were helping someone else and the person came right to me, one of them jumped up, saying, 'I'll be with you in just a second,' in a tone that made it clear asking me would be a waste of time. The first few times this happened, I'd figured they were just letting me get my feet under me. After a while, though, it was obvious. In their minds, I didn't belong there.

At noon, Amanda put a sign on the desk that said WILL RETURN AT 1:00 and drew a bagel in a Ziploc bag from her purse. Bethany followed suit, retrieving an apple and a gingko biloba bar from the drawer next to her.

'We'd invite you to join us,' Amanda said, 'but we're drilling for our Kaplan class. So just be back here in an hour, okay?'

'I can stay, if you want,' I said. 'And then take my lunch at one, so there's someone here.'

They both just looked at me, as if I'd suggested I could explain quantum physics while juggling bowling pins.

'No,' Amanda said, turning to walk out from behind the desk. 'This is better.'

Then they disappeared into a back room, so I picked up my purse and went outside, walking past the parking lot to a bench by the fountain. I took out the peanut butter and jam sandwich I'd brought, then laid it in my lap and took a few deep breaths. For some reason, I was suddenly sure that I was about to cry.

I sat on the bench for an hour. Then I threw out my sandwich and went back inside. Even though it was 12:55, Bethany and Amanda were already back at the desk, which made me seem late. As I navigated a path between their chairs to get to my seat, I could feel them looking at me.

The afternoon dragged. The library was mostly empty, and I suddenly felt like I could hear everything: the buzzing of the fluorescent lights over my head, the squeak of Bethany's chair as she shifted position, the tappety-tap of the online card catalogue station just round the corner. I was used to quiet, but this felt sterile, lonely. I could have been working for my mom, or even flipping crab cakes with a spatula, and I wondered if I'd made the wrong choice. But this was what I had agreed to.

At three o'clock, I pushed my chair back and stood up, then opened my mouth to say my first words in over two hours. 'I guess I'll see you guys tomorrow.'

Amanda turned her head, her braid sliding over her shoulder. She'd been reading some thick book on the history of Italy, licking her finger with each turn of a page. I knew this because I'd heard her, every single time.

'Oh, right,' she said, as Bethany gave me a forced smile. 'See you tomorrow.'

I could feel their gazes right around my shoulder blades as I crossed the reading room and pushed through the glass doors. There, suddenly, was the noise of the world: a car passing, someone laughing in the park across the street, the distant drone of a plane. One day down, I told myself. And only a summer to go.

'Well,' my mother said, handing me the salad bowl, 'if you were supposed to love it, they wouldn't call it work. Right?'

'I guess,' I said.

'It'll get better,' she said, in the confident way of someone who has no idea, none at all. 'And it's great experience. That's what really matters.'

By now, I'd been at the library for three days, and things

were not improving. I knew that I was doing this for Jason, that it was important to him, but Bethany and Amanda seemed to be pooling their considerable IQs in a single-minded effort to completely demoralize me.

I was trying to keep my emails to Jason upbeat and reassuring, but after day two, I couldn't help but vent a little bit about Bethany and Amanda and the way they'd been treating me. That was even before another dressing down in front of a patron, this time from Bethany, who felt compelled to point out – twice – that, to her trained ear, I'd mispronounced Albert Camus' name while directing a sullen summer-school student to the French literature section.

'Cam-oo,' she'd said, holding her mouth in that pursed, French way.

'Cam-oo,' I repeated. I knew I'd said it right and wasn't sure why I was letting her correct me. But I was.

'No, no.' She lifted up her chin again, then fluttered her fingers near her mouth. 'Cam-ooo.'

I just looked at her, knowing now that no matter how many times I said it, even if I trotted Albert himself up to give it a shot, it wouldn't matter. 'Okay,' I said. 'Thanks.'

'No problem,' she said, swivelling in her stupid chair, back to Amanda, who smiled at her, shaking her head, before going back to what she was doing.

So it was no wonder that when I got home that day, I was cheered, greatly, to see that Jason had written back to me. *He* knew how impossible those girls were; he would understand. *A little reassurance*, I thought, opening it with a double-click. Just what I needed.

After I scanned the first two lines, though, it was clear that my self-esteem and general emotional well-being were, to Jason anyway, secondary. *After your last email,* he wrote, *I'm concerned that you're not putting your full attention into the job. Two full paragraphs about the info desk, but you didn't answer the questions I asked you: did the new set of* Scientific Monthly Anthologies *come in? Have you been able to access the tri-county database with my password?* Then, after a couple of reminders about other things it was crucial I attend to, this: *If you're having problems with Bethany and Amanda, you should address them directly. There's no place in a working environment for these interpersonal issues.* He didn't sound like my boyfriend as much as middle management. Clearly I was on my own.

'Honey?'

I looked up. Across the table, my mother was looking at me with a concerned expression, her fork poised over her plate. We always ate at the dining-room table, even though it was just the two of us. It was part of the ritual, as was the rule that she fixed the entrée, I did the salad or vegetables, and we lit the candles, for ambiance. Also we ate at six sharp, and afterwards she rinsed the dishes and loaded them in the dishwasher, while I wiped down the counters and packed up leftovers. When we'd been four instead of two, Caroline and my dad had represented the sloppy, easy-going faction. With them gone, my mother and I kept things neat and organized. I could spot a crumb on the countertop from a mile off, and so could she.

'Yes?' I said.

'Are you okay?'

As I did every time she asked this, I wished I could answer her honestly. There was so much I wanted to tell my mother, like how much I missed my dad, how much I still thought about him. But I'd been doing so well, as far as everyone was concerned, for so long, that it seemed like it would be a failure of some sort to admit otherwise. As with so much else, I'd missed my chance.

I'd never really allowed myself to mourn, just jumped from shocked to fine-just-fine, skipping everything in between. But now I wished I had sobbed for my dad Caroline-style, straight from the gut. I wished that in the days after the funeral, when our house was filled with relatives and too many casseroles and everyone had spent the days grouped round the kitchen table, coming and going, eating and telling great stories about my dad, I'd joined in instead of standing in the doorway, holding myself back, shaking my head whenever anyone saw me and offered to pull out a chair. More than anything, though, I wished I'd walked into my mother's open arms the few times she'd tried to pull me close, and pressed my face to her chest, letting my sad heart find solace there. But I hadn't. I wanted to be a help to her, not a burden, so I held back. And after a while she stopped offering. She thought I was beyond that, when in fact I needed it now more than ever.

My dad had always been the more affectionate of the two of them, known for his tight-to-the-point-of-crushing bear hugs, the way he'd ruffle my hair as he passed by. It was part of his way of filling a room. I always felt close to him, even when there was a distance between us. My mom and I just weren't that effusive. As with Jason, I knew she loved me, even if the signs were subtle: a pat on my shoulder as she passed; her hand smoothing down my hair; the way she always seemed to be able to tell, with one glance, when I was tired or hungry. But sometimes I longed for that sense of someone pulling me close, feeling another heartbeat against mine, even though I'd often squirmed when my dad grabbed hold and threatened to squeeze the life out of me. It was another thing I never thought I'd miss, but did.

'I'm just tired,' I told my mother now. She smiled, nodding: this she understood. 'Tomorrow will be better.'

'That's right,' she replied, with certainty. I wondered if hers was an act too, or if she really believed this. It was so hard to tell. 'Of course it will.'

After dinner, I went up to my room and, after a few false starts and a fair amount of deleting, composed what I thought was a heartfelt yet not too cloying email to Jason. I answered all his questions about the job, and attached, as requested, a copy of the school recycling initiatives he'd implemented, which he wanted to show someone he'd met at camp. Then, and only then, did I allow myself to cross from the administrative to the personal.

I know it may seem petty to you, all this info desk drama, I wrote. *But I guess I just really miss you, and I'm lonely, and it's hard to go to a place where you're so spectacularly unwelcome. I'll just be really happy when you're home.*

This, I told myself, was the equivalent of touching his shoulder, or resting my knee against his as we watched TV. When you only had words, you had to make up for things, say what you might not need to otherwise. In fact, I felt so sure of this, I took it a step further, closing with *I love you, Macy*. Then I hit the send button before I had a chance to change my mind.

With that done, I walked over to my window, pushing it open, and crawled outside. It had rained earlier, one of those quick summer storms, and everything was still dripping and cool. I sat on the sill, propping my bare feet on the shingles. It was the best view, from my roof. You could see all Wildflower Ridge, and even beyond, to the lights of the Lakeview Mall and the university bell tower in the distance. In our old house, my bedroom had been distinct for a different reason. It had the only window that faced the street and a tree with branches close enough to step onto. Because of this, it got a lot of use. Not from me, but from Caroline.

She was wild. There was no other word for it. From seventh grade on, when she went, in my mother's words, 'boy crazy', keeping Caroline under control was a constant battle. There were groundings. Phone restrictions. Cuttings off of allowance, driving privileges. Locks on the liquor cabinet. Sniff tests at the front door. These were played out, in high dramatic form, over dinners and breakfasts, in stomping of feet and raising of voices across living rooms and kitchens. But other transgressions and offences were more secret. Private. Only I was witness to those, always at night, usually from the comfort of my own bed.

I'd be half sleeping, and my bedroom door would creak open, then close quickly. I'd hear the pat-pat of bare feet across the floor, then hear her drop her shoes on the carpet. Next, I'd feel the slight weight as she stepped up onto my bed.

'Macy,' she'd whisper, softly but firmly. 'Quiet. Okay?'

She'd step over my head, then hoist herself up on the sill that ran over my bed, slowly pushing open the window.

'You're going to get into trouble,' I'd whisper.

She'd stick her feet out of the window. 'Hand me my shoes,' she'd say, and when I did she'd toss them out onto the grass, where I'd hear them land with a distant, muted *thunk*.

'Caroline.'

She'd turn and look at me. 'Shut it behind me, don't lock it, I'll be back in an hour. Sweet dreams, I love you.' And then she'd disappear off to the left, where I'd hear her easing herself down the oak tree, branch by branch. When I sat up to shut the window she was usually crossing the lawn, her footsteps leaving dark spots in the grass, shoes tucked under her arm. By the stop sign a block down, a car was always waiting.

It was always more than an hour, sometimes several, before she appeared on the other side of the window, pushing it back up and tumbling in on top of me. All businesslike in the leaving, my sister was usually sloppy and sentimental, smelling of beer and sweet smoke, upon her return. She was often so sleepy she didn't even want to go back to her own room, instead just pushing her way under my blankets, shoes still on, make-up smearing my pillowcases. Sometimes she was crying, but she would never tell me why. Instead she'd just fall asleep beside me, and I'd doze in fits and spells before shaking her awake as the sun was rising and pushing her back to her own room, so she wouldn't be discovered. Then I'd crawl back into bed, smelling her all around me, and tell myself that next time I would lock that window. But I never did.

By the time we moved to Wildflower Ridge, Caroline was in college. She was still going out all the time, sometimes way late, but my parents had given up trying to stop her. Instead, in exchange for her living at home while she attended the local university and waited tables at the country club, they required only that she keep her GPA above a 3.0 and make her entrances and exits as quietly as possible. She didn't need to use my window, which was a good thing, because in the new house there was not a tree nearby and the drop was a lot further.

After my dad died, she sometimes didn't come home at all. My mind had raced with awful possibilities, picturing her dead on the highway, but the truth was actually much more innocuous. By then she'd already fallen hard for Wally from Raleigh, the once-divorced up-and-coming lawyer ten years her senior she'd been seeing for a while. She'd kept him, like so much else, secret from our parents, but after the funeral things got more serious, and before long, he asked her to marry him. All of this took longer than it sounds, summing it up. But at the time it seemed fast, really fast. One day Caroline was tumbling in my window; the next I was standing at the front of a church, all too aware of my uncle Mike walking her down the aisle towards Wally.

People made their comments, of course, about Caroline just needing a father figure, and how she was too young, getting married right after graduation. But she adored Wally, anyone could see that, and the quick nature of the wedding planning made it that much more of a happy distraction for all of us that spring. Plus, and best of all, their shared conviction that this had to be the Best Wedding Ever finally gave Caroline and my mother a solid common ground, and they'd got along pretty well ever since.

So after all that rebellion in her teens, my sister turned out to be surprisingly efficient, bagging a college diploma and a husband all within the same month. Now, as Mrs Wally Thurber, she lived in Atlanta, in a big house on a cul-de-sac where you could hear a highway roaring twenty-four hours a day. It was climate controlled, with a top-of-the-line thermostat system. She never had to open a window for anything.

As for me, I wasn't much for sneaking out, first because I was a jock and always had early practice, and then because Jason and I just didn't do stuff like that. I could only imagine how he'd react if I asked him to pick me up at midnight at the stop sign. Why? he'd say. Nothing would be open, I have yoga in the morning, God, Macy, honestly. And so on. He'd be right, of course. The sneaking out, the partying, all those long nights doing God-knows-what, were Caroline things. She'd taken them with her when she left, and there was no place for them here now. At least in my mind.

'Macy,' she'd say whenever she called and found me home on a Friday night, 'what are you doing? Why aren't you out?' When I'd tell her I was studying, or doing some work for school, she'd exhale so loudly I'd have to hold the phone away from my ear. 'You're young! Go out and live, for God sakes! There's time for all that later!'

My sister, unlike most of her new friends in the garden club and Junior League, did not gloss over her wild past, maintaining instead that it had been crucial to her development as a person.

In her view, my own development in this area was entirely too slow-going, if not completely arrested.

'I'm fine,' I'd tell her, like I always did.

'I know you are, that's the problem. You're a *teenager*, Macy,' she'd say, as if I weren't aware of this or something. 'You're supposed to be hormonal and crazy and emotional and wild. This is the best time of your life! You should be living it!'

So I'd swear that I was going out the next night, and she'd tell me she loved me, and then I'd hang up and go back to my SAT book, or my ironing, or the paper that wasn't due for another two weeks. Or sometimes I'd crawl out onto the roof and remember her wild days and wonder if I really was missing something. Probably not.

But the roof was still a nice sitting spot, at any rate. Even if my adventures in the outside world, my God-knows-what, started and ended there.

Work, despite my mother's assurances, did not improve. In fact, I'd come to realize that the cold treatment I'd received initially was actually Bethany and Amanda being *nice*. Now they hardly spoke to me at all, while keeping me as idle as possible.

By Friday, I'd had enough silence to last a lifetime. Which was too bad for me, because my mother was down at the coast for a weekend developer meet-and-greet conference. I had the entire house, every silent inch of it, to myself for two full days.

She'd invited me to come along, offering the opportunity to lie on the beach or by the pool, all that fun summer beach stuff.

But we both knew I'd say no, and I did. It was just one more thing that reminded me of my dad.

We had a house at the beach, in a little town called Colby that was just over the bridge. It was a true summer house, with shutters that creaked when the wind blew hard, and a front porch that was always covered in the thinnest layer of sand. While we all went down for the big summer weekends, it was mostly my dad's place. He'd bought it before he met my mom, and all the bachelor touches pretty much remained. There was a dartboard on the pantry door, a moose head over the fireplace and the utensil drawer held everything my dad considered crucial to get by: a beer opener, a spatula and a sharp fillet knife. Half the time the stove was on the fritz, not that my dad even noticed unless my mom was there. As long as the grill was gassed up and working, he was happy.

It was his fishing shack, the place he took his buddies to catch red drum in October, mahimahi in April, bluefin tuna in December. My dad always came home with a hangover, a coolerful of fish already cleaned and a sunburn despite the SPF 45 my mom always packed for him. He loved every minute of it.

I wasn't allowed on these trips – they were, traditionally, oestrogen-free – but he often took me down on other weekends, when he needed to work on the house or just felt like getting away. We'd cast off from the beach or take out his boat, play chequers by the fire, and go to this hole-in-the-wall place called the Last Chance, where the waitresses knew him by name and the hamburgers were the best I'd ever tasted. More than our old house, or our Wildflower Ridge place, the beach shack *was* my dad. I knew if he were haunting any place, it would be there, and for that reason I'd stayed away.

None of us had been down, in fact, since he died. His old Chevy truck was still there, locked in the garage, and the spare key it was always my job to fish out from the conch shell under the back porch had probably not been touched either. I knew my mom would probably sell the house and the truck eventually, but she hadn't yet.

So, on Friday afternoon, I came home to find the house completely and totally quiet. This would be good, I told myself. I had a lot of stuff I wanted to get done over the weekend: emails to send out, research on colleges to do and my closet had got really cluttered. Maybe this would be the perfect time to organize my winter sweaters and get some stuff to the thrift shop. Still, the silence was a bit much, so I walked over and turned on the TV, then went upstairs to my room to the radio, flipping past the music channels until I landed on a station where someone was blathering on about science innovations in our century. Even with all those voices going, though, I was acutely aware that I was alone.

Luckily, I got proof otherwise when I checked my email and there was one from Jason. By the second line, though, I knew a bad week had just got much, much worse.

Macy,
I've taken some time before writing back, because I wanted to be clear and sure of what I was going to say. It's been a concern of mine for a while that we've been getting too serious, and since I've been gone I've been thinking hard about our respective needs and

whether our relationship is capable of filling them. I care about you, but your increasing dependency on me – made evident from the closing of your last email – has forced me to really think about what level of commitment I can make to our relationship. I care about you very much, but this upcoming senior year is crucial in terms of my ideological and academic goals, and I cannot take on a more serious commitment. I will have to be very focused, as I'm sure you will be, as well. In view of all these things, I think it's best for us to take a break from our relationship, and each other, until I return at the end of the summer. It will give us both time to think, so that in August we'll know better whether we want the same things, or if it's best to sever our ties and make this separation permanent.

I'm sure you can agree with what I've said here: it just makes sense. I think it's the best solution for both of us.

I read it through once, then, still in shock, again. *This isn't happening*, I thought.

But it was. The world was still turning: if I needed proof, there was the radio across the room, from which I could hear headlines. A war in some Baltic country. Stocks down. Some TV star arrested. And there I sat, staring at the flickering screen, at these words. Words that, like the first ones Jason had read to me from *Macbeth*, were slowly starting to make awful sense.

A break. I knew what that meant: it was what happened right before something was officially and finally broken. Finished. Regardless of the language, it was most likely I was out, all for saying *I love you*. I'd thought we'd said as much to each other in the last few months, even if we never said it aloud. Clearly I'd been wrong.

I could feel my sudden aloneness in my gut, like a punch, and I sat back in my chair, dropping my hands from the keyboard, now aware of how empty the room, the house, the neighbourhood, the world, was all around me. It was like being on the other side of a frame and seeing the camera pull back, showing me growing smaller, smaller, smaller still until I was just a speck, a spot, gone.

I had to get out of there. So I got in my car and drove.

And it helped. I don't know why, but it did. I wound through Wildflower Ridge, cresting the hills and circling the ground that had just been broken for the newest phase, then ventured further, onto the main road and towards the mall. I drove in silence, since every song on the radio was either someone shrieking (not good for my nerves) or someone wailing about lost love (not good, period). In the quiet I'd been able to calm down as I focused on the sound of the engine, of gears shifting, brakes slowing, all things that, at least for now, were working just as they were supposed to.

On my way back, traffic was thick – everyone out for their Friday night. At stoplights I looked at the cars around me, taking in families with kids in car seats, probably heading home from dinner, and college girls in club make-up, blasting the radio and dangling cigarettes out of their open windows. In the middle lane, surrounded by all these strangers, it seemed even more awful that I was going back to an empty house, up to my room to face my computer screen and Jason's email. I could just see him typing it out at his laptop, so methodical, somewhere between condensing the notes he'd taken that day and logging onto his environmental action Listservs. To him, I was a commitment that had become more of a burden than an asset, and his time was just too precious to waste. Not that I had to worry about that. From now on, clearly, I would have plenty of time on my hands.

As I approached the next intersection, I saw the wishbone.

Same bold black strokes, same white van. It was passing in front of me now, and I could see Delia driving, someone else in the passenger seat. I watched them move across the intersection, bumping over the slight dip in the middle. WISH, it said on the back, two letters on each door.

I am not a spontaneous person. But when you're alone in the world, really alone, you have no choice but to be open to suggestions. Those four letters, like the ones that I'd written to Jason, had many meanings and no guarantees. Still, as the van turned onto a side street, I read that WISH again. It seemed as good a time as any to believe, so when my light dropped to green and I could go, I put myself in gear and followed them.

Chapter FOUR

'So I say, I *know* that you're not insulting my outfit. I mean, I can take a lot – already have taken a lot – but I won't tolerate that. You're my sister. You know. A girl has got to draw the line somewhere, right?'

Okay, I thought. *Maybe this was a bad idea.*

After almost turning back three times, two drive-bys and one final burst of courage, I was standing in front of McKimmon House, a mansion in the historical district. In front of me was the Wish Catering van, now parked crookedly against the kerb, the back doors flung open to reveal several racks of serving pans, blocks of packaged napkins and a couple of dented rolling carts. Inside, I could hear a girl's voice.

'So I do it: I draw the line. Which means, in the end, that I have to walk, like, two miles in my new platform sandals, which gave me blisters you would not believe,' she continued, her voice ringing out over the quiet of the street. 'I mean, we're talking deserted roads, no cars passing, and all I could think was – grab those spoons, no, not those, the other ones, right there – that this has got to officially be the worst first date *ever*. You know?'

I took a step backwards, retreating. What had I been thinking, anyway? I started to turn back to my car, thinking at least it wasn't too late to change my mind.

Just then, though, a girl walked to the open doors of the van and saw me. She was small, with a mass of blonde ringlets spilling down her back, and with one look I just knew it was she I'd heard. It was what she had on that made it obvious: a short, shiny black skirt, a white blouse with a plunging neck, tied at the waist, and thigh-high black boots with a thick heel. She had on bright red lipstick, and her skin, pale and white, was glittering in the glow of the streetlight behind me.

'Hey,' she said, seeing me, then turned her back and grabbed a pile of dishtowels before hopping out of the van.

'Hi,' I said. There was more I was going to say, entire words, maybe even a sentence. But for some reason I just froze, as if I'd got this far and now could go no further.

She didn't seem to notice, was too busy grabbing more stuff out of the van while humming under her breath. When she turned round and saw me still standing there, she said, 'You lost or something?'

Again I was stuck for an answer. But this time, it was for a different reason. Her face, which before had been shadowed in the van, was now in the full light, and my eyes were immediately drawn to two scars: one, faint and curving along her jaw line, like an underscore of her mouth, and the other by her right temple, snaking down to her ear. She also had bright blue eyes and rings on every finger, and smelled like watermelon bubble-gum, but these were things I noticed later. The scars, at first, were all I could see.

Stop staring, I told myself, horrified at my behaviour. The girl, for her part, didn't even seem to notice, or be bothered. She was just waiting, patiently, for an answer.

'Um,' I said finally, forcing the words out, 'I was looking for Delia?'

The front door of the van slammed shut, and a second later Monica, the slow girl from my mother's party, appeared. She was carrying a cutting board, which, by the expression of weariness on her face, must have weighed about a hundred pounds. She blew her long bangs out of her face as she shuffled along the kerb, taking her time.

The blonde girl glanced at her. 'Serving forks too, Monotone, okay?'

Monica stopped, then turned herself round slowly – a sort of human three-point turn – and disappeared back behind the van at the same snail's pace.

'Delia's up at the house, in the kitchen,' the girl said to me now, shifting the towels to her other arm. 'It's at the top of the drive, round the back.'

'Oh,' I said, as Monica reappeared, now carrying the cutting board and a few large forks. 'Thanks.'

I started over to the driveway, getting about five feet before she called after me.

'If you're headed up there anyway,' she said, 'would you please please please take something with you? We're running late – and it's kind of my fault, if you want the whole truth – so you'd be really helping me out. If you don't mind.'

'Sure,' I said. I came back down the driveway, passing Monica, who was muttering to herself, along the way. At the back of the van, the blonde girl had pulled out two of the wheeled carts and was piling foil pans onto them, one right after another. When she was done she stuck the towels on top of one, then rolled the other over to me.

'This way,' she said, and I followed her, pushing my cart, to the bottom of the driveway. There we stopped, looking up. It was steep, really steep. We could see Monica still climbing it, about halfway up: it looked like she was walking into the wind.

The girl looked at me, then at the driveway again. I kept noticing her scars, then trying not to, which seemed to make it all that more obvious. 'God,' she said, sighing as she pushed her hair out of her face, 'doesn't it seem, sometimes, that the whole damn world's uphill?'

'Yeah,' I said, thinking about everything that had already happened to me that night. 'It sure does.'

She turned her head and looked at me, then smiled: it changed her whole face, like a spark lighting into a flame, everything brightening, and for a second I lost track of the scars altogether. 'Oh well,' she said, leaning over her cart and tightening her fingers round its handle. 'At least we know the way back will be easy. Come on.'

Her name was Kristy Palmetto.

We introduced ourselves about halfway up the hill, when we stopped, wheezing, to catch our breath. 'Macy?' she'd said. 'Like the store?'

'Yes,' I replied. 'It's a family name, actually.'

'I like it,' she said. 'I intend to change my name as soon as I get to a place where nobody knows me, you know, where I can reinvent myself. I've always wanted to do that. I think I want to be a Veronique. Or maybe Blanca. Something with flair, you know. Anybody can be a Kristy.'

Maybe, I thought, as she started to push her cart again. But even five minutes into our friendship, I knew that this Kristy was different.

As we came up to the side door it opened, and Delia stuck her head out. She had a red Wish Catering apron on and there was a spot of flour on her cheek. 'Are those the ham scones? Or the shrimp and grits?'

'The scones,' Kristy said, pushing her cart up against the side of house and gesturing for me to do the same. 'Or the shrimp.'

Delia just looked at her.

'It's definitely one or the other,' Kristy said. 'Definitely.'

Delia sighed, then came out and started peering into the various pans on the carts.

Kristy leaned against the wall, crossing her arms over her chest. 'That hill is a killer,' she said to Delia. 'We've got to get the van up here or we'll never get everything in on time.'

'If we'd left when we were supposed to,' Delia said, lifting the lid of one pan, 'we could have.'

'I said I was sorry!' Kristy said. To me she added, 'I was having a fashion crisis. Nothing looked good. Nothing! Don't you hate it when that happens?'

'And anyway,' Delia continued, ignoring this tangent, 'they have strict rules about service vehicles up here by the garden. The grass is apparently very fragile.'

'So are my lungs,' Kristy said. 'And if we do it fast, they'll never notice.'

Monica appeared in the open door, holding a cookie sheet. 'Mushrooms?' she asked.

'Meatballs,' Delia said, without looking up. 'Put three trays in, get another three ready.'

Monica turned her body slowly, glancing at the oven behind her. Then she looked at Delia again. 'Meatballs,' she repeated, like it was a foreign word.

'Monica, you do this every weekend,' Delia said. 'Try to retain some knowledge, please God I'm begging you.'

'She retains knowledge,' Kristy said, a little defensively. 'She's just mad at me for holding us up, and that's how she expresses it. She's not good at being forthright about her emotions, you know that.'

'Then go help her, please,' Delia said in a tired voice. 'With the meatballs, not her emotions. Okay?'

'Okay,' Kristy said cheerfully, pulling open the door and going inside.

Delia put her hand on the small of her back and looked at me. 'Hi,' she said, sounding a little surprised. 'It's Macy, right?'

'Yes,' I said. 'I know this is probably a bad time –'

'It's always a bad time,' Delia said with a smile. 'It's a bad business. But I chose it, so I can't really complain. What can I do for you?'

'I just wondered,' I said, then stopped. I felt stupid now for holding her up, when so much else was going on. Maybe she had just been being nice when she'd said she would hire me. But then again, I was already here. I'd climbed that hill. The worst she could do was send me back down. 'I just wondered,' I said again, 'if the offer still stood. About the job.'

Before Delia could answer, Kristy reappeared in the doorway. 'Meatballs are in,' she said. 'Can I get the van now?'

Delia looked down the driveway, then shot a glance in the front window of the house. 'Can *you*? No,' she said.

'It's just one hill.' Kristy rolled her eyes. To me she said, 'I'm a terrible driver. But the fact that I admit it, shouldn't that count for something?'

'No,' Delia said. She looked down the driveway, then at the house, as if weighing the pros and cons, before digging into the pocket of her apron to pull out some keys. 'Once it's up here, unload fast,' she said to Kristy. 'And if anyone starts freaking, pretend you had no idea about the rules.'

'What rules?' Kristy said, reaching for the keys.

Delia shifted them out of her reach, holding them out to me instead. 'And Macy drives. Period. No argument.'

'Fine,' Kristy said. 'Let's just do it, okay?'

She turned on her heel and started down the driveway, bouncing a bit with each step. Even from a distance, you couldn't help but watch her: maybe it was the boots or the hair or the short skirt, but somehow to me it was something else. Something so electric, alive, that I recognized it instantly, if only because it was so lacking in myself.

Delia was watching her too, a resigned expression on her face, before turning her attention back to me. 'If you want a job, it's yours,' she said, dropping the keys into my hand. 'Payday's every other Friday, and you'll usually know your schedule a week in advance. You'll want to invest in a few pairs of black trousers and some white shirts, if you don't have a few already, and we don't work on Mondays. There's probably more you need to know but we're off to a rocky start here, so I'll fill you in later. Okay?'

'Sounds good,' I said.

Kristy, already halfway down the driveway, turned her head and looked up at us. 'Hey, Macy!' she yelled. 'Let's go!'

Delia shook her head, pulling the screen door open. 'Which is to say,' she said to me, 'welcome aboard.'

At the library, I'd had two weeks of training. Here, it was two minutes.

'What's most important,' Kristy said to me, as we stood side by side at the counter, piling mini ham scones onto trays, 'is that you identify what you're carrying and keep all crumpled-up napkins off your tray. No one will pick up anything and stick it in their mouth if it's next to a dirty napkin.'

I nodded, and she continued.

'Here's what you need to remember,' she continued, as Delia bustled past behind us, putting down another sheet of meatballs. 'You don't exist. Just hold out your tray, smile, say, "Ham scones with Dijon mustard," and move on. Try to be invisible.'

'Right,' I said.

'What she means,' Delia clarified from the stove, 'is that as a server, it's your job to blend in and make the partygoer's experience as enjoyable as possible. You are not attending the event: you are facilitating it.'

Kristy handed me the tray of ham scones, plunking down a stack of napkins on its edge. This close to her, I still found my eyes wandering to her scars, but slowly I was getting used to them, my eyes drawn now and then to other things: the glitter on her skin, the two tiny silver hoops in each of her ears. 'Work the edge of the room first. If you cross paths with a gobbler, pause for only a second, then smile and keep moving, even if they're reaching after you.'

'Gobbler?' I said.

'That's someone who will clear your whole tray if you let them. Here's the rule: two and move. When they reach for a third, you're gone.'

'Two and move,' I said. 'Right.'

'If they don't let you move on,' she continued, 'then they cross over to grabber status, which is completely out-of-line behaviour. Then you are wholly within your rights to stomp on their foot.'

'No,' Delia said, over her shoulder. 'Actually, you're not. Just excuse yourself as politely as possible, and get out of arm's reach.'

Kristy looked at me, shaking her head. 'Stomp them,' she said, under her breath. 'Really.'

The kitchen was bustling, Delia moving from the huge stove to the counter, Monica unwrapping one foil tray after another, revealing the salmon, steaks, whipped potatoes. There was a crackling energy in the air, as if everything was on a higher speed than normal, the total opposite of the info desk. If I'd wanted something other than silence, I'd surely found it. In spades.

'If there are old people,' Kristy said now, glancing at the door, 'make sure you go to them, especially if they're sitting down. People notice when Grandma's starving. Watch the room, keep an eye on who's eating and who's not. If you've done a full walk of the room and the goats' cheese currant stuffed celery sticks aren't finding any takers, don't keep walking around.'

'Goats' cheese currant?' I said.

Kristy nodded gravely.

'It was just one time, one job!' Delia hissed from behind us. 'I wish you all would just let that go. God!'

'If something sucks,' Kristy said, 'it sucks. When in doubt, grab some meatballs and get back out there. *Everybody* loves meatballs.'

'What time is it?' Delia asked, as the oven shut with a bang. 'Is it seven?'

'Six forty-five,' Kristy told her, tucking a piece of hair behind her ear. 'We need to get out there.'

I picked up my tray, then stood still while Kristy adjusted one scone that was close to falling off the edge. 'You ready?' she asked me.

I nodded.

She pushed the door open with one hand, and some people standing nearby waiting for drinks at the bar turned and looked at us, their eyes moving immediately to the food. *Invisible*, I thought. After all the attention of the last year or so, I was pretty sure I could get used to that. So I lifted my tray up, squared my shoulders and headed in.

Thirty minutes later, I'd discovered a few things. First, everybody does love meatballs. Second, most gobblers position themselves right by the door, where they have first dibs on anything you bring out, and if you try to sidestep them, they quickly move into grabber mode, although I'd yet to have to stomp anyone. And it's true: you are invisible. They'll say anything with you standing there. Anything.

I now knew that Molly and Roger, the bride and groom, had lived together for three years, a fact that one gobbler relative was sure contributed to the recent death of the family matriarch. Because of some bachelorette party incident, Molly and her maid of honour weren't currently speaking, and the father of the groom, who was supposed to be on the wagon, was sneaking martinis in the bathroom. And, oh yeah, the napkins were wrong. All wrong.

'I'm not sure I understand,' I heard Delia saying as I came back into the kitchen for a last round of goats'-cheese toasts. She was standing by the counter, where she and Monica were getting ready to start preparing the dinner salads, and next to her was the bride, Molly, and her mother.

'They're not right!' Molly said, her voice high pitched and wavery. She was a pretty girl, plump and blonde, and had spent the entire party, from what I could tell, standing by the bar with a pinched expression while people took turns squeezing her shoulder and making soothing it's-okay noises. The groom was outside smoking cigars, had been all night. Molly said, 'They were supposed to say *Molly and Roger*, then the date, then underneath that, *Forever*.'

Delia glanced around her. 'I'm sorry, I don't have one here . . . but don't they say that? I'm almost positive the one I saw did.'

Molly's mother took a gulp of the mixed drink in her hand, shaking her head. Kristy pushed back through the door, dumping a bunch of napkins on her tray, then stopped when she saw the confab by the counter.

'What's going on?' she said. Molly's mother was staring at the scars, I noticed. When Kristy glanced over at her, she looked away, though, fast. If Kristy noticed or was bothered, it didn't show. She just put her tray down, tucking a piece of hair behind her ear.

'Napkin problems,' I told her now.

Molly choked back a sob. 'They don't say *Forever*. They say *Forever* . . .' She trailed off, waving her hand. 'With that dot-dot-dot thing.'

'Dot dot dot?' Delia said, confused.

'You know, that thing, the three periods, that you use when you leave something open-ended, unfinished. It's a –' She paused, scrunching up her face. 'You know! That thing!'

'An ellipsis,' I offered, from across the room.

They all looked at me. I felt my face turn red.

'Ellipsis?' Delia repeated.

'It's three periods,' I told her, but she still looked confused, so I added, 'You use it to make a transition. Also, it's used to show a thought trailing off. Especially in dialogue.'

'Wow,' Kristy said from beside me. 'Go Macy.'

'Exactly!' Molly said, pointing at me. 'It doesn't say *Molly and Roger, Forever*. It says *Molly and Roger, Forever . . . dot dot dot*!' She punctuated these with a jab of her finger. 'Like maybe it's forever, maybe it's not.'

'Well,' Kristy said under her breath to me, 'it is a *marriage*, isn't it?'

Molly had pulled out a Kleenex from somewhere and was

dabbing her face, taking little sobby breaths. 'You know,' I said to her, trying to help, 'I don't think anyone would think that an ellipsis represents doubt or anything. I think it's more, you know, hinting at the future. What lies ahead.'

Molly blinked at me, her face flushed. Then she burst into tears.

'Oh, man,' Kristy said.

'I'm sorry,' I said quickly. 'I didn't mean –'

'It's not about the forever,' her mother told me, sliding her arm over her daughter's shoulders.

'It's all about the forever!' Molly wailed. But then her mother was steering her out of the kitchen, murmuring to her softly. We watched her go, all of us quiet. I felt completely and totally responsible. Clearly, this had not been the moment to show off my grammar prowess.

Delia wiped a hand over her face, shaking her head. 'Good Lord,' she said, once they were out of earshot. She looked at us. 'What should we do?'

Nobody said anything for a second. Then Kristy put down her tray. 'We should,' she announced definitively, 'make salads.' She started over to the counter, where she began unstacking plates. Monica pulled the bowl of greens closer, picking up some tongs, and they got to work.

I looked back over at the door, feeling terrible. Who knew three dots could make such a difference? Like everything else, a love or a wish or whatever, it was all in the way you read it.

'Macy.' I glanced up. Kristy was watching me. She said, 'It's okay. It's not your fault.'

And maybe it wasn't. But that was the problem with having

the answers. It was only after you gave them that you realized they sometimes weren't what people wanted to hear.

'All in all,' Delia said three hours later, as we slid the last cart, now loaded with serving utensils and empty coolers, into the van, 'that was not entirely disastrous. In fact, I'd even go so far as to say it was half decent.'

'There was that thing with the steaks,' Kristy said, referring to a panicked moment right after we distributed the salads, when Delia realized half the fillets were still in the van and, therefore, ice cold.

'Oh, right. I forgot about that.' Delia sighed. 'Well, at least it's over. Next time, everything will go smoothly. Like a well-oiled machine.'

Even I, as the newbie, knew this was unlikely. All night there'd been one little problem after another, disasters arising, culminating, and then somehow getting solved, all at whiplash speed. I was so used to controlling the unexpected at all costs that I'd felt my stress level rising and falling, reacting constantly. For everyone else, though, this seemed perfectly normal. They honestly seemed to believe that things would just work out. And the weirdest thing was, they *did*. Somehow. Eventually. Although even when I was standing right there I couldn't say how.

Now Kristy reached into the back of the van, pulling out a fringed black purse. 'Hate to say it,' she said, 'but I give the marriage a year, tops. There's cold feet, and then there's oh-God-don't-do-it. That girl was *freaking*.'

Monica, sitting on the bumper, offered what I now knew to

be one of her three default phrases, 'Mmm-hmm.' The other two were 'Better quit,' and 'Don't even,' both said with a slow, drawled delivery, the words running together into one: 'Bettaquit,' and 'Donneven.' I didn't know who had christened her Monotone, but they were right on the money.

'When you get home,' Delia said to me, running her hands over her pregnant belly once and then resting her spread fingers there, 'soak that in cold water and some Shout. It should come out.'

I looked down at my shirt and the stain there I'd completely forgotten about. 'Oh, right,' I said. 'I'll do that.'

About halfway through dinner, some overeager groomsman, leaping up to make a toast, had spilled a full glass of Cabernet on me. I'd already learned about gobblers and grabbers: at that moment, I got a full tutorial on gropers. He'd pawed me for about five minutes while attempting to dab the stain out, resulting in me getting arguably more action than I ever had from Jason.

Jason. As I thought his name, I felt a pull in my gut and realized that for the last three hours or so, I'd forgotten all about our break, my new on-hold girlfriend status. But it had happened, was still happening. I'd just been too busy to notice.

A car turned onto the road, its headlights swinging across us, then approaching slowly, very slowly. As it crept closer, I squinted at it. It wasn't a car but more like some sort of van, painted white with grey splotches here and there. Finally it reached us, the driver easing over to the kerb carefully before cutting off the engine. A second later, a head popped out of the window.

'Ladies,' a voice came, deep and formal, 'witness the Bertmobile.'

For a second, no one said anything. Then Delia gasped.

'Oh, my God,' Kristy said. 'You've got to be joking.'

The driver's side door swung open with a loud creak, and Bert hopped out. 'What?' he said.

'I thought you were getting Uncle Henry's car,' Delia said, taking a few steps towards him as Wes climbed out of the passenger door. 'Wasn't that the plan?'

'Changed my mind,' Bert said, jingling his keys. In a striped shirt with a collar, khaki trousers with a leather belt and loafers, he looked as if he were dressed up for something.

'Why?' Delia asked. She walked up to the Bertmobile, her head cocked to the side. A second later, she took a step back, putting her hands on her hips. 'Wait,' she said slowly. 'Is this an –'

'Vehicle that makes a statement?' Bert said. 'Yes. Yes it is.'

'– ambulance?' she finished, her voice incredulous. 'It is, isn't it?'

'No way,' Kristy said, laughing. 'Bert, only you would think you could get action in a car where people have *died*.'

'Where did you get this?' Delia said. 'Is it even legal to drive?'

Wes, now standing by the front bumper, just shook his head in a don't-even-ask kind of way. Now that I looked closer at the Bertmobile, I could in fact make out the faintest trace of an A and part of an M on the front grille.

'I bought it from that auto salvage lot by the airport,' Bert said. You would have thought it was a new-model Porsche by the way he was beaming at it. 'The guy there got it from a town auction. Isn't that the *coolest*?'

Delia looked at Wes. 'What happened to Uncle Henry's Cutlass?'

'I tried to stop him,' Wes told her. 'But you know how he is. He insisted. And it *is* his money.'

'You can't make a statement with a Cutlass!' Bert said.

'Bert,' Kristy said, '*you* can't make a statement, period. I mean, what are you *wearing*? Didn't I tell you not to dress like someone's dad? God. Is that shirt polyester?'

Bert, hardly bothered by this or any of her other remarks, glanced down at his shirt, brushing a hand over the front pocket. 'Poly-*blend*,' he said. 'Ladies like a well-dressed man.'

Kristy just rolled her eyes, while Wes ran a hand over his face. Monica, from behind me, said, 'Donneven.'

'It's an ambulance,' Delia said flatly, as if saying it aloud might get her used to the idea.

'A former ambulance,' Bert corrected her. 'It's got history. It's got personality. It's got –'

'Final sale status,' Wes said. 'He can't take it back. When he drove it off the lot, that was it.'

Delia sighed, shaking her head.

'It's what I wanted,' Bert said. It was quiet for a second: no one, it seemed, had an argument for this.

Finally Delia walked over and put her arms round Bert, pulling him close to her. 'Well, happy birthday, little man,' she said, ruffling his hair. 'I can't believe you're already sixteen. It makes me feel *old*.'

'You're not old,' he said.

'Old enough to remember the day you were born,' she said, pulling back from him and brushing his hair out of his face. 'Your mom was so happy. She said you were her wish come true.'

Bert looked down quickly, turning his keys in his fingers. Delia leaned close to him, then whispered something I couldn't hear, and he nodded. When he looked up again, his face was flushed, and for a second, I saw something in his face I recognized, something familiar. But then he turned his head, and just like that, it was gone.

'Did you guys officially meet Macy?' Delia asked, nodding at me. 'Macy, these are my nephews, Bert and Wes.'

'We met the other night,' I said.

'Bert sprung at her from behind some garbage cans,' Wes added.

'God, are you two still doing that?' Kristy said. 'It's so stupid.'

'I only did it because I'm down,' Bert said, shooting me an apologetic look. 'By three!'

'All I'm saying,' Kristy said, pulling a nail file out of her purse, 'is that the next person who leaps out at me from behind a door is getting a punch in the gut. I don't care if you're down or not.'

'Mmm-hmm,' Monica agreed.

'I thought she was Wes,' Bert grumbled. 'And I wouldn't jump out from behind a door anyway. That's basic. We're way beyond that.'

'Are you?' Kristy asked, but Bert acted like he didn't hear her. To me she said, 'It's this stupid gotcha thing; they've been doing it for weeks now. Leaping out at each other and us, scaring the hell out of everyone.'

'It's a game of wits,' Bert said to me.

'Half-wits,' Kristy added.

'There's nothing,' Bert said reverently, 'like a good gotcha.'

Delia, yawning, put a hand over her mouth, shaking her head. 'Well, I hate to break this up, but I'm going home,' she announced. 'Old pregnant ladies have to be in bed by midnight. It's the rule.'

'Come on!' Bert said, sweeping his hand across the ambulance's hood. 'The night is young! The Bertmobile needs *christening*!'

'We're going to ride around in an ambulance?' Kristy said.

'It's got all the amenities!' Bert told her. 'It's just like a car. It's *better* than a car!'

'Does it have a CD player?' she asked him.

'Actually –'

'No,' Wes told her. 'But it does have a broken intercom system.'

'Oh, well, then,' she said, waving her hand. 'I'm sold.'

Bert shot her a look, annoyed, but she smiled at him, squeezing his arm as she started over to the Bertmobile. Monica stood up and followed her, and they went round to the back, pulling open the rear doors.

'Have a fun night,' Delia called after them. 'Don't drive too fast, Bert, you hear?'

This was greeted with uproarious laughter from everyone but Wes – who looked like he would have laughed but was trying not to – and Bert, who just ignored it as he walked over to the driver's side door.

'Wes,' Delia called out, 'can you come here for a sec?'

Wes started over towards her, but I was in the way, and we did that weird thing where both of us went to one side, then the other, in tandem. During this awkward dance I noticed he was even better looking up close than from a distance – with those dark eyes, long lashes, hair curling just over his collar, his jeans low on his hips – and he had a tattoo on his arm, something Celtic-looking that poked out from under the sleeve of his T-shirt.

Finally I stopped moving, and he was able to get past me. 'Sorry about that,' he said, smiling, and I felt myself flush for some reason as I watched him disappear round the side of the van.

'Where are we supposed to sit?' I could hear Kristy asking from the back of the Bertmobile. 'Oh, Jesus, is that a gurney?'

'No,' Bert said. 'It's where the gurney used to be. That's just a cot I put in until I find something more comfortable.'

'A cot?' Kristy said. 'Bert, you're *entirely* too confident about this car's potential. Really.'

'Just get in, will you?' Bert snapped. 'My birthday is ticking away. Ticking!'

Wes was walking back to the Bertmobile as I dug out my keys and started towards my car, passing the van on my way.

'Have a good night,' he said to me, and I nodded, my tongue fumbling for a response, but once I realized that saying the same thing back would have been fine – God, what was wrong with me? – it was too late, and he was already getting into the Bertmobile.

As I passed the van, Delia was in the driver's seat fastening her seat belt. 'You did great, Macy,' she said. 'Just great.'

'Thanks.'

She grabbed a pen off the dashboard, then reached into her pocket and pulled out a crumpled napkin. 'Here,' she said, writing something on it, 'this is my number. Give me a call on Monday and I'll let you know when I can use you next. Okay?'

'Okay,' I said, taking the napkin and folding it. 'Thanks again. I had a really good time.'

'Yeah?' She smiled at me, surprised. 'I'm glad. Drive safe, you hear?'

I nodded, and she cranked the engine, then pulled away from the kerb, beeping the horn as she turned the corner.

I'd just unlocked my door when the Bertmobile pulled up beside me. Kristy was leaning forward from the back seat, hand on the radio: I could hear the dial moving across stations, from static to pop songs to some thumping techno bass beat. She looked across Wes, who was digging in the glove compartment, right at me.

'Hey,' she said, 'you want to come out with us?'

'Oh, no,' I said. 'I really have to go –'

Kristy twisted the dial again, and the beginning of a pop song blasted out, someone shrieking '*Baaaaby!*' at full melodic throttle. Bert and Wes both winced.

'– home,' I finished.

Kristy turned down the volume, but not much. 'Are you sure?' she said. 'I mean, do you really want to pass this up? How often do you get to ride in an ambulance?'

One time too many, I thought.

'It's a refurbished ambulance,' Bert grumbled.

'Whatever,' Kristy said. To me she added, 'Come on, live a little.'

'No, I'd better go,' I said. 'But thanks.'

Kristy shrugged. 'Okay,' she told me. 'Next time, though, okay?'

'Right,' I said. 'Sure.'

I stood there and watched them, noting how carefully Bert turned round in the opposite driveway, the way Wes lifted one hand to wave as they pulled away. Maybe in another life I might have been able to take a chance, to jump into the back of an ambulance and not remember the time I'd done it before. But risk hadn't been working out for me lately; I needed only to go home and see my computer screen to know that. So I did what I always did these days, the right thing. But, before I did, I glanced in my side mirror, catching one last look at the Bertmobile as it turned a far corner. Then, once they were gone, I started my engine and headed home.

Chapter FIVE

Dear Jason,

I received your email, and I have to say I was surprised to learn that you felt I'd been

Dear Jason,

I received your email, and I can't help but feel that maybe you should have let me know if you felt our relationship was

Dear Jason,

I received your email, and I can't believe you'd do this to me when all I did was say I love you, which is something most people who've been together can

No, *no*, I thought, and definitely, *no*.

It was Monday morning, and even with two full days to craft a response to Jason's email, I had nothing. The main problem was that what he'd written to me was so cold, so lacking in emotion, that each time I started to reply, I tried to use the same tone. But I couldn't. No matter how carefully I worked at it, by the time I finished all I could see was the raw sadness in the lines as I scanned them, all my failings and flaws cropping up in the spaces between the words. So, finally, I decided that the best response – the safest – was none at all. Since I hadn't heard from him, I assumed he'd accepted my silence as agreement. It was probably just what he wanted anyway.

As I drove to the library to begin another week at the info desk, I got stuck behind an ambulance at a stoplight, which made me think, as I had pretty frequently since Friday, about Wish Catering. I'd already had to confess about my new job to my mother, after she found my wine-stained shirt in the laundry room soaking in Shout. That's what I get for following instructions.

'But, honey,' she said, her voice more questioning than disapproving, but it was early yet, 'you already have a job.'

'I know,' I said as she took another doubtful look at the shirt, eyeing the stain, 'but I bumped into Delia on Friday at the supermarket, and she was all frazzled and short-handed, so I offered to help her out. It just kind of happened.' This last part, at least, was true.

She shut the washer, then turned and looked at me, crossing her arms over her chest. 'I just think,' she said, 'that you might get overwhelmed. Your library job is a lot of responsibility. Jason is trusting you to really give it your full attention.'

This would have been, in any other world, the perfect time to tell my mother about Jason's decision and our break. But I didn't. I knew my mother thought of me as the good daughter, the one she could depend on to be as driven and focused as she was. For some reason, I was sure that Jason's breaking up with me would make me less than that in her eyes. It was bad enough that *I* assumed I wasn't up to Jason's standards. Even worse would be for her to think so.

'Catering is just a once in a while thing,' I said now. 'It's not a distraction. I might not even do it again. It was just . . . for fun.'

'Fun?' she said. Her voice was so surprised, as if I'd told her that driving nails into my arms was, also, just that enjoyable. 'I would think it would be horrible, having to be on your feet all the time and waiting on people . . . plus, well, that woman just seemed so disorganized. I'd go crazy.'

'Oh,' I said, 'that was just when they were here. On Friday night, they were totally different.'

'They were?'

I nodded. Another lie. But my mother would never have understood why, in some small way, the mayhem of Delia's business would appeal to me. I wasn't even sure I could explain it myself. All I knew was that the rest of the weekend had been a stark contrast to those few hours on Friday night. During the days, I'd done all the things I was supposed to: I went to yoga class, did laundry, cleaned my bathroom and tried to compose an email to Jason. I ate lunch and dinner at the same time both days, using the same plate, bowl and glass, washing them after each meal and stacking them neatly in the dish rack, and went to bed by eleven, even though I rarely fell asleep, if at all, before two. For forty-eight hours, I spoke to no one but a couple of telemarketers. It was so quiet that I kept finding myself sitting at the kitchen table listening to my own breathing, as if in all this order and cleanliness I needed that to prove I was alive.

'Well, we'll just see how it goes, okay?' my mother had said as I reached over and turned on the washer. The water started gurgling, tackling the wine stain. 'The library job is still your first priority. Right?'

'Right,' I agreed, and that was that.

Now, however, as I walked in to begin my second week of work – even though our shifts began at nine, and it was only eight fifty, Bethany and Amanda were, naturally, already there and in place in their chairs – I felt a sense of inescapable dread. Maybe it was the silence. Or the stillness. Or the way Amanda raised her head and looked at me as I approached, her brow furrowing.

'Oh, Macy,' she said, with the same slightly surprised tone she'd used every day I'd showed up, 'I wondered if you would make it in today . . . considering.'

I knew what she meant, of course. Jason wasn't one to spill secrets, but there were a couple of other people from our high school at Brain Camp, one of whom, a guy named Rob who squinted all the time, was good friends with both Amanda and Jason. Whatever way it had gone, clearly this break wasn't just my secret any more. Now, it was Information and, as they were with everything else, Bethany and Amanda were suddenly experts.

'Considering,' Amanda said, repeating the word slowly as if, by not rising to the bait, I must not have heard her, 'what happened with you and Jason.'

I turned so I was facing her. 'It's just a break. And it has nothing to do with my job.'

'Maybe so,' she said as Bethany put a pen to her lips. 'We were just concerned it might, you know, affect your performance.'

'No,' I said. 'It won't.' And then I turned back to my computer screen. I could see their faces reflected there, the way Amanda shook her head in a she's-so-pathetic way, how Bethany pursed her lips, silently agreeing, before slowly swivelling back to face forward.

And so began my longest day yet. I didn't do much of anything, other than answer an all-time high of two questions (one from a man who stumbled in, unshaven and stinking of liquor, to ask about a job opening, and another from a six-year-old concerning how to find Mickey Mouse's address, both of which were, at least in Bethany and Amanda's opinion, not worth their time, but fully suited to mine). All this made it more than clear that last week, I'd been an annoyance to be tolerated. Now I was one easily, and rightfully, ignored.

It was just after dinner and I was following routine, wiping down the kitchen countertops, when the phone rang. I didn't even reach for it, assuming it was a client calling for my mother. But then I heard her office door open.

'Macy? It's for you.'

The first thing I heard when I picked up the kitchen phone was someone sobbing, in that blubbering, gaspy kind of way.

'Oh, Lucy, honey, please,' I heard a voice saying over it.

'You only do this when I'm on the phone, why is that? Hmmm? Why –'

'Hello?' I said.

'Macy, hi, it's Delia.' The crying started up again fresh, climbing to a full-out wail. 'Oh, Lucy, sweetie, please God I'm begging you, just let Mommy talk for five seconds . . . Look, here's your bunny, see?'

I just sat there holding the phone, as the crying subsided to sniffling, then to hiccuping, then stopped altogether.

'Macy,' she said, 'I am so sorry. Are you still there?'

'Yes,' I told her.

She sighed, that world-weary exhale I already associated with her, even though we hardly knew each other. 'The reason I'm calling,' she began, 'is that I'm kind of in a bind and I could use an extra pair of hands. I've got this big luncheon thing tomorrow, and currently I'm about two hundred finger sandwiches behind. Can you help me out?'

'Tonight?' I said, glancing at the clock on the stove. It was 7:05, the time when I usually went upstairs to check my email, then brushed and flossed my teeth before reviewing a few pages of my SAT word book so that I wouldn't feel too guilty about camping out in front of the TV until I was tired enough to try sleeping.

'I know it's short notice, but everyone else already had plans,' Delia said now, and I heard her running water. 'So don't feel bad about saying no . . . It was just a shot in the dark, you know. I dug out your mom's business card and thought I'd at least try to woo you over here.'

'Well,' I said, and the no, I can't, I'm sorry, was perched

right there on my tongue, so close to my saying it that I could feel my lips forming the words. But then I looked around our silent, perfectly clean kitchen. It was summer, early evening. Once this had been my favourite time of year, my favourite time of night. When the fireflies came out, and the heat cooled. How had I forgotten that?

'. . . don't know why you'd want to spend a few hours up to your elbows in watercress and cream cheese,' Delia was saying in my ear as I snapped back to reality. 'Unless you just had nothing else to do.'

'I don't,' I said suddenly, surprising myself. 'I mean, nothing that can't wait.'

'Really?' she said. 'Wonderful. Oh, God. You're saving my life! Here, let me give you directions. Now, it's kind of a ways out, but I'll pay you from right now, so your driving time will be on the clock.'

As I picked a pen out of the jar by the phone, pulling a notepad closer to me, I had a sudden pang of worry thinking about this deviation from my routine. But this was just one night, one chance to vary and see where it took me. The fireflies were probably already out: maybe it wasn't just a season or a time but a whole world I'd forgotten. I'd never know until I stepped out into it. So I did.

Delia's directions were like Delia: clear in places, completely frazzled in others. The first part was easy. I'd taken the main road through town then past the city limits, where the scenery turned from new subdivisions and office buildings to smaller farmhouses to big stretches of pasture and dairy lands, plus cows. It was the turn off from that road, however – which led to Delia's street – where I got stuck. Or lost. Or both. It just wasn't *there*, period, no matter how many times I drove up and down looking for it. Which became sort of embarrassing, as there was a produce stand I kept driving by – its sign, painted in bright red, said, TOMATOES FRESH FLOWERS PIES – where an older woman was sitting in a lawn chair, a large flashlight in her lap, reading a paperback book. The third time I passed her, she put the book down and watched me. The fourth, she got involved.

'You lost, sugar?' she called out as I crept past, scanning the scenery for the turn off – 'It's a narrow dirt road, blink and you'll miss it,' Delia had said – wondering if this was some sort of induction process for new employees or something, like an initiation ritual or catering boot camp. I stopped my car, then backed up slowly. By the time I reached the stand, the woman had got out of her chair and was coming to bend down into my passenger window. She looked to be in her early fifties, maybe, with greying hair pulled back at her neck, and was wearing jeans and a white tank top, with a shirt tied round her ample waist. She still had the paperback in her hand, and I glanced at the title: *The Choice*, by Barbara Starr. There was a shirtless man on the cover, a woman in a tight dress pressed against him. Her place was held with a nail file.

'I'm looking for Sweetbud Drive,' I said. 'It's supposed to be off this road, but I can't –'

'Right there,' she said, turning and pointing to a gravel strip to the right of the produce stand, so narrow it looked more like a driveway than a real street. 'Not your fault you missed it; the sign got stolen again last night. Bunch of damn potheads, I swear.' She indicated a spot on the other side of the drive where, in fact, there was a metal pole, no sign attached. 'And that's the *fourth* time this year. Now nobody can find my house until the DOT gets someone out here to replace it.'

'Oh,' I said. 'That's terrible.'

'Well,' she replied, switching her paperback to the other hand, 'maybe not terrible. But it sure is inconvenient. Like life isn't complicated enough. You should at least be able to follow the *signs*.' She stood up, stretching. 'Oh, and on your way, watch out for the big hole. It's right past the sculpture, and it's a doozy. Stick to the left.' Then she patted my hood, smiled at me and walked back to her lawn chair.

'Thank you,' I called out after her, and she waved at me over her shoulder. I turned round in the road and started down Sweetbud Drive, mindful that somewhere up ahead there was both a sculpture and a big hole. I saw the sculpture first.

It was on the side of the narrow drive, in a clearing between two trees. Made of rusted metal, it was huge – at least six feet across – shaped like an open hand. It was encircled by a piece of rebar with a bicycle chain woven round its edges, like some sort of garland. In the palm of the hand, a heart shape had been cut out, and a smaller heart, painted bright red, hung within it, spinning slightly in the breeze that was blowing. I just sat there, my car barely crunching over the gravel, and stared at it. I couldn't help but think I had seen that design somewhere before.

And then I hit the hole.

Clunk! went my front left wheel, disappearing into it entirely.

O-kay, I thought, as my entire car tilted to one side, this *must be why she called it a doozy*.

I was sitting there, trying to think of a way I could get myself out somehow and save the embarrassment of having to make such an entrance, when I looked up ahead and saw someone walking towards me from a house at the end of the road. It was just getting dark, so at first it was hard to make them out. Only when he was right in front of my wildly slanting front bumper did I realize it was Wes.

'Whatever you do,' he called out, 'don't try and reverse out of it. That only makes it worse.' Then, as he got closer, he looked at me and started slightly. I wasn't sure who he'd been expecting, but obviously it was a surprise seeing me. 'Hey,' he said.

'Hi.' I swallowed. 'I'm, um –'

'Stuck,' he finished. He disappeared for a second, ducking down to examine the hole and my tyre within it. Leaning out of my window, at the odd angle I was, I found myself almost level with the top of his head. A second later, when he looked up at me, we were face to face, and again, even under these circumstances, I was struck by how good looking he was, in that accidental, doesn't-even-know-it kind of way. Which only made it worse. Or better. Or whatever. 'Yup,' he said, as if there'd been any doubt, 'you're in there, all right.'

'I was warned too,' I told him as he stood up. 'I just saw that sculpture, and I got distracted.'

'The sculpture?' He looked at it, then at me. 'Oh, right. Because you know it.'

'What?' I said.

He blinked, seeming confused, then shook his head.

'Nothing. I just thought maybe, um, you'd seen it before, or something. There are a few around town.'

'No, I haven't,' I said. The breeze had stopped blowing now, and in the stillness the heart was just there in the centre of the hand, suspended. 'It's amazing, though.'

I heard a door slam off to my right and glanced over to see Delia standing on the front porch of a white house, her arms crossed over her chest. 'Macy?' she called out. 'Is that you? Oh, God, I forgot to tell you about the hole. Hold on, we'll get you out. I'm such an idiot. Just let me call Wes.'

'I'm on it,' Wes yelled back, and she put a hand on her chest, relieved, then sat down on the steps. Then, to me, he added, 'Hold tight. I'll be back in a second.'

I sat there, watching as he jogged down the street, disappearing into the yard of the house at the very end. A minute later an engine started up, and a Ford pickup truck pulled out to face me, then drove down the side of the road, bumping over the occasional tree root. Wes drove past me, then backed up until his back bumper was about a foot from mine. I heard a few clanks and clunks as he attached something to my car. Then I watched in my side mirror as he walked back up to me, his white T-shirt bright in the dark.

'The trick,' he said, leaning into my window, 'is to get the angle just right.' He reached over, putting his hands on my steering wheel, and twisted it slightly. 'Like that,' he said. 'Okay?'

'Okay,' I said, putting my hands where his had been.

'Have you out in a sec,' he said. He walked back to the truck, got in and put it in gear. I sat there, hands locked where he'd said to keep them, and waited.

The trucked revved, then moved forward, and for a second, nothing happened. But then, suddenly, I was moving. Rising. Up and out, bit by bit, until, in my headlights, I could see the hole emerging in front of me, now empty. And it was huge. More like a crater, like something you'd see on the moon. A doozy, indeed.

Once I was back on level ground, Wes hopped out of the truck, undoing the tow rope. 'You're fine now,' he called from somewhere near my bumper. 'Just keep to the left. *Way* left.'

I stuck my head out of the window. 'Thank you,' I said. 'Really.'

He shrugged. 'No problem. I do it all the time. Just pulled out the FedEx guy yesterday.' He tossed the tow rope into the truck bed, where it landed with a thunk. 'He was not happy.'

'It's a big hole,' I said, taking another look at it.

'It's a monster.' He ran a hand through his hair, and I saw the tattoo on his arm again, but he was too far away for me to make it out. 'We need to fill it, but we never will.'

'Why not?'

He glanced over to Delia's house. I could now see her coming down the walk. She had on a long skirt and a red T-shirt, her feet bare. 'It's a family thing,' he said. 'Some people believe everything happens for a reason. Even massive holes.'

'But you don't,' I said.

'Nope,' he said. He looked over my car at the hole, studying it for a second. I was watching him, not even aware of it until he glanced at me. 'Anyway,' he said, as I focused back on my steering wheel, 'I'll see you around.'

'Thanks again,' I said, shifting into first.

'No problem. Just remember: left.'

'Way left,' I told him, and he nodded, then knocked the side of my bumper, *rap-rap*, and started back to the truck. As he climbed in, I turned my wheel and eased round the hole, then drove the fifty feet or so to Delia's driveway, where she was waiting for me. Right as I reached to open my door, Wes's truck blurred past in my rearview mirror: I could see him in silhouette, his face illuminated by the dashboard lights. Then he disappeared behind a row of trees, gravel crunching, and was gone.

'The thing about Wes,' Delia said to me, unwrapping another package of turkey, 'is that he thinks he can fix anything. And if he can't fix it, he can at least do something with the pieces of what's broken.'

'That's bad?' I asked, dipping my spreader back into the huge, industrial-size jar of mayonnaise on the table in front of me.

'Not bad,' she said. 'Just – different.'

We were in Delia's garage, which served as Wish Catering central. It was outfitted with two industrial-size ovens, a large fridge and several stainless-steel tables, all of which were piled with cutting boards and various utensils. We were sitting on opposite sides of one of the tables, assembling sandwiches. The garage door was open, and outside I could hear crickets chirping.

'The way I see it,' she continued, 'is that some things are just meant to be the way they are.'

'Like the hole,' I said, remembering how he'd glanced at her, saying this.

She put down the turkey she was holding and looked at me. 'I know what he told you,' she said. 'He said that I was the reason the hole was still there, and that if I'd just let him fill it we wouldn't have the postman pissed off to the point of sabotaging our mail, and I wouldn't be facing yet another bill from Lakeview Auto for some poor client who busted their Goodyear out there.'

'No,' I said slowly, spreading the mayonnaise in a thin layer on the bread in front of me, 'he said that some people believe everything happens for a reason. And some people, well, don't.'

She thought for a second. 'It's not that I believe everything happens for a reason,' she said. 'It's just that . . . I just think that some things are meant to be broken. Imperfect. Chaotic. It's the universe's way of providing contrast, you know? There have to be a few holes in the road. It's how life *is*.'

We were quiet for a second. Outside, the very last of the sunset, fading pink, was disappearing behind the trees.

'Still,' I said, putting another slice of bread on the one in front of me, 'it *is* a big hole.'

'It's a huge hole,' she conceded, reaching for the mayonnaise. 'But that's kind of the point. I mean, I don't want to fix it because to me, it's not broken. It's just here, and I work around it. It's the same reason I refuse to trade in my car, even though, for some reason, the A/C won't work when I have the radio on. I just choose: music, or cold air. It's not that big a deal.'

'The A/C won't work when the radio is on?' I asked. 'That's so weird.'

'I know.' She pulled out three more slices of bread, putting mayonnaise, then lettuce on them assembly-line style. 'On a bigger scale, it's the reason that I won't hire a partner to help me with the catering, even though it's been chaos on wheels with Wish gone. Yes, things are sort of disorganized. And, sure, it would be nice to not feel like we're close to disaster every second.'

I started another sandwich, listening.

'But if everything was always smooth and perfect,' she continued, 'you'd get too used to that, you know? You have to have a little bit of disorganization now and then. Otherwise, you'll never really enjoy it when things go right. I know you think I'm a flake. Everyone does.'

'I don't,' I assured her, but she shook her head, not believing me.

'It's okay. I mean, I can't tell you how many times I've caught Wes out there with someone from the gravel place, secretly trying to fill that hole.' She put another row of bread down. 'And Pete, my husband, he's tried twice to lure me to the car dealership to trade in my old thing for a new car. And, as far as the business, well . . . I don't know. They leave me alone on that. Because of Wish. Which is so funny, because if she was here, and saw how things are . . . she'd flip out. She was the most organized person in the *world*.'

'Wish,' I said, reaching for the mayonnaise. 'That's such a cool name.'

She looked up at me, smiling. 'It is, isn't it? Her real name was Melissa. But when I was little, I mispronounced it all the time, you know, Ma-wish-a. Eventually, it just got shortened to Wish, and everyone started calling her that. She never minded.

I mean, it fitted her.' She picked up the knife at her elbow, then carefully sliced the sandwiches into halves, then quarters, before stacking them onto the tray beside us. 'This was her baby, this business. After she and the boys' dad divorced, and he moved up North, it was like her new start, and she ran it like a well-oiled machine. But then she got sick . . . breast cancer. She was only thirty-nine when she died.'

It felt so weird, to be on the other side, where you were the one expected to offer condolences, not receive them. I wanted my 'sorry' to sound genuine, because it was. That was the hard thing about grief, and the grieving. They spoke another language, and the words we knew always fell short of what we wanted them to say.

'I'm so sorry, Delia,' I told her. 'Really.'

She looked up at me, a piece of bread in one hand. 'Thank you,' she said, then placed it on the table in front of her. 'I am too.' Then she smiled at me sadly, and started to assemble another sandwich. I did the same, and neither of us said anything for a few minutes. The silence wasn't like the ones I'd known lately, though: it wasn't empty as much as chosen. There's an entirely different feel to quiet when you're with someone else, and at any moment it could be broken. Like the difference between a pause and an ending.

'You know what happens when someone dies?' Delia said suddenly, startling me a bit. I kept putting my sandwich together, though, not answering: I knew there was more. 'It's like, everything and everyone refracts, each person having a different reaction. Like me and Wes. After the divorce, he fell in with this bad crowd, got arrested, she hardly knew what to do with him. But then, when she got sick, he changed. Now he's totally different, how he's so protective of Bert and focused on his welding and the pieces he makes. It's his way of handling it.'

'Wes does welding?' I asked, and then, suddenly, I thought of the sculpture. 'Did he do –'

'The heart in hand,' she finished for me. 'Yeah. He did. Pretty incredible, huh?'

'It is,' I said. 'I had no idea. I was talking about it with him and he didn't even tell me.'

'Well, he'll never brag on it,' she said, pulling the mayonnaise over to her. 'That's how he is. His mom was the same way. Quiet and incredible. I really envy that.'

I watched her as she cut another two sandwiches down, the knife clapping against the cutting board. 'I don't know,' I said. 'You seem to be pretty incredible. Running this business with a baby, and another on the way.'

'Nah.' She smiled. 'I'm not. When Wish died, it just knocked the wind out of me. Truly. It's like that stupid thing Bert and Wes do, the leaping-out thing, trying to scare each other: it was the biggest gotcha in the world.' She looked down at the sandwiches. 'I'd just assumed she'd be okay. It had never occurred to me she might actually just be . . . gone. You know?'

I nodded, just barely. I felt bad that I didn't tell her about my dad, chime in with what I knew, how well I knew it. With Delia, though, I wasn't that girl, the one whose dad had died. I wasn't anybody. And I liked that. It was selfish but true.

'And then she was,' Delia said, her hand on the bread bag. 'Gone. Gotcha. And suddenly I had these two boys to take care of, plus a newborn of my own. It was just this huge loss, this huge *gap*, you know.'

'I know,' I said softly.

'Some people,' she said, and I wasn't even sure she'd heard me, 'they can just move on, you know, mourn and cry and be done with it. Or at least seem to be. But for me . . . I don't know. I didn't want to fix it, to forget. It wasn't something that was broken. It's just . . . something that happened. And, like that hole, I'm just finding ways, every day, of working around it. Respecting and remembering and getting on at the same time. You know?'

I nodded, but I didn't know. I'd chosen instead to just change my route, go miles out of the way, as if avoiding it would make it go away once and for all. I envied Delia. At least she knew what she was up against. Maybe that's what you got when you stood over your grief, facing it finally. A sense of its depths, its area, the distance across, and the way over or around it, whichever you chose in the end.

Chapter SIX

'Okay,' Wes said under his breath. 'Watch and learn.'

'Right,' I said.

We were at the Lakeview Inn, finishing up appetizers for a retirement party, and Wes and I were in the coat closet, where he was teaching me the art of the gotcha. I'd been sent by a woman to hang up her wrap and found him there, perfectly positioned and silent, lying in wait.

'Wes?' I'd said, and he'd slid a finger to his lips, gesturing for me to come closer with his other hand. Which I'd done, unthinkingly, even as I felt that same fluttering in my stomach I always felt when I was around Wes. Even when we weren't in an enclosed, small space together. Goodness.

In the next room, I could hear the party: the clinking of forks against plates, voices trilling in laughter, strains of the piped-in violin music that the Lakeview Inn had played at my sister's wedding as well.

'Okay,' Wes said, his voice so low I would have leaned closer to hear him if we weren't already about as close as we could get. 'It's all in the timing.'

An overcoat that smelled like perfume was hanging in my face: I pushed it aside as quietly as possible.

'Not now,' Wes was whispering. 'Not now . . . not now . . .'

Then I heard it: footsteps. Muttering. Had to be Bert.

'Okay . . .' he said, and then he was moving, standing up, going forward, 'now. *Gotcha!*'

Bert's shriek, which was high pitched to the point of ear-splitting, was accompanied by him flailing backwards and losing his footing, then crashing into the wall behind him. 'God!' he said, his face turning red, then redder as he saw me. I couldn't really blame him: there was no way to be splayed on the floor and still look dignified. He said, sputtering, 'That was –'

'Number six,' Wes finished for him. 'By my count.'

Bert got to his feet, glaring at us. 'I'm going to get you so good,' he said darkly, pointing a finger at Wes, then at me, then back at Wes. 'Just you wait.'

'Leave her out of it,' Wes told him. 'I was just demonstrating.'

'Oh no,' Bert said. 'She's part of it now. She's one of us. No more coddling for you, Macy.'

'Bert, you've already jumped out at her,' Wes pointed out.

'It's *on*!' Bert shouted, ignoring this. Then he stalked down the hallway, again muttering, and disappeared into the main room, letting the door bang shut behind him. Wes watched him go, hardly bothered. In fact, he was smiling.

'Nice work,' I told him as we started down the hallway to the kitchen.

'It's nothing,' he said. 'With enough practice, you too can pull a good gotcha someday.'

'Frankly,' I said, 'I'm a little curious about the derivation of all this.'

'Derivation?'

'How it started.'

'I know what it means,' he said. For a second I was horrified, thinking I'd offended him, but he grinned at me. 'It's just such an SAT word. I'm impressed.'

'I'm working on my verbal,' I explained.

'I can tell,' he said, nodding at one of the Lakeview Inn valets as he passed. 'Truthfully, it's just this dumb thing we started about a year ago. It pretty much came from us living alone in the house after my mom died. It was really quiet, so it was easy to sneak around.'

I nodded as if I understood this, although I couldn't really picture myself leaping out at my mother from behind a door or potted plant, no matter how perfect the opportunity. 'I see,' I said.

'Plus,' Wes continued, 'there's just something fun, every once in a while, about getting the shit scared out of you. You know?'

This time I didn't nod or agree. I could do without scares, planned or unplanned, for a while. 'Must be a guy thing,' I said.

He shrugged, pushing the kitchen door open for me. 'Maybe,' he said.

As we walked in, Delia was standing in the centre of the room, hands pressed to her chest. Just by the look on her face, I knew something was wrong.

'Wait a second,' she said. 'Everyone freeze.'

We did. Even Kristy, who normally ignored most directives,

stopped what she was doing, a cheese cracker dangling in midair over her tray.

'Where,' Delia said slowly, taking a look around the room, 'are the hams?'

Silence. Then Kristy said, her voice low, 'Uh-oh.'

'Don't say that!' Delia moved down the counter, hands suddenly flailing as she pulled all of the cardboard boxes we'd lugged in closer to her, peering into each of them. 'They have to be here! They have to be! We have a *system* now!'

And we did. But it was new, only implemented since the night before, when, en route to a cocktail party, it became apparent that no one had packed the glasses. After doubling back and arriving late, Delia had used her current pregnancy insomnia to compile a set of checklists covering everything from appetizers to napkins. We were each given one, for which we were wholly responsible. I was in charge of utensils. If we were lacking tongs, it was all on me.

'This is not happening,' Delia said now, plunging her hands into a small box on the kitchen island hardly big enough for half a ham, let alone the six we were missing. 'I remember, they were in the garage, on the side table, all ready to go. I *saw* them.'

On the other side of the kitchen door, I could hear voices rising: it was getting more crowded, which meant soon they'd be expecting dinner. Our menu was cheese crackers and goats'-cheese toasts to start, followed by green bean casserole, rice pilaf, rosemary dill rolls and ham. It was a special request. Apparently, these were pork people.

'Okay, okay, let's just calm down,' Delia said, although,

rustling through the plastic bags full of uncooked rolls with a panicked expression, she seemed like the only one really close to losing it. 'Let's retrace our steps. Who was on what?'

'I was on appetizers, and they're all here,' Kristy said, as Bert came through the swinging door from the main room, an empty tray in his hand. 'Bert. Were you on ham?'

'No. Paper products and serving platters,' he said, holding the one in his hand up as proof. 'Why? Are we missing something?'

'No,' Delia said firmly. 'We're not.'

'Monica was on ice,' Kristy said, continuing the count. 'Macy was utensils and Wes was glasses and champagne. Which means that the ham belonged to –' She stopped abruptly. 'Oh. Delia.'

'What?' Delia said, jerking her head out of a box filled with loaves of bread. 'No, wait, I don't think so. I was on –'

We all waited. It was, after all, her system.

'Main course,' she finished.

'Uh-oh,' Bert said.

'Oh, God!' Delia slapped a hand to her forehead. 'I did have the hams on the side table, and I remember being worried that we might forget them, so while we were packing the van I put them –'

Again, we all waited.

'On the back of my car,' Delia finished, placing her palm square in the middle of her forehead. 'Oh, my God,' she whispered as if the truth, so horrible, might deafen us all, 'they're still at the house. On my *car*.'

'Uh-oh,' Bert said again. He was right: it was a full thirty minutes away, and these people were expecting their ham in ten.

Delia leaned back against the stove. 'This,' she said, 'is awful.'

For a minute, no one said anything. It was a silence I'd grown to expect when things like this happened, the few seconds as we accepted, en masse, the crashing realization that we were, in fact, screwed.

Then, as always, Delia pushed on. 'Okay,' she said, 'here's what we're going to do . . .'

So far, I'd done three jobs with Wish since that first one, including a cocktail, a brunch and a fiftieth-anniversary party. At each, there was one moment – an old man pinching my butt as I passed with scones; the moment Kristy and I collided and her tray bonked me in the nose, showering salmon and crudités down my shirt; the time when Bert had hit me with another gotcha, jumping out from behind a coat rack and sending the stacks of plates I was carrying, as well as my blood pressure, skyrocketing – when I wondered what in the world I'd been thinking taking this on. At the end of the night, though, when it was all over, I felt something strange, a weird calmness. Almost a peace. It was like those few hours of craziness relaxed something held tight in me, if only for a little while.

Most of all, though, it was fun. Even if I were still learning things, like to duck when Kristy yelled, 'Incoming!' meaning she had to get something – a pack of napkins, some tongs, a tray – across a room so quickly that only throwing it would suffice, or never to stand in front of swinging doors, ever, as Bert always pushed them open with too much gusto, without taking into consideration that there might be anything on the other side. I learned that Delia hummed when she was nervous, usually 'American Pie', and that Monica never got nervous at all, was in fact capable of eating shrimp or crab cakes, hardly bothered, when the rest of us were in total panic mode. And I learned that I could always count on Wes for a raised eyebrow, an under-the-breath sarcastic remark or just a sympathetic look when I found myself in a bind: no matter where I was in the room, or what was happening, I could look over at the bar and feel that someone, at least, was on my side. It was the total opposite of how I felt at the library, or how I felt anywhere else, for that matter. Which was probably why I liked it.

But then, after the job was over and the van packed up to go home, after we'd stood around while Delia got paid, everyone laughing and trading stories about grabbers and gobblers and grandmas, the buzz of rushing around would wear off. As I'd begin to remember that I had to be at the library the next morning, I could feel myself starting to cross back to my real life, bit by bit.

'Macy,' Kristy would say, as we put the last of the night's supplies back in Delia's garage, 'you coming out with us tonight?'

She always extended the invitation, even though I said no every time. Which I appreciated. It's nice to have options, even if you can't take them.

'I can't,' I'd tell her. 'I'm busy.'

'Okay,' she'd say, shrugging. 'Maybe next time.'

It went like that, our own little routine, until one night when she squinted at me, curious. 'What do you do every night, anyway?' she'd asked.

'Just, you know, stuff for school,' I'd told her.

'Donneven,' Monica said, shaking her head.

'I'm prepping for the SATs,' I said, 'and I work another job in the mornings.'

Kristy rolled her eyes. 'It's *summertime*,' she told me. 'I mean, I know you're a smarty-pants, but don't you ever take a break? Life is long, you know.'

Maybe, I thought. *Or maybe not.* Out loud I said, 'I just really, you know, have a lot of work to do.'

'Okay,' she'd said. 'Have fun. Study for me, while you're at it. God knows I need it.'

So while at home I was still fine-just-fine Macy, wiping up sink splatters immediately and ironing my clothes as soon as they got out of the dryer, the nights when I arrived home from catering, I was someone else, a girl with her hair mussed, a stained shirt, smelling of whatever had been spilled or smeared on me. It was like Cinderella in reverse: if I was a princess for my daylight hours, at night I let myself and my composure go, just until the stroke of midnight, when I turned back to princess again, just in time.

The ham disaster was, like all the others, eventually averted. Wes ran to the gourmet grocery where Delia was owed a favour, and Kristy and I just kept walking through with more appetizers, deflecting all queries about when dinner was being served with a bat of the eyelashes and a smile (her idea, of course). When the ham was finally served – forty-five minutes late – it was a hit, and everyone went home happy.

It was ten thirty by the time I finally pulled into Wildflower Ridge, my headlights swinging across the town common and into our cul-de-sac, where I saw my house, my mailbox, everything as usual, and then something else.

My dad's truck.

It was in the driveway, right where he'd always parked, in front of the garage, left-hand side. I pulled up behind it, sitting there for a second. It *was* his, no question: I would have known it anywhere. Same rusty bumper, same EAT . . . SLEEP . . . FISH bumper sticker, same chrome toolbox with the dent in the middle from where he'd dropped his chainsaw a few years earlier. I got out of my car and walked up to it, reaching out my finger to touch the licence plate. For some reason I was surprised that it didn't just vanish, like a bubble bursting, the minute I made contact. That was the way ghosts were supposed to be, after all.

But the metal handle felt real as I pulled open the driver's side door, my heart beating fast in my chest. Immediately, I could smell that familiar mix of old leather, cigar smoke and the lingering scent of ocean and sand you carry back with you from the beach that you always wish would last, but never does.

I loved that truck. It was the place my dad and I spent more time together than anywhere else, me on the passenger side, feet balanced on the dashboard, him with one elbow out the window, tapping the roof along with the beat on the radio. We went out early Saturday mornings to get bacon and eggs and drive around checking on job sites, drove home from meets in the dark, me curled up in that perfect spot between the seat and window where I always fell asleep instantly. The air conditioner hadn't worked for as long as I'd been alive, and the heat cranked enough to dehydrate you within minutes, but it didn't matter. Like the beach house, the truck was dilapidated, familiar, with its own unique charm: it *was* my dad. And now it was back.

I eased the door shut, then went up to the front door of my house. It was unlocked, and as I stepped inside, kicking off my shoes as I always did, I could feel something beneath my feet. I crouched down, running my finger over the hardwood: it was sand.

'Hello?' I said, then listened to my voice bounce around our high ceilings back to me. Afterwards, nothing but silence.

My mother was at the sales office, had been there since five. I knew this because she'd left a message around ten on my cell phone, telling me. Which meant that either sometime in the last five hours my father's truck had driven itself from the coast, or there was another explanation.

I went back down the hallway and looked up to the second floor. My bedroom door, which I always left closed to keep it either cooler or warmer, was open.

I wasn't sure what to think as I climbed the stairs, remembering how many times I'd wished my dad would just turn up at the house one day, this whole thing one big misunderstanding we could all laugh about together. If only.

When I got to my room, I stopped in the open door and

noticed, relieved, everything familiar: my computer, my closed closet door, my window. There was the SAT book on my bedside table, my shoes lined up by the wastebasket. All as it should be. But then I looked at the bed and saw the dark head against my pillow. Of course my father wasn't back. But Caroline was.

She'd just stopped in for a visit. But, already, she was making waves.

'Caroline,' my mother said. Her voice, once polite, then stern, was now bordering on snappy. 'I'm not discussing this. This is not the place or time.'

'Maybe this isn't the place,' Caroline told her, helping herself to another breadstick. 'But, Mom, really. It's time.'

It was Monday, and we were all at Bella Luna, a fancy little bistro near the library. For once, I wasn't eating lunch alone, instead taking my hour with my mother and sister. Now, though, I was realizing maybe I would have preferred to eat my regular sandwich on a bench alone, as it became increasingly clear that my sister had come with An Agenda.

'I just think,' she said now, glancing at our waitress as she passed, 'that it's not what Dad would have wanted. He loved that house. And it's sitting there, rotting. You should see all the sand in the living room, and the way the steps to the beach are sagging. It's horrible. Have you even been down to check on it since he died?'

I watched my mother's face as she heard this, the way, despite her best efforts, she reacted to the various breaches of the conduct we'd long ago agreed on concerning my father and how he was mentioned. My mother and I preferred to focus on the future: this was the past. But my sister didn't see it that way. From the minute she'd arrived – driving his truck because her Lexus had blown a gasket while at the beach – it was like she'd brought him with her as well.

'The beach house is the least of my concerns, Caroline,' my mother said now, as our waitress passed by again with a frazzled expression. We'd been waiting for our entrees for over twenty minutes. 'I'm doing this new phase of townhouses, and the zoning has been extremely difficult . . .'

'I know,' Caroline said. 'I understand how hard it has been for you. For both of you.'

'I don't think you do.' My mother put her hand on her water glass but didn't pick it up or take a sip. 'Otherwise you would understand that this isn't something I want to talk about right now.'

My sister sat back in her chair, twisting her wedding ring round her finger. 'Mom,' she said finally, 'I'm not trying to upset you. I'm just saying that it's been a year and a half . . . and maybe it's time to move on. Dad would have wanted you to be happier than this. I know it.'

'I thought this was about the beach house,' my mother said stiffly.

'It is,' Caroline said. 'But it's also about living. You can't hide behind work forever, you know. I mean, when was the last time you and Macy took a vacation or did something nice for yourselves?'

'I was at the coast just a couple of weeks ago.'

'For work,' Caroline said. 'You work late into the night, you get up early in the morning, you don't do anything but think about the development. Macy never goes out with friends, she spends all her time holed up studying and she's not going to be seventeen forever –'

'I'm fine,' I said.

My sister looked at me, her face softening. 'I know you are,' she said. 'But I just worry about you. I feel like you're missing out on something you won't be able to get back later.'

'Not everyone needs a social life like you had, Caroline,' my mother said. 'Macy's focused on school, and her grades are excellent. She has a wonderful boyfriend. Just because she's not out drinking beer at two in the morning doesn't mean she isn't living a full life.'

'I'm not saying her life isn't full,' Caroline said. 'I just think she's awfully young to be so serious about everything.'

'I'm fine,' I said again, louder this time. They both looked at me. 'I am,' I said.

'All I'm saying is that you both could use a little more fun in your lives,' Caroline said. 'Which is why I think we should fix up the beach house and all go down there for a few weeks in August. Wally's working this big case all summer, he's gone all the time, so I can really devote myself to this project. And then, when it's finished, we'll all go down there together, like old times. It'll be the perfect way to end the summer.'

'I'm not talking about this now,' my mother said, as the waitress, now red-faced, passed by again. 'Excuse me,' my mother said, too sharply, and the girl jumped. 'We've been waiting for our food for over twenty minutes.'

'It will be right out,' the girl said automatically, and then scurried towards the kitchen. I glanced at my watch: five minutes until one. I knew that Bethany and Amanda were most likely in their chairs already, the clock behind them counting down the seconds until they finally had something legitimate to hold against me.

My mother was focusing on some distant point across the restaurant, her face completely composed. Looking at her in the light falling across our table, I realized that she looked tired, older than she was. I couldn't remember the last time I'd seen her really smile, or laugh a big belly laugh like she always did when my dad made one of his stupid jokes. No one else ever laughed – they were more groan-inducing than anything else – but my mother always thought they were hysterical.

'When I first got to the beach house,' Caroline said as my mother kept her eyes locked on that distant spot, 'I just sat in the driveway and sobbed. It was like losing him all over again, I swear.'

I watched my mother swallow, saw her shoulders rise, then fall, as she took a breath.

'But then,' my sister continued, her voice soft, 'I went inside and remembered how much he loved that stupid moose head over the fireplace, even though it smells like a hundred old socks. I remembered you trying to cook dinner on that stove top with only one burner, having to alternate pans every five minutes just to make macaroni and cheese and frozen peas, because you swore we wouldn't eat fish one more night if it killed you.'

My mother lifted up her hand to her chin, pressing two

fingertips there, and I felt a pang in my chest. Stop it, I wanted to say to Caroline, but I couldn't even form the words. I was listening too. Remembering.

'And that stupid grill that he loved so much, even though it was a total fire hazard,' Caroline continued, looking at me now. 'Remember how he always used to store stuff in it, like that frisbee or the spare keys, and then forget and turn it on and set them on fire? Do you know there are still, like, five blackened keys sitting at the bottom of that thing?'

I nodded, but that was all I could manage. Even that, actually, was hard.

'I haven't meant to let the house go,' my mother said suddenly, startling me. 'It's just been one more thing to deal with . . . I've had too much happening here.' *It can't be that easy*, I thought, *to get her to talk about this*. To bring her closer to the one thing that I'd circled with her, deliberately avoiding, for months now. 'I just –'

'It needs some new shingles,' Caroline told her, speaking slowly, carefully. 'I talked to the guy next door, Rudy? He's a carpenter. He walked through with me. It needs basic stuff, a stove, a screen door and those steps fixed. Plus a coat of paint in and out wouldn't hurt.'

'I don't know,' my mother said, and I watched as Caroline put her hand on my mother's, their fingers intertwining, Caroline's purposefully, my mother's responding seemingly without thinking. This reaching out to my mom was another thing I'd been working up to, never quite getting the nerve, but she made it look simple. 'It's just so much to think about.'

'I know,' my sister said, in that flat-honest way she had

always been able to say anything. 'But I love you, and I'll help you. Okay?'

My mother blinked, then blinked again. It was the closest I'd seen her come to crying in over a year.

'Caroline,' I said, because I felt like I had to, someone had to.

'It's okay,' she said to me as if she were sure. No question. I envied her that too. 'It's all going to be okay.'

Even though I scarfed down my linguini pesto in record time and ran the two blocks back to the library, it was one-twenty by the time I got back to work. Amanda, seated in her chair with her arms crossed over her chest, narrowed her eyes at me as I let myself behind the desk and, as I always did, battled around their thrones to reach my crummy little station in the back.

'Lunch ends at one,' she said, enunciating each word carefully as if my tardiness was due to a basic lack of comprehension. Beside her, Bethany smiled, just barely, before lifting a hand to cover her mouth.

'I know, I'm sorry,' I said. 'It was unavoidable.'

'Nothing is unavoidable,' she said snippily before turning back to her computer monitor. I felt my face turn red, that deep burning kind of shame, as I sat down.

Then, about a year and half too late, it hit me. I was never going to be perfect. And what had all my efforts got me, really, in the end? A boyfriend who pushed me away the minute I cracked, making the mistake of being human. Great grades that would still never be good enough for girls who Knew Everything. A quiet, still life, free of any risks, and so many sleepless nights to spend within it, my heart heavy, keeping secrets my sister had empowered herself by telling. This life was fleeting, and I was still searching for the way I wanted to spend it that would make me happy, full, okay again. I didn't know what it was, not yet. But something told me I wouldn't find it here.

So a few days later, back at Delia's after working a late-afternoon bridal shower (in a log-cabin lodge, no less, very woody) and encountering another disaster of sorts (soda water dispenser explosion during toasts), I'd made it through another day with Wish that was pretty much like all the others. Until now.

'Hey, Macy,' Kristy said, wiping something off the hem of her black fringed skirt, part of the gypsy look she was sporting, 'You coming out with us tonight?'

It was our routine now, how she always asked me. As much part of the schedule as everything in my other life was, dependable, just like clockwork. We both knew our parts. But this time I left the script, took that leap and improvised.

'Yeah,' I said. 'I am.'

'Cool,' she said, smiling at me as she hitched her purse over her shoulder. The weird thing was how she didn't even seem surprised. Like she knew, somehow, that eventually I'd come round. 'Come on.'

Chapter SEVEN

'Oh, man,' Kristy said, carefully guiding another section of my hair over the roller, 'Just wait. This is going to be *great*.'

Personally, I wasn't so sure. If I'd known that going out with Kristy meant subjecting myself to a makeover, I probably would have thought twice before saying yes. Now, though, it was too late.

I'd had my first reservations when she'd insisted I shed my work clothes and put on a pair of jeans she was absolutely sure would fit me (she was right) and a tank top that she swore would not show off too much cleavage (she was wrong). Of course, I couldn't really verify either of these things completely, as the only objective view was the mirror on the back of the closet door, which was now facing the wall so that, in her words, I wouldn't see myself until I was 'done'. All I had to go on was Monica, who was sitting in a chair in the corner of the room, smoking a cigarette she had dangling out the window and making occasional mmmm-hmm noises whenever Kristy needed a second opinion.

Clearly, this was a different sort of Friday night than I was used to. But then everything was different here.

Kristy and Monica's house wasn't a house at all but a trailer, although, as we approached it, Kristy explained that she preferred to call it a 'doublewide', as there was less redneck association with that moniker. To me, it looked like something out of a fairy tale, a small structure painted cobalt blue with a big sprawling garden beside it. There her grandmother Stella, whom I'd met the night I was lost, grew the flowers and produce she sold at her stand and to local restaurants. I'd seen lots of gardens before, even fancy ones in my neighbourhood. But this one was incredible.

Green and lush, it grew up and around the doublewide, making the structure, with its bright cobalt colour and red door, look like one more exotic bloom. Along the front, sunflowers moved lazily in the breeze, brushing a side window: beneath them were a row of rosebushes, their perfume-like scent permeating the air. From there, the greenery spread sideways. I saw a collection of cacti, all different shapes and sizes, poking out from between two pear trees. There were blueberry bushes beside zinnias and daisies and coneflowers, woolly lamb's ears up against bright purple lilies and red hot pokers. Instead of set rows, the plots were laid out along narrow paths, circling and encircling. Bamboo framed a row of flowering trees that led into one small garden plot with tiny lettuces poking up through the ground, followed by pecan trees next to geraniums, and beside them a huge clump of purple irises. And then there was the smell: of fruit and flowers, fresh soil and earthworms. It was incredible, and I found myself just breathing it in, the smell lingering on me long after we'd gone inside.

Now Kristy slid another bobby pin over a curler, smoothing with her hand to catch a stray piece of hair that was hanging over my eyes.

'You know,' I said warily, 'I'm not really a big-hair person.'

'Oh, God, me neither.' She picked up another roller. 'But this is going to be wavy, not big. Just trust me, okay? I'm really good with hair. It was, like, an obsession with me when I was bald.'

Because she was behind me, fussing with the rollers, I couldn't see her face as she said this. I had no idea if her expression was flippant or grave or what. I looked at Monica, who was flipping through a magazine, not even listening. Finally I said, 'You were bald?'

'Yup. When I was twelve. I had to have a bunch of surgeries, including one on the back of my head, so they had to shave all my hair off,' she said, brushing out a few of the loose tendrils around my face. 'I was in a car accident. That's how I got my scars.'

'Oh,' I said, and suddenly I was worried I had been staring at them too much, or she wouldn't have brought it up. 'I didn't –'

'I know,' she said easily, hardly bothered. 'But it's hard to miss them, right? Usually people ask, but you didn't. Still, I figured you were probably wondering. You'd be surprised how many people just walk right up and ask, point-blank, like they're asking what time it is.'

'That's rude,' I said.

'Mmm-hmm,' Monica agreed, stubbing her cigarette out on the windowsill.

Kristy shrugged. 'Really, I kind of prefer it. I mean, it's

better than just staring and acting like you're not. Kids are the best. They'll just look right at me and say, "What's wrong with your face?" I like that. Get it out in the open. I mean, shit, it's not like it isn't anyway. That's one reason why I dress up so much, you know, because people are already staring. Might as well give them a show. You know?'

I nodded, still processing all this.

'Anyway,' Kristy continued, doing another roller, 'it happened when I was twelve. My mom was on one of her benders, taking me to school, and she ran off the road and hit this fence, and then a tree. They had to cut me out of the car. Monica, of course, was smart enough to have the chicken pox so she didn't have to go to school that day.'

'Donneven,' Monica said.

'She feels guilty,' Kristy explained. 'It's a sister thing.'

I looked at Monica, who was wearing her normal impassive expression as she examined her fingernails. She didn't look like she felt particularly bad to me, but then again so far I'd only seen her with one expression, a sort of tired blankness. I figured maybe it was like a Rorschach inkblot: you saw in it whatever you needed or wanted to.

'Besides the scars on my face,' Kristy was saying, 'there's also one on my lower back, from the fusion, and a big nasty one on my butt from the skin graft. Plus there are a couple on my scalp, but you can't see those since my hair grew back.'

'God,' I said. 'That's horrible.'

She picked up another curler. 'I did not like being bald, I can tell you that much. I mean, there's only so much you can do with a hat or a scarf, you know? Not that I didn't try. The day my hair started to come in for real, I cried I was so happy. Now I can't bring myself to cut it more than just a tiny bit every few months. I *relish* my hair now.'

'It is really nice,' I told her. 'Your hair, I mean.'

'Thanks,' she said. 'I'm telling you, I think I appreciate it more than most people. I never complain about a bad-hair day, that's for sure.'

She climbed off the bed, tucking the hairbrush in her pocket before crouching down in front of me to secure a few loose wisps of hair with a bobby pin. 'Okay,' she said, 'you're almost set, so let's see . . . Monotone.'

'Nuh-uh,' Monica said, sounding surprisingly adamant.

'Oh, come on! If you'd just let me try something, for once, you'd see that –'

'Donneven.'

'*Monica.*'

Monica shook her head slowly. 'Bettaquit,' she warned.

Kristy sighed, shaking her head. 'She refuses to take fashion risks,' she said, as if this were a true tragedy. Turning back to her sister, she held up her hands in a visualize-this sort of way. 'Look. I've got one word for you.' She paused, for dramatic effect. 'Pleather.'

In response to this, Monica got up and started towards the door, shaking her head.

'Fine,' Kristy said, shrugging, as Monica went down the hallway, grabbing her purse off the floor by the door, 'just wear what you have on, like you always do. But you won't be dynamic!'

The front door slammed shut, responding to this, but

Kristy hardly seemed bothered, instead just walking back to her closet and standing in front of it, her hands on her hips. Looking out of the window beside me, I could see Monica start up the driveway, altogether undynamically and, as usual, exceptionally slowly.

Kristy bent down, pulling a pair of scuffed penny loafers out from under the hanging clothes and tossing them to me. 'Now, I know what you're thinking,' she said, as I looked down at them. 'But penny loafers are entirely underrated. You'll see. And we can do your cleavage with this great bronzer – I think it's in the bathroom.'

And then she was gone, pulling open the bedroom door and heading down the hallway, still muttering to herself. My head felt heavy under the rollers, my neck straining as I looked down at the tank top she'd given me to wear. The straps had tiny threads of glitter woven throughout, and the neckline plunged much further than anything I owned. It was way too dressy to go with the jeans, which were faded, the cuffs rolled up and frayed at the ankle; a heart was drawn on the knee in ballpoint pen. Looking at it, the solid blackness at its centre, the crooked left edge, not quite right, all I could think was that these weren't my clothes, this wasn't who I was. I'd been acting out against Bethany and Amanda, but I was the one who would really pay if this went all wrong.

I have to get out of here, I thought, and stood up, pulling one of the curlers by my temple loose and dropping it on the bed. A single corkscrew curl dropped down over my eyes and I stared at it, surprised, as it dangled in my field of vision, the smallest part of me transformed. But I was leaving. I was.

My watch said 6:15. If I left now, I could get home in time to be back on my schedule as if I'd never strayed from it. I'd tell Kristy my mom had called me on my phone, saying she needed me, and that I was sorry, maybe another time.

I stood up, pulling another curler out, then another, dropping them on the bed as I hurriedly slung my purse over my shoulder. I was almost to the door when Kristy came back down the hallway, a small compact in her hands.

'This stuff is great,' she said. 'It's like an instant tan, and we'll just put it –'

'I've just realized,' I said, plunging right in to my excuses, 'I really think –'

She looked up at me then, her eyes widening. 'Oh, God, I totally agree,' she said, nodding. 'I didn't see it before, but yeah, you're absolutely right.'

'What?'

'About your hair,' she said as she came into the room. I found myself backing up until I bumped against the bed again. Kristy reached past me, grabbing a white shirt that was lying on one of the pillows and, before I could stop her, she'd slid my arm inside one sleeve. I was too distracted to protest.

'My hair?' I said as she eased my other arm in, then grabbed the shirttails, knotting them loosely round my waist. 'What?'

She reached up, spreading her fingers and pulling them through my hair, stretching out the curls. 'I was going to brush it out, but you're right, it looks better like that, all tousled. It's great. See?'

And then she walked over to the closet door, pushing it shut, and I saw myself.

Yes, the jeans were faded and frayed, the heart on the leg crooked, too dark. But they fitted me really well: they could have been mine. And the tank top was a bit much, glittering in so many places from the overhead light, but the shirt over it toned it down, giving only glimpses here and there. The shoes, which had looked dorky when I put them on, somehow went with the jeans, which hit in such a way that they showed a thin sliver of my ankle. And my hair, without the clear, even parting that I worked so hard for every morning, drawing a comb down the centre with mathematical precision, was loose and falling over my shoulders, softening my features. None of it should have worked together. But, somehow, it did.

'See? I told you,' Kristy said from behind me, where she was standing smiling, proud of her handiwork, as I just stared, seeing the familiar in all these changes. How weird it was that so many bits and pieces, all diverse, could make something whole. Something with potential. 'Perfect.'

It took Kristy considerably longer to assemble her own look, a retro sixties outfit consisting of white go-go boots, a pink shirt and a short skirt. By the time we finally went out to meet Bert, he'd been waiting for us in the doublewide's driveway for almost a half-hour.

'It's about time,' he snapped as we came up to the ambulance. 'I've been waiting forever.'

'Does twenty minutes constitute forever now?' Kristy asked.

'It does when you're stuck out here waiting for someone who is selfish, ungrateful and thinks the whole world revolves around her,' Bert said, then cranked up the music he was playing – a woman wailing, loud and dramatic – ensuring that any retort to this would be drowned out entirely.

Kristy tossed her purse inside the ambulance, then grabbed hold of the side of the door, pulling herself up. The music was still going, reaching some sort of climax, with a lot of thundering guitars. 'Bert,' she yelled, 'can you *please* turn that down?'

'No,' he yelled back.

'Pink Floyd. It's my punishment; he knows how much I hate it,' she explained to me. To Bert she said, 'Then can you at least turn on the lights back here for a second? Macy can't see anything.'

A second later, the fluorescent light over her head flickered, buzzed, and then came on, bathing everything in a grey, sallow light. It was so hospital-like I felt the nervousness that had been simmering in my stomach since we'd left the house – ambulance phobia – begin to build. 'See, he'll do it for *you*,' she said. She stuck out her hand to me. 'Here, just grab on and hoist yourself up. You can do it. It's not as bad as it looks.'

I reached up and took her hand, surprised at her strength as she pulled me up, and the next thing I knew I was standing inside the ambulance, ducking the low ceiling, hearing the buzz of that light in my ear. There was now an old brown plaid sofa against one wall, and a small table wedged between it and the back of the driver's seat. *Like a travelling living room*, I thought, as Kristy clambered around it, grabbing her purse on the way, and slid into the passenger seat. I sat down on the couch.

'Bert, please turn that down,' Kristy yelled over the music, which was now pounding in my ears. He ignored her, turning his head to look out the window. 'Bert. Bert!'

Finally, as the shrieking reached a crescendo, Bert reached over, hitting the volume button. And suddenly it was quiet. Except for a slow, knocking sound. *Thunk. Thunk. Thunk.*

I realized suddenly that the sound was coming from the back doors, so I got up, pushing them open. Monica, a cigarette poking out of one side of her mouth, looked up at me.

'Hand,' she said.

'Put that out first,' Bert said, watching her in the rearview mirror. 'You know there's no smoking in the Bertmobile.'

Monica took one final drag, dropped the cigarette to the ground and stepped on it. She stuck her hand out again, and I hoisted her up, the way Kristy had done for me. Once in, she collapsed on the couch, as if that small activity had taken just about everything she had.

'Can we go now, please?' Bert asked as I pulled the doors shut. Up in the passenger seat, Kristy was messing with the radio, the wailing woman now replaced by a boppy pop beat. 'Or would you like another moment or two to make me insane?'

Kristy rolled her eyes. 'Where's Wes?'

'He's meeting us there. If we ever *get* there.' He pointed, annoyed, at the digital clock on the dashboard, which said 7:37. 'Look at that! The night is just ticking away. Ticking!'

'For God sakes, it's early,' Kristy said. 'We've got plenty of time.'

Which, I soon found out, was a good thing. We'd need it, with Bert behind the wheel.

He was a slow driver. More than slow, he was also incredibly cautious, a driver's ed teacher's dream. He paused for green lights, came to full stops before railroad crossings that hadn't seen trains in years, and obeyed the speed limit religiously, sometimes even dropping below it. And all the while, he had both hands on the wheel in the ten-and-two position, watching the road like a hawk, prepared for any and all obstacles or hazards.

So it seemed like ages later that we finally turned off the main road and onto a gravel one, then began driving on grass, over small rises and dips, towards an area where several cars were parked, encircling a clearing with a few wooden picnic tables in the centre. People were sitting at them, on them, grouped all around, and there were several flashlights scattered across the surfaces of the tables, sending beams of light in all directions. Bert backed in, so we were facing the tables, then cut the engine.

'Finally,' Kristy said, unbuckling her seat belt with a flourish.

'You could have walked,' Bert told her.

'I feel like we did,' she said. Then she pushed her door open, and I heard voices nearby, someone laughing. 'I'm going to get a beer. Anybody else want one?'

'Me,' Monica said, standing up and pushing open the back doors. She eased herself out with a pained expression, then started across the grass.

'Macy?' Kristy asked.

'Oh, no thanks,' I said. 'I'm fine.'

'Okay.' She climbed out the front door, letting it fall shut behind her. 'Be right back.'

I watched them cross into the clearing and walk past one of the picnic tables to a keg that was under some nearby trees. Two guys were standing by it, and one of them, who was tall with a shock of red hair, immediately went to work getting Kristy a beer, eyeing her appreciatively as he did so. Monica was standing by with a bored expression, while the redhead's friend shot her sideways looks, working up to saying something.

Bert was sitting on the back bumper of the ambulance, scanning the crowd, and I joined him, letting my feet dangle down. Most of the faces here were new to me, which made sense, since this was more of a Talbert High crowd, while I went to Jackson, on the other side of town. Still, I did recognize a few people I knew from school. I wondered if any of them knew me.

I looked across the clearing then, and saw Wes. He was standing with a group of guys around an old Mustang, talking, and seeing him I felt that same sort of lurch in my stomach as I had the first night I'd met him, and the night he'd pulled me out of the hole, and just about every time we'd crossed paths since. I couldn't explain it, had never felt it before: it was completely out of my control. *So idiotic*, I thought, and yet there I was again, staring.

After a minute or two he broke off from the group and started across the clearing. While I was making a pointed effort not to watch him – or, okay, not watch him the entire time – it was hard not to notice, as I took a quick glance around the circle, that I was not alone in my observations. I counted at least three other girls doing the same thing. I wondered if they felt as stupid as I did. Probably not.

'Hey,' he said. 'What took you guys so long?'

Bert rolled his eyes, nodding towards Kristy, who was now coming back over to us with Monica. 'What do you think?'

'I heard that,' she said. 'You know, it takes time to look like this. You can't just throw this sort of outfit together.'

Bert narrowed his eyes, looking at her. 'No?'

Ignoring this, she said, 'A fat lot of good it's doing me here, though. There aren't any good prospects.'

'What about that guy at the keg?' Bert asked.

'Please.' She sighed. 'Can't a girl have high standards? I don't want an *ordinary* boy.'

There was bout of laughter from the jeep parked beside us, and a second later a blonde girl in a halter top suddenly stumbled over. 'Hey,' she said, pointing at me. 'I know you. Don't I know you?'

'Um, I'm not sure,' I said, but I did know her. It was Rachel Newcomb: we'd run middle-school track together. We hadn't spoken in years.

'I do, I do,' she said, snapping her fingers, hardly seeming to notice everyone else looking on. Kristy raised her eyebrows.

'You know me, Rachel,' Bert said quickly. 'Bert? I tutored you last summer at the Kaplan centre, in maths?'

Rachel looked at him briefly, then turned her attention back to me. 'Oh shit, I know! We used to run together, right? In middle school? And now you date that guy, the one who's always yelling at us about bicycling!'

It took me a second.

'Recycling?' I said.

'Right!' She clapped her hands. 'That's it!'

There was hysterical laughter from the jeep, followed by someone yelling, 'Rachel, you're so freaking stupid!'

Rachel, hardly bothered, plopped herself down between me and Bert. 'God,' she said, tipping her head back and laughing, 'remember how much fun we used to have at meets? And you, shit, you were *fast*. Weren't you?'

'Not really,' I said, instinctively reaching to smooth my hair before realizing it wasn't even parted. I could feel Kristy watching me, listening to this.

'You were!' she poked Bert in the arm. 'You should have seen her. She was so fast, like she could . . .'

There was an awkward silence as we all waited for whatever verb was coming.

'. . . fly,' Rachel finished, and I heard Kristy snort. 'Like she had freaking wings, you know? She won everything. You know, the only way anyone else ever got to win anything was when you quit.'

'Well,' I said, willing her to get up and move on, before she said anything else. Whatever anonymity I'd enjoyed so far this summer had been based on everyone from Wish not being from my school and therefore not knowing anything about me. I had been a clean slate, and now here was Rachel Newcomb, scribbling out my secrets for everyone to see.

'We were the Running Rovers,' Rachel was saying to Monica now, slurring slightly. 'I always thought that name was so dumb, you know? It made us sound like dogs. Go Rovers! Woof! Woof!'

'Good God,' Kristy said, to no one in particular. Still, I felt my face burn, and that was even before I glanced up to see Wes looking at me.

'Look,' Rachel said, slapping a hand on my knee. 'I want you to know something, okay?'

Even though I knew what was coming – how, I have no idea – I could think of no way to stop her. All I could do was stand off to the side and watch everything fall apart.

'And what I want you to know is,' she said earnestly, as if this was private and we didn't have an audience, 'that I don't care what anyone says, *I* don't think you're all weird since that thing happened with your dad. I mean, that was messed up that you were there. Most people couldn't handle that, you know? Seeing someone die like that.'

I just sat there, looking at her: at her flushed face, the sloshy cup of beer in her hand, the white of her tan line that was visible, just barely, beneath the straps of her halter top. I could not bring myself to look at the others. So much for my fairy tale, however brief, my luxury of scars that didn't show. Somewhere, I was sure I could hear a clock chiming.

'Rachel!' someone yelled from the next car over. 'Get over here or we're leaving you!'

'Oh, gotta go!' Rachel stood up, flipping her long hair over her shoulder. 'I'm going,' she said, redundantly. 'But I meant what I said, okay? Remember that. Remember what I said. Okay?'

I couldn't even nod or say a word. Rachel stumbled off to the jeep, where she was greeted with more laughter and a few bicycling jokes. Then someone turned up the radio, some Van Morrison song, and they all started singing along, off-key.

It was one of those moments that you wish you could just disappear, every particle in you shrinking. But that, I knew, was impossible. There was always an After. So I lifted my head, and looked at Kristy, seeing Bert watching me, Wes and Monica's faces in my peripheral vision. Then I took a breath, to say what, I didn't know. But before I could Kristy had walked over and sat down beside me.

'That girl,' she said, wrapping her hand round mine, 'is as dumb as a bag of hammers.'

'No kidding,' Bert said softly, and when I looked at him I saw not The Face, but instead a good-humoured sort of disgust, not directed at me, not about me at all.

Kristy leaned across me, saying, 'Wasn't she the one you had to explain the concept of odd numbers to during that summer maths tutoring thing you did?'

Bert nodded. 'Twice,' he said.

'Moron.'

'Mmm-hmm,' Monica said, nodding.

Kristy rolled her eyes, then took a sip of her beer. Her palm felt warm against mine, and I realized how long it had been since anyone had held my hand. I looked at Wes, remembering his sculpture, the heart cut into the palm. He was looking at me, just as I'd thought he would be, but, like Bert's, his look was not what I expected. No pity, no sadness: nothing had changed. I realized all those times I'd felt people stare at me, their faces had been pictures, abstracts. None of them were mirrors, able to reflect back the expression I thought only I wore, the feelings only I felt. Until now, this moment, as our eyes met. If there was a way to recognize something you'd never seen but still knew by heart, I felt it as I looked at his face. Finally, someone understood.

'Still,' Kristy said wistfully, 'I did like her halter top. I have a black skirt that would look just *great* with that.'

We just sat there for a second, none of us talking. In the middle of the clearing, someone was playing with a flashlight, the beam moving across the trees overhead, showing bits and pieces of branches and leaves, a glimpse here and there, then darkness again. I knew that in the last few minutes everything had changed. I'd tried to hold myself apart, showing only what I wanted, doling out bits and pieces of who I was. But that only works for so long. Eventually, even the smallest fragments can't help but make a whole.

An hour later, we were in the back of the Bertmobile on the couch, being honest. It might have been the beer.

I was not a drinker, never had been. But after what had happened with Rachel, I'd felt shaken enough to agree when Kristy offered to go get me a very small beer, which I was, she assured me, under absolutely no obligation to drink. After a few sips, we'd started talking about boys, and it just went from there.

'Here's the thing,' she said, crossing one white boot over the other. 'My last boyfriend left me for dead out in the middle of nowhere. It's not like that should be so hard to improve upon. I want a nice boy. You know?'

It was strange to me to be sitting there as if the whole thing with Rachel had never happened. But after we'd sat there for just a second, Wes said he had someone he had to find who had promised him some rebar, Bert tagged along and Kristy, Monica, and I moved onto the couch to discuss other things. My secret, released, did not hover over like a dark cloud. Instead, it dissipated, grew fainter, until it seemed, if not forgotten, left behind for the time being.

'What I really would like,' Kristy said now, pulling me back to the present conversation, 'is a smart boy. I'm sick of guys who can't even remember my name, much less spell it. Someone really focused and brainy. That's what I want.'

'No, you don't,' I said, taking another sip of my beer. Only when I swallowed did I realize they were both looking at me, waiting for me to elaborate. 'I had a boyfriend like that,' I explained. 'Or have. Or sort of have.'

'Oh, those are the worst,' she said sympathetically, nodding.

I was confused. 'What are?'

'Sort-of boyfriends.' She sighed. 'You know, they sort of like you, then they sort of don't. The only thing they're absolutely sure of is that they want to get into your pants. I *hate* that.'

'Mmm-hmm,' Monica agreed adamantly.

'Actually,' I said, 'it's not like that, exactly. We're more sort of not together, and not broken up. We're on a break.'

'A break,' Kristy repeated, sounding out the word as if it was foreign, one she'd never heard before. 'Meaning . . .' She moved her hand in a motion that meant I was supposed to jump in, any time now.

'Meaning,' I told her, 'that there were some concerns about us not wanting the same things, not having the same expectations. So we've agreed to not be in contact until the end of the summer, and then we're going to see where we stand.'

She and Monica contemplated this for a moment. 'That,' Kristy said finally, 'is just so very mature.'

'Well, that's Jason,' I told her. 'It was his idea, really.'

'How long has this break been going on?' she asked.

I thought for a second. 'Since the night I met you,' I told her, and her eyes widened, surprised. 'He'd just emailed me about it, like, an hour earlier.'

'That is so funny,' she said, 'because that night, I was picking up on something, like you had a boyfriend or were in some sort of situation.' She pointed at Monica. 'Didn't I say that, that night?'

'Mmm-hmm,' Monica said.

'You just looked . . .' she said, searching for the word, '*taken*, you know? Plus you hardly reacted to Wes. I mean, you did a little, but nothing like most girls. It was a little swoon. Not a *sa-woon*, you know?'

I said, 'Sa-woon?'

'Oh, come on,' she said, shaking her head. 'Even a blind girl could tell he's amazing.'

Beside me, Monica sighed wistfully in agreement.

'So why haven't you gone out with him?' I asked her.

'Can't,' she said flatly. 'He's too much like family. I mean, after the accident, when my mom flaked out and took off to find herself and we came to live with Stella, I was crazy for him. We both were.'

'Bettaquit,' Monica said darkly.

'It's still a sore subject,' Kristy explained, while Monica

turned her head, exhaling. 'Anyway, I did everything I could to get his attention, but he'd just gotten back from Myers School then, was still dealing with his mom dying and all that. So he had a lot on his mind. At least I told myself that's why he could resist me.'

'Myers School?' I said.

Kristy nodded. 'Yeah. It's a reform school.'

I knew this. Jason had tutored out there, and I'd often ridden along with him, then sat in the car doing homework while he went inside. Delia had said Wes had been arrested: I supposed this was the punishment. Maybe he'd even been there those days, as I sat in the car, looking up at the loops of barbed wire along the fence, while cars whizzed by on the highway behind me.

'Okay,' Kristy said, tapping her foot to the music, 'tell us about the sort-of boyfriend.'

'Oh,' I said, 'we've been dating for a year and a half.'

I took a sip of my beer, thinking this would suffice. But they were sitting there, expectant, waiting for more. *Oh, well,* I thought. *Here goes nothing.*

'He went away for the summer,' I continued, 'and a couple of weeks after he left, he decided maybe it was better that we take this break. I was really upset about it. I still am, actually.'

'So he found someone else,' Kristy said, clarifying.

'No, it's not like that,' I said. 'He's at Brain Camp.'

'Huh?' Monica asked.

'Brain Camp,' I repeated. 'It's like a smart-kid thing.'

'Then he found someone else at Brain Camp,' Kristy said.

'No, it's not about someone else.'

'Then what is it about?'

It just seemed wrong to be sitting here discussing this. Plus I was embarrassed enough by what had happened, what I'd done to freak him out, so embarrassed I hadn't even told my mother, whom I should have been able to tell anything. I could only imagine what these girls would think.

'Well,' I said, 'a lot of things.'

Another expectant pause.

I took a breath. 'Basically, it came down to the fact that I ended an email by saying I loved him, which is, you know, big, and it made him uncomfortable. And he felt that I wasn't focused enough on my job at the library. There's probably more, but that's the main stuff.'

They both just looked at me. Then Monica said, 'Donneven.'

'Wait a second.' Kristy sat up against the edge of the couch, as if she needed her full height, small though it was, to say what was coming next. 'You've been dating for a year and a half and you can't tell the guy you love him?'

'It's complicated,' I said, taking a sip of my beer.

'And,' she continued, 'he broke up with you because he didn't think you were focused enough on your job performance?'

'The library,' I said, 'is very important to him.'

'Is he ninety years old?'

I looked down at my beer. 'You don't understand,' I said. 'He's been, like, my life for the last year and a half. He's made me a better person.'

This quieted her down, at least temporarily. I ran my finger around the rim of my cup.

'How?' she said finally.

'Well,' I began, 'he's perfect, you know? Great in school, smart, all these achievements. He can do anything. And when I was with him, it was, like, good for me. It made me better too.'

'Until . . .' she said.

'Until,' I said, 'I let him down. I pushed too hard, I got too attached. He has high standards.'

'And you don't,' she said.

'Of course I do.'

Monica exhaled, shaking her head. 'Nuh-*uh*,' she said adamantly.

'Sure doesn't seem like it,' Kristy said, seconding this. She took a sip of her beer, never taking her eyes off me.

'Why not?' I asked.

'Listen to yourself,' she said. 'God! Are you actually going to sit there and say he was justified in dumping you because you dared to get attached to him after a year and a half? Or because you didn't take some stupid job at the library as seriously as he thought you should?'

I knew this was, pretty much, what I'd just said. But somehow it sounded different now, coming from her.

'Look,' she said, as I struggled with this, trying to work it out, 'I don't know you that well. I'll admit that. But what I see is a girl any guy, especially some library nerd who's off at Cranium Camp –'

'Brain Camp,' I muttered.

'– would totally want to hear say she loved him. You're smart, you're gorgeous, you're a good person. I mean, what makes him such a catch, anyway? Who is he to judge?'

'He's Jason,' I said, for lack of a better argument.

'Well, he's a fuckhead.' She sucked down the rest of her beer. 'And, if I were you, I'd be glad to be rid of him. Because anyone that can make you feel that bad about yourself is toxic, you know?'

'He doesn't make me feel bad about myself,' I said, knowing even as my lips formed the words this was exactly what he did. Or what I let him do. It was hard to say.

'What you need,' Kristy said, 'what you *deserve*, is a guy who adores you for what you are. Who doesn't see you as a project, but a *prize*. You know?'

'I'm no prize,' I said, shaking my head.

'Yes,' she said, and she sounded so sure it startled me: like she could be so positive while hardly knowing me at all. 'You *are*. What sucks is how you can't even see it.'

I turned my head, looking back out at the clearing. It seemed no matter where I turned, someone was telling me to change.

Kristy reached over and put her hand on mine, holding it there until I had to look up at her. 'I'm not picking on you.'

'No?' I said.

She shook her head. 'Look. We both know life is short, Macy. Too short to waste a single second with anyone who doesn't appreciate and value you.'

'You said the other day life was long,' I shot back. 'Which is it?'

'It's both,' she said, shrugging. 'It all depends on how you choose to live it. It's like forever, always changing.'

'Nothing can be two opposite things at once,' I said. 'It's impossible.'

'No,' she replied, squeezing my hand, 'what's impossible is that we actually think it could be anything *other* than that. Look, when I was in the hospital, right after the accident, they thought I was going to die. I was really fucked up, big time.'

'Uh-huh,' Monica said, looking at her sister.

'Then,' Kristy continued, nodding at her, 'life was very short, literally. But now that I'm better, it seems so long I have to squint to see even the edges of it. It's all in the view, Macy. That's what I mean about forever too. For any one of us our forever could end in an hour, or a hundred years from now. You can never know for sure, so you'd better make every second count.'

Monica, lighting another cigarette, nodded. 'Mmm-hmm,' she said.

'What you have to decide,' Kristy said to me, leaning forward, 'is how you want your life to be. If your forever was ending tomorrow, would this be how you'd want to have spent it?' It seemed like it was a choice I had already made. I'd spent the last year and a half with Jason, shaping my life to fit his, doing what I had to in order to make sure I had a place in his perfect world, where things made sense. But it hadn't worked.

'Listen,' Kristy said, 'the truth is, nothing is guaranteed. You know that more than anybody.' She looked at me hard, making sure I knew what she meant. I did. 'So don't be afraid. Be *alive*.'

But then I couldn't imagine, after everything that had happened, how you could live and not constantly be worrying about the dangers all around you. Especially when you'd already had the scare of your life.

'It's the same thing,' I told her.

'What is?'

'Being afraid and being alive.'

'No,' she said slowly, and now it was as if she were speaking a language she knew at first I wouldn't understand, the very words, not to mention the concept, being foreign to me. 'Macy, no. It's not.'

It's not, I repeated in my head, and looking back later it seemed to me that was the moment everything really changed. When I said these words, not even aloud, and in doing so made my own wish: that for me this could somehow, someday, really be true.

A little bit later Kristy and Monica headed off to the keg again, but I stayed behind, sitting on the back bumper of the ambulance. I was feeling a bit woozy from the small amount of beer I'd had, not to mention everything Kristy had said. Too much to contemplate even under the best of conditions, now it was close to impossible.

I looked up after a few minutes to see Wes coming towards me from across the clearing. He had a bunch of metal rods under his arm – the rebar he'd been promised, I assumed. I just sat there watching him approach, his slow loping gait, and wondered what it would be like if he were coming to see me, coming to be with me. It wasn't what I thought when I saw Jason; that was more a reassurance. With him in sight, I could always get my bearings. If anything, Wes was the opposite. One look, and I had no idea what I was doing.

'Hey,' he said as he got closer, and I made myself look up at him, as if surprised, oh look, there you are. Which worked fine, until he sat down next to me, and again I felt that looseness, something inside me coming undone. He put the rods down beside him. 'Where is everybody?'

'The keg,' I said, nodding towards it.

'Oh. Right.'

Talk about forever: the next silent minute seemed to go on for that and longer. I had a picture of a school clock in my mind, those final seconds of the hour when the minute hand just trembles, as if willing itself to jump to the twelve. Say something, I told myself, sneaking a glance at Wes. He hardly seemed to be noticing this lapse, instead just watching the crowd in the middle of the clearing, his arms hanging loosely at his sides. Once again I could see the very bottom of the tattoo on his upper arm. Kristy had told me to live, whatever that meant in all its variations, and her words were still resonating. *Oh well*, I thought, *here goes*.

'So what is that?' I asked him, forcing the words out, then immediately realized I was looking at him, not at his arm, so this question could concern just about anything. He raised his eyebrows, confused, and I added – face flushing, God help me – 'Your tattoo, I mean. I've never been able to see what it is.'

This full sentence, an enquiry to boot, seemed to me on a par with Helen Keller finally signing W-A-T-E-R. I mean, really.

'Oh,' he said, pushing up his shirtsleeve. 'It's just this design. You saw it that first day you came out to Delia's, right?'

I felt myself nodding, but truthfully I was just staring at the black, thick lines of the design, now fully revealed: the heart in the hand. This one was, of course, smaller, and contained within a circle bordered by a tribal pattern, but otherwise it was the same. The flat palm, fingers extended, the red heart in its centre.

'Right,' I said. Like the first time I'd seen it, I couldn't help think that it was familiar, something pricking my subconscious, as weird as that sounded. 'Does it mean something?'

'Sort of.' He looked down at his arm. 'It's something my mom used to draw for me when I was a kid.'

'Really.'

'Yeah. She had this whole thing about the hand and the heart, how they were connected.' He ran a finger over the bright red of the heart, then looked at me. 'You know, feeling and action are always linked, one can't exist without the other. It's sort of a hippie thing. She was into that stuff.'

'I like it,' I said. 'I mean, the idea of it. It makes sense.'

He looked down at the tattoo again. 'After she died I started tinkering with it, you know, with the welding. This one has the circle, the one on the road has the barbed wire. They're all different, but with the same basic idea.'

'Like a series,' I said.

'I guess,' he said. 'Mostly I'm just trying to get it right, whatever that means.'

I looked across the clearing, catching a sudden glimpse of Kristy as she moved through the crowd, blonde head bobbing.

'It's hard to do,' I said.

Wes looked at me. 'What is?'

I swallowed, not sure why I'd said this out loud. 'Get it right.'

He must think I'm so stupid, I thought, vowing to keep my mouth shut from now on. But he just picked up one of the rods he'd carried over, turning it in his hands. 'Yeah,' he said, after a second. 'It is.'

Kristy was now almost at the keg. I could see her saying something to Monica, her head thrown back as she laughed.

'I'm sorry about your mom,' I said to Wes. I didn't even think before saying this, the connotation, what it would or wouldn't convey. It just came out, all on its own.

'I'm sorry about your dad,' he replied. We were both looking straight ahead. 'I remember him from coaching the Lakeview Zips, when I was a kid. He was great.'

I felt something catch in my throat, a sudden surge of sadness that caught me unaware, almost taking my breath away. That was the thing. You never got used to it, the idea of someone being gone. Just when you think it's reconciled, accepted, someone points it out to you and it just hits you all over again, that shocking.

'So,' he said suddenly, 'why'd you stop?'

'Stop what?' I said.

'Running.'

I stared down into my empty cup. 'I don't know,' I said, even as that winter day flashed in my mind again. 'I just wasn't into it any more.'

Across the clearing, I could see Kristy talking to a tall blond guy who was gesturing, telling some kind of elaborate story. She kept having to lean back, dodging his flailing fingers.

'How fast were you?' Wes asked me.

I said, 'Not that fast.'

'You mean you couldn't . . . fly?' he said, smiling at me.

Stupid Rachel, I thought. 'No,' I said, a flush creeping up my neck, 'I couldn't fly.'

'What was your best time for the mile?'

'Why?' I said.

'Just wondering,' he said, turning the rod in his hands. 'I mean, I run. So I'm curious.'

'I don't remember,' I said.

'Oh, come on, tell me,' he said, bumping my shoulder with his. *I cannot believe this*, I thought. 'I can take it.'

Kristy was glancing over at us now, even as finger guy was still talking. She raised her eyebrow at me, then turned back to face him.

'Okay, fine,' I said. 'My best was five minutes, five seconds.'

He just looked at me. 'Oh,' he said finally.

'What? What's yours?'

He coughed, turning his head. 'Never mind.'

'Oh, see,' I said, 'that's not fair.'

'It's more than five-five,' he told me, leaning back on his hands. 'Let's leave it at that.'

'That was years ago,' I said. 'Now I probably couldn't even do a half a mile in that time.'

'I bet you could.' He held the rod up, squinting at it. 'I bet,' he said, 'you'd be faster than you think. Though maybe not fast enough to fly.'

I felt myself smile, then bit it back. 'You could outrun me easily, I bet.'

'Well,' he said, 'maybe someday we'll find out.'

Oh, my God, I thought, and I knew I should say something,

anything. But now Kristy, Bert and Monica were walking towards us, and I missed my chance.

'Twenty minutes to curfew,' Bert announced as he got closer, looking at his watch. 'We need to go.'

'Oh, my God,' Kristy said, 'you might actually have to go over twenty-five to get us home in time.'

Bert made a face at her, then walked to the driver's side door, opening it. Monica climbed up into the ambulance, plopping herself on the couch, and I followed her, with Kristy right behind me.

'What were you two talking about?' she whispered as Wes pulled the doors shut.

'Nothing,' I said. 'Running.'

'You should have seen your face,' she said, her breath hot in my ear. 'Sa-woooon.'

Chapter EIGHT

'Okay,' Caroline said, pushing a button on the camera and then coming over to sit next to my mother. 'Here we go.'

It was Saturday morning. My sister had arrived the night before, having spent the day in Colby meeting with the carpenter about the renovations and repairs to the beach house. This was familiar ground to her, as she'd already done her own house, plus the place she and Wally had in the mountains. Decorating, she claimed, was her calling, ever since one of her college art professors told her she had a 'good eye', a compliment that she took to mean she was entitled to redo not only her own house but also anyone else's.

So although my mother was just barely on board – which was itself miraculous, in my opinion – Caroline was moving full steam ahead, showing up with not only most of her extensive library on home decorating but also pictures she'd taken with Wally's digital camera, so she could walk us through the suggested changes with visual aids.

'These things are a real lifesaver when you're doing long-distance remodelling,' she explained as she hooked the camera up to the TV. 'I don't know what we ever did without them.'

She pushed a button, and the screen went black. Then, just like that, the beach house appeared. It was the front view, the way it looked if you had your back to the ocean. There was the deck, with its one rickety wooden bench. There were the stairs that led over the dunes. There was the old gas grill, beneath the kitchen window. It had been so long since I'd seen it, but still I felt a lurch in my stomach at how familiar it was. It seemed entirely possible that if you leaned in closer, peering in the back window, you'd see my dad on the couch reading the paper and turning his head to look as you called his name.

My mother was just staring at it, holding her coffee cup with both hands, and I wondered again if she was going to be able to handle this. But then I looked at my sister, and she was watching my mom too. After a second she said, very carefully, 'So this is the way it looks now. You can see that the roof is sagging a bit. That's from the last big storm.'

My mother nodded. But she didn't say anything.

'It needs to be braced, and we have to replace some shingles as well. The carpenter was saying as long as we're shoring it up we might want to consider adding a skylight, or something . . . since the living room gets so little light from those front windows. You know how much you always complained about that.'

I remembered. My mother was forever turning on lights in the living room, complaining it was like a dungeon. ('All the better for naps!' my father would claim, just before falling asleep on the couch with his mouth open.) She preferred to spend her time in the front bedroom, which had a big window.

Plus the moose gave her the creeps. I wondered what she was thinking now. It was hard for her; it was hard for me too. But I kept remembering everything Kristy had said two nights before, about not being afraid, and how if I'd come home when I got scared, I would have missed everything that had happened.

'But I've never dealt with skylights,' Caroline said. 'I don't know how much they run, or if they're even worth the trouble.'

'It depends on the brand,' my mother said, her eyes on the screen. 'And the size. It varies.'

I had to hand it to my sister. For all her pushing, she knew what she was doing. Take one small step – show the picture, which she knew would be hard for my mother – and pair it with something she'd feel entirely sure about: work.

It went the same way for the next half-hour, as Caroline carefully guided us through the beach house, room by room. At first it was all I could do to swallow over the lump in my throat when I saw the view from the deck of the ocean, or the room with the bunk beds where I always slept. Even worse were the pictures of the main bedroom, where a pair of my dad's beat-up running shoes was still parked against the wall by the door.

But slowly, carefully, Caroline kept bringing us back. For every sharp intake of breath, every moment I was sure I couldn't bear it, there was a question, something logical to grab onto. I'm thinking maybe glass blocks in place of that window in the bathroom, she'd say, what do you think? Or, see how the linoleum's coming up in the kitchen? I found some great blue tile I think we could replace it with. Or would tile be too expensive? And each time, my mother would reply, grabbing the answer as if it were a life preserver in a choppy sea. Once she had her breath back, they'd move on.

When the slideshow was over, I left them in the living room discussing skylights and went to pull my laundry out of the dryer so I could iron something for the info desk the next day. I was almost done when my mother appeared in the doorway, leaning against it with her arms crossed over her chest.

'Well,' she said, 'your sister sure seems to have found herself a project, hasn't she?'

'Where is she?'

'Out in her car. She's got some swatches she wants to show me.' She sighed, running her hand over the edge of the door frame. 'Apparently, corduroy upholstery is all the rage these days.'

I smiled, smoothing a crease out of the trousers I was holding. 'She is an expert at this,' I said. 'You know what a great job she did with her place, and the mountain house.'

'I know.' She was quiet for a second, watching as I folded a shirt and put it in the basket at my feet. 'But I can't help but think it's a lot of money and work for such an old house. Your father always said the foundation would probably go in a few years . . . I just wonder if it's worth it.'

I pulled Kristy's jeans out of the dryer and folded them. The black heart on the knee was just as dark as ever. 'It might be fun,' I said, picking my words carefully. 'To have a place to go again.'

'I don't know.' She pulled a hand through her hair. 'I wonder if it would be easier, if the foundation might be flawed, to just take it down. Then we'd have the lot and could start over.'

I was bent over, peering into the dryer to pull out the last things in there, and for a second I just froze. Minutes ago, I'd had my first look at the beach house in over a year. To think that it, like so much else, might one day just be gone – I couldn't even imagine. 'I don't know,' I said. 'I bet the foundation's not that bad.'

'Mom?' Caroline called from the living room. 'I've got the swatches . . . Where are you?'

'Coming,' my mother said over her shoulder. 'It was just an idea,' she added, more quietly, to me. 'Just a thought.'

It shouldn't have surprised me, really. My mother trafficked in new houses, so of course the idea of everything being perfect and pristine, even better than before, would appeal to her. It was the dream she sold every day. She had to believe in it.

'Is that new?' she asked me suddenly.

'Is what new?'

She nodded at the tank top I'd just finished folding. 'I haven't seen it before.'

Of course she hadn't: it was Kristy's, and here, in the bright light of the laundry room, I knew it looked even more unlike something I'd wear than it had when I'd first agreed to put it on. You could plainly see the glittery design on the straps, and it was clear it was lower cut than my mother was most likely comfortable with. In Kristy's room, in Kristy's world, it was about as shocking as a plain white T-shirt. But here, it was completely out of place.

'Oh, this isn't mine,' I said. 'I just, um, borrowed it from a friend.'

'Really?' She looked at it again, trying to picture, I was sure, one of my student-council friends sporting such a thing. 'Who?'

Kristy's face immediately popped into my mind, with her wide smile, the scars, those big blue eyes. If the tank top was enough to cause my mother concern, I could only imagine how Kristy, in one of her full outfits, would go over, not to mention any of my other Wish friends. It seemed simpler, and smarter, to just say, 'This girl I work with. I spilled some salad dressing on my shirt last night so she lent me this, to drive home in.'

'Oh,' she said. It wasn't that she sounded relieved, but clearly, this was an acceptable explanation. 'Well. That was nice.'

'Yeah,' I said as she left the doorway, heading to the kitchen, where my sister and her swatches were waiting. 'It was.'

I left them downstairs, my mother listening dubiously as Caroline explained about how corduroy wasn't just for overalls any more, and went up to my room, putting my laundry basket on the bed. After I'd stacked all my T-shirts, shorts and jeans in the bureau, and laid out my info-desk clothes for the week to be ironed, the only things left were Kristy's jeans and the tank top. I went to put them on my desk, where I'd be sure to see them the next time I was leaving for work and could return them, but then, at the last minute, I stopped myself, running the thin, glittery strap of the tank top between my thumb and forefinger. It was so different from anything of mine, it was no wonder my mother had noticed it instantly. That was why I should have returned it immediately.

And that was why, instead, I slipped it into my bottom drawer, out of sight, and kept it.

On Sunday, my sister was cooking dinner, and she needed arugula. I wasn't entirely sure what that was. But I still got recruited to go look for it with her.

We'd just started down the second aisle of the farmer's market, my sister deep into an explanation of the difference between lettuce and arugula, when suddenly, there was Wes. *Yikes*, I thought, my hand immediately going to my hair, which I hadn't bothered to wash (so unlike me, but Caroline, convinced there was going to be some mass rush on exotic greens, had insisted we leave right after breakfast), then to my clothes – an old Lakeview Mall 5K T-shirt, shorts and flip-flops – which I'd thrown on without considering the fact I might see anyone I knew, much less Wes. It was one thing for him to see me catering, when, even if I was in disarray, at least I wasn't alone. Here, in broad daylight, though, all my old anxieties came rushing back.

'. . . not to be confused with field greens,' Caroline was saying, 'which are an entirely different thing altogether.'

He was at the very end of the row, with a bunch of sculptures set up all around him, talking to a woman in a big floppy hat, who was holding her chequebook. Looking more closely, I saw one big piece, which was sporting a SOLD sign, as well as several smaller ones. They were all whirligigs, a part of each spinning in one direction or another in the breeze.

I took a sudden left, finding myself facing a table full of

pound cakes and crocheted pot holders, as Caroline kept walking, still talking about various types of greens. It took her a second to realize I'd ditched her, and she doubled back looking annoyed.

'Macy,' she said, entirely too loudly, at least to my ears, 'what are you doing?'

'Nothing.' I picked up one of the pot holders. 'Look, aren't these nice?'

She looked at the pot holder – which was orange and spangled and not nice at all – then at me. 'Okay,' she said. 'Tell me what's going on.'

I glanced back down at Wes, hoping he'd gone to look for arugula too, or had maybe gone to help the woman get the sculpture to her car. But no. Now, in fact, he was looking our way.

My way, to be exact. The woman with the floppy hat was gone, and he was just standing there, watching me. He lifted his hand and waved, and I felt my face flush as I put the pot holder back with its hideous brethren.

'Macy, what on earth is wrong with you? Are you okay?' Caroline squinted at me from behind her entirely too expensive designer sunglasses, then turned her head to see what, exactly, had made me turn bright red. I watched her gaze move across the tables of fresh corn, goats' cheese and hammocks, until, finally: 'Oh.'

I knew what she was thinking, could hear Kristy's voice in my head: *Sa-wooon.*

'Do you know that guy?' she asked me, still staring.

'Sort of,' I said. Now that we'd all seen each other, there

was no amount of pot holders, or hammocks, that could save me. Thinking this, I took Caroline by the elbow. 'Come on.'

As we got closer, I looked at the sculptures and realized there were no heart in hands on display. Instead, I noticed another theme: angels and halos. The smaller pieces were all stick figures made of various bits of metal and steel, with gears for faces and tiny nails for fingers and toes. Above the heads of each was a sculpted circle, each decorated in a different way. One was dotted with squares of different coloured glass, another had long framing nails twisting off in all directions, an angel Medusa. On the large sculpture with the SOLD sign, barbed wire was threaded around the halo, much the same as on the sculpture on Sweetbud Drive, and I thought of the Myers School again, the way the wire there had curved the same way round the fence, roped like ribbon.

'Hey,' Wes said as we came up. 'I thought that was you.'

'Hi,' I said.

'These are amazing,' Caroline said, reaching out her hand to the large sculpture and running a finger along the edges of the gear that made up its midsection. 'I just love this medium.'

'Thanks,' Wes said. 'It's all from the junkyard.'

'This is Wes,' I said as she walked around the sculpture, still examining it. 'Wes, this is my sister, Caroline.'

'Nice to meet you,' Caroline said in her socialite voice, extending her hand. They shook hands, and she went back to circling the sculpture, taking off her sunglasses and leaning in closer. 'What's great about this,' she said as if we were in a museum and she was leading the tour, 'is the contrast. It's a real juxtaposition between subject matter and materials.'

Wes looked at me, raising his eyebrows, and I just shook my head, knowing better than to stop my sister when she was on a roll. Especially about art, which had been her major in college.

'See, it's one thing to do angels,' she said to me, while Wes looked on, 'but what's crucial here is how the medium spells out the concept. Angels, by definition, are supposed to be perfect. So by building them out of rusty pieces, and discards and scraps, the artist is making a statement about the fallibility of even the most ideal creatures.'

'Wow,' I said to Wes, as she moved on to the smaller pieces, still murmuring to herself. 'I'm impressed.'

'Me too,' he replied. 'I had no idea. I just couldn't afford new materials when I started.'

I laughed, surprising myself, then was surprised even more – no, shocked – when he smiled at me, a heartbreaker's smile, and for a second I was just in the moment: me and Wes, surrounded by all those angels, in the sunshine, on a Sunday.

'Oh, wow,' Caroline called out, shaking me back to attention, 'is this sheet metal you used here? For the face?'

Wes looked over to where she was squatting in front of a figure with a halo studded with bottle caps. 'That's an old Coke sign,' he told her. 'I found it at the dump.'

'A Coke sign!' she said, awed. 'And the bottle caps . . . it's the inevitable commingling of commerce and religion. I love that!'

Wes just nodded: a fast learner, he already knew to just go along with her. 'Right,' he said. Then, in a lower voice to me he added, 'Just liked the Coke sign, actually.'

'Of course you did,' I said.

A breeze blew over us then, and some of the halos on the smaller pieces began to spin again. A small one behind us was decorated with jingle bells, their ringing like a whistling in the air. As I bent down closer to it, the bells whizzing past, I saw the one behind it, which was turning more slowly. It was a smaller angel with a halo studded with flat stones. As I touched one as it turned, though, I realized it wasn't a stone but something else that I couldn't place at first.

'What is this?' I asked him.

'Sea glass,' Wes said, bending down beside me. 'See the shapes? No rough edges.'

'Oh, right,' I said. 'That's so cool.'

'It's hard to find,' he said. The breeze was dying down, and he reached out and spun the halo a bit with one finger, sending the light refracting through the glass again. He was so close to me, our knees were almost touching. 'I bought that collection at a flea market, for, like, two bucks. I wasn't sure what I was going to use it for then, but it seemed too good a thing to pass up.'

'It's beautiful,' I said, and it was. When the halo got going fast, the glass all blurred, the colours mingling. *Like the ocean*, I thought, and looked at that angel's face. Her eyes were washers, her mouth a tiny key, the kind I'd once had for my diary. I hadn't noticed that before.

'You want it?'

'I couldn't,' I said.

'Sure you can. I'm offering.' He reached over and picked it up, brushing his fingers over the angel's tinny toes. 'Here.'

'Wes. I can't.'

'You can. You'll pay me back somehow.'

'How?'

He thought for a second. 'Someday, you'll agree to run that mile with me. And then we'll know for sure whether you can kick my ass.'

'I'd rather pay you for it,' I said, as I reached into my back pocket for my wallet. 'How much?'

'Macy, I was kidding. I know you could kick my ass.' He looked at me, smiling. *Sa-woon*, I thought. 'Look. Just take it.'

I was about to protest again, but then I stopped myself. *Maybe for once I should just let something happen*, I thought. I looked down at the angel in his hand, at those sparkling bits of glass. I did want it. I didn't know why, couldn't explain it if I had to. But I did.

'Okay,' I said. 'But I am paying you back somehow, sometime.'

'Sure.' He handed it to me. 'Whatever you want.'

Caroline was coming back over to us now, picking her way through the smaller sculptures and stopping to examine each one. She had her purse open, her phone to her ear. '. . . no, it's more like a yard art thing, but I just think it would look great on the back porch of the mountain house, right by that rock garden I've been working on. Oh, you should just see these. They're so much better than those iron herons they sell at Attache Gardens for hundreds of dollars. Well, I know you liked those, honey, but these are better. They are.'

'Iron herons?' Wes said to me.

'She lives in Atlanta,' I told him, as if this explained everything.

'Okay, honey, I'm going. I'll talk to you later. Love you, bye!' She snapped the phone shut, then dropped it into her purse before slinging it back over her shoulder. 'All right,' she said to Wes, 'let's talk prices.'

I hung back, holding my angel, as they walked through the various pieces, Caroline stopping the negotiations every so often to explain the meaning of this or that piece as Wes stood by politely, listening. By the time it was all over she'd bought three angels, including the Coke bottle cap one, and had taken Wes's number to set up an appointment for her to come see the bigger pieces he had out at his workshop.

'A steal,' she said, ripping her sizeable cheque out of her chequebook and handing it to him. 'Really. You should be charging more.'

'Maybe if I show someplace else,' he told her, folding the cheque and sticking it in his front pocket, 'but it's hard to get pricey when you have baked goods on either side of you.'

'You will show someplace else,' she told him, picking up two of her angels. 'It's only a matter of time.' She looked at her watch. 'Oh, Macy, we have to run. I told Mom we'd be home for lunch so we could look at the rest of those colour swatches.'

Something told me my mother, who that morning had picked out windows and a skylight with about as much enjoyment as someone getting a root canal, would not be broken up to miss that conversation. But I figured it wasn't worth pointing that out to Caroline, who was already distracted checking out another angel with a thumbtack halo, which she'd somehow missed earlier. 'Well,' I said to Wes, 'thank you again.'

'No problem,' he said, glancing over at my sister. 'Thanks for the business.'

'That's not me,' I told him. 'It's all her.'

'Still,' he said. 'Thanks anyway.'

'Excuse me,' a woman by the big sculpture called out, her voice shrill, 'do you have others like this?'

Wes looked over. 'I should go, I guess.'

'Go,' I said. 'I'll see you later.'

'Yeah. See you around.'

I stood there watching as he walked over to the woman, nodding as she asked her questions, then looked down at the angel in my arms, running a finger over the smooth sea glass dotting her halo.

'Ready?' Caroline said from behind me.

'Yeah,' I said. 'I'm ready.'

Chapter NINE

'Now this,' Delia said to me, her voice low, '*really* makes me nervous.'

Looking out from the kitchen, I could only nod in agreement. But while Delia was referring to the fact that we were in a house where delicate antiques crowded just about every level surface and Monica had just been sent out with a trayful of full wine glasses, for me it was something else entirely. Namely the fact that a mere two feet from the door in which we were standing, in prime grabber location, were Jason's parents.

Since we'd arrived I'd been in the kitchen with Wes, shelling shrimp as fast as humanly possible because Delia, distracted by another crisis involving the ovens not lighting, had forgotten to get it done earlier. Suddenly, I'd heard a trilling laugh I recognized. As Kristy pushed through from the living room, her tray picked clean of the crackers she'd walked out with only minutes earlier, I saw Mrs Talbot. And as the door swept shut, I was almost certain she saw me.

'Unbelievable,' Wes said.

'What?' For a second I thought he meant Mrs Talbot.

'Look at that.' I followed his gaze, realizing he meant the

shrimp in my hands, as well as the pile in front of me, which was twice the size of his. 'How are you doing those so fast?'

'I'm not,' I said, sliding the shrimp out of the shell and dropping it on my pile.

He just looked at me, then down at the one he was holding. 'I've been watching you,' he said, 'and while I've been working on this one, you've done five. At least.'

I picked up another one, ripped the legs off, then slid off the shell in one piece, dropping the shrimp onto my pile.

'Six,' he said. 'This is getting embarrassing. How'd you learn to do that?'

Starting another one, I said, 'My dad. In the summers, we used to buy a couple of pounds of shrimp to steam and eat for dinner. He loved shrimp, and he was super fast. So, if you wanted to eat, you had to keep up.' I dropped the shrimp onto my pile. 'It was a Darwinian thing.'

He finally finished the one in his hand, putting it on the pile. 'In my house,' he said, 'it was the opposite. You did everything you could to keep from eating.'

'Why?'

'After the divorce,' he said, picking up another one and, eyeing how I was doing it, ripping all the legs off at once, 'my mom got into natural foods. Part of the whole cleanse-your-life, cleanse-your-body thing. Or something. No more hamburgers, no more hot dogs. It was lentil loaf and tofu salad, and that was a good day.'

'My dad was the total opposite,' I told him, starting another one. 'He was a firm believer in the all-meat diet. To him, chicken was a vegetable.'

'I wish,' he said.

'Shrimp! I need shrimp!' Delia hissed from behind us. I scooped the pile in front of me onto a plate, then ran to the sink, rinsing them quickly and patting them dry as she hurriedly piled toothpicks, napkins, and cocktail sauce onto a platter.

'Those crackers are going fast,' Kristy reported as she came back through the door, balancing her tray on her upturned palm. Today, she was in her most striking outfit yet: a black leather skirt and motorcycle boots paired with a loose white peasant blouse. Her hair was held back at the back of her head with a pair of red chopsticks. 'That crowd is all professor types, and they're so weird that way, ultra polite but really grabby at the same time. Like they say, 'Oh, my, doesn't that look tasty,' and then clean out your whole tray.'

'Two and move,' I said.

'Don't I know it.' She blew a piece of hair out of her face. 'It's just work, is all I'm saying.'

There was a crash from the other room, just as Delia handed off the shrimp tray. We all froze.

'Shit,' Delia said. 'I mean, shoot. No, actually, I mean shit. I really do.'

Kristy eased open the door a tiny bit. 'It wasn't anything of theirs,' she reported, and I saw Delia visibly relax. 'But a couple of wine glasses bit it on the carpet.'

'Red or white?' Delia asked.

'Ummm,' Kristy said. 'Looks like red.'

'*Shit*,' Delia said again, crossing the room to the plastic Tupperware container she always brought with us. 'And Bert would pick today to have other plans.'

I looked at Wes quizzically, and he said, 'Bert's a whiz with stains. He can get anything out of anything.'

'Really,' I said.

'Oh yeah.' Wes nodded, slowly de-shelling another shrimp. 'He's a legend.'

Delia yanked a bottle of carpet cleaner and a rag out of the container. 'And how are you?' she asked me, handing them to me.

'How am I what?'

'At getting out stains.'

I looked down at the rag and cleaner in my hands, as Kristy pushed out the door.

'Um,' I said. Through the still open door, I could see Monica down on the floor, slowly picking up pieces of broken glass as the hostess of the party stood by, watching. 'I'm not –'

'Good,' Delia said, pushing me through the door. 'Go to it!' She'd given me such a nudge I actually stumbled over the threshold: luckily, I was able to catch myself right before doing a face plant into a nearby end table. I caught my breath, then crossed the room over to Monica, who'd made what looked like very little headway in the cleaning-up effort.

'Hey,' I said, starting to kneel down beside her. 'You okay?'

'Mmm-hmm,' she said. But then she stood up, wiping her hands on her apron and starting across the floor to the kitchen, leaving me and the tray behind her. *So much for teamwork*, I thought, as I dropped the cloth and cleaner beside me and began to pick up the broken glass as fast as I could. I'd just got what I hoped was all of it and begun spraying the carpet when I heard a voice.

'Macy? Is that you?'

For a second, I just kept spraying, as if doing so long enough might remove not only the stain, but me and this entire situation as well. After I gave the carpet a good dousing, though, it was clear I had no choice but to look up.

'Hi,' I said to Mrs Talbot, who was standing over me holding a napkin piled with shrimp. 'How are you?'

'We're well,' she said, glancing a bit hesitantly over at Mr Talbot, who was helping himself to shrimp from Kristy's tray as she tried, unsuccessfully, to move on. 'Are you . . . working here?'

Even though I knew this was a valid question, the fact that I was wearing a Wish Catering apron, holding a rag and on my knees on the carpet fighting a stain made me wonder if Mrs Talbot was really all that smart after all. 'Yes,' I said, tucking a piece of hair behind my ear. 'I, um, just started.'

'But you're still at the information desk,' she said, suddenly serious, and I could see Jason in her features, this automatic concern that all be As It Should. 'Aren't you?'

I nodded. 'I'm just doing this occasionally,' I said. 'For extra money.'

'Oh.' She glanced over again at Mr Talbot, who was standing in place chewing, his napkin piled with what, to my eye, looked like a lot more than two shrimp. 'Well. That's wonderful.'

I ducked my head back down, and after a second a woman came up to her, asking about some research trip, and thankfully, they moved on. I'd been dousing, then patting, then dousing for a good five minutes when a pair of motorcycle boots appeared right at my eye level, foot tapping.

'You know,' Kristy said, her voice low, 'it doesn't look so good for you to be on the floor like this.'

'There's a stain,' I said. 'And Monica just abandoned me to deal with it.'

She squatted down across from me, moving her knees to one side in a surprisingly ladylike way. 'It's very hard for her,' she said to me, her voice serious. 'She's self-conscious about her clumsiness, so a lot of the times rather than acknowledge it she just shuts down. It's a defence mechanism. You know, she's very emotional, Monica. She really is.'

As she said this, Monica pushed through the door from the kitchen, carrying a trayful of goats'-cheese toasts. She started across the room, her face flat and expressionless, walking right past us without even a glance.

'See?' Kristy said. 'She's *upset*.'

'Macy,' a man's voice boomed from over our heads. 'Hello down there!'

Kristy and I both looked up at the same time. It was Mr Talbot, of course, and he was smiling widely, although I assumed it had more to do with Kristy's shrimp tray than us reuniting. As she and I both stood, he proved me right by immediately reaching for one and popping it into his mouth.

'Hi, Mr Talbot,' I said as Kristy looked on, annoyed. 'It's good to see you.'

'And you,' he replied. 'Martha tells me you've taken on this job in addition to your library work. That's very ambitious of you. I know Jason finds the information desk to be a full-time commitment.'

'Oh, well,' I said, bending down to retrieve my cleaner and

rag, as the stain looked, miraculously, like it was actually fading, 'I'm sure for him, it is.'

Mr Talbot, reaching for another shrimp, raised his eyebrows.

'I mean,' I said quickly, as Kristy switched her tray to the other hand, 'that Jason just gives such a big commitment to everything. He's very, you know, focused.'

'Ah, yes, he really is,' he said, nodding. Then he lowered his voice, adding, 'I'm so glad that you understand that, considering the decision he had to make recently about your relationship.' He dabbed his lips with a napkin. 'I mean, he is fond of you. But Jason just has so much on his plate. He has to be very careful not to get distracted from his goals.'

I just stood there, wondering how, exactly, he expected me to react to this. I was a distraction from his goals? I felt my face flush.

'At any rate,' Mr Talbot continued, 'I know he hopes, as we do, that you two can work things out once he returns.'

And with that, he started to reach for another shrimp. But as his fingers neared the edge of the tray, zeroing in, Kristy yanked it away with such force that a couple actually slid off the other side and hit the carpet, *thud thud*. Mr Talbot looked confused. Then he looked at the shrimp on the floor, as if actually wondering if the two-second rule applied here.

'So sorry,' Kristy said smoothly, turning on her heel, 'but we're on goal to get out another round of appetizers, and we can't allow ourselves to be distracted.'

'Kristy,' I hissed.

'Come on,' she said, and then she was starting across the

floor, and there was really nothing I could think of to do but follow her. Which I did, not looking back, although whether it was to save my pride or save myself the sight of Mr Talbot eating shrimp off the floor, I wasn't sure.

Kristy knocked the kitchen door open, walked to the opposite counter, and put down her tray with a bang. Wes and Delia, who were arranging more wine glasses on two platters, looked up at us.

'You are not going to believe,' she said, 'what just went down out there.'

'Did something else break or spill?' Delia asked. 'God! What is going on today?'

'No,' Kristy said. Looking at her, I realized that I was upset, even hurt: but Kristy, she was *pissed*. 'Do you know who's out there?'

Delia looked at the door. 'Monica?'

'No. Macy's jerkwad boyfriend's father. And do you know what he did out there, in front of God and me and everybody?'

This time, neither Wes nor Delia offered any theories, instead just looking at me, then back at Kristy. Outside, I heard Mrs Talbot trilling again.

'He said,' she said, 'that his stupid asshole son put their relationship on hold because she wasn't in line with his *goals*.'

Delia raised her eyebrows. I had no idea what Wes's reaction was, as I was making a concentrated effort not to look at him.

'And then,' Kristy continued, reaching full throttle, 'he ate half my shrimp plate. He insults my friend – to her face! – and then tries to go for shrimp. I wanted to sock him.'

'But,' Delia said carefully, 'you didn't. Right?'

'No,' Kristy replied, as Delia visibly relaxed again, 'but I did cut him off. He's on crustacean restriction, from here on out. He tries another grab, he's getting a foot stomp.'

'Oh, don't do that,' Delia said as I concentrated on a spot on the opposite wall, still trying to calm myself from the various shames that had been thrown my way in the last few minutes, 'please God I'm begging you. Can't you just avoid him?'

'It's the principle of the thing,' Kristy replied, piling more shrimp on her tray by the handful, 'and no, I can't.'

The door swung open again, and Monica ambled in, blowing her bangs out of her face. 'Shrimp,' she said flatly, looking at Kristy.

'I'm sure they do,' she shot back, plunking another container of cocktail sauce and some napkins onto her tray. 'Bastards.'

'Kristy,' Delia said, but she was already pushing back out the door, her tray on her palm, rising to shoulder level. As it swung shut, Delia looked around, somewhat desperately, then picked up a tray of filled wine glasses, lifting it carefully with both hands.

'Just to be on the safe side,' she said, nudging the door open with her toe and glancing out at the living room, where I could see Kristy zipping past a group of people who were reaching, in vain, for her shrimp, 'I'm going to make a pass around the room and keep an eye on her. Wes, grab that other tray of glasses. Monica, get another trayful of toasts out here. And Macy –'

I turned and looked at her, glad to have something else to focus on.

'I'm sorry,' she said, and smiled at me so kindly I felt like it was a third shame, the biggest of all, even though I knew that wasn't how she intended it. Still, I felt something hurt in my heart as the door swung shut again, as if all the inadequacies I'd felt since Jason's email were no longer hidden away inside me but were as clear on my face as if they were written there.

After Delia left, the room seemed to feel smaller. Monica was slowly moving toasts onto her tray, while Wes finished pouring the wine behind me. I could see out through the kitchen door to the garden and the road beyond it, and for a second I considered just pushing it open and walking out, could almost feel the grass under my feet, the sun on my face as I just left this behind.

Monica picked up her tray, then brushed past me and out of the door. As it swung open, I heard a second of party noises and voices, and then it was quiet again. When I turned round to look at Wes he was already lifting his tray, arranging the glasses on it, clearly more concerned with keeping them balanced than with my various shortcomings. But then he looked at me.

'Hey,' he said, and I felt some part of me brace, preparing for what came next, 'are you –'

'I'm fine,' I told him, my easy, knee-jerk answer. 'It was nothing, just some stupid thing somebody said.'

'– gonna be able to grab that other tray?' he finished.

Then we both shut up, abruptly: it was one of those moments when you're not sure what to respond to first, like a conversational photo finish where you're still waiting for the judges to weigh in.

'Yeah.' I nodded at the tray behind him. 'Go ahead, I'm right behind you.'

'All right,' he said. And then, for one second, he looked at me, as if maybe he should say more. But he didn't. He just walked to the door, pushing it open with his free hand. 'I'll see you out there.'

As he disappeared into the living room I caught another quick, slicing glimpse of the party, not enough to see much, but then I didn't have to, really. I knew Kristy was probably exacting the revenge she thought I was due, while Delia moved right behind her, making apologies and smoothing rough edges. Monica was most likely following her own path, either oblivious or deeply emotionally invested, depending on what you believed, while Wes worked the perimeter, always keeping an eye on everything. There was a whole other world out there, the Talbots' world, where I didn't belong now, if I ever had. But it was okay not to fit in everywhere, as long as you did somewhere. So I picked up my tray, careful to keep it level, and pushed through the door to join my friends.

'Delia,' Kristy said, 'just go, would you please? Everything's fine.'

Delia shook her head, pressing one finger to her temple. 'I'm forgetting something, I just know it. What is it?'

Her husband, Pete, who was standing by his car with his keys in hand, said patiently, 'Is it that our dinner reservations were for ten minutes ago?'

'No,' she snapped, shooting him a look. 'It's something else. God, think, Delia. *Think.*'

Beside me, Kristy yawned, then looked at her watch. It was eight thirty and, finally done with the academic cocktail party, we were amassed in the client's driveway, waiting to leave. We'd been all ready to go, and then Delia had that feeling.

'You know what I mean,' she said now, snapping her fingers, as if that action might cause some sort of molecular shift that would jog her memory. 'When you just know you're forgetting something?'

'Are you sure it's not a pregnancy thing?' Kristy asked.

Delia glared at her. 'Yes,' she said. 'I'm sure.'

We all exchanged looks. The closer Delia got to her due date, the angrier she became when anyone attributed anything – loss of memory, mood swings, her conviction that every room was always too hot, even when everyone else's teeth were chattering – to her condition.

'Honey,' Pete said gently, tentatively reaching to put his hand on her arm, 'our sitter is costing us ten bucks an hour. Can we please go to dinner? Please?'

Delia closed her eyes, still trying to remember, then shook her head. 'Fine,' she said, and with that one word, everyone began to scatter, Pete opening the door to their car, Kristy digging out her own keys, Wes starting towards the van, 'but then I'll remember in five minutes, and it will be too late.'

She was still muttering as she eased herself into the passenger seat of Pete's car, then pulled the seat belt across her belly, struggling to make it reach. As I got into the van with Wes, I watched them pull out of the driveway, then start down the road. I wondered, as they reached the stop sign there, if she'd already remembered. Probably.

'When is that baby due?' Kristy called out as she and Monica pulled up beside us. About fifteen minutes earlier, when the van was packed and we'd been paid, she'd disappeared for a few minutes into the garage, emerging in an entirely different outfit: a short denim skirt, a blouse with ribboned sleeves, and high-heeled platform sandals, her hair held up in a high ponytail. Not only was she versatile, I'd marvelled as she did a little spin, showing it off, but quick. Clark Kent becoming Superman had nothing on her, and he didn't even have to worry about hair.

'July tenth,' Wes told her, cranking the van's engine.

'Which leaves us,' she said, squinting as she attempted to do the maths for a second before giving up, 'entirely too long before she gets normal again.'

'Three weeks,' I said.

'Exactly.' She sighed, checking her reflection in the mirror. 'Anyway, so listen. This party is in Lakeview. Take a right on Hillcrest, left on Willow, house at the end of the cul-de-sac. We'll see you guys there. Hey, and, Macy?'

'Yeah?'

She leaned further out of the window, as if we were sharing a confidence, even though there was a fair amount of space, not to mention Wes, between us. 'I have it on good authority,' she said, her voice low, 'that there will be extraordinary boys there. You know what I mean?'

Wes, beside me, was fiddling with his visor. 'Um, no,' I said.

'Don't worry.' She put her car in gear, then pointed at me. 'By the end of the night, you will. See you there!' And then, in a cloud of dust, the radio blasting, she was gone, hardly slowing for the stop sign at the end of the road.

'Well,' Wes said as we pulled out of the driveway with slightly less velocity, 'to the party then. Right?'

'Sure.'

I tried, for the first five minutes or so of the drive, to come up with a witty conversation starter. Topics, from the inane to slightly promising, flitted through my brain as we moved along the quiet, mostly deserted country roads. Finally, when I couldn't stand the silence any more, I opened my mouth, not even knowing what I was going to say.

'So,' I began, but that was as far as I got. And, as it turned out, as far as we got.

The engine, which had been humming along merrily up until that point, suddenly began to cough. Then lurch. Then moan. And then: nothing. We were stopped dead in the middle of the road.

For a second, neither of us said anything. A bird flew by overhead, its shadow moving across the windshield.

'So,' Wes said, as if picking up where I'd left off, '*that's* what Delia forgot.'

I looked at him. 'What?'

He lifted his finger, pointing at the gas gauge, which was flat on the E. Empty. 'Gas,' he said.

'Gas,' I repeated, and in my mind, I could hear Delia's voice, echoing this, finally remembering with a palm slapped to her forehead. *Gas.*

Wes already had his door open and was getting out, letting it fall shut behind him. I did the same, then walked round the van to the deserted road, looking both ways.

I'd heard people talk about being in the middle of nowhere, but it had always been an exaggeration. Now, though, as I took in the flat pastureland on either side of us, it seemed completely appropriate. No cars were in sight. I couldn't even see any houses anywhere nearby. The only light was from the moon, full and yellow, halfway up the sky.

'How far,' I said, 'would you say it is to the nearest gas station?'

Wes squinted back the way we'd come, then turned and looked ahead, as if gathering facts for a scientific guess. 'No idea,' he said finally. 'Guess we'll find out, though.'

We pushed the van over to the side of the road, then rolled up the windows and locked it. Everything sounded loud in the quiet: our footsteps, the door shutting, the owl that hooted overhead, making me jump. I stood in the middle of the road while Wes did a last check of the van, then walked over, his hands in his pockets, to join me.

'Okay,' he said, 'now we decide. Left or right?'

I looked one way, then the other. 'Left,' I said, and we started walking.

'Green beans,' Wes said.

'Spaghetti,' I replied.

He thought for a second, and in the quiet all I could hear was our footsteps. 'Ice cream,' he said.

'Manicotti.'

'What's with all the *I* words?' he said, tipping his head back and staring up at the sky. 'God.'

'I told you,' I said. 'I've played this game before.'

He was quiet for a minute, thinking. We'd been walking for about twenty minutes, and not one car had passed. I had my cell phone with me, but Kristy wasn't picking up, Bert wasn't home and my mother was at a meeting, so we were pretty much on our own, at least for the time being. After going along in silence for a little while, Wes had suggested that we play a game, if only to make the time pass faster. It was too dark for I Spy, so I suggested Last Letter, First Letter, which he'd never heard of. I even let him pick the category, food, but he was still struggling.

'Instant breakfast,' he said finally.

'That's not food.'

'Sure it is.'

'Nope. It's a drink.'

He looked at me. 'Are you seriously getting competitive about this?'

'No,' I said, sliding my hands in my pockets. A breeze blew over us, and I heard the leaves on the trees nearby rustling. 'But it is a drink, not a food. That's all I'm saying.'

'You're a rule person,' he said.

'My sister was a cheater. It sort of became necessary.'

'She cheated at this game?'

'She cheated at *everything*,' I said. 'When we played Monopoly, she always insisted on being banker, then helped herself to multiple loans and 'service fees' for every real estate transaction. I was, like, ten or eleven before I played at someone else's house and they told me you couldn't do that.'

He laughed, the sound seeming loud in all the quiet. I felt myself smiling, remembering.

'During staring contests,' I said, 'she always blinked. *Always*. But then she'd swear up and down she hadn't, and make you go again, and again. And when we played Truth, she lied. Blatantly.'

'Truth?' he said, glancing over his shoulder as something – another owl, I hoped – hooted behind us. 'What's that?'

I looked at him. 'You never played Truth, either?' I asked. 'God, what did you guys do on long car trips?'

'We,' he said, 'discussed politics and current events and engaged in scintillating discourse.'

'Oh.'

'I'm kidding,' he said, smiling. 'We usually read comics and beat the crap out of each other until my dad threatened to pull over and "settle things once and for all". Then, when it was just my mom, we sang folk songs.'

'You sang folk songs,' I said, clarifying. Somehow I couldn't picture this.

'I didn't have a choice. It was like the lentil loaf, no other options.' He sighed. 'I know the entire Woody Guthrie catalogue.'

'Sing something for me,' I said, nudging him with my elbow. 'You *know* you want to.'

'No,' he said flatly.

'Come on. I bet you have a lovely singing voice.'

'I don't.'

'Wes,' I said, my voice serious.

'Macy,' he replied, equally serious. 'No.'

For a minute we walked in silence. Far, far off in the distance, I saw headlights, but a second later they turned off in another direction, disappearing. Wes exhaled, shaking his head, and I wondered how far we'd walked already.

'Okay, so Truth,' he said. 'How do you play?'

'Is this because you can't think up another *I* food?' I asked.

'No,' he said indignantly. Then, 'Maybe. How do you play?'

'We can't play Truth,' I told him, as we crested a small hill, and a fence began on one side of the road.

'Why not?'

'Because,' I said, 'it can get really ugly.'

'How so?'

'It just can. You have to tell the truth, even if you don't want to.'

'I can handle that,' he said.

'You can't even think of an *I* food,' I said.

'Can you?'

'Ice milk,' I said. 'Italian sausage.'

'Okay, fine. Point proved. Now tell me how to play.'

'All right,' I said. 'But you asked for it.'

He just looked at me. *Okay*, I thought. *Here we go.*

'In Truth,' I said, 'there are no rules other than you have to tell the truth.'

'How do you win?' he asked.

'That,' I said, 'is such a boy question.'

'What, girls don't like to win?' He snorted. 'Please. *You're* the one who got all rule driven on me claiming Instant Breakfast isn't a food.'

'It's not,' I told him. 'It's a beverage.'

He rolled his eyes. *I can't believe this*, I thought. A week or two ago putting a full sentence together in front of Wes was a challenge. Now we were arguing about liquids.

'Okay,' he said, 'back to Truth. You were saying?'

I took in a breath. 'To win, one person has to refuse to answer a question,' I said. 'So, for example, let's say I ask you a question and you don't answer it. Then you get to ask me a question and, if I answer it, I win.'

'But that's too simple,' he said. 'What if I ask you something easy?'

'You wouldn't,' I told him. 'It has to be a really hard question, because you don't want me to win.'

'Ahhh,' he said, nodding. Then, after mulling it for a second he said, 'Man. This is diabolical.'

'It's a girl's game,' I explained, tilting my head back and looking up at the stars. 'Always good for a little drama at the slumber party. I told you, you don't want to play.'

'No. I do.' He squared his shoulders. 'I can handle it.'

'You think?'

'Yup. Hit me.'

I thought for a second. We were walking down the centre line of the road, the moonlight slanting across us. 'Okay,' I said. 'What's your favorite colour?'

He looked at me. 'Don't coddle,' he said. 'It's insulting.'

'I'm trying to ease you in,' I said.

'Don't ease. Ask something real.'

I rolled my eyes. 'Okay,' I said. And then, without even really thinking about it, I said, 'Why'd you get sent to Myers School?'

For a second, he was quiet, and I was sure I'd overstepped.

But then he said, 'I broke into a house. With a couple of guys I used to hang out with. We didn't take anything, just drank a couple of beers, but a neighbour saw us and called the cops. We ran but they caught us.'

'Why'd you do that?'

'What, run?'

'No,' I said, although I had to admit I was curious about that too. 'Break in.'

He shrugged. 'I don't know. These guys I was friends with, they'd done it a couple of times, but I never had before. I was there, so I went along.' He ran a hand through his hair. 'It was my first offence, my only offence, but the county was on this whole thing where they were punishing right off, to scare you out of doing more, so I got sent away. Six months, let out after four.'

'My boyfriend,' I said, then, feeling the need to correct myself, added, 'sort-of boyfriend, he used to tutor there.'

'Really.'

I nodded. 'Yup.'

'So what's the deal with that,' he asked. 'The boyfriend.'

'What?'

'I get to ask a question now,' he said. 'That's how the game goes, correct?'

'Um,' I said. 'Yes. I guess.'

He waved his hand at me in a take-it-away sort of motion. *Great*, I thought, scanning the horizon for headlights. No such luck.

'I'm waiting,' Wes said. 'Does this mean you pass?'

'No,' I snapped. 'I mean, no. I'm answering. I'm just collecting my response.'

Another few seconds passed.

'Is there a time limit for this?' he asked. I shot him a look. 'Just wondering.'

'Fine,' I said, taking a breath. 'We've been dating for about a year and a half. And he's just, you know, a genius. Really smart, and driven. He went away for the summer, and I was just, you know, being a little too clingy or something I guess, and it sort of freaked him out. He's very independent.'

'Define clingy,' he said.

'You don't know what clingy is?'

'I know what it means to me,' he said. 'But it's different for different people.'

'Well,' I said, then stopped, not sure how to explain. 'First, he was upset that I wasn't taking my job, which had been his job, more seriously. And then, I said I loved him in an email, and that made him a little skittish.'

'Skittish?'

'Do you need a definition of that too?' I said.

'Nope. Know it.' He tipped his head back, looking up at the moon. 'So things went sour because you said those three words, and because you weren't as serious about the library as he wanted you to be.'

'Right,' I said. Again, it sounded stupid, but of course everything does when you're just getting the bare-bones facts, only the basics, without – and then it hit me. 'Wait,' I said. I stopped walking. 'I never said anything about the library.'

'Yeah, you did,' he said. 'You –'

'Nope.' I was sure of it. 'I didn't.'

For a second we just stood there.

'Kristy,' I said finally.

'Not exactly. I just heard you guys talking that night, out at the clearing.'

I started walking again. 'Well, now you've heard it twice. Although I think you should be penalized in some way, because you asked a question you already knew the answer to, and that is totally against the rules.'

'I thought the only rule was you had to tell the truth.'

I made a face at him. 'Okay, so there are two rules.'

He snorted. 'Next you'll tell me there are service charges too.'

'What is your problem?' I asked.

'All I'm saying,' he said, shrugging, 'is that I vote that the second one be done away with.'

'You don't get to *vote*,' I said. 'This is an established game.'

'Clearly it isn't.' He was so freaking stubborn, or so I was noticing. 'You seem to be making up rules as you go.'

'I am not,' I said indignantly. He just looked at me, obviously not believing this, so I said, 'Fine. If you're proposing a rule change, you have to at least present a case for it.'

'That is so student council,' he said with a laugh.

I was pretty sure this was an insult. 'I'm waiting,' I told him.

'You should be allowed to occasionally ask a question you know the answer to,' he said, as I reflected how it was so like a guy to change the rules when he'd only just started playing, 'so that you can be sure the other person is telling the truth.'

And then we both saw it: headlights, in the distance. They came closer, even closer, and then finally swung left, disappearing down a side road. So close, and yet so far.

Wes sighed, shaking his head, then looked at me. 'Okay, forget it,' he said. 'I drop my case. We tell the truth, or else. Okay?'

I nodded. 'Fine with me.'

'Go ahead then,' he said. 'It's your turn.'

I thought for a second, really wanting to come up with something good. Finally I said, 'Okay, fair's fair. What was the story with your last girlfriend?'

'My last girlfriend,' he said, 'or the girlfriend I have now?'

I had to admit I was surprised. Not just surprised, I realized, gauging the sudden drop in my stomach, but disappointed. But only for a second. Of course a boy like him had a girlfriend.

'The current girlfriend,' I said. 'What's the story there?'

'Well,' he said. 'To begin with, she's incarcerated.'

I looked at him. 'You're dating a prisoner?'

'Rehab.' He said this so easily, the way I'd told people Jason was at Brain Camp, as if it were just that normal. 'I met her at Myers. She was in for shoplifting, but since then she got busted with some pot, so now she's at Evergreen Care Centre. At least until her dad's insurance runs out.'

'What's her name?'

'Becky.'

Becky. Becky the shoplifting pothead, I thought, and then immediately told myself I was being petty. 'So it's serious,' I said.

He shrugged. 'She's been in and out of trouble for the last year, so we've hardly been able to see each other. She says she hates me to see her at Evergreen, so we're sort of waiting until she gets out to see what happens.'

'And when's that?' I asked.

'End of the summer.' He kicked at a rock, sending it skittering across the pavement. 'Until then, everything's just sort of on hold.'

'That's me too,' I said. 'We're supposed to get together in August, when we'll know better whether we want the same things, or if it's best to make this break permanent.'

He winced, listening to this. 'That sounds verbatim.'

I sighed. 'It is. Right off the email he sent me.'

'Ouch.'

'I know.'

So there we were, me and Wes, still walking, in the dark, on a break. It was weird, I thought, how much you could have in common with someone and, from a distance, never even know it. That first night at my mom's he'd just been a good-looking boy, one I figured I'd never see again. I wondered what he'd thought of me.

'Okay,' he said, as we started up a hill lined by trees, 'my turn.'

I slid my hands into my pockets. 'Okay, shoot.'

'Why'd you really stop running?'

I felt myself take in a breath, like this had hit me in my gut: it was that unexpected. Questions about Jason I could handle, but this was something else. Something more. But we were playing Truth, and so far he'd played fair. It was dark and quiet, and we were alone. And suddenly, I found myself answering.

'The morning my dad died,' I said, keeping my eyes on the road ahead, 'he came into my room to wake me up for a run, and I was sleepy and lazy, so I waved him off and told him to go without me.'

This was the first time, ever, that I'd told this story aloud. I couldn't even believe I was doing it.

'A few minutes later, though, I changed my mind.' I stopped, swallowing. I didn't have to do this. I could pass, and if I lost, no big deal. But for some reason I kept going. 'So I got up and went to catch up with him. I knew the route he'd take, it was the same one we always did. Out our neighbourhood, a right on Willow, then another right onto McKinley.'

Wes wasn't saying anything, but I knew he was listening. I could just tell.

'I was a little less than halfway into that first mile when I came over this ridge and saw him. He was lying on the sidewalk.'

I felt him look at me, but I knew if I turned to face him I'd stop. So I just kept talking. My footsteps, our footsteps, were so steady. *Keep going*, I thought. *Keep going*.

'At first,' I said, 'it didn't even compute, you know? I mean, my mind couldn't put it together, even though it was right in front of my face.'

The words kept coming, almost too fast, tumbling over my tongue like they'd been held back for so long that now, finally free, nothing could stop them. Not even me.

'I started running faster. I mean, faster than I ever had. It was adrenalin, I guess. I'd never run that fast in my life. Never.'

All I could hear were our footsteps. And the quiet dark. And my voice.

'There was this man,' I went on. 'He was just some random guy who'd been on his way to the store, and he'd stopped and was trying to give my dad CPR. But, by the time I got to him, he'd already given up. The ambulance came, and we went to the hospital. But it was too late.'

And then it was done. Over. I could feel my breath coming quickly, through my teeth, and for a second I felt unsteady, as if with this story no longer held so closely against me, I'd lost my footing. Grief can be a burden, but also an anchor. You get used to the weight, to how it holds you to a place.

'Macy,' he said quietly.

'Don't,' I said, because I knew what came next, some form of I'm sorry, and I didn't want to hear it, especially now, especially from him. 'Please. Just –'

And then, suddenly, there was light. Bright yellow light, rising over the other side of the hill, splashing across us: instantly, we had shadows. We were both squinting, Wes raising one hand to shield his eyes. The car had a rumbling engine, and it seemed like it took forever to pull up beside us and slow to a stop.

'Hey.' A man's voice came from behind the wheel. After all the brightness, I couldn't make out his face. 'You kids need a ride someplace? What you doing out here?'

'Ran out of gas,' Wes told him. 'Where's the nearest station?'

The man jerked his thumb in the opposite direction. 'About three miles that way. Where'd you break down?'

'About two miles that way,' Wes told him.

'Well, get in then,' he said, reaching to unlock the back door. 'I'll run you up there. You about scared me to death, though, walking out here in the dark. Thought you were deer or something.'

Wes pulled the door open for me, holding it as I climbed in, then sliding in beside me. The car smelled like cigar smoke and motor oil, and as the man began to drive I could make out his profile: he had white hair and a crook nose, and drove slowly, almost as slowly as Bert. It was amazing we hadn't seen him coming. He'd just appeared, as if he'd dropped out of the sky or something.

As I leaned back against the seat, my heart felt like it was shaking: I couldn't believe what I'd just done. There was no way to take the story back, folding it neatly into the place I'd kept it all this time. No matter what else happened, from here on out, I would always remember Wes, because with this telling, he'd become part of that story, of my story, too.

'That you?' the man asked, glancing back at us in the rearview mirror as we passed the Wish van.

'Yes, sir,' Wes replied.

'Well, you had no way to know, I guess,' he said, and I wasn't sure what he meant until about a minute later, when we crested a hill, took a corner, and there was a gas station, all lit up. The neon sign in the window said, almost cheerfully, OPEN. 'Had no idea how close you were.'

'No,' Wes said. 'I guess we didn't.'

As we pulled up to the station I turned to look at him, to say something, but he was already pushing open the door and getting out of the car, walking round to the trunk, where the man had a gas can. I sat there, the fluorescent light flickering overhead, as the man went inside to buy cigarettes and Wes pumped gas, his back to me, eyes on the numbers as they clicked higher and higher.

I turned my head and saw he was looking at me. In this, my first true glimpse of his face in over an hour, I braced myself for what I might see. After all, with Jason, any time I'd opened up, he'd pulled back. I was prepared, even expecting it to happen again.

But as I looked at Wes I saw only those same familiar features, even more so now, that same half-smile. He motioned for me to roll down the window.

'Hey,' he said.

'Hey.'

I waited. What came next? I wondered. What words would he say to try and make this better? 'I thought of one,' he said.

For a second, I just blinked at him. 'What?'

'Iceberg lettuce,' he said. Then he added, quickly, 'And don't say it's not a food, because it is. I'm willing to fight you on it.'

I smiled. 'No fight,' I told him. 'It's a keeper.'

The pump stopped then, and he hung the hose back up, screwing the top on the gas can. 'Need anything?' he asked, and when I shook my head, he started towards the store.

I heard a buzzing under my feet: my phone. I unzipped my purse and pulled it out, hitting the Talk button as I raised it to my ear. 'Hel–'

'Where *are* you?' Kristy demanded. I could hear party noises behind her, music and loud voices. 'Do you know how worried we are? Monica's about sick, she's almost inconsolable –'

'We ran out of gas,' I told her, switching the phone to my other ear. 'I left you a message. We were stuck out in the middle of nowhere.'

'Message? I didn't get any –' A pause as, presumably, she actually checked for the first time. 'Oh. Well. God! Where are you? Are you okay?'

'We're fine. We got a ride and we're getting gas for the van right now.'

'Well, thank goodness.' I heard her cover up the phone and relay this information to Monica, who, upset or not, I imagined would receive it with her same flat, bored expression. Then Kristy came back on. 'Look, I gotta tell you, if I were you guys, I'd just go straight home. This party is a bust. And I was totally misled. There are *nothing* but ordinary boys here.'

I turned and looked into the gas station, where Wes was now paying, as the man who'd driven us looked on. 'That's too bad,' I said.

'It's okay, though,' she assured me. 'Someday I'll show you an extraordinary boy, Macy. They do exist. You just have to believe me.'

'Don't worry,' I said. 'I do.'

Chapter TEN

My mother was stressed.

Truthfully, my mother was *always* stressed. I couldn't remember the last time I'd seen her actually relax and sit still in a way that made it obvious she wasn't already thinking about the next six things she had to do, and maybe the six after that. Once, she'd been a pro at decompressing, loved to sit on the back deck of the beach house in one of our splintery deck chairs for hours at a time, staring at the ocean. She never had a book or the paper or anything else to distract her. Just the horizon, but it kept her attention, her gaze unwavering. Maybe it was the absence of thought that she loved about being out there, the world narrowing to just the pounding of the waves as the water moved in and out.

Everything about Wildflower Ridge led back to my mom. The original proposal for the development, the floor plans for each phase, the landscaping, the community organization; every decision was hers. So I was used to her cell phone joining us for dinner every night, sitting on the third place mat, accustomed to her being at the model-home office late into the night, entirely unsurprised when I came home to find contractors, local business owners or prospective home buyers sitting in our living room listening to a spiel about what makes Wildflower Ridge special.

Her current project was the townhouses, and for my mother they were especially important. She'd taken a risk by going for luxury, adding all kinds of fancy accoutrements like heated garages, marble bathrooms, balconies and high-end appliances, all for the discerning, affluent professional. But just as she began building, the economy took a slide: there were layoffs, the stock market plummeted and suddenly everyone was tentative with their dollars, especially when it came to real estate. Since she'd already started, she had no choice but to keep going, but her nervousness had driven her to work harder at making contacts and sales. Considering how many of her waking hours (i.e., all of them) were devoted to this already, it seemed close to impossible. Hence stress. Lots of it.

'I'm fine,' she said to Caroline one morning a couple of days after my late night with Wes, as the three of us sat at the kitchen table. My sister was spending most of her time shuttling between her house in Atlanta, making sure Wally was eating enough vegetables while he battled some corporation in his law case, and the coast, where she conferred with the carpenter, dickered over fabric and paint chips, and, by the looks of the receipts I'd seen, bought up most of the inventory at Home Depot. In between, she'd taken to dropping in to show us pictures of the progress, ask for our opinions on decorating decisions, and tell my mother, repeatedly, that she needed to relax and take a vacation. Yeah, right.

'Mom,' she said now, as I took a bite of cereal, 'you're not fine. Are you even sleeping?'

'Of course I am,' my mother said, shuffling through some papers. 'I sleep like a baby.'

That is, if she was sleeping at all. More than once lately I'd come downstairs at two or three in the morning only to see her in her office, still in her work clothes, typing away, or leaving voicemail messages for her contractors or subs. I didn't know when she went to bed, but by the next morning when I was getting up for work she was always in the kitchen, showered and dressed in new clothes, already talking on her cell phone.

'I just want to be sure that when the house is done, you'll commit to this vacation,' my sister said now, opening one of her beach-house folders and sorting through some photographs. 'It looks like it's going to be August, probably the second week.'

'Any time after the seventh is fine,' my mother said, moving her coffee cup aside to make a note on something with the pencil in her hand. 'That's the gala for the opening of the townhouses.'

'You're having a gala?' I said.

'Well, it's a reception,' she told me, picking up her cell phone, then putting it down, 'but I'm planning for it to be nicer and bigger than the sales events we've had here before. I'm renting a tent, and I've found this fantastic French caterer . . . Oh, that reminds me, I've *got* to call about the kitchen faucets if I want to change them from ruby to diamond class.'

And then she was up, pushing back her chair and starting across the kitchen, still muttering to herself. How she'd got to faucets from caterers was hard to say, but it was hard keeping up with her these days.

'So the eighth?' Caroline called after her. 'Of August? I can write that down, it's firm?'

My mother, halfway through the door, turned her head. 'The eighth,' she said, nodding, 'firm. Absolutely.'

Caroline smiled, pleased with herself, as my mother disappeared down the hallway. She picked up her folder, tapping it on the tabletop to straighten its contents, then put it down in front of her again. 'So it's set,' she said. 'The eighth to the fifteenth, we're officially on vacation.'

I put my spoon down in my now empty bowl, finally realizing why this date had been ringing a bell in my head. It was the day after Jason was returning from Brain Camp: by then I'd know whether we were together or really over. But now it was only the end of June. The townhouses still needed windows, fixtures, landscaping. The beach house was going to be painted, the floors sanded, the new décor installed under my sister's watchful eye. The new would be new, the old, new again. What I'd be, on a break, broken or otherwise, I had no idea. Luckily for all of us, though, we still had time.

Wes and I were friends now. And, really, no one was more surprised than me.

Initially, the only thing we shared, other than working for Wish, was that we had both lost a parent. This was a lot to have in common, but it wasn't just about that any more, either. The truth was, since our night stranded together, I felt comfortable around Wes. When I was with him, I didn't have to be perfect, or even try for perfect. He already knew my secrets, the things I'd kept hidden from everyone else, so I could just be myself. Which shouldn't have been such a big deal. But it was.

'Okay,' he said to me one night, as we sat on the back deck rail at a party in the Arbours, a neighbourhood just down from my own, 'what's *that* about?'

I followed his gaze to the open sliding glass door that led into the kitchen, where three girls I recognized from my school – the sort of girls who hung out in the parking lot after late bell, wearing sunglasses and cupping their hidden cigarettes against their palms – were staring at us. Or, more specifically, at me.

'Well,' I said, taking a sip of the beer I was holding, 'I think they're just surprised to see me here.'

'Really.'

I nodded, putting my beer back on the rail. Inside, over the girls' heads, I could see Kristy, Bert and Monica playing quarters at a long oak table in the dining room, the fancy centrepiece of which had been pushed aside and was now piled high with beer cans. More often than not at parties lately, I ended up sitting with Wes off to the side, while Kristy and everyone else trolled for extraordinary boys or, in Bert's case, desperate freshman girls. While they tried their luck and bemoaned the prospects, we on-a-break types just sat and shot the breeze, watching the party unfold around us.

'And they're surprised to see you here because . . .' Wes said, nodding at a guy in a baseball hat who passed by, saying his name.

'Because,' I said, 'they think I'm Miss Perfect.'

'You?' he said, sounding so surprised I felt obligated to shoot him a look. 'I mean, ah, I see.'

I picked up my beer, taking another sip. 'Shut up,' I said.

'No, seriously, this is interesting,' he said as the girls moved out onto the deck, disappearing behind a clump of people waiting in line at the keg. 'Perfect as in . . .'

'Goody-goody,' I said, 'by association. Jason would never be here.'

'No?'

'God, no.'

Wes considered this for a second as I noted at least six different girls around the deck checking him out. As much as I was getting used to this happening whenever I was with him, it was still a little unnerving. I'd lost count of how many dirty looks I'd got just by sitting next to him. We're not like that, I wanted to say to the girls who stared at me, slit-eyed, their eyes following me whenever I went to the bathroom or to find Kristy, waiting for me to be far enough away to move in. By now, though, I could spot who was and wasn't his type a mile off. The girl in the tight black dress and red lipstick, leaning against the keg? Nope. The one in the denim skirt and black T with the tan? Maybe. The one who kept licking her lips? Ugh. No. No. No.

'Let's say Jason was here,' he said now. 'What would he be doing?'

I considered this. 'Probably complaining about the smoke,' I said, 'and getting very concerned about whether all these cans are going to be properly recycled. What about Becky?'

He thought for a second, pulling a hand through his hair. In the dining room, I could hear Kristy laughing loudly. 'Passed out someplace. Or behind the bushes sneaking a smoke that she'd deny to me later.'

'Ah,' I said.

'Ah.'

The girl in the tight black dress was passing by us now, eyeing Wes and walking entirely too slowly. 'Hi,' she said, and he nodded at her but didn't reply. *Knew it*, I thought.

'Honestly,' I said.

'What?'

'Come on. You have to admit it's sort of ridiculous.'

'What is?'

Now that I had to define it, I found myself struggling for the right words. 'You know,' I said, then figured Kristy had really summed it up best. 'The sa-woon.'

'The what?'

'Wes, come on,' I said. 'Are you seriously not aware of how girls stare at you?'

He rolled his eyes, leaning back on his palms. 'Let's get back to the idea of you being perfect.'

'Seriously. What's it like?'

'Being perfect? I wouldn't know.'

'Not being perfect.' I sighed. 'Being . . .'

As I tried to come up with something, he flicked a bug off his arm.

'. . . gorgeous,' I finished. Two weeks earlier, this would have mortified me: I could just see myself bursting into flames from the shame. But now, I only felt a slight twinge as I took another sip of my beer and waited for him to answer.

'Again,' he said, as the parking lot girls passed by, eyeing both of us, 'I wouldn't know. You tell me.'

'Donneven,' I said, in my best Monica imitation, and he laughed. 'We're not talking about me.'

'We could be,' he said as I watched Bert take note of a group of what looked like ninth graders who had just come into the living room.

'I'm not gorgeous,' I said.

'Sure you are.'

I just shook my head, knowing this was him evading the question. 'You,' I said, 'have this whole tall, dark stranger thing going on. Not to mention the tortured artist bit.'

'Bit?'

'You know what I mean.'

He shook his head, clearly discounting this description. 'And you,' he said, 'have that whole blonde, cool and collected, perfect smart girl thing going on.'

'You're the boy all the girls want to rebel with,' I said.

'You,' he replied, 'are the unattainable girl in homeroom who never gives a guy the time of day.'

There was a blast of music from inside, a thump of bass beat, then quiet again.

'I'm not perfect,' I said. 'Not even close.'

'I'm not tortured. Unless you count this conversation.'

'Okay.' I picked up my beer. 'What do *you* want to talk about?'

'How about,' he said, 'that we've got an ongoing game of Truth to get back to?'

'How about,' I said, as a guy from my English class

stumbled by, looking sort of queasy, 'not. I can't handle Truth tonight.'

'You're only saying that,' he said, 'because it's my turn.'

'It isn't. It's mine.'

'It's –'

I said, 'I asked you about Myers School, then you asked me about Jason. I countered with a question about Becky, and you asked me about running. Two rounds, my turn.'

'See, *this* is why I don't hang out with smart girls,' he said. Then he rubbed his hands together, psyching himself up, while I rolled my eyes. 'Okay, go ahead. I'm ready.'

'All right,' I said, tucking a piece of hair behind my ear. 'What's it like to always have girls swooning over you?'

He turned and looked at me. 'Macy.'

'You're the one who wanted to play.'

He didn't say anything for a minute, and I wondered if he was going to pass. *Too competitive*, I thought, and I was right. 'I don't know,' he said. 'It's not something I notice, if it's even happening.'

'The name of the game,' I told him, 'is *Truth*.'

He turned and looked at me, annoyed. 'Fine. It's weird. I mean, it's not like it counts or anything. They don't know me by looking, nobody does. It's totally surface. It's not real.'

'Tell that to her,' I said, nodding at the girl in the far corner, who was still ogling him.

'Funny,' he muttered, making it a point to look away. 'Is it my turn yet?'

'No, I have a follow-up question.'

'Is that legal?'

'Yes,' I said, with authority. Now I was Caroline, making up my own rules. 'Okay, so if that's not real, what is? What counts, to you?'

He thought for a second, then said, 'I don't know. Just because someone's pretty doesn't mean she's decent. Or vice versa. I'm not into appearances. I like flaws, I think they make things interesting.'

I wasn't sure what answer I'd expected. But this wasn't it. For a second, I just sat there, letting it sink in.

'You know,' I said finally, 'saying stuff like that would make girls even crazier for you. Now you're cute *and* somewhat more attainable. If you were appealing before, now you're off the charts.'

'I don't want to be off the charts,' he said, rolling his eyes. 'I do, however, want to be off this subject.'

'Fine,' I said. 'Go ahead, it's your turn.'

Inside, I could see Kristy chatting up some guy with dreadlocks, while Monica sat beside her, looking bored. Bert, for his part, was eyeballing the girl with the quarter, who, by my count, had now missed the cup six times in a row.

'Why is being perfect so important to you?'

I felt myself blink. 'It's not,' I said.

He narrowed his eyes at me. 'What's this game called again?'

'That's the truth,' I said. 'I don't care that much about being perfect.'

'Seems like you do.'

'How do you figure?'

He shrugged. 'Every time you've mentioned your boyfriend, you've said he was.'

'Well, he is,' I said. 'But I'm not. That was part of the problem.'

'Macy, come on.' He looked at me. 'I mean, what's perfect, anyway?'

I shook my head, lifting my beer to my lips. It was empty, but I needed something to do. 'It's not about being perfect, really. It's about . . . I don't know. Being in control.'

'Explain,' he said, and I sighed.

'I don't know if I can,' I told him. I glanced back at the dining room, looking for Kristy, a distraction, but she and Monica and Bert were gone, the table now deserted. 'When my dad died, it was like everything felt really shaky, you know? And trying to be the best I could be, it gave me something to focus on. If I could just do everything right, then I was safe.'

I couldn't believe I was saying this, not here, at a party packed with classmates and strangers. In fact, I couldn't imagine saying it anywhere, really, except in my own head, where it somehow made sense.

'That sucks, though,' Wes said finally, his voice low. 'You're just setting yourself up to fail, because you'll never get everything perfect.'

'Says who?'

He just looked at me. 'The world,' he said, gesturing all around us, as if this party, this deck encompassed it all. 'The universe. There's just no way. And why would you want everything to be perfect, anyway?'

'I don't want everything to be perfect,' I said. *Just me*, I thought. *Somehow*. 'I just want –'

'Curfew,' I heard from beside me, and I looked up to see

Monica standing there, blowing her bangs out of her face. She gestured to her watch, then to the kitchen, where I could see Bert and Kristy waiting for us.

'Saved by the bell,' Wes said, hopping down off the rail. I slid down too, taking my time, my last three words still hovering in my mind. Here was a boy who liked flaws, who saw them not as failings but as strengths. Who knew such a person could even exist, or what would have happened if we'd found each other under different circumstances? Maybe in a perfect world. But not in this one.

Oh, how I hated the info desk.

Before, it had been bad. Boring. Stifling. So quiet I was sure, if I listened hard enough, I could hear the blood moving through my veins, the plates of the earth shifting, time literally passing. Even if my day was going well, all it took was pushing open the doors of the library for everything to just stop. Sink. And stay that way for the full six hours I was stuck there.

One day, I was crossing to the periodical room, carrying a stack of mouldy old *Nature* magazines. I'd just passed one of the stacks when I heard it.

'Gotcha!'

I jumped, startled. Not scared, since it had been more of a whisper, a low-key gotcha, which made sense once I stopped and leaned back, craning my neck, and saw Kristy. She was dressed in a white pleather skirt, a pink short-sleeved fuzzy sweater, and her white go-go boots, her hair pulled up high on her head. She was also wearing sunglasses, huge white ones, and carrying a fringed purse. She looked like she should be at the rodeo. Or maybe dancing in a cage. But not in fiction A–P, which is where she was.

'Hey!' she said, entirely too loudly: a man at the next shelf, whose arms were full of books, peered through at us. 'How's it going?'

'What are you doing here?' I asked her, shifting the magazines to my other arm.

'Monica needed intellectual stimulation,' she said, nodding across the library, where I could see Monica, chewing gum and looking exhausted, examining some books in non-fiction. 'She's a total bookworm, inhales them. I'm more of a magazine gal myself, but I came along to see how you spent your days.'

I glanced over at the info desk, where I could see Bethany on the phone, typing away at her keyboard. Amanda was beside her, looking at us. Or, to be more specific, at Kristy. 'Well,' I said, 'this is it.'

'Who's the braid?' she asked me, pushing her sunglasses up onto her head and staring back at Amanda, who was not dissuaded. I wondered if she thought we couldn't see her or something.

'That's Amanda,' I said.

'Right.' Kristy raised an eyebrow. 'She's quite the starer, isn't she?'

'Apparently so.'

Kristy crossed her eyes at Amanda, who seemed taken aback, quickly dipping her head down and opening a book in front of her. 'I have to say, though, I'm digging that twin set. Is it merino wool?'

'I have no idea.'

'I bet it is.' She hitched her purse up on her shoulder. 'So look, Monica and I are going to that new wrap place for lunch. You want to come?'

'Wrap place?' I asked. Now Bethany was off the phone, and she and Amanda had their heads together, talking. Every once in a while one of them would look up at us, then say something to the other.

'Yeah. It's at the mall. They'll put, like, anything in a tortilla for you. I mean, within reason. Can you come?'

I glanced at the clock. It was 11:45. 'I don't know,' I said as Amanda pushed back from the info desk in her chair, sliding sideways, her eyes still on me, 'I probably shouldn't.'

'Why not? You do *get* lunch, don't you?'

'Well, yeah.'

'And you have to eat, right?'

'I guess so,' I said.

'So what's the problem?' she asked.

'It's complicated,' I told her. 'They don't like it when I take lunch.'

'Who doesn't?'

I nodded towards Amanda and Bethany.

'And you care about that because . . .' Kristy said slowly.

'They intimidate me,' I said. 'I'm a loser. I don't know, pick one.'

Kristy narrowed her eyes. 'Intimidated?' she said. 'Really?'

I fiddled with the magazines, embarrassed I'd even admitted this. 'It's complicated.'

'I just don't understand,' she said, shaking her head. 'I mean, they're so . . . unhappy. Why would they intimidate you?'

'They're not unhappy,' I said.

'They're totally miserable!' She looked at them, saw them staring and shook her head. 'Look at them. Really. Look. Look right now.'

'Kristy.'

'*Look.*' She reached up, cupping her fingers round my chin, and turned my head. Bethany and Amanda stared back at us. 'Can't you see it? They're all milky and uptight-looking. I mean, I like a twin set as much as the next person, but you don't have to wear it like you have a stick up your ass. Clearly all the smarts in the world don't translate to good fashion sense. And God, what's with the staring?' She cleared her throat. 'What,' she repeated, her voice carrying easily across the room, 'is with the staring. Huh?'

Bethany's face flushed, while Amanda's mouth opened, then shut again.

'Shh,' someone said from the next row over.

'Oh, you shush,' Kristy said, dropping her hand from my chin. 'Macy,' she said, her voice serious, 'if that's ideal, they can have it. Right?'

Hearing this, I had no idea what to say.

'Then it's decided,' Kristy said. 'You'll take lunch, because you're human and you're hungry and most of all, you are not intimidated. We'll meet you outside at . . . what, noon? Is that when you get off?'

'Yeah,' I said. Monica was walking across the library towards the front door now, a couple of books under her arm. 'At noon.'

'Cool. We'll see you in fifteen minutes.' She glanced around again before leaning in closer to me, her voice softening. 'I mean, you have to get out of here, right? Even if it's just for an hour. Too much time in a place like this could really do a person some damage. I mean, look what it's done to *them*.'

But I was thinking about what it had done to me. Being here, miserable, day after day. In so many ways, I was realizing, the info desk was a lot like my life had been before Wish and Kristy and Wes. Something to be endured, never enjoyed.

'I'll see you outside,' she said to me, dropping her sunglasses back down to her face. Then she squeezed my arm and started towards the front doors. As she passed underneath the huge central skylight, the sun hit her, and for a second, it was like she was sparkling, the light catching her hair and glinting off, winking. I saw it. Bethany and Amanda did too. So when I came back from lunch an hour later and walked up to the info desk to find them waiting for me, chairs aligned perfectly, it didn't bother me that they asked, haughtily, if I'd enjoyed lunch with my 'friends' in such a way that I could hear the quotation marks. I didn't care that they snickered when I answered yes, or spoke in hushed tones. Because now I didn't care what they thought. It wasn't new, this realization that I would never be like them. What was different now was that I was glad.

Chapter ELEVEN

'You know,' I said, for what had to be the hundredth time since I'd got to Kristy's house two hours earlier, 'I just think maybe I'll go home.'

'Macy.' Kristy turned round from the mirror, where she was examining the side view of her outfit: a short red skirt, a black strappy tank, and a pair of sandals that could only be described as ankle breakers. 'I told you, there's no commitment for you here. It's just a bunch of us going out, not a big deal.'

This was her latest version of the night's events. Every time I objected, it got more and more suspiciously innocuous. The basic gist was that Monica and Kristy had met a couple of guys at a day catering job while I'd been at the library who were, while not extraordinary, in Kristy's words, 'promising'. Both the guys worked delivering pizzas, so they could only meet up after curfew, which meant we had to wait until Stella dozed off in front of the TV, then sneak out. I'd been recruited that afternoon after we'd worked a job, when Kristy invited me over to spend the night. It wasn't until I was already there, under the impression we were actually going to stay in, that I'd been informed that the guys were bringing a third and had asked Kristy and Monica to do the same.

'I told you,' I said, 'I'm not interested –'

Monica, who was sitting by the window, about to light a cigarette, turned her head. 'Now,' she said, nodding out the screen at something I couldn't see. Kristy immediately moved over to stand behind her chair, bending down to peer out as well, waving her hand to indicate I should come join them.

'What is it?' I said, looking over Monica's head. It was barely getting dark, and all I could see was the end of the sunset and the side of Stella's garden, several rows of lettuce and some day lilies, with a path running between them.

'Just wait,' Kristy told me, her voice a whisper. 'It happens every night, right about this time.'

I expected to see a bird, or maybe some unusual flower that only bloomed at dusk. Instead, after a second of staring, I heard something. A *thump, thump, thump* noise that was so familiar, and yet I couldn't quite place it. But I knew it. It was –

'Mmm-hmm,' Monica murmured, just as Wes came into view on the path. He was running, his pace quick and steady. He was in shorts, his shirt off, staring ahead as he passed. His back was tan and gleaming with sweat.

Beside me, I heard Kristy sigh, a long one that lasted all the way until he disappeared through a row of trees and round a turn, where I could see his own house in the distance. 'Good God,' she said finally, fanning her face with her hand, 'I've seen it a million times, but it just never gets old. Never.'

'Come on,' I said, as Monica nodded, seconding this. 'It's *Wes*.'

'Exactly.' Kristy turned and walked back to the mirror, bending in to inspect her cleavage. 'I mean, there aren't a lot of benefits to living out here in the middle of nowhere. But that is definitely one of them.'

I shook my head, exasperated, as I went over and sat down on the bed. Monica lit her cigarette, reaching up to dangle it halfway out the window, the smoke curling up past the panes.

'Is that why you are being so difficult about tonight?' Kristy asked as she flopped down beside me, glancing through the open doorway down the hall at Stella. An hour earlier, when she'd settled in front of the TV, she'd begun dozing immediately. Now, by the looks of it, she'd moved on to full snooze.

'What?'

She nodded towards the window. 'Our Wesley. I know you guys have some sort of weird thing going on, with that game you play and everything –'

'It's called a friendship,' I said. 'And, no, it has nothing to do with that. I told you, I'm on a break. I'm not interested in hanging out with some new guy.'

'Unless it's Wes,' she said, clarifying.

I just looked at her. 'That's different. He's in a relationship too, so it's not weird or anything.'

Her eyes widened. 'Oh, my God!' she said, slapping a hand over her mouth. 'I *totally* get it now.'

'Get what?'

She didn't answer me. Instead, she leaned over the bed, rummaging beneath it for a few seconds. I could hear things clanking against each other – what did she have down there? –

and glanced at Monica, who just exhaled, shrugging. Then Kristy lifted up her head.

'You and Wes,' she said, triumphant, 'are just like *this*.'

She was holding a book, a paperback romance. The title, emblazoned in gold across the cover, was *Forbidden*, and the picture beneath it was of a man in a pirate outfit, eye patch and all, clutching a small, extremely busty woman to his chest. In the background, there was a deserted island surrounded by blue water.

'We're pirates?' I said.

She tapped the book with one fingernail. 'This story,' she said, 'is all about two people who can't be together because of other circumstances. But, secretly, they pine and lust for each other constantly, the very fact that their love is forbidden fuelling their shared passion.'

'Did you just make that up?'

'No,' she said, flipping the book over to read the back cover. 'It's right here! And it's totally you and Wes. You can't be together, which is exactly why you want to be. And why you can't admit it to us, because that would make it less secret and thus less passionate.'

I rolled my eyes. Monica, across the room, said, 'Hmmm,' as if all of this actually made sense.

Kristy put the book on the bed between us. 'I have to admit,' she said wistfully, crossing her arms over her chest, 'an unrequited love is so much better than a real one. I mean, it's perfect.'

'Nothing's perfect,' I said.

'Nothing *real*,' she replied. 'But as long as something is

never even started, you never have to worry about it ending. It has endless potential.' She sighed, the same way she'd sighed at seeing Wes running by without a shirt: with emphasis, and at length. 'So romantic. No wonder you don't want to go out with Sherman.'

I was distracted, thinking about what she'd said, until she got to this last part. 'Sherman?' I said.

She nodded. 'That's John and Craig's friend. He's visiting from Shreveport.'

'Sherman from Shreveport?' I said. 'This is the guy you're determined I go out with?'

'You can't judge a book by its cover!' she snapped. When I slid my eyes towards *Forbidden*, she grabbed, shoving it back under the bed. 'You know what I mean. Sherman might be very nice.'

'I'm sure he is,' I said. 'But I'm not interested.'

She just looked at me. 'Of course not,' she said finally. 'Why would you be, when you have your very own sexy, misunderstood pirate Silus Branchburg Turlock to pine for?'

'Who?'

'Oh, just forget it,' she said, getting up and stomping out of the room. A second later the bathroom door swung shut with a bang. I looked at Monica, who was staring out of the window, her face impassive as always.

'Sherman.' Saying it aloud, it sounded even more ludicrous. 'From Shreveport.'

'Donneven?' she said slowly, exhaling.

'Exactly.'

And so it was that at ten fifteen, when John and Craig and

Sherman from Shreveport pulled into the driveway, headlights flashing just once before going dark again, I crept outside, following Kristy down the stairs. Stella didn't stir as Monica eased the door shut behind us, then started over to the car, the guy in the passenger seat climbing out to meet her. Kristy waved at the driver, who waved back, then turned to me. There was someone else in the back seat, but I couldn't make out a face: just a form, leaning against the window.

'Last chance to change your mind,' she said to me, her voice low.

'Sorry,' I told her. 'Maybe another time.'

She shook her head, clearly not buying this, then pushed her purse up her arm. 'Your loss,' she said, but she squeezed my arm as she started over to the car. 'Call me tomorrow.'

'I'll do that,' I said.

As she got closer, the guy driving smiled at her, then opened the back door. 'Watch out for Sherman,' he said as she started to get inside. 'He started his night a few hours ago, and now he's already out.'

'What?' Kristy said.

'Don't worry,' the guy told her, getting back behind the wheel. 'We think he puked up everything he had in him already. So you should be okay.'

Kristy looked at the slumped body beside her, then at me, and I raised my eyebrows. She shrugged before pulling the door shut and waving to me as the car slowly backed out of the driveway and up to the road, the engine chugging softly.

Which left me alone in the quiet of Stella's garden. I was about to get into my car, then changed my mind, dropping my purse through my open window and instead starting down through the sunflowers and into the thick of the dark, fragrant foliage.

Everything in the garden felt so *alive.* From the bright white flowers that reached out like trailing fingers from dipping branches overhead all the way down to the short, squat berry bushes that lined the trail like stones, it was like you could feel everything growing, right before your eyes. I kept walking, taking in clumps of zinnias, petunias, a cluster of rosebushes, their bases flecked with white speckles of eggshells. I could see the roof of the doublewide over to my right, the road to my left, but the garden seemed thick enough to have pushed them back even further on the periphery, as if once you entered it moved in to surround you, crowding up close to hold you there.

I could see something else up ahead, something metallic, catching the moonlight: there was a clearing round it, rimmed by bobbing rambler roses. Stepping through them, I found myself at the back of a sculpture. It was a woman; her arms were outstretched to the side, palms facing the sky, and lying across them were slim pieces of pipe, the ends curving downwards. I moved around it and stood in its shadow, looking up at the figure's head, which was also covered in the thin, twisted pipes, and crowned with a garland made of the same. Of course this was one of Wes's, that much was obvious. But there was something different, something I couldn't quite put my finger on. Then I realized that the sculpture's hair and those bits of pipe it was holding all ended in a washer bisected by a tiny piece of metal: every one was a flower. Looking at it from the top, where the moonlight illuminated those curling pipes, to the bottom, where the sculpture's feet met the ground, I finally got it that this was Stella, the entire figure showing the evolution of that thick, loamy soil moving through her hands to emerge in bloom after bloom after bloom.

'Macy?'

It was the gotcha of all gotchas. The gotcha of all *time*, even. Which somewhat justified the shriek that came out of my mouth, the way my heart leaped in my chest, and how these two events then repeated themselves when a flock of tiny sparrows, startled by my startling, burst forth from the sculpture's base and flew in dizzy circles, rising over the rosebushes and disappearing into the dark.

'Oh,' I said, swallowing, 'my God.'

'Wow,' Wes said. He was standing by the path, his hands in his pockets. 'You really *screamed*.'

'You scared the shit out of me!' I said. 'What are you doing out here, lurking around in the dark?'

'I wasn't lurking,' he said. 'I've been calling your name for five minutes at least, ever since you walked in here.'

'You have not.'

'I really have been,' he said.

'You have not,' I said. 'You snuck up and got your big gotcha and now you're just so happy.'

'No,' he replied slowly as if I were a toddler having a totally unjustified tantrum, 'I was on my way out and I saw you dropping your purse through the window. I called your name. You didn't hear me.'

I looked down at the ground, my heart calming now. And then a breeze gusted up over us, the flowers behind Wes leaning one way, then the other. I heard a whirring noise above me and looked up at the sculpture. As the wind blew, the curved flowers in the figure's hands began spinning, first slowly, then faster, as the garland on her head began to do the same.

Wes and I just stood there, watching it, until the wind died down again. 'You really scared me,' I said to Wes, almost embarrassed now.

'I didn't mean to.'

'I know.'

Everything was settling back to how it had been: my heart, the flowers in the figure's hand and her garland, even the sparrows, which were now clustered on the rosebushes behind me, waiting to come back home. I started back over to the path, Wes holding aside one trailing branch so I could step through.

'Let me make it up to you,' he said as he fell in step behind me.

'You don't have to,' I said.

'I know I don't have to. I want to. And I know just the way.'

I turned back and looked at him. 'Yeah?' I asked.

He nodded. 'Come on.'

Apologies come in all shapes and sizes. You can give diamonds, candy, flowers or just your deepest heartfelt sentiment. Never before, though, had I got a pencil that smelled like syrup. But I had to admit, it worked.

'Okay,' I said. 'You're forgiven.'

We were at the World of Waffles, which was located in a small, orange building right off the highway. I'd driven by it a million times, but it had never occurred to me to actually stop there. Maybe it was the rows of eighteen-wheelers that were always parked in the lot, or the old, faded sign with its black letters spelling out Y'ALL COME ON. But now I found myself here, just before eleven on a Saturday night, holding my peace offering, a pencil decorated with waffles, scented with maple, that Wes had purchased for me at the gift shop for $1.79.

The waitress came up as I lifted my menu off the sticky table, pulling a pen out of her apron. 'Hey there, sugar,' she said to Wes. She looked to be about my mother's age, and was wearing thick support hose and nurses' shoes with squeaky soles. 'The usual?'

'Sure,' he said, sliding his menu to the edge of the table. 'Thanks.'

'And you?' she asked me.

'A waffle and a side of hash browns,' I told her, and put my menu on top of his. The only people in there other than us were an old man reading a newspaper and drinking endless cups of coffee and a group of drunken college students who kept laughing loudly and playing Tammy Wynette over and over on the jukebox.

I picked up my pencil, sniffing it. 'Admit it,' Wes said, 'you can't believe you've got this far in life without one of those.'

'What I can't believe,' I said, putting it back down on the table, 'is that you're *known* at this place. When did you start coming here?'

He sat back in the booth, running his finger along the edge of the napkin under his knife and fork. 'After my mom died. I wasn't sleeping much, and this is open all night. It was better than just driving around. Now I'm sort of used to it. When I need inspiration, I always come here.'

'Inspiration,' I repeated, glancing around.

'Yeah,' Wes said, emphatically, as if it were obvious I wasn't convinced. 'When I'm working on a piece, and I'm kind of stuck, I'll come here and sit for a while. Usually by the time I finish my waffle I've figured it out. Or at least started to.'

'What about that piece in the garden?' I said. 'What did that come from?'

He thought for a second. 'That one's different,' he said. 'I mean, I made it specifically for someone.'

'Stella.'

'Yeah.' He smiled. 'She made the biggest fuss over it. It was to thank her, because she was really good to Bert and me when my mom was sick. Especially Bert. It was the least I could do.'

'It's really something,' I told him, and he shrugged, that way I already recognized, the way he always did when you tried to compliment him. 'All of your pieces have the whirligig thing going on. What's that about?'

'Look at you, getting all meaning driven on me,' he said. 'Next you'll be telling me that piece is representative of the complex relationship between agriculture and women.'

I narrowed my eyes at him. 'I am not my sister,' I said. 'I just wondered, that's all.'

He shrugged. 'I don't know. The first stuff I did at Myers was just basic, you know, static. But then, once I did the heart-in-hand stuff, I got interested in how things moving made a piece look different, and how that changes the subject. How it makes it seem, you know, alive.'

I thought back to how I'd felt as I started into Stella's garden earlier that night, that tangible, ripe feeling of everything around you somehow breathing as you did. 'I can see that,' I said.

'What were you doing out there, anyway?' he asked. Across the restaurant, the jukebox finally fell silent.

'I don't know,' I said. 'Ever since the first day Kristy brought me there, it's sort of fascinated me.'

'It's pretty incredible,' he said, sipping his water. The heart in hand on his upper arm slid into view, then disappeared again.

'It is,' I said, running my finger down the edge of the table. 'Plus, it's so different from anything at my house, where everything is just so organized and new. I like the chaos in it.'

'When Bert was a kid,' Wes said, sitting back in his seat and smiling, 'he got lost in that garden, trying to take the shortcut back from the road. We could all hear him screaming like he was stranded in the jungle, but really he was about two feet from the edge of the yard. He just lost his bearings.'

'Poor Bert,' I said.

'He survived.' He slid his glass in a circle on the table. 'He's tougher than he seems. When my mom died, we were all most worried about him, since he was only thirteen. They were really close. He was the one who was there when she found out about the cancer. I was off at Myers. But Bert was a real trooper. He stuck by her, even during the bad parts.'

'That must have been hard for you,' I said. 'Being away and all.'

'I was back home by the time things really got bad. But, still, I hated being locked up when they needed me, all because of some stupid thing I'd done. By the time I got out, all I knew was that I never wanted to feel like that again. Whatever else happened, to Bert or anyone, I was going to be there.'

The waitress was approaching the table now, a plate in each hand. On cue my stomach grumbled, even though I hadn't thought I was hungry. She deposited the plates with a clank, gave us each a quick second to ask for something else, and then shuffled off again.

'Now, see,' Wes said, nodding at my plate, 'this is going to blow your mind.'

I looked at him. 'It's a waffle, not the second coming.'

'Don't be so sure. You haven't tasted it yet.'

I spread some butter on my waffle, then doused it with syrup before cutting off a small bite. Wes watched as I put it in my mouth. He hadn't even started his yet, as if, first, he wanted to hear my verdict. Which was, pretty good. Damn good, actually.

'Knew it,' he said, as if he'd read my mind. 'Maybe not the second coming, but a religious experience of sorts.'

I was on my second bite now, and tempted to totally agree with this. Then I remembered something, and smiled.

'What?' he said.

I looked down at my plate. 'What you just said, that's so funny. It reminded me of something my dad always used to say.'

He popped a piece of waffle in his mouth, waiting for me to go on.

'We never went to church,' I explained, 'even though my mother always thought we should, and she was always feeling guilty about it. But my dad loved to cook big breakfasts on Sunday. He said that was his form of worship, and the kitchen was his church, his offering eggs and bacon and hash browns and . . .'

'Waffles,' Wes finished for me.

I nodded, feeling a lump rise in my throat. *How embarrassing*, I thought, *to suddenly be on the verge of tears at a truck stop waffle house with Tammy Wynette in the background.* But then I thought how my dad would have loved this place, probably even loved Tammy Wynette, and the lump just grew bigger.

'My mom,' Wes said suddenly, spearing another piece of his own waffle, 'was the one who first brought me here. We used to stop on the way back from Greensboro, where my grandmother lived. Even during the health-food phase, it was a sort of ritual. This was the only place she'd ever eat something totally unhealthy. She'd get the Belgian waffle with whipped cream and strawberries and eat every bit of it. Then she'd complain the entire way home about how sick she felt.'

I smiled, taking a sip of my water. The lump was going away now. 'Isn't it weird,' I said, 'the way you remember things, when someone's gone?'

'What do you mean?'

I ate another piece of waffle. 'When my dad first died, all I could think about was that day. It's taken me so long to be able to think back to before that, to everything else.'

Wes was nodding before I even finished. 'It's even worse when someone's sick for a long time,' he said. 'You forget they were ever healthy, ever okay. It's like there was never a time when you weren't waiting for something awful to happen.'

'But there was,' I said. 'I mean, it's only been in the last few months that I've started remembering all this good stuff, funny stuff about my dad. I can't believe I ever forgot it in the first place.'

'You didn't forget,' Wes said, taking a sip of his water. 'You just couldn't remember right then. But now you're ready to, so you can.'

I thought about this as I finished off my waffle. 'It was hard too, I think, because after my dad died my mom kind of freaked and cleaned out all his stuff. I mean, she threw out just about everything. So in a way it was like he'd never been there at all.'

'At my house,' Wes said, 'it's the total opposite. My mom is, like, everywhere. Delia packed a lot of her stuff into boxes, but she got so emotional she couldn't do it all. One of her coats is still in the hall closet. A pair of her shoes is still in the garage, beside the lawn mower. And I'm always finding her lists. They're everywhere.'

'Lists?' I said.

'Yeah.' He looked down at the table, smiling slightly. 'She was a total control freak. She made lists for everything: what she had to do the next day, goals for the year, shopping, calls she had to return. Then she'd just stuff them somewhere and forget about them. They'll probably be turning up for years.'

'That must be sort of weird,' I said, and then, realizing this didn't sound right, added, 'or, you know, good. Maybe.'

'It's a little of both.' He sat back in the booth, tossing his napkin on his now empty plate. 'It freaks Bert out, but I kind of like it. I went through this thing where I was sure they meant something, you know? If I found one, I'd sit down with it and try to decipher it. Like picking up dry cleaning or calling Aunt Sylvia is some sort of message from beyond.' He shrugged, embarrassed.

'I know,' I said. 'I did the same thing.'

He raised his eyebrows. 'Really.'

I couldn't believe I was about to tell him this. But then the words were just coming. 'My dad was, like, addicted to those gadgets they sell on late-night TV. He was always ordering them, things like that doormat with the sensor that lets you know when someone's about to –'

'The Welcome Helper,' he finished for me.

'You know it?'

'No.' He smiled. 'Yes, of course. Everyone's seen that freaking commercial, right?'

'My dad bought all that stuff,' I told him. 'He couldn't help himself. It was like an addiction.'

'I've always wanted to order that coin machine that sorts things automatically,' he said wistfully.

'Got it,' I told him.

'No way.'

I nodded. 'Anyway, after he died, the company kept sending them. I mean, every month a new one shows up. But for a while, I was convinced it meant something. Like my dad was somehow getting them to me, like they were supposed to mean something.'

'Well,' Wes said now, 'you never know. Maybe they do.'

I looked at him. 'Do what?'

'Mean something,' he said.

I looked out the window, where car lights were blurring past distantly on the highway. It was after midnight, and I wondered where so many people were going. 'I keep them,' I said softly, 'just in case. I can't bear to throw them out. You know?'

'Yeah,' he said. 'I know.'

We stayed there for another hour. In that time, customers came and went all around us. We saw families with sleeping babies, truckers stopping in before the next leg, one young couple who sat in the booth across from us with a map spread out between them, tracing with their fingers the route that would take them to wherever they were going next. All the while, Wes and I just sat there, talking about anything and everything. I couldn't remember the last time I'd talked so much, really talked. Maybe I never had.

Still, I beat Kristy to Stella's by about ten minutes. I'd just waved goodbye to Wes and slipped inside, past where Stella was still sleeping, when the guys dropped her and Monica off in the driveway. By the time she got to her room, carrying her shoes, I'd already spread the sleeping bag she'd pulled out for me earlier on the floor next to her bed and changed into my pyjamas. She looked entirely unsurprised to see me.

'Good night?' I asked as she pulled off her skirt and top, exchanging them for a T-shirt and a pair of boxer shorts.

'No.' She sat down on the bed, pulled a container of cold cream out of the bedside table, and began smearing it all over her face. When it was half covered, she said, 'Let me just say this: Sherman, even though he was passed out the entire time, was the best of the lot.'

'Ouch.'

She nodded, screwing the cap back on the container.

'Those boys *wished* they were even ordinary. I mean, it's so disappointing. What's worse than ordinary? I feel like I'm working backwards now.'

'Oh, that's not true,' I told her. 'It was just one bad night.'

'Maybe so.' She stood up and went to the door. 'But a girl could lose heart in this world. That's all I'm saying, you know?'

As she went to the bathroom to wash her face, I stretched out on the sleeping bag. If I looked up through the window behind me, I could see the garden and the moon above it. Soon, though, I was too tired to do even that, instead just closing my eyes, only aware of Kristy returning by the sound of the door sliding shut and the loud sigh she emitted as she crawled into her bed.

'It just sucks,' she said, yawning, 'when a night is over and you have not one damn thing to show for it. Don't you hate that?'

'Yeah,' I said. 'I do.'

She harrumphed again, turning over and fluffing her pillow. 'Goodnight, Macy,' she said after a second of quiet. Her voice sounded sleepy. 'Sweet dreams.'

'You too. Goodnight.'

A minute later I could hear her breathing grow steady: she fell asleep that fast. I just lay there for a few minutes, staring up at that moon behind my head, then reached beside the sleeping bag for my purse, rummaging around until I found what I was looking for. Then, in the dark, I wrapped my fingers more tightly round what I had to show for my evening – a pencil that smelled like sugar and syrup. In the morning, when I woke up with the sun spilling over me, it was still in my hand.

• • •

'Macy? Is that you?'

I put my shoes down on the bottom step of the landing, laying my purse beside them. My mother was usually up first thing on weekend mornings, leaving soon after for the model home to greet potential homeowners. Now, though, it was almost ten, and I could see her in the recliner by the window, drinking a cup of coffee and reading a real-estate magazine. She looked idle and still, which she never was. Ever. So she had to be waiting for me.

'Um, yeah,' I said. As I walked across the foyer, I instinctively tucked in my shirt, then reached up to smooth my hair, running a finger down the part. 'Kristy made breakfast, so I stayed longer than I planned. What are you doing home?'

'Oh, I just decided to take an hour or so to get caught up here.' She put her magazine on the table beside her. 'Plus I just feel like it's been ages since we've had a chance to talk. Come sit down, tell me what's going on.'

I had a flashback, suddenly, to being at the top of the stairs and watching Caroline come down after a night out, then have to make her way to the living room, where my mom was always waiting to begin a 'discussion'. It was always a bit tense, that feeling of certain friction to come in the air. Kind of like this.

I came over and sat down on the couch. The sunlight was slanting through the window, bright and piercing, and in it I felt especially exposed, as if every little flaw, from my mussed hair to my chipped toenail polish, was especially noticeable. I wanted to scoot over to the chair or the ottoman, but thought this would attract even more attention. So I stayed where I was.

'So,' my mother said, 'how was work yesterday?'

'Good.' She was looking at me, waiting for more, so I said, 'Fun. It was a pre-wedding thing, which means everyone's either all hung over from the rehearsal dinner or freaking out about last-minute details. This time, it was both. So it was a little crazy. And then, you know, we had this whole thing with the crêpes catching on fire, but that really wasn't our fault. Entirely.'

My mother was looking at me with an expression of polite but detached interest, as if I were describing the culture of a foreign country she would never visit in a million years. 'Well,' she said, 'you certainly have been putting in a lot of hours catering lately.'

'Not that many,' I said. Then, realizing I sounded defensive – did I sound defensive? – I added, 'I mean, it's just been busy the last couple of weeks because Delia's booked a lot of jobs before the baby comes. Pretty soon I won't have anything to do, probably.'

My mother slid the magazine off her lap and onto the couch. 'You'll still have the info desk, though,' she said. 'Right?'

'Oh, yeah, right,' I said, too quickly. 'I mean, yes. Of course.'

A pause. Too long of a pause for my taste.

'So how is the library?' she said finally. 'You hardly mention it any more.'

'It's okay. Just, you know, the same.' This was definitely the truth. My days at the library had not improved at all in the last few weeks. The difference was it just bothered me less. I put in my time, avoided Bethany and Amanda as much as possible, and got out of there the minute the big hand hit three. 'It's work. If it was fun, they'd call it fun, right?'

She smiled, nodding. *Uh-oh*, I thought. I just knew there was something coming. I was right.

'I was out for a lunch meeting yesterday, and I saw Mrs Talbot,' she said now. 'She told me that Jason is really enjoying the Scholars' Retreat he's on this summer.'

'Really,' I replied, reaching up to smooth my part again.

'She also said,' she continued, crossing her legs, 'that Jason told her you two are taking a break from your relationship for the summer.'

Oh, great, I thought. 'Um, yeah,' I said. 'I mean, yes.'

For a second, it was so quiet I could hear the refrigerator humming. I remembered these awkward pauses from Caroline's homecomings, as well. It was now, in the empty spaces between accusations and defenses, that I had always wondered what, exactly, was happening.

'I was surprised,' she said finally, 'that you didn't mention it to me. She said this happened weeks ago.'

'Well, it *is* just a break,' I told her, trying to make my voice sound cheery, confident. 'We're going to talk as soon as he gets back. We both just thought for now it was the best thing to do.'

My mother put her hands in her lap, folding them round each other, and leaned forward slightly. I knew that stance. I'd seen it at a million sales cocktails. She was moving in. 'I have to say, Macy,' she began, and I felt something inside me start to deflate slightly, 'that I'm a little bit concerned about you right now.'

'Concerned?' I said.

She nodded, keeping her eyes on me. 'You've been out an

awful lot of nights lately with your new friends. You're working so many hours catering that I fear you're not giving your full attention to the library job, which is your most important commitment in terms of your college transcript.'

'I haven't missed a single day there,' I told her.

'I know you haven't. I'm just . . .' she trailed off, glancing out of the window. Now the sun was on her face, and I could immediately make out tiny lines around her eyes, how tired she looked. Not for the first time, I felt a stab of worry, totally overreacting I knew, that maybe she was pushing herself too hard. I hadn't noticed with my dad. Neither of us had. 'This coming year is so *important* for you, in terms of college and your future. It's crucial that you do well on your SATs and are focused on your classes. Remember how you told me you wanted to be working towards preparing for those goals this summer?'

'I am,' I said. 'I've been studying my words and taking practice tests online.'

Another glance out of the window. Then she said, 'You've also been spending nights out with your friend Christine –'

'Kristy,' I said.

' – as well as a bunch of other new friends I haven't met and don't know.' She looked down at her hands, folding and unfolding them in her lap. 'And then I hear this about you and Jason. I just wonder why you didn't feel like you could tell me about that.'

'It's just a break,' I said, 'and, besides, Jason doesn't have anything to do with my goals. They're totally separate things.'

'Are they, though?' she asked. 'When you were with Jason,

you were home more. Studying more. Now I hardly see you, and I can't help but wonder if the two are connected somehow.'

I couldn't argue with that. In the last few weeks, I *had* changed. But in my mind, those changes had been for the better: I was finally getting over things, stepping out of the careful box I'd drawn round myself all those months ago. *It was a good thing*, I thought. *Until now.*

'Macy,' she said, her voice softening, 'all I'm saying is that I want to be sure your priorities are straight. You've worked so hard to get where you are. I don't want you to lose that.'

Again, I could agree with this. But while for her it meant how I'd pushed myself to be perfect, got good grades, scored the smart boyfriend and recovered from my loss to be composed, together, fine just fine, for me, it worked in reverse. I'd been through so much, falling short again and again, and only recently had found a place where who I was, right now, was enough.

This was always the problem with my mother and me, I suddenly realized. There were so many things we thought we agreed on, but anything can have two meanings. Like sides of a coin, it just matters how it falls.

'I don't want that either,' I said.

'Good. Then we're on the same page. That's all I wanted to be sure of.' She smiled, then squeezed my hand as she stood up, our accepted sign of affection. As she started towards her office, I headed for the stairs and my room. I was halfway there when she called after me.

'Honey?'

I turned around. She was standing at her office door, her hand on the knob. 'Yes?'

'I just want you to know,' she said, 'that you can talk to me about things. Like Jason. I want you to feel like you can share things with me. Okay?'

I nodded. 'Okay.'

As I climbed the stairs, I knew that my mother had already moved on to the next challenge, this issue now filed under Resolved. But for me it wasn't that simple. Of course she'd think I could tell her anything: she was my mother. In truth, though, I couldn't. I'd been wanting to talk to her for over a year about what was bothering me. I'd wanted to reach out to her, hold her close, tell her I was worried about her, but I couldn't do that either. So it was just a formality, what we'd just agreed on, a contract I'd signed without reading the fine print. But I knew what it said. That I could be imperfect, but only so much. Human, but only within limits. And honest, to her or to myself, never.

When I got to my room, I found a shopping bag sitting in the centre of my bed with a note propped up against it. I recognized the loopy, flowing script even from a distance: Caroline.

Hi Macy,

Sorry I missed you. I'll be back in a couple of days, hopefully with a good progress report of the renovation. I forgot when I was here last time to drop this off for you. I found it in the bedroom closet of the beach house the last time I was there, when I was cleaning stuff out. I'm not sure what it is (didn't want to open it) but I thought you should have it. I'll see you soon.

It was signed with a row of *X*s and *O*s, as well as a smiley face. I sat down on the bed next to the bag, opening the top. I took one glance, then shut it, quick.

Oh, God, I thought.

In that one glimpse, I'd seen two things. Wrapping paper – gold, with some pattern – and a white card with my name written on it. In another hand I recognized, would know anywhere. My dad's.

More to come, the card he'd given me that Christmas Day, the last day I'd had with him, had said. *Soon*. So my missing present wasn't an EZ gift after all, but this.

I reached to open the bag, then stopped myself. As much as I wanted to, I couldn't unwrap it now, I realized, because no matter what it was, it would disappoint me. All this time it wasn't a gift I'd wanted: it was a sign. So maybe it was best to let this, of all things, have endless potential.

I pulled my chair over to the closet, took the bag, and pushed it up and over next to the box with the EZ products. Whatever it was, it had waited a long time to find me. A little bit longer wouldn't make that much of a difference.

Chapter TWELVE

'Whose turn is it to ask?'

'Yours,' Wes said to me.

'Are you sure?'

He nodded, cranking the van's engine. 'Go ahead.'

I sat back in my seat, tucking one foot underneath me as we pulled out of Delia's driveway and started down Sweetbud Drive. We'd won the toss, which meant we got to go wash the van, while Bert and Kristy were stuck making crab cakes. 'Okay,' I said, 'what's your biggest fear?'

As always, he took a second to think about his answer. 'Clowns,' he said.

'Clowns.'

'Yup.'

I just looked at him.

'What?' he said, glancing over at me.

'That is not a real answer,' I told him.

'Says who?'

'Says me. I meant a real *fear*, like of failure, of death, of regret. Like that. Something that keeps you awake nights, questioning your very existence.'

He thought for a second. 'Clowns.'

I rolled my eyes. 'Please.'

'That's my answer.' He slowed down, edging carefully around the hole. I glanced at the heart in hand, which was still, shimmering in the heat. 'I don't like clowns. They scare the shit out of me, ever since I went to the circus as a kid and one popped a balloon right in my face.'

'Stop it,' I said, smiling.

'I wish I could.'

We were at the end of the road now, a cloud of dust settling all around us.

'Clowns,' I repeated. 'Really?'

He nodded. 'Are you going to accept it as my answer, or not?'

'Is it the truth?'

'Yeah. It is.'

'Fine,' I said. 'Then it's your turn.'

I knew a lot about Wes now. That he'd got his first kiss from a girl in sixth grade named Willa Patrick. That he thought his ears were too big for his head. And that he hated jazz, wasabi and the smell of patchouli. And clowns.

The game we'd begun the night we were stranded was ongoing: whenever we found ourselves alone, driving to a job or prepping silverware or just hanging out, we picked it up automatically where we'd left off the last time. When everyone else from Wish was around, there was noise and drama and laughter and chaos. But times like these, it was just me, Wes and the truth.

When I'd first started playing Truth, back in my slumber-party days, it had always made me nervous. Wes was right in saying it was diabolical: the questions asked were always personal or embarrassing, preferably both. Often, playing with my friends or sister, I'd choose to pass on a question and lose rather than have to confess I was madly in love with my maths teacher. As I got older, the games were even more brutal, with questions revolving round boys and crushes and How Far You'd Gone. But with Wes Truth was different. He'd asked me the hardest question first, so all that followed were easier. Or somewhat easier.

'What,' he asked me one day, as we walked through Milton's Market looking for paper towels, 'is the grossest thing that's ever happened to you?'

'Ew,' I said, shooting him a look. 'Is this really necessary?'

'Answer or pass,' he told me, sliding his hands into his pockets.

He knew I wouldn't pass. He wouldn't either. We were both totally competitive, but, really, there was more to it than that, at least for me. I liked this way of getting to know him, these random facts and details, each one like a puzzle piece I examined carefully, figuring out how it fitted in with the rest. If either of us won, it would all be over. So I had to keep answering.

'Fifth grade,' I said, as we turned onto the paper-product aisle. 'It was December, and this woman came in to talk to us about Hanukkah. I remember she gave us gelt.'

'That's the gross part?'

'No,' I said, shooting him a look. 'I'm getting to it.' Being so economical with his own words, Wes was always prodding me to hurry up and get to the point, to which I responded by padding my story that much more. It was all part of the game. 'Her name was Mrs Felton, Barbara Felton's mom. Anyway, so we got gelt, we were talking about the menorah. Everything was fine.'

We were at the paper towels now. Wes pulled an eight-pack off the shelf, tucking it under his arm, then handed me another one, and we started towards the registers.

'Then,' I said, 'my teacher, Mrs Whitehead, comes up to Norma Piskill, who's sitting beside me, and asks if she's okay. And Norma says yes, although looking at her, I notice she's a little green.'

'Uh-oh,' he said, making a face.

'Exactly.' I sighed. 'So the next thing I know, Norma Piskill is trying to get up, but she doesn't make it. Instead, she pukes all over me. And then, as I'm standing there dripping, she does it again.'

'Yuck.'

'You asked,' I said cheerfully.

'I did,' he agreed, as we got in line. 'Your turn.'

'Right.' I thought for a second. 'What do you worry about most?'

As always, he paused, considering this. From vomit to deep introspection: this was how Truth worked. You either went with it, or you didn't. 'Bert,' he said flatly, after a second.

'Bert,' I repeated.

He nodded. 'I just feel responsible for him, you know? I mean, it's a big-brother thing. But also with my mom gone . . .

She never said so but I know she was counting on me to take care of him. And he's so . . .'

'So what?' I asked as the cashier scanned the towels.

He shrugged. 'So . . . Bert. You know? He's intense. Takes everything really seriously, like with all his Armageddon stuff. A lot of people his age, you know, they just don't *get* him. Everything he feels, he feels strongly. Too strongly, sometimes. I think he freaks people out.'

'He's not that bad,' I said as he handed the cashier a twenty and got change. 'He's just . . .' And now I was at a loss, unable to find the right word.

'Bert,' he finished for me.

'Exactly.'

And so it went. Question by question, answer by answer. Everyone else thought we were weird, but I was starting to wonder how I'd ever got to know anyone any other way. If anything, the game made you realize how little you knew about people. After only a few weeks, I knew what Wes worried about, what embarrassed him most, his greatest disappointment. I couldn't be sure of any of these things when it came to my mother, or Caroline, or Jason, and knew they'd be equally stymied if asked about me.

'I just think it's weird,' Kristy said to me after walking up on us a couple of times, only to catch the tail end of Wes detailing some seventh-grade trauma or me explaining why I thought my neck was strange-looking. 'I mean, Truth or Dare, that I understand. But this is just talking.'

'Exactly,' I said. 'Anyone can do a dare.'

'I don't know about *that*,' she said darkly. 'Everyone knew if you were smart, you always picked Truth over Dare. That way you could at least lie, if you had to.'

I just looked at her.

'What?' she said. She rolled her eyes. 'I wouldn't lie to you. I'm talking about cut-throat slumber-party ethics. Nobody tells the truth all the time.'

'You do in this game,' I said.

'Maybe *you* do. But how do you know he is?'

'I don't know,' I told her. 'I just do.'

And I did. It was why I liked being with Wes so much, that summer. He was the one person I could count on, unequivocally, to say exactly what he meant, no hedging around. He had no idea, I was sure, how much I appreciated it.

'Macy!'

I turned round, and there was Bert, standing at the top of his driveway in an undershirt and a pair of smart trousers. There was a piece of tissue stuck to his chin and another on his temple, both clearly shaving injuries, and he looked desperate. 'Can you come here for a second?'

'Sure,' I said, starting across the road. When I got within a few feet of him, I could smell his cologne. One step closer, and every step after that, it was all I could smell, which was saying something, considering I'd spent the last hour helping Delia peel garlic to make hummus and was pretty fragrant myself. 'What's going on?'

He turned round and started down the driveway towards his house, walking at such a fast, frenzied pace that I found myself struggling to keep up with him. 'I have an important engagement,' he said over his shoulder, 'and Kristy was supposed to help me get ready. She *promised.* But she and Monica had to take Stella to deliver bouquets, and she's not back yet.'

'Engagement?' I asked.

'It's my Armageddon club social. A *big* deal.' He looked at me pointedly, as if to emphasize this. 'It only happens once a year.'

'Right,' I said. As we walked up the steps to his front door, I watched as one of the pieces of tissue dislodged from his face, taking flight over his head and disappearing somewhere behind us. On the bright side, at least with us moving I couldn't smell the cologne. As much.

I'd never been inside Wes and Bert's house before. From the road, all you could see was that it was wood, cosy and cabinlike, but I was surprised, as I followed Bert in, by how open and bright it was. The living room was big, with beams across the ceiling and skylights, the furniture modern and comfortable looking. The kitchen ran against the back wall, and there were plants all along the counter, many of them leaning towards one large window above the sink. Also there was art everywhere: abstract paintings on the walls, several ceramic pieces, and two of Wes's smaller sculptures on display on either side of the fireplace. I'd expected it to look, well, like two teenaged guys lived there, with pizza boxes piled up on the counter and half-filled glasses cluttering every surface, but it was surprisingly neat.

'What's at issue here,' Bert said as we headed down the hallway, passing a closed door and another bedroom along the way, 'is dots or stripes. What do you think?'

He pushed open the door to his bedroom, going inside, but once I hit the threshold I just stood there, staring. Not at the two button-up shirts he was now holding out to me, but at the huge poster behind him, which took up the entire wall. It said, simply, ATTENTION: ARMAGEDDON and featured a graphic image of a blue earth being shattered to bits. The rest of the room was decorated the same way, with posters proclaiming THE END IS NEARER THAN YOU THINK and one that said simply MEGA-TSUNAMI: ONE WAVE, TOTAL ANNIHILATION. The remaining wall space was taken up by shelves, all of which were packed with books featuring similar titles.

'Stripes,' Bert said, shaking one shirt at me, 'or dots. Stripes or dots. Which one?'

'Well,' I said, still totally distracted, 'I think –'

Just then the door behind me opened, and Wes emerged from the bathroom, hair wet, rubbing his face with a towel. He had on jeans and no shirt, which, frankly, was almost as distracting as the mega-tsunami. Or even more so. He started to wave hello to me, then stopped. And sniffed. Twice.

'Bert,' he said, wincing, 'what did I tell you about cologne?'

'I'm hardly wearing any,' Bert said, as Wes put a hand over his nose, disputing this. He held up the shirts again, clearly willing to take all opinions. 'Wes, which should I wear? First impressions are important, you know.'

Wes's voice was muffled, through his hand. 'My point exactly. Were you going for overpowering?'

Bert ignored this, turning back to me. 'Macy. *Please.* Stripes or dots?'

As always, I found myself feeling a kind of affection for

Bert, in his weird bedroom, wearing his nerdy undershirt, one piece of tissue still stuck to his face. 'The stripes,' I told him. 'They're more grown-up looking.'

'Thank you.' He dropped the polka-dotted shirt on the bed, slipping on the other one and buttoning it quickly. Turning to face himself in the mirror, he said, 'That's what I thought too.'

'Are you wearing a tie?' Wes asked him, walking back into the bathroom and tossing the towel over the shower rod.

'Should I?'

I said, 'What kind of impression are you going for?'

Bert thought for a second. 'Mature. Intelligent. Handsome.'

'Overpowering,' Wes added.

'Then yes,' I told Bert, who was now scowling. 'Wear a tie.'

As Bert pulled open his closet door and began rummaging around, I turned to look at Wes, who'd walked into his own room and was now pulling on a grey T-shirt. Unlike Bert's, Wes's walls were bare, the only furnishings a futon against one wall, a milk crate stacked with books, and a bureau with a mirror hanging over it. There was a black-and-white picture of a girl taped to the mirror, but I couldn't make out her face.

'The thing about the Armageddon social,' Bert said to me now, as I turned round to see him struggling to knot a blue tie, 'is that it's the one time of the year EOWs from all over the state get together.'

'EOWs?' I asked, watching him loop the tie, start a knot, and then yank it too tight before dismantling it and starting over.

'End-of-worlders,' he explained, trying another knot. This

time, the front came out way too long, almost hanging to his belt buckle. 'It's a great opportunity to learn about new theories and trade research tips with like-minded enthusiasts.' He looked down at the tie. 'God! Why is this so hard? Do you know how to do this?'

'Not really,' I said. My father had never been the formal type, and Jason, who wore ties often, could do one with his eyes closed, so I'd had no reason to learn.

'Kristy promised she would help me,' he muttered, yanking on the tie, which only made the front go longer. His face was getting red. 'She *promised*.'

'Calm down,' Wes said, stepping round me into the room and walking up to Bert. He untangled the tie, smoothing the ends. 'Stand still.' Then Bert and I both stood and watched as, with one cross, a twist, and a yank, he tied the knot perfectly.

'Wow,' Bert said, looking down at it as Wes stepped back, examining his handiwork. 'When did you learn that?'

'When I had to go to court,' Wes told him. He reached up, plucking the piece of tissue off his brother's face, then straightened the tie again. 'Do you have enough money?'

Bert snorted. 'I prebought my ticket way back in March. There's a chicken dinner and dessert. It's all paid for.'

Wes pulled out his wallet and slid out a twenty, tucking it into Bert's pocket. 'No more cologne, okay?'

'Okay,' Bert said, looking down at the tie again. The phone rang and he picked up a cordless from the bed. 'Hello? Hey, Richard. Yeah, me too . . . Um, striped shirt. Blue tie. Poly-blend slacks. My good shoes. What about you?'

Wes stepped back into the hallway, shaking his head, and went into his room. I leaned against the doorjamb, taking another look at its sparse furnishings. 'So,' I said, 'I see you're a minimalist.'

'I'm not into clutter,' he replied, opening the closet and pulling out something, 'if that's what you mean. If you don't see it here, I don't need it.'

I stepped inside, then walked over to his bureau, leaning in to look at the girl in the picture. I knew I was probably being nosy, but I couldn't help myself. 'So, is this Becky?'

He turned round, glancing over at me. 'No. Becky's skinny, angular. That's my mom.'

Wish was beautiful. That's what I thought first. And in this picture, young, maybe her late teens or early twenties. I immediately recognized Bert's round face in her features, and Delia's dark curly hair and wide smile. But, more than anything, she reminded me of Wes. Maybe it was the way she was not looking at the camera but instead just beyond it, half-smiling, nothing posed or forced about her. She was sitting on the edge of a fountain, her hands resting easily in her lap. You could see water glittering behind her.

'She looks like you,' I said.

He came up behind me, a box in his hand, and then we were both framed in the mirror, peering in. 'You think?'

'Yeah,' I said. 'I do.'

Bert came out of his room, walking quickly, a lint roller in one hand. 'I'd better go,' he said. 'I want to be there right when the doors open.'

'You're taking the roller?' Wes asked him.

'There's always the possibility of car lint,' Bert told him, sticking it in his front pocket. 'So I look okay?'

'You look great,' I told him, and he smiled at me, genuinely pleased.

'I'm staying at Richard's tonight, so we can recap,' Bert said, pulling the door open. 'I'll see you tomorrow, okay?'

Wes nodded. 'Have fun.'

Bert disappeared down the hallway, and seconds later I heard the front door slam. Wes grabbed his keys and wallet off the bureau, shifting the box he was carrying to his other arm, and we started towards the living room, me taking one last look at Wish before he shut the door behind us.

'I should go too, I guess,' I said, as we came into the living room. Again, I was struck by how cosy it was, unlike my house, which, with its high ceilings and huge rooms, always seemed to feel empty.

'Don't tell me,' he said. 'You're going to the Armageddon social too?'

'How'd you guess?'

'Just a hunch.'

I made a face. 'No, I'll actually be studying. Doing laundry. I don't know, I might get really out of hand and iron some clothes. With *starch*.'

'Uh-oh,' he said. 'Now you're talking crazy.'

He pulled the door open and I stepped outside, stopping on the stairs as he locked it. 'Okay, fine, Mr Excitement. What's your plan?'

'Well,' he said, holding up the box in his hand, 'I have to drop by this party in Lakeview and give a friend of mine these car parts I found at the salvage yard.'

'A party *and* car parts?' I said. 'Don't hurt yourself, now.'

'I'll try not to.'

I smiled at him, digging my own keys out of my pocket.

'You want to ride along?'

I was sort of surprised that he asked me. And even more surprised how quickly I answered, no hesitation, as if this had been what I'd been planning to do all along. 'Sure.'

The party was big and in full swing by the time we pulled up twenty minutes later. As we walked up to the front door, dodging people grouped along the driveway and front lawn, I was, as always, aware of the fact that we were being stared at. Or that Wes was. He hardly seemed to notice, but I wondered how he'd ever got used to it.

Once inside, I'd barely crossed the threshold when someone grabbed my arm. Someone in a denim miniskirt, cowboy boots and a hot-pink bustier. One guess.

'Oh, my God,' Kristy hissed in my ear, yanking me sideways to the bottom of the stairs. 'I *knew* it! What are you doing? Macy, you'd better start talking. Now.'

Wes had stopped in the middle of the foyer and was looking around for me. When he finally spotted me and saw I was with Kristy, he mouthed he'd be right back, then disappeared down the hallway past a clump of cheerleaders, who watched him go with wistful expressions. Not that I could focus on this, as Kristy was about to break my arm.

'Will you stop?' I asked her, wrenching myself out of her grip. 'I think you sprained something.'

'I can't believe,' she said indignantly, not even hearing this, 'that you and Wes are out on a date and you didn't even tell me. What does this say about our friendship? Where is the *trust*, Macy?'

I felt someone bump my other side and looked over to see Monica, a bottled water in one hand, looking out at the crowd in the living room with a bored expression.

'Did you see who Macy is *with*?' Kristy said to her.

'Mmm-hmm,' Monica said.

'I am not *with* him,' I said, rubbing my elbow. 'He needed to drop something off, I was over there helping Bert get ready for the Armageddon social and he just –'

'Oh, shit!' Kristy put a hand to her mouth, her eyes wide. 'I forgot about the social. God, please tell me he didn't wear that polka-dot shirt.'

'He didn't,' I told her, and she visibly relaxed. 'Stripes.'

'Tie?'

I nodded. 'The blue one.'

'Good.' She took a sip of the beer she was holding, then pointed a finger at me. 'Now, let's get back to you and Wes. Do you swear there's nothing going on?'

'God, calm down,' I said. She was still looking at me as if this were not an acceptable answer. I added, 'I swear.'

'All right then,' she said, nodding towards the dining room, where I could see a bunch of guys gathered round the table. 'Prove it.'

'Prove it?' I said, but she was already dragging me down

into the foyer, across the living room and into the dining room, plopping me down in a chair, and perching herself on the arm. Monica, true to form, arrived about thirty seconds later, looking winded. Not that Kristy seemed to notice. Clearly she was on a mission.

'Macy,' she said, gesturing down the table to a heavy-set guy in a baseball cap, another in an orange shirt and, at the end, a hippie-looking type with blue eyes and a ponytail, 'this is John, Donald and Philip.'

'Hi,' I said, and they all said hello in return.

'Macy's currently sort of between relationships,' Kristy explained, 'and I am trying, *trying*, to show her that there is a whole world of possibilities out there.'

Everyone was looking at me, and I felt my face redden. I wondered when Wes was coming back.

'These guys,' Kristy continued, gesturing round the table, 'are totally undateable. But they're really nice.'

'The fact that we're undateable, however,' John, the one in the baseball hat, said to me, 'did not stop her from dating all of us.'

'That's how I know!' she said, and they all laughed. Donald handed her a quarter and she bounced, missing, and drank. 'Look,' she said to me, 'I'm going to go do a preliminary sweep. When I come back, I'll walk you through and introduce you to some prospects. Okay?'

'Kristy,' I said, but she was already walking away, patting John on the head as she passed him.

'Your turn,' he said, nodding at me.

I picked up the quarter. While I'd seen this game played

before, I'd never tried it myself. I bounced the quarter like Kristy had, and it landed in the cup with a splash, which was good. I thought. 'What happens now?' I asked Philip.

He swallowed. 'You pick someone to drink.'

I looked round the table, then pointed at John, who raised his cup, toasting me.

'Your turn again,' Philip said.

'Oh.' I bounced the quarter again: again, it went in.

'Watch out!' Donald said. 'She's on fire!'

Just barely: with my third bounce, I missed. Philip indicated that I should drink, which I did, and pushed the quarter on to John. 'Oh well,' I said. 'It was fun while it lasted.' He made it, of course, and pointed at me.

'Bottoms up,' he said, so I drank again.

And again. And again. The next twenty minutes or so passed quickly – or at least it seemed that way – as I missed just about every bounce I took *and* was picked to drink whenever anyone else landed one in. Dateable or not, these guys were ruthless. Which meant that by the time Wes slid into the seat beside me, things were seeming a little fuzzy. To say the least.

'Hey,' he said. 'Thought you were lost.'

'Not lost,' I told him. 'Kidnapped. And now, a colossal failure at quarters. Did you find your friend?'

He shook his head. 'He's not here. You about ready to go?'

'Beyond ready,' I said. 'In fact, I think I'm a little –'

'Macy.' I turned round to see Kristy, hands on hips, looking determined. 'It's time to do this.'

'Do what?' Wes asked, and I was wondering the same thing, having totally forgotten our earlier conversation. Not that it mattered, as she already had me on my feet, stumbling slightly, and was dragging me full force into the kitchen. *Oh, right*, I thought. *Prospects*.

'You know,' I said. 'I don't think I'm really –'

'Five minutes,' she said firmly. 'That's all I'm asking.'

Fifteen minutes later, I found myself still in the kitchen, which was now packed with people, talking to a football player who was named either Hank or Frank: it had been too loud to make it out exactly. I'd been trying to extract myself, but between the crowd pressed all around me and Kristy watching like a hawk as she talked to her own prospect, it was kind of hard. Plus I was feeling a bit unsteady. Make that a lot unsteady.

'Don't you date Jason Talbot?' he said to me, shouting to be heard over the music that was blasting from a nearby stereo.

'Well,' I began, pushing a piece of hair out of my face.

'What?' he yelled.

I said, 'Actually, we're –'

He shook his head, cupping a hand behind his ear. 'What?'

'No,' I said loudly, leaning in closer to him and almost losing my balance. 'No. I don't.'

Just then, someone bumped me from behind, pushing me into Hank/Frank. 'Sorry,' I said, starting to step back, but he put his hands on my waist. I felt dizzy and strange, too hot, entirely too hot.

'Careful there,' he said, smiling at me again. I looked down at his hands, spread over my hips: they were big and hammy. Yuck. 'You okay?'

'I'm fine,' I said, trying to step back again. But he moved

with me, sliding his arms further round my waist. 'I think I need some air,' I said.

'I'll come with you,' he said, and Kristy turned her head, looking at me.

'Macy?' she said.

'She's fine,' Hank/Frank said.

'You know,' I said to Kristy, but I lost sight of her as a tall girl with a pierced nose stepped between us, 'I think we should –'

'Me too,' Hank/Frank said. I could feel his fingers brushing under my shirt, touching my bare skin. I felt a chill, and not the good kind. He leaned in closer to me, his lips touching my ear just slightly, and said, 'Hey, let's go somewhere.'

I looked for Kristy again, but she was gone, nowhere I could see. Now I was feeling totally woozy as Hank/Frank leaned into my ear again, his voice saying something, but the music was loud, the beat pounding in my ears.

'Wait,' I said, trying to pull back from him.

'Shhh, calm down,' he said, moving his hands up my back. I yanked away from him, too hard, then stumbled backwards, losing my balance. I could feel myself falling fast, into the space behind me, even as I tried to right myself. And then, suddenly, there was someone there.

Someone who put his hands on my elbows, steadying me, pulling me back to my feet. The hands were cool on my hot skin, and I could just feel this presence behind me, solid, like a wall. Something to lean on, strong enough to hold me.

I turned my head. It was Wes.

'There you are,' he said, as Hank/Frank looked on, annoyed. 'You about ready to go?'

I nodded. I could feel his stomach against my back, and without even thinking about it I felt myself leaning back into him. His hands were still cupping my elbows, and even though I knew this was weird, that I'd never do it any other time, I just stayed where I was, pressed against him.

'Hey,' Hank/Frank said to me, but Wes had already started through the crowd. There were so many people, so much to navigate, and as the distance fluctuated between us his hand kept slipping, down my arm to my wrist. And maybe he was going to let go as people pressed in on all sides, but all I could think was how when nothing made sense and hadn't for ages, you just have to grab on to anything you feel sure of. So, as I felt his fingers loosening round my wrist, I just wrapped my own round them, tight, and held on.

The instant we walked out through the front door, someone yelled Wes's name, loud. It startled me, startled both of us, and I dropped his hand quickly.

'Where you been, Baker?' some guy in a baseball hat, leaning against a Land Rover, was yelling. 'You got that carburetor for me?'

'Yeah,' Wes yelled back. 'One second.'

'Sorry,' I said to him as he turned and looked at me. 'I just, it was so hot in there, and he –'

He put his hands on my shoulders, easing me down so I was sitting on the steps. 'Wait here,' he said. 'I'll be right back. Okay?'

I nodded, and he started across the grass towards the Rover. I took in a deep breath, which just made me feel dizzier, then cupped my head in my hands. A second later, I had the feeling that I was being watched. When I turned my head, I saw Monica.

She was standing just to my right, smoking a cigarette, the bottle of water tucked under her arm. I knew well she was not the type to creep up or move fast, which meant she'd seen us come out. Seen us holding hands. Seen everything.

She put her cigarette to her lips, taking a big drag, and kept her eyes on me, steady. Accusingly.

'It's not what you think,' I said. 'There was this guy in there . . . Wes rescued me. I grabbed *his* hand, just to get out.'

She exhaled slowly, the smoke curling up and rising between us.

'It was just one of those things,' I said. 'You know, that just happen. You don't think or plan. You just do it.'

I waited for her to dispute this with a 'Donneven,' or maybe a 'Mmm-hmm,' meant sarcastically, of course. But she didn't say a word. She just stared at me, indecipherable as ever.

'Okay,' Wes said, walking up, 'let's get out of here.' Then he saw Monica and nodded at her. 'Hey. What's going on?'

Monica took another drag in reply, then turned her attention back to me.

I stood up, tilting slightly, and then righted myself, not without effort. 'You okay?' Wes asked.

'I'm fine,' I said. He headed down the walk towards the truck, and I followed. At the bottom of the steps, I turned back to Monica. 'Bye,' I told her. 'I'll see you tomorrow, okay?'

'Mmm-hmm,' she answered. I could feel her still watching me as I walked away.

• • •

'If you could change one thing about yourself,' Wes asked me, 'what would it be?'

'How about everything I did between leaving your house and right now?' I said.

He shook his head. 'I told you, it wasn't that bad,' he said.

'You didn't have some football player pawing you,' I pointed out.

'No,' he said, 'you're right about that.'

I sat back against the side of the truck, stretching my legs out in front of me. Once we'd left the party, Wes had stopped at the Quik Zip, where I'd bought a big bottled water and some aspirin. Then he drove me back to my house, rebuffing my half-hearted protests by promising to get me back to my car the next morning. Once there, I'd expected him to just drop me off, but instead, ever since, we'd been sitting in my driveway, watching fireflies flit around the streetlights and telling Truths.

But not the one about why I'd grabbed his hand. Everything had been such a blur, so hot and crazy, that there were moments I wondered if I'd imagined the whole thing. But then I'd remember Monica, her flat sceptical look, and know it had happened. I kept thinking about Jason, how weird he'd always been about physical contact, how reaching out for him was always like taking a chance, making a wish. With Wes, it had come naturally, no thinking.

'I wouldn't be so afraid,' I said now. Wes, watching a firefly bob past, turned to look at me. 'If I could change anything about myself. That's what it would be.'

'Afraid,' he repeated. Once again, I was reminded how much I liked that he never judged, in face or in tone, always giving me a chance to say more, if I wanted to. 'Of . . .'

'Of doing things that aren't planned or laid out in advance for me,' I said. 'I'd be more impulsive, not always thinking about consequences.'

He thought about this for a second. 'Give me an example.'

I took a sip of my water, then set it down beside me. 'Like with my mother. There's so much I want to say to her, but I don't know how she'll react. So I just don't.'

'Like what?' he asked. 'What do you want to say?'

I ran my finger down the tailgate, tracing the edge. 'It's not as much what I'd say, but what I'd do.' I stopped, shaking my head. 'Forget it. Let's move on.'

'Are you passing?' he asked.

'I answered the question!' I said.

He shook his head. 'Only the first part.'

'That was not a two-part question,' I said.

'It is now.'

'You know you're not allowed to do that,' I said. When we'd started, the only rule was you had to tell the truth, period. Still, ever since, we'd been bickering over various addendums. There had been a couple of arguments about the content of questions, one or two concerning the completeness of answers, and too many to count about whose turn it was. This, too, was part of the game. It was considerably harder to play by the rules, though, when you were making them up as you went along.

He looked at me, shaking his head. 'Come on, just answer,' he said, nudging my arm with his.

I exhaled loudly, leaning back on my palms. 'Okay,' I said,

'I'd just . . . if I could, I'd just walk up to my mother and say whatever I felt like saying, right at that moment. Maybe I'd tell her how much I miss my dad. Or how I worry about her. I don't know what. Maybe it sounds stupid, but for once I'd just let her know exactly how I feel, without thinking first. Okay?'

It wasn't the first time I'd felt a wave of embarrassment pass over me in giving an answer, but this was more raw and real, and I was grateful for the near-dark for whatever it could hide of my expression. For a minute, neither of us said anything, and I wondered again how it was possible that I could confess so much to a boy I'd only known for half a summer.

'That's not stupid,' he said finally. I picked at the tailgate, keeping my head down. 'It's not.'

I felt that weird tickle in my throat and swallowed over it. 'I know. But just talking about anything emotional is hard for her. For us. It's like she prefers we just not do that any more.'

I swallowed again, then took a deep breath. I could feel him watching me.

'Do you really think she feels that way?' he asked.

'I have no real way of knowing. We don't talk about it. We don't talk about anything. That's the problem.' I ran my finger round the top of my water bottle. 'That's my problem, actually. I don't talk to anybody about what's going on in my head, because I'm afraid they might not be able to take it.'

'What about this?' he asked, waving his hand between us. 'Isn't this talking?'

I smiled. 'This is Truth,' I said. 'It's different.'

He pulled a hand through his hair. 'I don't know. The vomit story alone was *huge*.'

'Enough with the vomit story,' I said, exasperated. 'Please God I'm begging you.'

'The point is,' he continued, ignoring this, 'that you've told me a lot playing this game. And while some of it might be weird, or heavy, or downright gross –'

'Wes.'

'– it's nothing I couldn't handle.' He was looking at me now, his face serious. 'So you should remember that, when you're thinking about what other people can deal with. Maybe it's not so bad.'

'Maybe,' I said. 'Or maybe you're just really extraordinary.'

As this came out, it was like someone else had said it. I just heard the words, even agreed with them, and a second later realized it was my voice. *Oh, my God*, I thought. This is what happens when you don't think and just do.

We sat there, looking at each other. It was warm out, the fireflies sparkling around us, and he was close to me, his knee and mine only inches apart. I had a flash of how his hand had felt earlier, his fingers closing over mine, and for one crazy second I thought that everything could change, right now, if only I could let it. If he'd been any other boy, and this was any other world, I would have kissed him. Nothing would have stopped me.

'Okay,' I said, too quickly, 'my turn.'

He blinked at me, as if he'd forgotten we were even playing. So he'd felt it too.

'Right,' he said, nodding. 'Go ahead. Hit me.'

I took in a breath. 'What's the one thing you'd do,' I asked, 'if you could do anything?'

As always, he took a second to think, staring straight ahead out at the clearing. I had no idea what he'd say, but then I never did. Maybe he'd reply that he wished he could see his mom again, or suddenly be granted X-ray vision, or orchestrate world peace. I don't know what I was expecting. But it wasn't what I got.

'Pass,' he said.

For a second I was sure I'd heard wrong. 'What?'

He cleared his throat. 'I said, I pass.'

'Why?'

He turned his head and looked at me. 'Because.'

'Because why?'

'Because I just do.'

'You know what this means, right?' I said, and he nodded. 'You know how the game works?'

'You have to answer whatever question I ask next,' he said. 'And if you do, you win.'

'Exactly.' I sat up straighter, bracing myself. 'Okay. Go ahead.'

He drew in a breath, and I waited, ready. But all he said was, 'No.'

'No?' I said, incredulous. 'What do you mean, no?'

'I mean,' he repeated, as if I were slow, 'no.'

'You have to ask a question,' I told him.

'Not immediately,' he replied, flicking a bug off his arm. 'For a question this important, a question that carries the outcome of the game, you can take as long as you want.'

I could not believe this. 'Says who?'

'Says the rules.'

'We have more than covered the rules,' I told him. 'That is *not* one of them.'

'I'm making an amendment,' he explained.

I was truly stumped. In fact, everything that had happened in the last five minutes, from me calling him extraordinary, to that one moment I felt something shift, to this, felt like some sort of out-of-body experience.

'Okay, fine,' I said. 'But you can't just take forever.'

'I don't need that long,' he said.

'How long?'

'Considerably less than forever.' I waited. Finally he said, 'Maybe a week. You can't bug me about it, either. That will nullify the entire thing. It has to just happen when it happens.'

'Another new rule,' I said, clarifying.

He nodded. 'Yup.'

I just looked at him, still processing this, when suddenly there was a burst of light from the other end of the street as a car came over the hill. We both squinted, and I put my hand to my face, then lowered it as I realized it was my mother. She was on the phone – of course – and didn't seem to see us at first as she passed, pulling into the driveway and up to the garage. It was only when she got out of the car, the phone still between her ear and shoulder, that she looked over at us, squinting slightly.

'Macy?' she said. 'Is that you?'

'Yes,' I replied. 'I'm coming in, right now.'

She went back to her conversation, still walking, but not before taking another glance at me and at Wes's truck before climbing the stairs, finding her keys and letting herself inside.

A second later, the foyer light came on, followed by the ones in the kitchen and back hall as she moved towards her office.

'Well,' I said to Wes, hopping down from the tailgate. 'Thanks for a truly exciting evening. Even if you *are* leaving me hanging.'

'I think you can handle it,' he said as he walked round to the driver's side, climbing behind the wheel.

'All I'm saying,' I said, 'is that when this is all over, I'm going to submit, like, twenty amendments. You won't even recognize the rules once I'm done with them.'

He laughed out loud, shaking his head, and I felt myself smile. What I wouldn't have admitted to him, not then, maybe not ever, was that I was actually happy to have to wait a while. The game had become important to me. I didn't want it to end at all, much less right that second. Not that he had to know that. Especially since he hadn't asked.

'You know,' I told him, 'after all this build-up, it had better be a good question.'

'Don't worry,' he said, sounding sure of himself, as always. 'It will be.'

Chapter THIRTEEN

'Goodness,' my mother said, tracing her finger down one side of the picture on the table in front of her. 'It's really coming along.'

My sister beamed. 'Isn't it? The plumber's coming tomorrow to install the new toilet, and the skylights are in. We've just got to decide on paint colours and then they can start on the walls. It's going to be just *gorgeous*.'

I'd never thought it was possible for someone to be so enthusiastic about going over paint chips that, to my eye anyway, looked exactly alike. But Caroline had completely thrown herself into the beach-house project. And while there were new window treatments and skylights, the moose head was still over the fireplace (although it had been cleaned by a professional – hard to believe someone actually *did* such things for a living), and the same splintery chairs remained on the back deck, where they'd be joined by a new wrought-iron bench and a row of decorative flowerpots. All the things we loved about the beach house, she said, would still be there. It was, she said, what my dad would have wanted.

'What I'm thinking,' Caroline said now as my mother

moved on to another picture, squinting at it, 'is that once the kitchen is all painted, I can do some tiling along the moulding. Kind of a south-western look, with different patterns. I have it in here somewhere, hold on.'

I watched my mother as she looked through the latest round of pictures, picking up one showing the new sliding glass doors to examine it more closely. I could tell her mind was wandering to other houses, other paint chips, other fixtures: the ones in the townhouses, which were progressing on a parallel timeline to Caroline's project. I knew that to her the beach house was distant, past, while her projects were present and future, close enough to see from the top of our driveway, rising up over the next hill. Maybe you could go backwards and forward at the same time, but it wasn't easy. You had to want to. My sister, her mind dancing with images of plantation shutters and smooth blue kitchen tiles, might not have been able to see this. But I could. I only hoped that eventually my mother would come round.

A few nights later, I worked a fiftieth birthday party with Wish in the neighbourhood right next to Wildflower Ridge. They picked me up on their way there, and afterwards, dropping me off, Delia asked a favour.

'I *so* have to pee,' she said. 'Would it be all right if I came in for a second?'

'Sure,' I said.

'Delia!' Bert said, looking at his watch. 'We're in a hurry here!'

'And I'm pregnant and about to pee all over myself,' she replied, opening her door and swinging one leg out. 'I'll only be a second.'

But a second, to Bert, was too long. All night he'd been obsessing about how he needed to be home by ten at the very latest in order to see *Update: Armageddon*, a show that covered, in his words, 'all the latest doings in doomsday theory'. But the party had run long, and even though we'd rushed as much as we could, time was clearly running out, not only for the world, but for Bert as well.

'I'm coming too,' Kristy said now, unlocking the side door. 'Every time I tried to use the bathroom at that party someone was in it.'

'My show comes on in five minutes!' Bert said.

'Bert,' Wes said, pointing at the dashboard clock, which said 9:54, 'it's over. You're not going to make it.'

'Update: it's too late,' Kristy added.

Bert glared at both of them, then slumped in his seat, looking out of the window. For a second it was quiet, except for Delia grunting as she lowered herself onto the grass by the sidewalk. I looked at my dark house, looming up in front of us: my mother was at an overnight meeting in Greensboro, not due back until morning.

'You can come in and watch it here,' I said. 'I mean, if you want to.'

'Really?' Bert looked at me, surprised. 'You mean it?'

'Macy,' Kristy moaned, knocking me with her elbow, 'what are you *thinking*?'

'She's thinking that she's kind and considerate,' Bert said

as he quickly slid down the seat to the open door, 'unlike some people I could mention.'

'I'm sorry,' Delia said, putting her hand on my arm, 'but I'm really bordering on emergency status with my bladder here.'

'Oh, right,' I said. 'Come on, it's just inside.'

'So we're all going in?' Wes asked, cutting the engine.

'Yep,' Kristy said. 'Looks that way.'

As we approached the front steps, Delia waddling, Kristy eyeing the house, with Bert and Wes and Monica bringing up the rear, I told myself that even if my mother had been home, I could have done this, invited my friends in. But the truth was, ever since her talk with me about concerns for my priorities, I'd stopped talking about my job at Wish, or Kristy, or anything related to either. It just seemed smarter, as well as safer.

I unlocked the front door, then pointed Delia to the powder room. She moved across the foyer faster than I'd seen her go in weeks, the door shutting swiftly behind her. 'Oh, sweet Jesus,' we heard her say. Kristy laughed, the sound sudden and loud, bouncing off the high ceiling above us, and we all looked up at once, following it.

'See,' Bert said to her, 'I told you this place was huge.'

'It's a palace.' Kristy peered in the dining room, eyeing my sister's wedding portrait, which was hanging over the sideboard. 'How many bedrooms are there?'

'I don't know, five?' I said, walking to the bottom of the stairs and glancing up at the second floor. There were no lights on, and the rest of the house was dark.

'Is the TV this way?' Bert asked me, poking his head into the living room. Wes reached up and popped him on the back of his head, reminding him of his manners. 'I mean, is it okay if I find the TV?'

'It's in here,' I said, starting down the hallway to the kitchen, hitting light switches as I came upon them. I pointed to the right, to the family room. 'The remote should be on the table.'

'Thanks,' Bert said, crossing quickly to the couch. 'Oh, wow, this TV is *huge*!' Monica followed him, flopping down on the leather recliner, and a second later I heard the set click on.

I walked into the kitchen, pulling open the fridge. 'Does anybody want anything to drink?'

'Do you have Dr Pepper?' Bert called out. I saw Wes shoot him a look. 'I mean, no thanks.'

Kristy smiled, running her finger along the top of the island. 'Look at this, it's so cool. Like it has little diamonds in it. What's this called?'

'I don't know,' I said.

'Corian,' Wes told her, peering over her shoulder.

'Everything here is so *nice*,' Kristy said emphatically, looking around the kitchen. 'If Stella ever gets her fill of me, I'm moving in with Macy. She's got five bedrooms. I'd even sleep in that powder room. I bet it's nicer than my whole doublewide.'

'It's not,' I said.

From the living room, I could hear an announcer on the TV, speaking in a deep, important-sounding voice: 'This is the future. This is our fate. This is *Update: Armageddon.*'

'Come on, you guys, it's on!' Bert yelled.

'Bert, use your inside voice,' Kristy told him, turning on her stool to look out the sliding glass doors at the backyard. 'Wow! Monica, are you seeing this deck out here? And the pool?'

'Mmm-hmmm,' Monica replied.

'Monica loves pools,' Kristy told me. 'She's like a freaking fish; you can't get her out of the water. Me, I'm more of a lie-by-the-pool-drinking-something-with-an-umbrella-in-it kind of girl.'

I took a few cans of Coke out of the fridge, then pulled some glasses out of the cabinet, filling them with ice. Kristy was now flipping through a *Southern Living* my sister had left behind during her last stay, while Wes stood at the back glass doors, checking out the backyard. With the noise from the TV, and everyone there, I was suddenly aware of how quiet and still my house was normally. Just the addition of so many people breathing gave it a totally different feel, some sort of palpable energy that was never there otherwise.

'I,' Delia announced as she came down the hallway, her flip-flops smacking the tile floor, 'feel *so* much better. Never would I have imagined that peeing could make me so happy.'

From the TV, the announcer bellowed, 'What do you think will bring . . . the *end of the world*?'

'From the looks of it,' Kristy said, flipping a page, 'I'd put my money on this room decorated entirely in gingham. I mean, it's just hideous.'

'Macy?'

I jumped, startled. It was my mother, pulling a gotcha all her own. As I turned round, my heart thumping in my chest, I saw her standing in the open archway that led to the hallway to her office, file folder in hand. She'd been here the entire time.

'Mom,' I said, too quickly. 'Hi.'

'Hi,' she replied, but she wasn't looking at me, her eyes instead moving across the room to take in Bert and Monica in front of the TV, Wes by the back doors, Delia making her way over to the couch and, finally, Kristy, her head still bent over the magazine. 'I thought I heard voices.'

'We just got here.' I watched as she came into the room, sliding the file onto the counter. 'I invited everyone in to watch this show. I hope that's okay.'

'Of course it is,' she said. Her voice sounded up, cheery, forced. Fake. 'I've been wanting to meet your new friends.'

Hearing this, Kristy lifted up her head, sitting up straighter. 'Kristy Palmetto,' she said, sticking out her hand.

My mother, businesswoman that she was, reached for the hand first. Then she took her first good look at Kristy's face and saw the scars. 'Oh . . . hello,' she said, stumbling slightly on the second word. She recovered quickly, though, as I knew she would, and the next thing she said was smooth, absolutely not affected. 'I've heard a lot about you from Macy. It's so nice to meet you.'

'You have a beautiful home,' Kristy told her. She patted the island. 'I especially love this Coreal.'

'Corian,' Wes corrected from behind her.

'Right.' Kristy smiled at my mother, who was doing that thing where you try to look everywhere but where your eyes are drawn naturally. Luckily, Kristy, in her black velvet shirt and short skirt, wearing full make-up, with her hair piled up on her head, offered plenty of other options. 'It's just gorgeous. Anyway, I told Macy if she's not careful I'm moving in here. I heard you have extra bedrooms.'

My mother laughed politely, then glanced at me. I smiled, noting how forced it felt, like my lips weren't covering my teeth enough. This was the way I always used to smile, I thought. When I had to work at it.

'Mom,' I said, nodding towards Wes as he turned round from the glass doors, 'this is Wes.'

'Hi,' Wes said.

'And you know Delia,' I said, gesturing to where she was sitting on the couch.

'Of course! How are you?' my mother said.

'Very pregnant,' Delia called back, smiling. 'But other than that, fine.'

'She's due any second,' I explained, and when my mother looked slightly alarmed I added, 'I mean, any day. And that's Bert, and next to him is Monica.'

'Hello,' my mother called out, as Bert and Monica waved hello, 'nice to meet you.'

'Have you heard,' the announcer on the TV bellowed, 'the Big Buzz?'

'Bert really wanted to watch this show,' I explained. 'It's, um, about theories.'

'Crackpot theories,' Kristy said.

'These are backed up by science!' Bert yelled.

'Bert,' Wes said, walking over to the living room, 'inside voice.'

'By science,' Bert repeated, more quietly. 'The end of the world is no joke. It's not a matter of if. It's *when.*'

I looked at my mother. Something told me that the expression on her face – confusion, curiosity, maybe even shock – was not unlike the one I probably had the first day I'd been introduced to these people. But, seeing it there, I had a feeling this wasn't necessarily a good thing.

'Macy,' she said to me after a second, 'can I talk to you in my office for a moment?'

'Um, sure,' I said.

'Can you believe this?' Kristy asked me, holding up the magazine to show me a living room full of wicker furniture. 'Have you ever seen a more uncomfortable-looking couch?'

I shook my head, then followed my mother down the short hallway to her office. She shut the door behind us, then crossed to her desk and stood behind it. 'It's after ten,' she said, her voice low. 'Don't you think it's a little late to have people over?'

'Bert really wanted to see this show,' I said. 'It's only a half hour. Plus, I thought you were at that meeting.'

'You have to work in the morning, Macy,' she said, as if I didn't know this. 'And we've got a big day tomorrow as well, with the Fourth of July picnic, and you working the welcome booth. It's not a good night for company.'

'I'm sorry,' I said. 'They'll be gone soon.'

She looked down at her desk, riffling through some papers, but her disapproval was palpable. I could feel it all around me, settling, taste it in the air.

There was a burst of laughter from the living room, and I glanced at the door. 'I should go back out there,' I said. 'I don't want to seem rude.'

She nodded, running a hand through her hair. I stood up and started towards the door.

'What happened to Kristy?' she asked, just as I was about to push it open.

I had a flash of Kristy, just moments earlier, extending her hand to my mother so cheerfully. 'She was in a car accident when she was eleven.'

'Poor thing,' she said, shaking her head as she pulled a pencil out of the holder on her desk. 'It must be just horrible for her.'

'Why do you say that?' I asked. Truthfully, I hardly noticed Kristy's scars at all any more. They were just part of her face, part of who she was. Her outfits garnered more of my attention, maybe because they at least were always changing.

She looked at me. 'Well,' she said, 'only because of the disfigurement. It's hard enough being that age, without a handicap to deal with.'

'She's not handicapped, Mom,' I said. 'She just has a few scars.'

'It's just so unfortunate.' She sighed, picking up a folder, moving it to the other side of the desk. 'She'd be a pretty girl, otherwise.'

Then she started writing, opening the folder and jotting something down. Like I was already gone, this was the end of it, there could be no rebuttal, no other side. Of course Kristy wasn't beautiful: her flaws were right there, where anyone could see. Of course we were over my dad's passing: just look around, we were successful, good in school, fine just fine. I'd never spoken up to say otherwise, so I had no one to blame but myself.

Thinking this, I went back into the kitchen, where I found

Wes now sitting next to Kristy, both of them looking at *Southern Living*.

'See, this stuff isn't nearly as good as yours,' Kristy was saying, pointing at a page. 'I mean, what is that supposed to be, anyway?'

'An iron heron,' he said, glancing at me. 'I think.'

'A what?' Kristy said, squinting at it again.

'No way,' I said, coming over to look for myself. Sure enough, there was an iron heron, just like my sister had been talking about.

'They're big in Atlanta,' Wes explained to Kristy.

'Huge,' I said.

Kristy looked at him, then at me. 'Whatever,' she said, nodding, as she pushed her chair out and hopped down. 'I'm going to find out about that Big Buzz.'

I watched her as she walked into the living room, flopping down in our overstuffed chair. She ran her hands over the arms, settling in, then looked up at the ceiling before directing her attention to the TV.

Wes, across from me, turned a page of the magazine. 'Everything okay with your mom?' he asked, not looking up.

'Yeah,' I said, glancing down at one of the iron herons. 'I'm not getting the appeal of those,' I said.

He pointed at the picture. 'See, first, they're very clean and simple looking. People like that. Second, they have the wildlife thing going for them, so they fit in well with a garden. And thirdly,' he turned the page, indicating another picture, 'the artist takes himself, and the herons, very seriously. So that gives them a certain cachet as well.'

I looked at the artist. He was a tall guy with white hair pulled back in a ponytail, striking a pensive pose by a reflecting pond. *To me*, one of the quotes below it read, *my herons represent the fragility of life and destiny*. 'Ugh,' I said. 'If that's taking your work seriously, he can have it.'

'Exactly.'

'Just wait, though,' I said. 'Someday you'll be in *Southern Living*, with a picture just like that, talking about the deep true meaning of your work.'

'Unlikely,' he said. 'I don't think they pick people who got their start by being arrested and getting sent to reform school.'

'Maybe that could be your angle,' I suggested. He made a face at me. 'And, anyway, what kind of attitude is that?' I asked.

'A realistic one,' he told me, shutting the magazine.

'You,' I said, poking him, 'need a little positivity.'

'And you,' he said, 'need to stop poking me.'

I laughed, then heard something behind me and turned around. It was my mother again, standing in the doorway. How long had she been there, I wondered, but one look at the expression on her face – stern, chin set, clearly not happy – answered this question.

'Macy,' she said, her voice level, 'could you hand me that folder on the counter, please.'

I walked over to the counter by the fridge, feeling her watching me. Wes, who couldn't help but pick up on the sudden tension in the air, started towards the living room. As he got close, Kristy moved over in the big chair, making room, and he slid in beside her.

'A reverberation,' the announcer was saying from the living

room, 'that would cause a domino effect among the population, causing people to slowly go insane from the constant, unknown droning.'

'You can go crazy from vibrations?' Kristy said.

'Oh, yeah,' Bert said. 'You can go crazy from anything.'

'. . . a natural phenomenon,' the announcer was saying, 'or perhaps a tool used by extraterrestrials, who may communicate using sounds beyond our comprehension?'

'Interesting,' Delia murmured, rubbing her stomach.

'Mmm-hmm,' Monica echoed.

I picked up the folder and brought it to my mother. She stepped out into the darkness of the hallway, giving me a look that meant I should follow.

'Macy,' she said, 'did I just hear that boy say he's been arrested?'

'It was a long time ago,' I said. 'And –'

'Macy!' Kristy called out. 'You're going to miss the mega-hunami!'

'Tsunami,' Bert said.

'Whatever,' she said. 'It's the mega part that matters, anyway.'

But I could barely hear this. I was just watching my mother, the way she was staring at them, her judgement so clear on her face. From Delia's chaotic business practices to Kristy's scars to Wes's past, it was clear they were far from flawless.

'He's the boy you were with the other night, correct?' she asked.

'What?' I asked.

She looked at me, her face stern, as if I were talking back, which I wasn't. 'The other night,' she repeated, enunciating the words, 'when I came home and you were outside with someone. In a truck. Was that him?'

'Um,' I said, 'yeah, I guess it was. He just gave me a ride.' And here I'd thought she'd hardly noticed us. But now, as I watched her looking at Wes, I knew this was one more thing she would hold against me. 'It's not what you think. He's a nice guy, Mom.'

'When the show is over,' she said, as if I hadn't even said this, 'they leave. Understood?'

I nodded, and she stuck the folder under her arm as I headed back through the kitchen, towards the living room. I was almost there when I heard her call after me.

'I forgot to tell you,' she said, her voice loud and clear. 'Jason called. He's going to be in town for the weekend.'

'He did?' I said. 'He is?'

'His grandmother's taken ill, apparently,' she said. 'So he's coming down for the weekend. He said to tell you he gets in around noon, and he'll see you at the library.'

I just stood there, trying to process this information, as she turned and headed back to her office. Jason was coming home. And of course my mother had felt it necessary to announce this out loud, in front of everyone – especially Wes – while so much of our other business had been conducted in private. She'd told me she wanted me back on track: this was one way of nudging me there.

When I walked into the living room, the announcer on the TV was talking about the mega-tsunami, describing in detail how all it would take was one volcano blowing to set off the chain reaction of events that would end with that big wave crashing over our extended coastline. What other proof, I thought, did you need that life was short. That volcano could already be rumbling, magma bubbling up, pressure building to an inevitable, irrevocable burst.

Kristy scooted over on the wide arm of the oversized chair, making a space for me between herself and Wes, who was studying the screen intently. He didn't say anything as I sat down, and I wondered if he'd heard my mother say Jason was coming home. Not that it mattered. We were just friends, after all.

'Everything okay?' Kristy asked me, and I nodded, my eyes on the TV, which was showing a computer simulation of the mega-wave. There was the volcano blowing, there was the land falling into the ocean, all of these events that led up to this one, huge After as the wave rose up and began to move across the ocean, crossing the space between Africa and where we were. All I could think was that right there, in every passing second, was the future winding itself down. Never would forever, with all its meanings, be so clear and distinct as in the true, guaranteed end of the world.

Chapter FOURTEEN

The next day, I woke up in the mother of all bad moods. I'd tossed and turned all night, having one bad dream after another. But the last one was the worst.

In it, I'd been walking down the sidewalk outside the library during my lunch break, carrying my sandwich, and a car pulled up beside me, beeping its horn. When I turned my head, I saw my dad was behind the wheel. He motioned for me to get in, but when I reached for the door handle the car suddenly lurched forward, tyres squealing. My dad kept looking back at me, and I could tell that he was scared, but there was nothing I could do as it headed into the intersection, which was filling up with cars from all directions. In my dream, I started to run, and it felt so real: the little catch I always felt in my ankle right after a start, that certain feeling that I'd never get my pace right. Each time I got close to my dad, he'd slip out of my reach, and everything I grabbed thinking it was the car or a part of the car slipped through my hands.

I woke up gasping, my sheets tangled around my legs. Unfurling them slowly, I could feel my pulse banging in my wrist as I struggled to calm down. *Not a good start*, I thought.

My mother was on the phone as I came into the kitchen, dealing with some last-minute details for the Wildflower Ridge Independence Day Picnic and Parade she'd been planning for weeks now. After my shift at the library, which was open special holiday hours until one, I was supposed to be there at the neighbourhood information table, to smile and answer any and all questions. Even if I'd had a good night's sleep – or any sleep at all – it would have been a long day. Now, with Jason and everything else still to get through before that even began, it felt like there was no way for it to be anything but positively endless.

I was sitting at the kitchen table, forcing down some porridge and trying not to think about it, when my mother hung up the phone and came over to sit beside me, her coffee in hand. 'So,' she said, 'I think we should talk about last night.'

I put my spoon down in my bowl. 'Okay,' I said.

She took a breath. 'I've already conveyed to you –'

And then the phone rang. She got up, pushing out her chair, and crossed the kitchen, picking it up on the second ring.

'Deborah Queen,' she said. She listened for a second, turning her back to me. 'Yes. Oh, wonderful. Yes. Three thirty at the latest, please. Thanks so much.' She hung up the phone, jotting something down, then came back over to her chair. 'Sorry about that,' she said, picking up her coffee cup and taking a sip. 'As I was saying, we've already discussed my unhappiness with some recent changes I've noticed in you. And, last night, it seemed that some of my concerns were well founded.'

'Mom,' I said. 'You don't –'

There was a shrill ringing sound from her purse, which was

on the island: her cell phone. She turned round, digging it out, then pushed a button, pressing it to her ear. 'Deborah Queen. Oh, Marilyn, hello! No, it's a perfect time. Let me just run and get those figures for you.' She held up her finger, signalling for me to stay put, then got up, disappearing down the hallway to her office. It was bad enough to be having to have this conversation; the fact that it was getting dragged out was excruciating. By the time she returned and hung up, I'd washed out my bowl and put it in the dishwasher.

'The bottom line is,' she said, sitting down again and picking right up where we'd left off, 'that I don't want you hanging around with those people outside work.'

Maybe it was that I was tired. Or the fact that she couldn't even commit to this conversation without interruptions. But whatever the reason, what I said next surprised us both.

'Why?'

It was just one word. But with it, I'd taken a stand against my mother, albeit small, for the first time in as long as I could remember.

'Macy,' she said, speaking slowly, 'that boy has been *arrested*. I don't want you out riding around with someone like that, out at all hours –'

The phone rang again, and she started to push herself up out of her chair, then stopped. It rang again, then once more, before falling silent.

'Honey, look,' she said, her voice tired. 'I know what can happen when someone falls into a bad crowd. I've already been through this before, with your sister.'

'That's not fair,' I said. 'I haven't done anything wrong.'

'This isn't about punishment,' she said. 'It's about prevention.'

Like what was happening to me was a forest fire, or a contagious disease. I turned my head, looking out of the window at the backyard, where the grass was shimmering, wet under the bright sun.

'You have to realize, Macy,' she said, her voice low. 'The choices you make now, the people you surround yourself with, they all have the potential to affect your life, even who you are, forever. Do you understand what I'm saying?'

In fact, I knew this to be true now more than ever before. With just a few weeks of being friends with Kristy, and more importantly, Wes, I had changed. They'd helped me to see there was more to the world than just the things that scared me. So they *had* affected me. Just not in the ways she was afraid of.

'I do understand,' I said, wanting to explain this, 'but –'

'Good,' she said, just as the phone rang again. 'I'm glad we see eye to eye.'

And then she was up. Walking to the phone, picking it up, already moving on. 'Deborah Queen,' she said. 'Harry. Hello. Yes, I was just thinking that I needed to consult you about . . .'

She walked down the hallway, still talking, as I just sat there, in the sudden quiet of the kitchen. Everyone else could get through to my mother: all they had to do was dial a number and wait for her to pick up. *If only*, I thought, *it were that easy for me.*

When I went to leave for work, I found myself blocked in by a van that was filled with folding chairs. I went back inside, pulling my mother away from another phone call, only to find out some salesman had taken the keys home with him after parking it there.

'I'll drive you,' she said, grabbing her purse off the counter. 'Let's go.'

Silences are amplified by small spaces, we found out once we were not only in the car but stuck in a traffic jam, with other annoyed commuters blocking us in on all sides. Maybe my mother had no idea I was upset with her. Until we'd got in the car, I hadn't really realized it either, but now, with each passing second, I could feel myself getting angrier. She'd taken my dad's stuff from me, his memories. Now she wanted to take my friends too. The least I could do was fight back.

'Honey, you look tired,' she said, after we'd been sitting in silence for a few minutes. I'd felt her glancing at me, but hadn't looked back. 'Did you not sleep well?'

My *I'm fine* was poised on my lips, about to come automatically. But then, I stopped myself. *I'm not fine*, I thought. So instead I said, 'No. I didn't. I had bad dreams.'

Behind us, someone honked.

'Really,' she said. 'What about?'

'Actually,' I said, 'Dad.'

I was watching her carefully as I said this, saw her fingers, curled round the steering wheel pulse white at the tips, then relax. I had that twinge in my stomach, like I was doing something wrong.

'Really,' she said, not taking her eyes off the road as the traffic began to pick up.

'Yeah,' I said slowly. 'It was scary. He was driving this car, and –'

'Your room was probably too hot,' she said, reaching forward and adjusting her vent. 'And you do have an awful lot of blankets on your bed. Whenever you get hot, you have nightmares.'

I knew what this was: a conversational nudge, her way of easing me back between the lines.

'It's weird,' I made myself say, 'because right after he died, I had a lot of dreams about him, but I haven't lately. Which is why last night was so disturbing. He was in trouble, and I couldn't save him. It scared me.'

These four sentences, blurted out too fast, were the most I had said to my mother about my dad since he'd died. The very fact they had been spoken, were able to bridge the gap from my mind to the open air, was akin to a miracle, and I waited for what would come next, partly scared, partly exhilarated.

My mother took in a breath, and I curled my fingers into my palms.

'Well,' she said finally, 'it was only a dream.'

And that was it. All this build-up to a great leap, and I didn't fall or fly. Instead I found myself back on the edge of the cliff, blinking, wondering if I'd ever jumped at all. *It's not supposed to be like this*, I thought. My mother was looking straight ahead, her eyes focused on the road.

As she pulled up to the library, I got my purse and opened the door, feeling the already thick heat hit my face as I stepped out onto the kerb.

'Can you find a way home?' she asked me. 'Or should I pick you up?'

'I'll get a ride,' I said.

'If I don't hear from you,' she told me, 'be at the Commons at six sharp. Okay?'

I nodded, then shut my door. As she drove off, I just stood there watching her go, realizing how similar my dream had been to this, me standing in this exact spot, a car moving away. Like I'd never woken up at all, and soon I'd open my eyes to another morning, another way of all this happening. But as my mother pulled out onto the street she wasn't looking back at me scared, or needing me. She was fine. Just fine.

I walked into the library at exactly 9:12. Bethany and Amanda both looked up from the info desk. Bethany turned her head slightly, eyeing the clock over her head, then looked back at me.

'There was a big traffic jam on Cloverdale,' I said, pushing open the swinging door and immediately whacking my knee on the back of her chair. I waited for her to slide sideways, so I could pass, but she didn't, so I had to step round her, which put me in a direct line with Amanda's chair. Of course.

'I come that way,' she said coolly, pushing herself a bit more in my path, the wheels squeaking. 'I didn't hit any hold-ups this morning.'

I moved round her, having to sidestep the garbage can in the process, and put my bag on the floor next to my seat, which was piled high with periodicals. I moved them onto the table beside my computer, then sat down. I had been putting up with this for weeks. Weeks. Why? Because I had an obligation? To whom? Not to Jason, who'd shed his commitment to me as easily as a second, ill-fitting skin. And certainly not my mother, who, for all the time I'd suffered here, still thought I wasn't dedicated enough.

It just wasn't worth it. Not even close.

Clearly, I wasn't the only one who'd been alerted to Jason's homecoming visit. All morning long, Bethany and Amanda bustled and chattered as they updated the database and organized the invoices for all the periodicals that had come in during his absence. I, however, was exiled to the back room to organize mildewed magazines. I had about two full hours to think about Jason and what I would say to him once he arrived. But as much as I tried to focus on formulating a plan, my mind kept slipping back to Wish and Wes and everything that had happened in the last few weeks. The night Jason had announced our break, all I could think about was how to fix things between us. But now, I wasn't sure what I wanted.

After the magazines were done, I sat facing the wall outside my window, knowing that the time was ticking down to his arriving. *Any minute now*, I kept thinking, *that door will open and something will happen*. I just didn't know what.

Beside me, Amanda and Bethany were busy practising their conversational French for a school club trip they were taking at the end of the summer. All those guttural sounds on top of my anxious mood were about to drive me crazy. Which was probably why, when they finally, abruptly, shut up, I noticed.

Oh, God, I thought. *Here we go*. One moment Amanda was saying something about the Champs Élysées, and the next they were both staring at the library's front entrance, speechless.

I looked up, already picturing Jason in my mind. But it wasn't him. It was Wes.

He'd just come in and was standing by the front door, looking around as if getting his bearings. Then he saw me and started towards the desk with that slow, loping walk that I knew so well.

As he approached, I could hear the wheels of Bethany and Amanda's chairs moving; they were pushing up closer, arranging their postures. But he came right to me.

'Hey,' he said.

I had never been so happy to see anyone in my entire life. 'Hey.'

'So look,' he began, leaning over the desk, 'I was –'

'Excuse me?' Bethany said. Her voice was loud, even.

Wes turned and looked at her. As he did so, I watched his profile, his arm, that little bit of the heart in hand peeking out from his sleeve.

'We can help you over here,' Bethany said to him. 'Did you have a question?'

'Um, sort of,' Wes said, glancing at me, a mild smile on his face. 'But –'

'I can answer it,' Bethany said solidly, so confidently. Amanda, beside her, nodded, seconding this.

'Really, it's fine,' he said, then looked at me again. He raised his eyebrows, and I just shrugged. 'Okay, so –'

'She's only a trainee; she won't know the answer,' Bethany told him, pushing her chair over closer to where he was, her voice too loud, bossy even. 'It's better if you ask me. Or ask us.'

Then, and only then, did I see the tiniest flicker of annoyance on Wes's face. 'You know,' Wes said, 'I think she'll know it.'

'She won't. Ask me.'

Now it wasn't just a flicker. Wes looked at me, narrowing his eyes, and for a second I just stared back. *Whatever happens*, I thought, *happens*. For the first time, time at the info desk was flying.

'Okay,' he said slowly, moving down the counter. He leaned on his elbows, closer to Bethany, and she sat up even straighter, readying herself, like someone on *Jeopardy* awaiting the Daily Double. 'So here's my question.'

Amanda picked up a pen, as if there might be a written portion.

'Last night,' Wes said, his voice serious, 'when the supplies were being packed up, what happened to the big tongs?'

The sick part was that Bethany, for a second, looked as if she were actually flipping through her mental Rolodex for the answer. I watched her swallow, then purse her lips. 'Well,' she said. But that was all.

I could feel myself smiling. A real smile.

Wes looked at Amanda. 'Do you know?'

Amanda shook her head slowly.

'All right,' he said, turning back to look at me. 'Better ask the trainee then. Macy?'

I could feel Amanda and Bethany looking at me. 'They're in the bottom of that cart with the broken back wheel, under the aprons,' I said. 'There wasn't room for them with the other serving stuff.'

Wes smiled at me. 'Oh,' he said, shaking his head like this was just so obvious. 'Of *course*.'

I could hear wheels squeaking as Bethany and Amanda pushed themselves further down the counter. Wes watched them go, hardly bothered, then leaned over the counter and looked down at me.

'Nice co-workers,' he said under his breath.

'Oh, yeah,' I said, not as quietly. 'They hate me.'

The chairs stopped moving. Silence. *Oh, well*, I thought. *It's not like it was a secret.*

'So anyway,' I asked him. 'What's going on?'

'Typical Wish chaos,' he said, running a hand through his hair. 'Delia's freaking out because one of the coolers broke last night and everything in it's gone bad. Kristy and Monica are at the beach, so now she and Bert and I have to make five more gallons of potato salad on the fly *and* work this job with just three of us. Then, I'm on my way back from a mayonnaise run when Delia calls up, hysterical, saying we have no tongs and I should come here and ask you.' He took a deep breath, then said, 'So how's your day so far?'

'Don't ask,' I said.

'Has the boyfriend shown up yet?'

So he did hear, I thought. I shook my head. 'Nope. Not yet.'

'Well, just think, it could be worse,' he said. 'You could be having to make potato salad. Just imagine being up to your elbows in mayonnaise.'

I made a face. He was right – this wasn't a pretty picture.

'The point is, we could really use you,' Wes said, running a hand over the counter between us. 'It's too bad you can't get out of here.'

A moment passed, during which all I could hear was the silence of the library. The ticking of the clock. The slight squeak of Bethany's chair. And after everything that had happened, from the first day until the last five minutes, that was the last straw.

'Well,' I said. 'Maybe I can.'

I turned round and looked at Bethany and Amanda, who were pretending to be huddled over some periodical while listening to every word we were saying. 'Hey,' I called out, and they looked up, in tandem, like a creature with two heads. 'You know, I think I'm going to go.'

A moment passed as this sunk in.

Amanda's eyes widened. 'But you don't get off for another hour,' she said.

'Your shift,' Bethany added, 'ends at one.'

'Well,' I said, picking up my purse, 'something tells me you're not really going to miss me.'

I stood up and pushed in my chair. Wes was watching me, curious, his hands in his pockets, as I took one last look around my pitiful little workstation. *This could be a big mistake*, I thought, but it was already happening. I was not a girl with all the information, but I knew one thing. If this was my forever, I didn't want to spend another second of it here.

'If you leave now,' Bethany said under her breath, 'you can't come back.'

'You're right,' I told her. And I was so glad that she was. Right, that is. 'I can't.'

I started to walk towards the swinging door, but, as usual, her chair was in my way. And beyond that was Amanda's. It had been so hard to come in here that first day, and every day since. I figured that by now I'd earned a clear path out.

So I picked up my purse and tossed it over the desk. It hit the carpet with a thud, right by Wes's feet. Then, in a fashion my sister the rebel would have appreciated, I hoisted myself up, throwing one leg over, and jumped the counter, while Bethany and Amanda watched, stunned.

'Wow,' Wes said, raising his eyebrows as I picked up my purse. 'Nice dismount.'

'Thanks,' I said.

'Macy,' Bethany hissed at me. 'What are you *doing*?'

But I didn't answer her, didn't even look back as we started across the library, everyone staring, to the exit. This felt right. Not just leaving, but how I was doing it. Without regret, without second guessing. And with Wes right there, holding the door open for me as I walked out into the light.

Chapter FIFTEEN

Lucy picked up a crayon, gripping it in her short, chubby fingers. When she put it to the paper she pressed hard, as if only by doing so would the colour transfer. 'Tree,' she announced as a squiggle emerged, stretching from one end of the paper to the other.

'Tree,' I repeated, glancing at Wes. Even now, a full hour after I'd jumped the info desk, he was still looking at me the way he had the entire ride back to Sweetbud Drive, with an expression that was half impressed, half outright incredulous. 'Stop it,' I said to him.

'Sorry.' He shrugged as if this would help him to shake it, once and for all. 'I just can't get that visual out of my head. It was –'

'Crazy,' I finished for him, as Lucy, sitting between us on Wes's side porch, exhaled loudly before picking up another crayon.

'More like kick-ass,' he said. 'I mean, that's the way I've always wanted to quit jobs but never had the nerve, you know?'

'It wasn't kick-ass,' I said, embarrassed.

'Maybe not to you.'

Truthfully, for me, it just hadn't sunk in yet. I knew that across town something bigger than the mega-tsunami had hit and was already reverberating, sending shockwaves that would eventually ripple out to meet me. I could just see Jason at the library, listening with that same incredulous expression, as my desk leap was described, in SAT verbal perfect words, by Amanda and Bethany. He was probably already calling my cell phone to demand an explanation, which was why I'd turned it off, deciding to give myself at least until six, when I had to meet my mother, to try not to think about what happened next. For now, I just wanted to do something else. Like colouring.

Thinking this, I glanced at Lucy again. When we'd come back with the mayonnaise, Delia had been beyond frazzled, frantically boiling huge kettles of water while she and Bert chopped a small mountain of potatoes in the garage. Lucy, hot and bored, was underfoot, and Delia had handed her off to us, asking us to just entertain her until it was time to start mixing everything up. Now I watched as she pushed one of her tight black curls out of her face and pressed an orange crayon to the paper, zigzagging across it. 'Cow,' she said with authority.

'Cow,' I said.

A breeze blew over the porch then, ruffling the trees, and suddenly there was a flash, something glinting round the side of the house, that I caught out of the corner of my eye. I leaned back on my palms, craning my neck, and saw that in the side yard there were several angels, big and small, as well as a few works in progress: large pieces of rebar twisted and sculpted, a couple of whirligigs that were still only gigs, missing their moving parts. Behind them, lining the fence, was what looked like a small salvage yard, pile after pile of pieces of pipe, metal car parts and hardware, gears in every size from enormous to small enough to fit in the palm of your hand.

'So,' I said, nodding towards that side of the house, 'that's where the magic happens.'

'It's not magic,' he replied, watching Lucy scribble orange all across the top of the page.

'Maybe not to you,' I said as he made his modest face. 'Can I see?'

As we came round the corner of the porch, Lucy, who was toddling along ahead of us, immediately ran down the stairs and towards a large piece that was made up of hubcaps attached to a twisted centre pipe. 'Push! Push!' she demanded, slapping at one of the lower parts with her hand.

'Say please,' Wes told her. When she did, he gave one of the top hubcaps a big push, and the entire piece began spinning, some of the circles rising up, while others moved down, all of it circular, catching the light again and again. Lucy stepped back, watching entranced and silent until it slowed a couple of minutes later, then creaked to a stop.

'More!' she said. She was so excited she was hopping up and down. 'Wes, more!'

Wes looked at me. 'This,' he said dryly, 'can go on for hours.' But he pushed it again anyway.

'Wes?' Delia's voice carried over the trees. 'Can you come over here? I need something heavy lifted.'

'I *said* I can do it,' I heard Bert protest. 'I'm stronger than I look!'

'Wes?' Delia called again. *Poor Bert*, I thought.

'Coming,' Wes replied. To me he said, 'You okay with her for a minute?' When I nodded, he headed round the side of the house. Lucy watched him go, and I wondered if she was going to start screaming. But instead she began walking across the yard with what for a two-year-old seemed like a strong sense of purpose.

When I finally caught up with her, she was at the back fence. Looking over her shoulder, I saw a row of three small heart-in-hand sculptures, miniatures of the one by the side of the road. Each one was slightly different: in the first, the heart had a zigzag across it, like it was broken. In another, the edges of the heart were jagged, pointy and sharp looking. My favourite was the one on the very end, where the heart in the centre of the palm had another, smaller, hand cut into its centre, reminding me of the little nesting dolls I'd had as a kid. All the sculptures were especially rusted and dirty: clearly they'd been there for a while before Lucy pushed aside the grass covering them.

Now, she turned her head and looked at me. 'Hands,' she said.

'Hands,' I repeated. I watched as she took her small hand and pressed it to the hand in the first sculpture, her fingers overlapping the rusted ones, the pale smoothness of her skin contrasting with the dark, ragged metal. Then she glanced back at me and I did the same, pressing my hand to the one beside it.

I felt a shadow fall over us and looked up to see Wes coming back across the yard, with Delia beside him. Lucy turned her head and, seeing her mother, scrambled to her feet and darted across the grass, hurling herself at Delia's knees. Delia looked down at her, shaking her head, and pulled her fingers through Lucy's dark curls.

'What are you guys doing?' Wes asked me.

'She was showing me these,' I told him, nodding towards the sculptures. 'I never knew you made small ones.'

'Just for a little while,' he said dismissively. 'They never really caught on.'

'So,' I said, standing up, 'is it time for potato duty?'

'Nope,' Wes told me. 'False alarm.'

'Really?'

Delia pressed Lucy against her legs. 'It's the strangest thing,' she said, shaking her head. 'Right as we're about to start boiling all those potatoes, I get this phone call from the client. Turns out that they don't want potato salad after all, that they'd rather do coleslaw and macaroni and cheese, which we have plenty of, instead.'

'I tried to tell her,' Wes said, 'that this is a *good* thing.'

'Of course it is,' I told her. 'Why wouldn't it be?'

She smoothed her hand over Lucy's head. 'It's just . . . weird. I don't know. It makes me suspicious.'

Wes just looked at her. 'You know, sometimes things do go the way they're supposed to. It's not unheard of.'

'It is for us,' Delia said with a sigh. 'Anyway, now we at least we have plenty of time to get ready. Which I guess, you know, is good.' She still didn't sound convinced.

'Don't worry,' Wes said as we started back towards her house. 'I'm sure disaster will strike any minute now.'

Delia reached down, taking Lucy's hand. 'Yeah,' she said, seeming encouraged. 'You're probably right.'

As we packed for the job, though, things kept happening. Or, more accurately, *not* happening. Whereas we usually had to cram all the carts in and hope they'd fit, for some reason this time Delia had managed to organize the items in the coolers so economically that we were able to take one less, so everything went in easily, with even (gasp!) room left over. The best round serving platter, which had been missing for weeks, suddenly turned up in the garage, behind one of the freezers. And, most amazing of all, instead of racing down Sweetbud Drive already late, we finished with time to spare and actually found ourselves having to kill time instead of scramble for it. It was a little weird, I had to admit.

Delia and I ended up on the front steps fanning ourselves, while Bert and Wes milled around the garage, packing the last few things. 'So,' she said, leaning back on her hands in an effort to get comfortable. 'I heard you quit your job.'

I glanced at Wes, who was passing by with a box of napkins. 'Couldn't help it,' he said. 'It's just too good not to tell.'

'Maybe you should tell my mom then,' I said, pulling my hair back behind my neck.

'No thanks,' he said, before disappearing back into the garage.

'You really think she'll be mad?' Delia asked me. 'From what you've said about that job, you were miserable there.'

'I was,' I said. 'But to her it's not about that. It's about the fact that I made a commitment.'

'Ah.'

'And that this job would look good on my transcript.'

'I see.'

'And,' I finished, 'it fits right in with what she wants me to be.'

'Which is?'

I ran the fabric of my shirt between my thumb and forefinger, remembering our conversation that morning, as well as the one the night before. 'Perfect,' I said.

Delia shook her head. 'Come on,' she said, waving her hand as if brushing this very thought aside, 'I'm sure she doesn't want that.'

'Why wouldn't she?' I asked.

'Well, for starters, because it's impossible.' She leaned back again, shifting her weight a little bit. 'And, secondly, because she's your mother. And mothers, of all people, are the least likely to care about such things.'

'Yeah, right,' I said glumly.

'I'm serious.' She stretched her feet out in front of her, smoothing her hands over her belly. 'I know something about this, okay? All I care about for Lucy, and Wes and Bert, is that they be happy. Healthy. And good people, you know? I'm not perfect, not by a long shot. So why would I expect them to be?'

'My mom's not like that,' I told her, shaking my head.

'Okay,' she said. 'Then what *is* she like?'

I sat there for a second, considering this, surprised, as the seconds passed, that the answer didn't come more easily. 'She works too much,' I began, then stopped. 'I mean, since my dad died she's had to carry the whole business. There's always so much to do. I worry about her. A lot.'

Delia didn't say anything. I could feel her watching me.

'And I think she works so much because she can be in control of it, you know?' I said. She nodded. 'It makes her feel, I don't know, safe.'

'I can understand that,' Delia said softly. 'Losing someone can make you feel very out of control. Totally so.'

'I know,' I said. 'But it's not really fair. Like, after my dad died, I wanted to be okay for her. So I was. Even when I had to fake it. But now, when I really do feel okay, she's not happy with me. Because I'm not perfect any more.'

'Grieving doesn't make you imperfect,' Delia said quietly as Bert came back out to the van, adjusting one of the carts inside. 'It makes you human. We all deal with things differently, Macy. Your mom is missing your dad in her own way, every day. Maybe you should ask her about it.'

'I can't,' I said. 'I can't even bring him up. I tried this morning for the first time in ages, and she just shut down.'

'Then try again.' She moved closer to me, putting an arm round my shoulder. 'Look, everyone mourns at their own pace. Maybe you're just a little bit ahead of her, but she'll get to you eventually. The important thing is that you keep trying to talk to each other, even if it's difficult at first. It gets easier. I promise.'

I felt so tired all of a sudden that I just relaxed into her shoulder, leaning my head there. She smoothed her hand over my hair, saying nothing. 'Thank you,' I said.

'Oh, sweetie,' she replied, her voice vibrating under my cheek. 'You're so welcome.'

We sat there like that, not talking, for a good minute or two. Then, from the garage, we heard it.

'*Gotcha!*'

It was Bert who shrieked in response to this. I knew it instantly.

Delia sighed loudly. 'Honestly,' she said.

'That's ten,' I heard Wes say, and Bert grumbled something I couldn't make out in return. 'And counting.'

Once we got to the party, our good-luck trend continued. It seemed at first that we were off to a normal start when we arrived to find that the large gas grills Delia had ordered from her equipment company would not, no matter how many times Wes tried, ignite with any sort of flame.

'Oh, my God!' she was hissing at me as people started arriving. 'This is a cookout. A *cookout.* You have to cook outside. It's part of the definition!'

'Delia, just –'

And then, suddenly, there was a whoosh, and we had fire. It turned out that the gas tanks just hadn't been hooked up. No problem.

Then, about an hour later, as I was doing a last round of appetizers before the grilled items came out, Bert noticed that we'd only brought one case of hamburger patties instead of two, which left us about, oh, a hundred or so short.

'Okay,' Delia said, putting her hands to her face, 'God, just let me think . . . think . . .'

'What's wrong?' Wes said as he passed through, picking up more ginger ale for the bar.

'We didn't bring enough hamburgers,' I told him. To Delia I said, 'Look, it's fine, most people probably won't even –'

'Three cases isn't enough?' Wes said.

Delia took her hands off her face. 'There were supposed to be two,' she said, speaking slowly.

'You said three,' he told her. 'I remember.'

'I said two,' she said, sounding out the words carefully.

'I don't think so.'

'Two!' Delia held up two fingers, waving them in the air. 'Two boxes is what I said.'

'But there *are* three,' he told her, speaking equally slowly. 'One in the first cart, two in the cooler. Go check. They're there.'

I did, and they were. Not only were we not scrambling for beef, we had a surplus. And that wasn't all. Bert and I almost collided and spilled condiments all over each other, but I was able to step aside at the last second, disaster averted. The ice-cream scoopers were nowhere to be found, until they magically appeared, in the drawer beneath where they were supposed to be. And so on.

'I'm telling you,' Delia said to me later as we stood in the back of the kitchen, surveying the yard, which was full of happy, well-fed people enjoying food, beverage and each other's company without incident, 'this just makes me *very* nervous.'

'Delia,' I said, watching as Wes poured a glass of wine for a woman in a strappy sundress who was gesturing grandly, talking to him. He was just nodding, in an oh-sure-absolutely way, as if what she was saying was fascinating. As he bent down to scoop ice though, out of her sight, I saw him roll his eyes.

'I know, I know.' She chewed on her pinkie nail. 'It's just so weird. Everything is going too well.'

'Maybe you've just earned it,' I offered. 'You know, the cumulative effect of all those bad nights.'

'Maybe,' she said. 'I just wish we'd have one little mishap. It would be reassuring.'

The weirdest thing was, I could see her point. Once, this sort of night had been all I aspired to, everything going like clockwork, just perfect. But now it was a little eerie. Not to mention, well, boring.

I couldn't help but think, though, as the hour crept from four to four thirty to five, that maybe this was a trend that could work in my favour. After all, in about a half hour I'd get dropped off at the Commons, where I'd have to face my mother and explain quitting the info desk. The closer it got, the more nervous I became. Each time my stomach jumped, though, I reminded myself of what Delia had said to me, about how it might be hard to tell my mother how I really felt, but I had to try anyway. It wouldn't be easy, but it was a start. And like my dad always said, the first step is always the hardest.

I was mulling over this as I stood by the buffet, spatula in hand, when a hand blurred across my vision. 'Hello?' Wes said as I blinked, looking at him. 'Man, where were you?'

'The land of truth and consequences,' I said, poking at the vegetarian option (grilled marinated peppers and spicy black-bean burgers) which had, so far, had no takers. 'Less than an hour before everything hits the fan.'

'Ah, right,' he said, eyeing the veggie burgers disdainfully, 'Jason.'

'Not Jason,' I said. 'God. He's the least of my problems. My *mother*.'

'Oh.' He nodded. 'Right.'

'I haven't even thought about Jason,' I told him, using the spatula to stack the burgers so that maybe they'd look more appetizing. 'I mean, I was dreading seeing him at the library, because that was not going to be a good scene. But now . . . now, everything's different. I mean, we're . . .'

Wes waited, not saying anything, as I searched for the right word. A woman passed by, eyeing the peppers before loading up from the next pan, which was full of steaks.

'Over,' I finished, realizing this myself just as I said it. I could only imagine Jason's response to me quitting the info desk: he'd never want me back now, and that, I realized, was just fine with me. 'It's over,' I said again, testing how I felt as my mouth formed the word. Okay, actually. 'We're over.'

'Wow,' Wes said slowly. 'Are you –'

'Excuse me, are these vegetarian?' I looked up to see a short, squat woman in a bright print dress, holding a plateful of potato chips. She had on thick, wire-rimmed glasses, which clearly were not strong enough for her to make out the sign that said VEGETARIAN ENTRÉE.

'Yes,' I said. 'They are.'

'Are you sure?'

I nodded, then scooped up one of the burgers and put it on her plate. She squinted down at it, then moved on. To Wes I said, 'What were you –'

'Lady at the corner table wants a white-wine spritzer,' Bert reported as he passed by with a trayful of crumpled napkins and empty cups. 'Pronto!'

Wes started round the table, glancing back at me. 'Um, nothing,' he said. 'I'll tell you later.'

As he went back to the bar, Delia moved down the table, rearranging the items in the pans. 'It is just so weird,' she said, taking in the black-bean burgers, 'because I meant to bring more of those, and forgot them. I was so worried we wouldn't have enough!'

'Nope,' I said, waving off a fly that was buzzing over them. 'Plenty.'

'See, again,' she said, sighing. 'Too good. Too good! I don't like this. I need a sense of balance. I never thought I'd admit this, but I need *chaos*.'

Just as we were leaving, she got her wish.

It happened as we were packing the last of our stuff into the van. Wes and I were pushing in the carts, and Delia was at the top of the driveway, getting her cheque from the client, who was so entirely happy with her catering experience that she was paying full price *and* adding a bonus, which was another first. So all was great, wonderful: perfect. And then I heard a shriek.

It wasn't Delia. Nope. It was the client, reacting to the fact that Delia's water had just broken. The baby was on its way.

Chapter SIXTEEN

'Are you okay?'

I nodded. 'I'm fine. Fine.'

This was my mantra, the thing I kept saying in my mind. Actually, though, I wasn't entirely certain. All I knew for sure was that I was at the hospital: everything beyond that, like the last time I'd been here, was a bit of a blur.

After the initial shock of the water breaking, we'd done what we did best: gathered our wits, got a plan and went into action. It wasn't until we'd piled into the van and were on our way to the hospital, Delia beside me, my hand gripped in hers, that I'd glanced at the clock on the dashboard. It was five forty-five, which meant that in fifteen minutes, I was supposed to be meeting my mother at the Commons. Considering how things were going, this should have been my biggest concern. But instead my mind kept drifting back to another ride, not so long ago.

Then, I'd been holding a hand too. My father's, though, had been limp, my fingers doing all the work to hold our palms to each other. Instead of Bert, who was breathing loudly through his nose while Delia waved him off, annoyed, there'd been a paramedic across from me, his hands moving swiftly to attach an oxygen mask and prepare the defibrillator. And instead of the wind whooshing past from Wes's open window, and Delia on her cell phone calmly making arrangements with Pete and the babysitter, there had been an eerie, scary silence, punctuated only by the sound of my heart beating in my ears. Then, a life was ending. Here, one was about to begin. I didn't believe in signs. But it was hard to ignore the fact that someone, somewhere, might have wanted me to go through this again and see there was another outcome.

The memories were everywhere. When we pulled up at the kerb, it was in the same spot. Entering emergency, the doors made that same smooth *swish* noise. Even the smell was the same, that inexplicable mix of disinfectant and florals. For a second, I'd thought for sure I couldn't do it, and found myself hanging back. But then Wes turned back and looked at me, offering the same question he'd been asking ever since. I'd nodded, then fallen in beside him. He was pushing Delia in a wheelchair and she was taking deep, slow breaths, so I did too. When we got on the elevator and the doors slid shut, I finally relaxed and felt myself rise.

What I felt now was a different kind of scared. For the past two and a half hours, I'd sat on the bench in the hallway a few feet down from Delia's room, watching as doctors and nurses first ambled in and out, as if there were a million years before anything really happened, then started moving more quickly, and even more so, and then suddenly everything was a commotion. Machines were beeping, voices calling out names overhead, the floor beneath my feet reverberating as a doctor jogged down the hallway, his stethoscope thumping against his chest.

In my opinion, everyone else was entirely too calm. Especially Wes, who, when he wasn't asking if I were all right, was eating one of the many snack foods he kept disappearing to buy from the vending machine downstairs. Now, as he unwrapped a package of little chocolate doughnuts, offering me one, I shook my head.

'I don't see how you can turn down a chocolate doughnut,' he said, popping one into his mouth. From Delia's doorway, I was sure I heard a groan or a moan, followed by Pete's voice, soothing.

'I don't see how you can *eat*,' I replied as a nurse emerged from the room, her arms full of some sort of linens, and started down the hallway towards the desk.

He chewed for a second, then swallowed. 'This could go on for ages,' he said as Bert, who was sitting on his other side, jerked awake from the nap he'd been taking for the last half hour, blinking. 'You have to keep your strength up.'

'What time is it?' Bert asked sleepily, rubbing his eyes.

Wes handed him a doughnut. 'Almost seven,' he said.

I felt my stomach do a flip-flop, although I wasn't sure it was from hearing that I was now officially an hour late to meet my mother, or from the shriek that came from Delia's room, this one loud and extended enough that we all looked at the slightly open door until it abruptly stopped. In the quiet that followed, I pushed myself to my feet.

'Macy?' Wes said.

'I'm fine,' I said, knowing that was his next question. 'I'm just going to call my mom.'

I'd left my cell phone in the van, so I walked to the line of pay phones, digging some change out of my pocket. The first time, the line was busy and I hung up and tried again. Still busy. I pushed open a door that led outside to a small patio, where I sat for a few minutes, looking at the sky, which was slowly growing darker. It was perfect fireworks weather. Then I went back inside and called again, getting the solid busy beep once more. This time, I held on for her voicemail, then cleared my throat and tried to explain.

'It's me,' I said, 'I know you're probably worried, and I'm really sorry. I was on my way to meet you but Delia went into labour so now I'm at the hospital. I have to wait until someone can drive me, but I'll get there as soon as I can. I'm sorry, again. I'll see you soon.'

There, I thought as I hung up the phone. *Done*. I knew it wouldn't solve everything, or even anything. But I'd deal with that when the time came.

When I came back to the bench where Wes and Bert and I had been sitting, it was empty. In fact, there was nobody in the hallway at all, or at the nurses' station, and for a second I just stood there, feeling totally creeped out. Then Wes stuck his head out of Delia's room. He was grinning.

'Hey,' he said. 'Come see.'

He held the door for me as I stepped inside. Delia was sitting up in the bed, the sheets gathered around her midsection. Her face was flushed, and in her arms was this tiny little thing with dark hair. Pete was sitting on her right, his arm over her shoulders, and they were both looking down at the baby. The room was so quiet, but in a good way. By the window, even Bert, pessimist of pessimists, was smiling.

Then Delia looked up and saw me. 'Hey,' she said softly, waving me over. 'Come say hello.' As I came round the bed, she shifted her arms, so the baby was closer to me. 'Look. Isn't she beautiful?'

Up close, the baby looked even smaller: her eyes were closed, and she was making these little snuffly noises, like she was dreaming about something amazing. 'She's perfect,' I said, and for once it was the exact right word to use.

Delia trailed her finger over the baby's cheek. 'We're calling her Avery,' she said. 'It's Pete's mom's name. Avery Melissa.'

'I like it,' I said.

I stared down at the baby's face, her little nose, the tiny nails on her tiny fingers, and suddenly it all came back to me: getting here, the walk across the lobby, how scared I'd been remembering everything about being with my dad. I could feel it rushing over me and I wanted to block it out, but I steeled myself, tightening my fingers into my palms. Avery's eyes were open now, and they were dark and clear. As she looked at me, I wondered what it was like for the world to be so new, everything a first. Today I hadn't had that luxury: each thing that happened since the moment we pulled up was an echo of something else.

Now I watched Delia study her daughter, smiling and slightly teary, and I had a flash of my own mother, all those months ago, walking out of the waiting room downstairs towards me. More than anything I'd wanted to see something in her expression that gave me hope, but there was nothing. Just the same overwhelming sadness and shock, reflected back at me. That had been when this all began, the shift between us, everything changing.

I felt something ache in my chest, and suddenly I knew I was going to cry. For me, for my mother. For what we'd had taken from us, but also for what we'd given up willingly. So much of a life. And so much of each other.

I swallowed, hard, then backed away from the bed. 'I, um,' I said, and I could feel Wes watching me, 'I need to go try my mom again.'

'Tell her I couldn't have done it without you,' Delia said. 'You were a real pro.'

I nodded, barely hearing this, as Delia bent her head back over the baby, smoothing the blanket round her head.

'Macy,' Wes said as I moved past him, out into the hallway.

'It's just,' I said, swallowing again. 'I . . . need to talk to my mom. I mean, she's worried probably, and she's wondering where I am.'

'Okay,' he said. 'Sure.'

Suddenly I just missed my mother – who once stared at the ocean, who laughed huge belly laughs – so much it was like a pain, something throbbing. I gulped down some air. 'So I'll just do that,' I said to Wes. 'Call my mom. And I'll be back.'

He nodded. 'All right.'

I crossed my arms over my chest as I started towards the elevators, walking quickly, struggling to stay calm, even as tears began to sting my eyes. I could feel my heart beating as I ducked round the next corner to an empty alcove. I barely made it before I was sobbing, hands pressed to my face as the tears just flowed, tumbling over my fingers.

I don't know how long I was there before Wes came. It could have been seconds, or minutes, or hours. He said my name and I wanted to collect myself, but I just couldn't.

When he first put his arms round me, it was tentative, like maybe he expected I'd pull away. When I didn't, he moved in closer, his hands smoothing over my shoulders, and in my mind I saw myself retreating a million times when people tried to do this same thing: my sister or my mother, pulling back and into myself, tucking everything out of sight, where only I knew where to find it. This time, though, I gave in. I let Wes pull me against him, pressing my head against his chest, where I could feel his heart beating, steady and true. I felt someone pass by, looking at us, but to them I was just another person crying in a hospital. I couldn't believe it had taken me this long to finally understand. Delia was right: it was fine, okay, expected. This was what you were supposed to do. And it happened all the time.

We caught the last of the fireworks, the biggest and best, as we walked to the Wish van in the hospital parking lot. As they burst overhead, Wes and Bert and I all stopped to look up at them, the whiz and pop as they shot upwards, and the trailing, winding sparks that fell afterwards. Avery was lucky, I thought. She'd always have a party on her birthday.

After everything that had happened, I'd thought that maybe things would be weird between Wes and me when I finally emerged from the ladies' room, having splashed my face with cold water in an attempt to compose myself somehow. But as usual, he surprised me, walking me back to Delia's room to say our goodbyes as if nothing really out of the ordinary had happened. And maybe it hadn't.

When we turned into Wildflower Ridge, he pulled up at the far edge of the Commons, a decent distance from the picnic and fireworks area, as if he knew I'd need a little bit of a walk to get my head together and prepare myself for the next challenge. In the back seat, Bert was asleep, snoring with his mouth open. Before I opened my door and hopped out, I eased my purse from under his elbow, careful not to wake him.

Wes got out too, stretching his arms over his head as he came to meet me in front of the van. Looking more closely, I could see the party was breaking up, people gathering their blankets and strollers and dogs, chatting with each other as they rounded up the children who weren't already sleeping in arms or over shoulders.

'So,' Wes said, 'what are you doing tomorrow?'

I smiled, shaking my head. 'No idea. You?'

'Not much. Got a few errands to take care of in the afternoon. I'm thinking about running in the morning, maybe trying that loop in this neighbourhood.'

'Really,' I said. 'Are you going to ask me *the* question? Maybe shout it from the street?'

'Maybe,' he said, smiling. 'You never know. So you'd better be ready. I'll probably pass by around nine or so. I'll be the one moving really slowly.'

'Okay,' I said. 'I'll keep an eye out.'

He started back to the driver's side. 'Have a good night.'

'You too,' I said. 'And thanks.'

Once he was gone, I took a deep breath, then started across the Commons to find my mother. There was so much I wanted to say to her, and for once I wouldn't overthink, instead just letting the words come. Delia had convinced me that my mother only wanted me to be happy. It was up to me to show her that I was now, and why.

After picking my way through the crowd, dodging little kids and various dogs, I spotted my mother talking to Mrs Burcock, the president of the homeowner's association. I watched her as she listened, waving now and then at people passing by. The night had clearly been a success, and she seemed relaxed as I walked up to stand beside her. She turned and glanced at me, smiling, then redirected her attention back to what Mrs Burcock was saying.

'. . . and bring it up at the meeting next week. I just really think a pooper-scoop rule would improve things for everyone, especially out here on the Commons.'

'Absolutely,' my mother replied. 'Let's bring it to the table and see how everyone responds.'

'Well, Macy,' Mrs Burcock said to me. She was an older woman with a prim haircut. 'Did you have a good evening?'

'I did,' I said. I could feel my mother watching me. 'Did you?'

'Oh, it was just wonderful. We'll have to start planning next year, right, Deborah?'

My mother laughed. 'Starting tomorrow,' she said. 'First thing.'

Mrs Burcock smiled, then waved and started across the

Commons towards her house. My mother and I stood there for a second, not talking, as more neighbours passed on either side of us.

'So,' I said. 'Did you get my message?'

She turned her head and looked at me, and I saw, in that one moment, that she was mad. Beyond mad. Furious. I couldn't believe I'd missed it before.

'Not now,' she said, her lips hardly moving as she formed the words.

'What?'

'We are not,' she said, and this time I could hear, clearly, the absolute rigidness in her voice, 'going to discuss this now.'

'Great event, Deborah!' A man in khakis and a golf shirt called out as he passed us, a couple of kids in tow.

'Thanks, Ron,' my mother replied, smiling. 'Glad you enjoyed it!'

'Mom, it wasn't my fault,' I said. I took a breath: this wasn't how I wanted this to go. 'Delia went into labour, and I couldn't –'

'Macy.' Never before had I flinched at the sound of my own name. But I did now. Big time. 'I want you to go home, get changed and get into bed. We'll discuss this later.'

'Mom,' I said. 'Just let me explain; you don't understand. Tonight was –'

'Go.' When I didn't, she just stared at me, then said, '*Now.*'

And then she turned her back and walked away. Just walked away from me, her posture straight, crossing over to where her employees were waiting for her. I watched her as she listened to them, giving her full attention, nodding, all the things she hadn't, for even one second, done for me.

I walked home, still in shock, and went up to my room. As I passed my mirror I stopped, seeing my shirt was untucked, my jeans had a barbecue-sauce stain on them, my hair and face were all mussed and wild from crying. I looked different, absolutely: even if I hadn't been able to explain it, all that had happened showed on my face, where my mother had seen it, instantly. *Get changed*, she said, which was ironic, because all I'd wanted to tell her was that I already had.

I was so screwed.

It wasn't just that I hadn't showed up for the picnic. It was also the fact that Jason, arriving at the info desk to find I'd quit, had immediately called my cell phone, then my house. Not finding me available, he discussed the situation with my mother, who had been trying to reach me ever since. I'd forgotten to turn my phone back on, then left it in the van, never checking it afterwards. Until late that night, when I finally pulled it out of my bag. I had ten messages.

Put plainly, I was in big trouble. Luckily, I had someone around who knew that area, could recognize the landmarks and knew the best road out.

'When you first get down there, just let her talk,' Caroline said. She'd been unlucky enough to stop in that morning en route from the beach house, walking right into this maelstrom. Now we were in the bathroom, where I was devoting twice as much time as usual to brushing my teeth as I attempted to put off the inevitable. 'Sit and listen. Don't nod. Oh, and don't smile. That really makes her mad.'

I rinsed, then spat. 'Right.'

'You have to apologize, but don't do it right off, because it seems really ungenuine. Let her blow it out of her system, and then say you're sorry. Don't make excuses, unless you have a really valid one. Do you?'

'I was at the *hospital*,' I said, picking up the bottle of mouthwash. If I was going down, at least I'd have nice breath. 'My friend was giving birth.'

'Was there not a phone there?' she asked.

'I called her!' I said.

'An *hour* after you were supposed to be at the picnic,' she pointed out.

'God, Caroline. Whose side are you on?'

'Yours! That's why I'm helping you – can't you see?' She sighed impatiently. 'The phone thing is so basic, she'll go to that right off. Don't even try to make an excuse; there isn't one. You can always find a phone. *Always*.'

I took in a mouthful of Listerine, then glared at her.

'Tears help,' she continued, leaning against the doorjamb and examining her fingernails, 'but only if they're real. The fake cry only makes her more angry. Basically, you just have to ride it out. She's always really harsh at first, but once she starts talking she calms down.'

'I'm not going to cry,' I told her, spitting.

'And, oh, whatever you do,' she said, 'don't interrupt her. That's, like, *lethal*.'

She'd barely finished this sentence when my mother's voice came from the bottom of the stairs. 'Macy?' she said. 'Could you come down here, please.'

It wasn't a question. I looked at Caroline, who was biting

her lip, as if experiencing some sort of post-traumatic flashback.

'It's okay,' she said. 'Take a deep breath. Remember everything I told you. And now –' she put her hands on my shoulders, squeezing them as she turned me round – 'go.'

I went. My mother who was waiting at the kitchen table, already dressed in her work clothes, did not look up until I sat down. *Uh-oh*, I thought. I put my hands on the table, folding them over each other in what I hoped was a submissive pose, and waited.

'I'm extremely disappointed in you,' she said, her voice level. '*Extremely*.'

I felt this. In my gut, which burned. In my palms, which were sweating. It was what I had worked to avoid for so long. Now it was crashing over me like a wave, and all I could do was swim up towards the surface and hope there was air there.

'Macy,' she said now, and I felt myself blinking, 'What happened last night was unacceptable.'

'I'm sorry,' I blurted, too early, but I couldn't help it. I hated how my voice sounded, shaky, not like me. The night before I'd been so brave, ready to say all and everything. Now, all I could do was sit there.

'There are going to be some changes,' she said, her voice louder now. 'I can't count on you to make them, so I will.'

I wondered fleetingly if my sister were sitting on the steps, knees pulled to her chest, as I had been so many times, hearing her addressed this way.

'You will not be catering any more. Period.'

I felt a 'but' rising in my throat, then bit it back. Ride it out, Caroline had said, the worst is always first. And Delia was going to be out of commission for a while anyway. 'Okay,' I said.

'Instead,' she said, dropping her hand to the arm of her chair, 'you'll be working for me, at the model home, handing out brochures and greeting clients. Monday through Saturday, nine to five.'

Saturday? I thought. But of course. It was the busiest day as far as walk-in traffic went. And all the better to keep me under her thumb. I took a breath, holding it in my mouth, then let it out.

'I don't want you seeing your friends from catering,' she continued. 'All of the issues I have with your behaviour – staying out late, showing less concern about your commitments – began when you took that job.'

I kept looking at her, trying to remember everything I'd felt the night before, that sudden welling of emotion that had made me miss her so much. But each time I did, I just saw her steely, professional façade, and I wondered how I could have been so mistaken.

'From now until school starts, I want you in by eight every night,' she continued. 'That way, we can be sure that you'll be home and rested enough to focus on preparing for the school year.'

'Eight?' I said.

She levelled her gaze at me, and I saw my sister was right. Interruptions were lethal. 'It could be seven,' she said. 'If you'd prefer.'

I looked down at my hands, silent, shaking my head. All

around us the house was so quiet, as if it, too, was just waiting for this to be over.

'You have half a summer left,' she said to me, as I studied my thumbnail, the tiny lines running along it. 'It's up to you how it goes. Do you understand?'

I nodded, again. When she didn't say anything for a minute I looked up to see her watching me, waiting for a real answer. 'Yes,' I said. 'I understand.'

'Good.' She pushed back her chair and stood up, smoothing her skirt. As she passed behind me, she said, 'I'll see you at the model home in an hour.'

I just sat there, listening to her heels clack across the kitchen, then go mute as she hit the carpet, heading to her office. I stayed in place as she gathered her briefcase, then called out a goodbye to Caroline as she left, the door shutting with a quiet thud behind her.

A few seconds later I heard my sister come down the stairs. 'That,' she said, 'was pretty bad.'

'I can't see my friends,' I said. 'I can't do anything.'

'She'll ease up,' she told me, glancing towards the door. She didn't sound entirely convinced, though. 'Hopefully.'

But she wouldn't. I knew that already. My mother and I had an understanding: we worked together to be as much in control of our shared world as possible. I was supposed to be her other half, carrying my share of the weight. In the last few weeks, I'd tried to shed it, and doing so sent everything off kilter. So of course she would pull me tighter, keeping me in my place, because doing so meant she would always be sure, somehow, of her own.

I went up to my room and sat down on my bed, listening to the sounds of the neighbourhood: a lawn mower, someone's sprinkler whirring, kids riding their bikes in a nearby cul-de-sac. And then, later, the sound of footsteps coming down the sidewalk. I looked at my watch: it was 9:05. The footsteps approached, getting louder and louder, and then slowed as they passed my house. I peered under my shade and, sure enough, it was Wes. He was still moving, but slowly, as if maybe he was hoping I'd come out and join him, or at least wave hello. Maybe he might have even asked that question. But I didn't do anything. I couldn't. I just sat there, as the rest of my summer began to sink in and, a second later, he picked up the pace and moved on.

Chapter SEVENTEEN

It was Tuesday night, six fifteen on the nose. My mother and I were having dinner and making conversation. Now that we worked together, this was even easier, since we always had something safe to talk about.

'I think we're going to see a real upswing in the townhouse sales this week,' she said to me as she helped herself to more bread. She offered me the bowl, but I shook my head. 'The interest has been higher lately, don't you think?'

When my punishment had first started, I'd sulked openly, making sure my mother knew how much I disagreed with what she'd done to me. Pretty soon I'd figured out this didn't help my case, though, so I'd progressed to the cold but polite stage, which meant I answered when addressed, but offered no more than the most basic of responses.

'There have been a lot of walk-ins,' I said.

'There really have.' She picked up her fork. 'We'll just have to see, I guess.'

By the time we finished eating, I'd have about an hour and a half before curfew. If I didn't go out to yoga class or to the bookstore to browse and drink a mocha (basically the only two allowed options for my 'free' time), I'd watch TV or get my clothes ready for work the next day, or just sit on my bed, the window open beside me, and study my SAT word book. It was weird how if I flipped back enough pages, I could see the way I'd carefully made notes, earlier in the summer, next to the harder words, or underlined their prefixes or suffixes neatly. I couldn't even remember doing that now: it was like it was another person, some other girl.

Once, this had been the life I'd wanted. Even chosen. Now, though, I couldn't believe that there had been a time when this kind of monotony and silence, this most narrow of existences, had been preferable. Then again, once, I'd never known anything else.

'Caroline should be coming into town again next week,' my mother said, putting her fork down and wiping her mouth with a napkin.

'Thursday, I think,' I replied.

'We'll have to plan to have dinner, so we can all catch up.'

I took a sip of my water. 'Sure.'

My mother had to know I was unhappy. But it didn't matter: all she cared about was that I was her Macy again, the one she'd come to depend on, always within earshot or reach. I came to work early, sat up straight at my desk and endured the monotony of answering phones and greeting potential homebuyers with a smile on my face. After dinner, I spent my hour and a half of free time alone, doing accepted activities. When I came home afterwards, my mother would be waiting for me, sticking her head out of her office to verify that, yes, I was just where I was supposed to be. And I was. I was also miserable.

'This salad,' she said now, taking a sip from her wine glass, 'is just wonderful.'

'Thanks,' I told her. 'The chicken's good too.'

'It is, isn't it?'

Around us, the house was dark and quiet. Empty.

'Yes,' I said. 'It really is.'

I missed Kristy. I missed Delia. But, most of all, I missed Wes.

He'd called the first night of my punishment, my cell phone buzzing as I sat on my bed, contemplating the rest of my summer, which now seemed to stretch out ahead of me, endless and flat. I'd been feeling sorry for myself all day, but it really kicked into overdrive the minute I punched the TALK button and heard his voice.

'Hey,' he said. 'How's it going?'

'Don't ask.'

He did though, as I knew he would, just as I knew he would listen, making sympathetic noises, as I outlined my restrictive curfew and the very real possibility that I might not see him again, ever. I didn't go so far as to tell him that he and everyone else from Wish were off limits, although I had a feeling he probably knew that too.

'You'll be okay,' he said. 'It could be worse.'

'How?'

The only noise was the buzzing of the line as he considered this. 'Could be forever,' he said finally.

'It's until the end of the summer,' I said. 'It *is* forever.'

'Nah. It just seems like it now, because it's the first day. You'll see. It'll go fast.'

This was easy for him to say. While my life had slowed to a near stop, Wes's was now busier than ever. When he wasn't working on sculptures to keep up with increasing demand, he was driving to garden art places to drop off pieces and take new orders. At night, he was working the job he'd taken delivering for A la Carte, a store that specialized in high-end, restaurant-quality dinner entrées brought right to your door. Most of our conversations lately had taken place while he was en route to one delivery or another. While I sat in my room, staring out the window, he was constantly in motion, crisscrossing town with bags of chicken parmigiana and shrimp scampi riding shotgun beside him. I was always happy to hear his voice. But it wasn't the same.

We didn't talk about our Truth game, other than to agree to keep it on hold until we got to see each other face to face. Sometimes, at night, when I sat out on my roof alone, I'd run over the questions and answers we'd traded back and forth in my head. For some weird reason, I was afraid I might forget them otherwise, like they were vocabulary words or something else I had to study to keep close at hand.

Kristy had been in touch as well, calling to extend invitations to come over and sunbathe, or go to parties (she knew I was grounded, but like 'free time' for my mother, this was clearly a flexible term for her), or just to talk about her new boyfriend. His name was Baxter, and they'd met when he stopped by the produce stand while she was sitting in for Stella one day. He'd talked to her for over an hour, then, besotted, bought an entire bushel of cucumbers. This was clearly extraordinary, or at least notable, and now she was busy much of the time too. That was the thing about being on the inside: the world was just going on, even when it seemed like time for you had stopped for good.

I was bored. Sad. Lonely. It was only a matter of time before I cracked.

I'd had a long day at the model home, stapling Welcome packets and listening to my mother give her sales spiel to six different prospective clients. It was the same thing I'd done the day before, and the day before that. Which was bad enough even before you factored in that I'd eat the same dinner (chicken and salad) with the same person (my mother) at the same time (six sharp), then fill the hours before bedtime the same way (yoga and studying). With all of this combined, the monotony hit lethal levels. So it was no wonder I was feeling totally hopeless and trapped, even before I went home and found an email from Jason.

Macy,
I've been wanting to get in touch with you, but I haven't been sure what to say. I don't know if your mom told you, but I came on the Fourth because my grandmother had a stroke, and she's been deteriorating ever since. We're very close, as you know, but even so dealing with this, and the very real possibility that she may not make it, has been harder for me than I expected. I was disappointed to hear that you quit the info desk, and while I have a few ideas on the subject, I'd like to know, in your own words, what it was that precipitated that decision.

That's not really why I'm writing, however. I guess with everything that's happening in my own family right now I feel like I've had some added insight into how things must have been for you in the last couple of years. I think I was hard on you about the info desk earlier this summer, and for that I apologize. I know I suggested that we be on a break until I return, but I hope that whatever happens we can at least stay in contact, and stay friends. I hope you'll write back. I'd really like to hear from you.

I had read it twice, but it still didn't really make sense. I'd thought that quitting the info desk would be the final proof he needed that I would never be the girl for him. Now, though, with the prospect of loss hovering over him, he seemed to think the opposite. If anyone understood, I could see him reasoning, with that even, cool logic, it was me. Right?

'No,' I said aloud. My mind was spinning. A week and a half earlier it had seemed like my life had changed for good. That *I* had changed it. But now it was all slipping away. I was back to being my mother's daughter, and, with this, it seemed maybe I could be Jason's girlfriend too. If I didn't take action, somehow, by the fall everything that had happened with Wish, and with Wes, would be smoothed over, forgotten, no more than a dream. So that night, after I'd wiped the counters down and put away the leftovers, I picked up my yoga mat, told my mother I'd be back by eight, and broke her rules, driving off to Sweetbud Drive.

I pulled in to the still signless road, and dodged the hole

unthinkingly, glancing at the heart in hand as I passed it. I was looking at everything, surprised that it didn't seem all that different until I realized it had only been about ten days since I'd last been there.

First I pulled into Wes's driveway, but his truck was gone, the house dark. I walked round the side of the house to his workshop. There were more pieces than ever grouped in the yard: I saw angels, a few large whirligigs, and one piece that was medium sized, barely begun, with only the frame of a stick figure with some brackets attached to the back.

On my way to Kristy's, I slowed down in front of Delia's house, peering through the front window. I could see Pete walking with Avery in his arms, rocking her, and Delia beyond him, stirring something on the stove as Lucy sat at her feet, stacking blocks on top of each other. I knew she would have been happy to see me, but instead I just watched them for a second, feeling sort of sad. It was as if everything had closed up and grown over my absence, like I'd never been there at all.

When I pulled in the driveway of the doublewide, I could see the light of the TV through the window. As I got out of my car and started up the steps, Bert came out of the front door. He was in khakis and a collared golf shirt that looked to be polyester, and he reeked of cologne. I actually smelled him before I saw him.

'Hey,' I said. I was trying not to wince. 'You look nice.'

He smiled, obviously pleased. 'Got a date,' he said, hooking his fingers in his pockets and leaning back on his heels. 'Going out to dinner.'

'That's great,' I said. 'Who's the girl?'

'Her name's Lisa Jo. I met her at the Armageddon social. She's, like, an expert on the Big Buzz. Last summer, she went out west with her dad and recorded evidence of it.'

'Really.' A female Bert. I couldn't even imagine.

'Yup.' He hopped off the step and started down the walk. 'See you later.'

'Bye,' I said, watching as he cut through the garden, down the winding path that led back to his house. 'Have fun.'

I pulled open the doublewide door and called out a hello, then stepped inside. There was no answer, and I glanced down the hallway to Kristy's room: the door was open, the light off. Looking the other way, I saw only Monica sitting on the couch, staring at the TV.

'Hey,' I said again, and she turned her head slightly, finally seeing me. 'Where's Kristy?'

'Out,' she replied.

'With Baxter?' She nodded. 'Oh,' I said, crossing the room and sitting down on the ottoman in front of Stella's chair. 'I thought maybe she'd be in tonight.'

'Nope.'

It was just too damn ironic that, in desperately seeking conversation, I'd ended up with, of all people, Monica. What was even sadder was that I stayed where I was, making various stabs at it anyway.

'So,' I said, as she flipped channels, 'what's been going on?'

'Nothing.' She paused on a rap video, then moved on. 'You?'

'I've been grounded,' I said, a bit too eagerly. 'I mean, I still am grounded, technically. I'm not supposed to be here . . . but

I got this email from my boyfriend, and it kind of flipped me out. It's just . . . I feel like everything's changing, you know?'

'Mmm-hmm,' she said sympathetically.

'It's just weird,' I said, wondering why I was telling her all this, and yet fully unable to stop, 'I don't know what to do.'

She took in a breath, and for a second I thought I might actually get a full sentence. But then she sighed and said, 'Uh-huh.'

Clearly, this was not what I needed. So I said my goodbyes, leaving Monica still flipping channels, and drove back into town. And there, at a traffic light by the Lakeview Mall, I finally found what I was looking for.

Wes. He was across the way, facing me, and I flicked my lights at him. When the light changed, he pulled into the lot in front of Milton's Market while I turned round and doubled back to meet him.

'I thought you were grounded,' he said, as I got out of my car and walked over to where he was standing in front of the truck. I couldn't believe how happy I was to see him.

'I am,' I said. 'I'm at yoga.'

He looked at me, raising his eyebrows, and I felt myself smile, suddenly feeling reassured. Of course I wouldn't go back to Jason. Of course I wasn't the same girl again. It had just taken seeing Wes to remind me.

'Okay, so I'm not at yoga,' I said. I shook my head. 'God, this night has just been . . . I don't know. Weird. I just needed to get out. Too much to think about.'

He nodded, running a hand through his hair. 'I know the feeling.'

'So what are you doing?' I asked. 'Working?'

'Um,' he said, glancing at the truck, 'not really. I took the night off. I have a bunch of stuff I have to get done.'

I looked at my watch, then said, 'I have another hour before I'm due home. You want company?'

'Um,' he said again. I noticed this, for some reason. In fact, as I stood there, I noticed that he was jumpy, nervous even. 'Better not. I've got to meet with this client at seven thirty. You'd be late.'

'Oh.' I tucked a piece of hair behind my ear, and neither of us said anything for a minute, a silence more awkward than any I'd ever felt between us. *Something's going on*, I thought, and immediately I flashed back to that night at the hospital, when I'd cried. Maybe it had been too much, and had freaked him out. We'd only talked on the phone since then, hadn't seen each other. For all I knew, this change had happened ages ago, and I was only just catching up with it now.

'It's just,' he said, as I turned my head, watching a car pass by, 'just this thing I have to do. You wouldn't want to come.'

I felt my body reacting, my posture straightening, as I shifted into the defensive mode I knew so well. 'Yeah, I should go anyway,' I said.

'Well, hang out for a second,' he said. 'What's been going on?'

'Not much.' I looked at my watch. 'God, I'm gonna go. It's stupid for me to even be risking this, with everything that's happened. And I have this email from Jason to answer.'

'Jason?' He looked surprised. 'Really.'

I nodded, flipping my car keys in my hand. 'I don't know,

he's having some problems, we're in touch. He wants to get back together, I think.'

'Is that what you want?'

'I don't know,' I said, even though I knew it wasn't. 'Maybe.'

He was looking at me now: I had his full attention. Which was why I turned my back and started walking to my car.

'Macy,' he said, 'hold on a second.'

'I really have to go,' I told him. 'I'll see you around.'

'Wait.' I was still walking, but I could hear him coming up behind me, knew he'd put his hand on my shoulder even before he did. 'Are you okay?'

'Yes,' I said, and started walking again. 'I'm fine.' Even when I got to my car and opened the door, he hadn't moved, stayed there as I drove away. I would have thought this would make me feel better, for once getting to be the one to leave and not the one left behind. But it didn't. Not at all.

I was almost all the way home when I turned round.

But he was gone. I sat at the light for a second, the big time and temperature sign at Willow Bank blinking above me: 7:24, 78 degrees. I kept looking from the red stoplight to the numbers, then back again, and all of a sudden I knew where to go.

Call it a gut feeling, but all the way to the World of Waffles I was sure that, somehow, I could fix this. Maybe I'd just been too sensitive. He had a lot on his mind. It probably had nothing to do with me. But he *had* been acting so weird, checking his watch. That I knew I hadn't imagined. But, regardless, he needed to know why I'd been so cold to him, how important he was to me. Maybe that would freak him out too. But it was the Truth. And we'd always held to that.

As soon as I saw his truck parked in the lot, I felt myself relax. *I can do this*, I thought, as I pulled in two spaces down and cut my engine, then pushed my door open. The air was full of that sweet, doughy smell, and as I started towards the front door, I reminded myself that this, too, was proof that I had changed. Once, I would have just let Wes go. But I was different now.

I was different all the way across the parking lot, to the edge of the kerb, almost to the door. But then I saw him, sitting in the same booth against the window. He wasn't alone.

Gotcha, I thought, and it was weird that it felt exactly the same way, a sudden shock, a jump of the heart, like your entire system shuts down, and then, as you stand there gasping, somehow reboots. Somehow.

I hadn't heard a lot about Becky, but I recognized her with just one look. Like Wes had said, she was skinny, angular, with a short haircut, the ends of which barely touched her collarbone. She had a thin black tank top on, a rosary necklace and dark-red lipstick, which had already stained the rim of the coffee mug she was holding between her hands. Wes was sitting opposite her, talking, and she was looking at him intently, her gaze steady, as if what he was saying were the most important thing in the world. And it probably was. Maybe he was telling her his deepest secrets. Or asking her the question I'd been waiting for. I'd never know.

I got back in my car, starting the engine, then drove off. It wasn't until I pulled onto the highway that it all really sunk in, how temporary our friendship had been. We'd been on our breaks, after all, but it wasn't our relationships that were on pause: it was us. Now we were both in motion again, moving ahead. So what if there were questions left unanswered. Life went on. We knew that better than anyone.

Chapter EIGHTEEN

For weeks, my mother had been concerned about me. Now, it was my turn to really worry.

My mother had always worked hard. But I'd never seen her like this. Maybe it was just that I was up close now, for six or seven hours each day, where I could hear the constant string of phone conversations, the clattering of her answering emails and watch the constant stream of contractors, realtors and salespeople coming in and out of her office. It was now July twenty-third, which meant the townhouse opening and the gala celebrating it were a little over two weeks away. Everyone else seemed to think things were going well, but my mother wasn't happy with the pre-sales. Or the marble tubs that had been installed so far. Or several of her contractors, who, at least in her view, cared more about little things like sleeping and the occasional Sunday off than getting everything done exactly right, ahead of schedule. I'd been aware for a while of how tired she looked, and how she hardly ever seemed to smile. But all of a sudden I began to see that things were worse than I'd realized.

Maybe I should have noticed earlier, but I'd been distracted with my own problems. After what happened with Wes, though,

I'd stopped resisting my punishment. It was weird how, with things pretty much done between us, I could so easily go back to the life I'd had before. I found myself forgetting the girl I'd become, who'd been, if not fearless, not as afraid.

My life was quiet, organized and silent. My mother's, however, was fast and frenetic. She never seemed to sleep, and she was losing weight, the dark circles under her eyes clearly visible, despite her always careful application of concealer. More and more I found myself watching her, worrying about the toll her stress was taking on her body. Sometimes you had signs: sometimes you didn't. But I kept a close eye anyway.

'Mom,' I said one day, as I stood in her open door, the chicken salad sandwich I'd ordered for her in my hand. It was now two thirty, which meant it had been sitting on the corner of my desk, the mayonnaise in it certainly courting food poisoning, for almost three hours. 'You have to eat. Now.'

'Oh, honey, I will,' she said, picking up some pink message slips and flipping through them. 'Bring it in. I'll get to it as soon as I finish this.'

I came in just as she started talking on the phone again, clicking away at her keyboard. Arranging her sandwich on a paper plate, I listened as she talked with the chef she'd hired for the gala, who called himself Rathka. He'd come highly recommended, but so far he and my mother had butted heads repeatedly, about his erratic schedule (he never seemed to answer the phone), the expensive china dishes he insisted she rent (because only they allowed the full culinary experience) and the menu, about which he'd so far declined to give specifics.

'What I mean,' my mother was saying as I poured her a Diet Coke, putting it next to her sandwich, 'is that because I am inviting seventy-five people, and because this is a most important event, I'd like to have a bit more of a concrete idea of what we'll be eating.'

I folded a napkin, sliding it under the edge of her paper plate, then nudged both closer to her elbow. Only when they bumped it did she look up at me, mouthing a thank you. But then she only took a sip of the Diet Coke, ignoring the sandwich altogether.

'Yes, I understand there will be lamb,' she said, rolling her eyes. Lately it seemed like my mother was battling with everyone. 'But lamb does not a full menu make . . . It means, I need more details.' There was a pause. 'I understand that you're an artiste, Rathka. But I am a businesswoman. And I need some idea of what I'm paying for.'

I went back to my desk and sat down, swivelling in my chair, and punched a few keys, calling up my own email account. While working for my mother kept me busier than the info desk ever had, there was the occasional bit of downtime. It was then that I always seemed to find myself staring at another email from Jason.

The night I'd seen Wes, I'd come home to find Jason's message still on my screen. While my first thought was to just delete and ignore it, I reconsidered. So I sat down, my fingers poised over the keyboard. Being pushed back to this life was one thing. Now at least I felt like I was choosing it. And it wasn't like I had other options, anyway.

I wrote to Jason that I hated the info desk, that I just felt like it wasn't the job for me and I probably should have quit right away instead of staying. I told him how his other email, announcing our break, had hurt me, and how I wasn't sure how I felt about us getting back together at the end of the summer, or ever. But I also told him I was sorry about his grandmother, and that if he needed to talk, I was here. It was the least I could do, I figured. I wasn't going to turn my back on someone in their moment of weakness.

So now we were in contact, if you could call it that. Our emails were short and to the point: he talked about Brain Camp, how it was stimulating but a lot of work, and I wrote about my mother and how stressed out she was. I didn't worry so much about what he thought of what I wrote, what he might read between the lines. I didn't race to answer him either, sometimes letting a day or two go before I replied, letting the words come at their own pace. When they did, I'd just type them up and hit Send, trying not to overthink. He always wrote back faster than I did, and had even started hinting about us seeing each other the day he got back, the seventh, which was also the day of the gala. The more I pulled back, the more he seemed to move forward. I wondered if it was really because he cared about me, or if now I was just another challenge.

I still thought about Wes a lot. It had been about two weeks now, and we hadn't talked. The first few days afterwards he tried to call me on my cell phone, but when I saw his number pop up on the screen I just slid it aside, letting it ring, and eventually turned it off entirely. I knew what he'd think: we'd just been friends, after all, and we'd always talked about Becky and Jason before, so why not now? I didn't know the answer to this, just as I didn't know why it had bothered me so much to see him with Becky. She'd come back to him, just like Jason had come back to me, and I knew he was probably happy about that. I should have been happy too, but I just wasn't.

Occasionally I heard from Kristy, who had in this interim gone from smitten with Baxter to positively lovesick. 'Oh, Macy,' she'd sigh in my ear, sounding so wistful and happy I could have hated her, if I hadn't thought she so deserved it. 'He's just extraordinary. Truly extraordinary.'

I kept waiting for her to bring up Becky, and her and Wes being back together, but she never did, knowing, probably, that it was a sore subject. She did, however, say that Wes had been asking about me, and she wondered if something had happened between us. 'Is that what he said?' I asked her.

'No,' she'd replied, switching the phone to her other ear. 'It's Wes. He never says anything.'

Once he had, I thought. Once he'd said a lot, to me. 'It's nothing,' I told her. 'We just, you know, don't have that much in common.' And maybe this was true, after all.

It was a Friday, which was supposed to be a good thing. For me, though, and the concrete guy in my mother's office, things were just going from bad to worse.

'. . . and I will not be paying any overtime for a job that was guaranteed to be done over a week ago!' I could hear my mother say. This was the fourth meeting she'd had with a subcontractor today, and they'd all gone pretty much the same way. As in, not well.

'The weather,' the concrete guy inside said, 'was –'

'The weather,' my mother shot back, interrupting him, 'is something that you, as a professional who deals with it as a factor in all jobs, should take into consideration when submitting a bid for work. This is summer. It rains!'

My mother's voice, so brittle and shrill these days, sent a chill down my spine. I could only imagine how the concrete guy felt.

There was a bit more back and forth, and then their voices dropped, which meant this meeting was almost over. Sure enough, a second later the door opened, and the concrete guy, heavy-set and irritated-looking, mumbled past my desk and slammed out of the office, the windows rattling in his wake.

My phone buzzed, and I picked it up. 'Macy,' my mother said. She sounded exhausted. 'Could you bring me a water, please?'

I reached into the small fridge beside my desk to get one, then pushed out my chair and walked to her door. For once, my mother was not on the phone or staring at the computer screen. Instead, she was sitting back in her desk chair, looking out the window at the sign across the street advertising the townhouses. There was a truck parked in front of it, so you could see only the last part: AVAILABLE AUGUST 8TH. SIGN UP FOR YOURS NOW!

I twisted the cap off the water, then slid it across the desk to her. I watched her take a sip, closing her eyes, then said, 'You okay?'

'I'm fine,' she said automatically, unthinkingly. 'It's always like this at the end of a project. It was like this with the houses, and the apartments. It doesn't matter if it's fifty million-dollar townhouses or one spec house. Everything always gets crazy at the end. You just have to keep going, regardless of how awful it gets. So that's what I do.' She sipped at her water again. 'Even on days like this, when I'm sure it's going to kill me.'

'Mom,' I said. 'Don't even say that.'

She smiled again, a tired smile, the only smile I ever saw from her lately. 'It's just an expression,' she said, but I still felt uneasy. 'I'm fine.'

For the rest of the afternoon, I busied myself with the gala guest list. At four forty-five, I sat back in my chair, grateful I only had fourteen minutes and counting before I got to escape. Then, though, two things happened. The phone rang, and my sister walked in.

'Wildflower Ridge Sales,' I said, waving at her as she shut the door behind her and walked up to my desk.

'Meez Queensh pleeze es Raffka,' the voice on the other end said. Rathka, besides having an accent that made him almost completely incomprehensible, always seemed to talk with his mouth pressed right up to the receiver.

'Right, hold please.' I hit the button, then looked up at Caroline, who was standing in front of me, hands clasped together, her face expectant. 'Hey,' I said. 'What's up?'

She took a breath to answer, but then my mother opened her office door, sticking her head out. 'Is line one for me?' she asked, then saw my sister. 'Caroline, hello. When did you get here?'

My sister looked at her, then back at me. Clearly, she was working up to something. She took in another breath, smiled, then said, 'It's done.'

There was a second or two of silence as my mother and I processed this. On the phone in front of me, the red light was blinking.

'It's done,' my mother repeated slowly.

Caroline was still looking at us, expectant.

'The beach house,' I said finally. 'Right?'

'Yes!' Caroline clapped her hands, three times fast, like this was a game show and I'd won the showcase showdown. 'It's done! And it's fabulous. Fabulous! You have to come and see it. Right now.'

'Now?' My mother glanced at the clock, then back at my blinking phone. 'But it's –'

'Friday. Quitting time. The weekend.' Caroline, clearly, had thought this through. 'I've gassed up my car and bought sandwiches so we won't even have to stop for dinner. If we leave in the next half hour, we might even get there for the last of the sunset.'

My mother put her hand on my desk. I watched her fingers curl round the edge. 'Caroline,' she said slowly, 'I'm sure it's just wonderful. But I can't get away this weekend. There's just too much work to do.'

It took Caroline a second to react to this. 'It's just one night,' she said after a minute. 'You can come back first thing tomorrow.'

'I have a meeting in the morning with my superintendents. We're on a very tight schedule. I can't get away.'

Caroline lowered her hands to her sides. 'But you've been saying that all summer.'

'That's because it's been true all summer. It's just a bad

time.' My mother looked at the phone again, that blinking light, still so insistent. 'Who is that holding?'

'Rathka,' I said quietly.

'I should take it. It's probably important.' She started back to her office, then turned and looked at my sister, who was just standing there, like she was in shock. I felt a pang of pity, thinking of her buying sandwiches, stocking a cooler, how excited she must have been to show us the house. 'Honey,' my mother said, pausing in the doorway, 'I know how much you've put into this, and I so appreciate everything you've done.'

I wasn't sure that she did, though. That either of us did. For the past few weeks, my sister had been in constant transit between the beach house and her own, stopping during each trip to give us an update. My mother and I, concerned with our own problems, had given what attention we could, but neither of us was ever as involved as she would have liked us to be.

Now, she stood in the doorway, biting her lip. I'd never thought I had that much in common with my sister, but now, watching her, I felt some sense of solidarity. Caroline, in the last few weeks, had engineered an amazing transformation, one she wanted more than anything to share with us, but especially my mother.

'Mom,' Caroline said now, 'you're going to love it. Just take twelve hours off and come and see. Please.'

My mother sighed. 'I'm sure I will. And I'll get there, okay? Just not today.'

'Fine,' Caroline said, in a voice that made it clear it really wasn't. She walked over and sat down in one of the chairs by the window, crossing one leg over the other. My mother was edging into her office, as if that red light was pulling her closer, when my sister said, 'I guess it was kind of spur of the moment, thinking we could do this today. I mean, since we're going next Sunday anyway.'

'Next Sunday,' my mother repeated. She seemed confused. 'What's happening then?'

Caroline was looking at her, and I had a bad feeling. Really bad. 'We're going to the beach house for the week,' I said quickly, looking from her to my mother, then back at Caroline. 'On the eighth. Right?'

I was waiting for Caroline to agree. Instead, my mother said, 'Next Sunday? The day after the party? That's impossible. The phase will have just opened. When did you decide this?'

'I didn't,' Caroline said, finally speaking. Her voice was level, even. '*We* did. Weeks ago.'

My mother looked at me. 'But that's impossible,' she said, running a hand through her hair. 'I wouldn't have agreed to that, it's too soon. The sales will have just started, and we have a meeting that Monday on breaking ground for the next phase . . . I have to be here.'

'I can't believe this,' my sister said, shaking her head. 'I can't believe you.'

'Caroline, you have to understand,' my mother told her. 'This is important.'

'No!' my sister screamed, the word suddenly just filling the room. 'This is *work*, and for you, it's never done. You promised me we'd take this vacation, and I've killed myself getting ready on time so we could have this week together as a family. You said you'd be done, but you're never done. All this summer it's been about these stupid townhouses, and two days after they open, you're breaking ground for something else? God! You'll do *anything* to avoid it.'

'Avoid what?' my mother said.

'The past,' Caroline said. 'Our past. I'm tired of acting like nothing ever happened, of pretending he was never here, of not seeing his pictures in the house, or his things. Just because you're not able to let yourself grieve.'

'*Don't*,' my mother said, her voice low, 'talk to me about grief. You have no idea.'

'I do, though.' Caroline's voice caught, and she swallowed. 'I'm not trying to hide that I'm sad. I'm not trying to forget. You hide here behind all these plans for houses and townhouses because they're new and perfect and don't remind you of anything.'

'Stop it,' my mother said.

'And look at Macy,' Caroline continued, ignoring this. 'Do you even know what you're doing to her?'

My mother looked at me, and I shrank back, trying to stay out of this. 'Macy is fine,' my mother said.

'No, she's not. God, you *always* say that, but she's not.' Caroline looked at me, as if she wanted me to jump in, but I just sat there. 'Have you even been paying the least bit of attention to what's going on with her? She's been miserable since Dad died, pushing herself so hard to please you. And then, this summer, she finally finds some friends and something she likes to do. But then one tiny slip-up, and you take it all away from her.'

'That has nothing to do with what we're talking about,' my mother said.

'It has everything to do with it,' Caroline shot back. 'She was finally getting over what happened. Couldn't you see the change in her? I could, and I was barely here. She was *different.*'

'Exactly,' my mother said. 'She was –'

'Happy,' Caroline finished for her. 'She was starting to live her life again, and it scared you. Just like me redoing the beach house scares you. You think you're so strong because you never talk about Dad. Anyone can hide. Facing up to things, working through them, *that's* what makes you strong.'

'I've given everything I have to support this family,' my mother replied, biting off the words. 'And for you, it's still not enough.'

'I'm not asking for everything you have.' Caroline put her hands to her face, breathing in, then lowered them. 'I'm asking you to allow me, and Macy, and especially yourself to remember Dad –'

My mother exhaled loudly, shaking her head.

'– and I'm asking you for one week of your time to begin doing it.' Caroline looked at me, then back at my mother. 'That's all.'

The pause that followed this was long enough that I started to think maybe, just maybe, my mother was going to agree. She was just standing there, arms crossed over her chest, looking out of the front window of the model home at the houses across the street.

'I have to be here,' she said finally. 'I can't just leave.'

'It's one week,' Caroline said. 'It's not forever.'

'I can't leave,' my mother repeated. 'I'm sorry.' And she

walked back into her office, stiffly, and shut the door behind her. I listened for the familiar noises – the squeak of her chair rollers, the phone being picked up so she could deal with Rathka, the keyboard clacking – but heard nothing. It was like she'd just disappeared.

My sister, gulping back tears, turned and pushed the front door open. 'Caroline,' I said, but she was already outside, walking down the front steps.

I thought about going after her. I wanted to be able to say something that would make everything okay, but I had no idea what that might be. *It's not forever*, she'd said, but to my mother, it might as well have been. She had made her choice, and this was it, where she felt safe, in a world she could, for the most part, control.

My sister was in her car now, wiping her eyes: I watched her as she cranked the engine, then drove away from the kerb. As she moved away, I could see the sign across the street in full view now, and I read the rest of it. NEW PHASES COMING SOON! it said. And then, as if it were easy, or a good thing, always: COME CHANGE WITH US.

My mother was still in her office, silent, when the clock hit five and I stood up to leave. I thought about knocking at her door, even asking if she were okay, but instead I just gathered up my things and slipped out the front door, shutting it behind me hard enough so that she'd hear it and know I was gone.

As I came up our front walk, I saw the box on the front porch: small, square, parked in the direct centre of our welcome mat. *Waterville, Maine*, I thought, even before I got close enough to check the return address. I picked it up and took it inside with me.

The house was quiet, cool, as I went into the kitchen, put the box on the counter, then found the scissors and cut it open.

Inside, there were two pictures: the first was of a belt loop sporting a huge, cluttered key ring that looked like it weighed about a hundred pounds. Then in the second picture, there was the same belt loop, but now attached to it was a square plastic box that looked sort of like a tape measure. Along one side, though, was a series of tabs, each a different colour. *Frustrated with your old, clunky key chain?* asked the bright print below. *Get rid of it! Get organized. Get the EZ-Key!*

Apparently, with the EZ-Key, you could colour code each of your keys, then attach them to a retracting cord, so that you only had to pull them out, unlock whatever needed unlocking, and zip! they shot right back into place. It was a good idea, really, I thought as I turned the box in my hand, rereading its breathless copy, but then they all were, at least on the surface.

About an hour later, as I was sliding some chicken breasts into the oven, my mother called.

'Macy,' she said, 'I need you to get me a phone number.'

'Okay,' I said, starting towards her office. 'Let me just get your phone book.'

'No, I think you know it. It's for that woman, Delia. The woman you worked for.'

'Delia?' I said.

'Yes.'

I just stood there for a second, waiting for her to offer an explanation. When she didn't, I said, 'Why . . .?'

'Because,' she said, 'Rathka has just quit, and every other catering company is already booked for next Saturday or on vacation. This is a last resort.'

'Rathka quit?' I asked, incredulous.

'Macy,' she said. 'The number, please.'

I knew there was no way Delia would do it: she hadn't booked any jobs since Avery had been born, and it was way short notice. But with the way my mother's day had been going, I figured it was better not to point this out. 'It's 555-7823,' I said.

'Thank you,' she said. 'I'll be home soon.' And then there was a click, and she was gone.

Chapter NINETEEN

My sister stayed away for a full week, completely and totally incommunicado. She stopped answering her cell phone and ignored all emails, and when we finally got through on her home phone, it was always Wally who answered, his voice stiff and forced enough that it was immediately clear not only that he had been coached to say she was out but that she was standing right there behind him as he did so.

'She'll get over it,' my mother kept saying, each time I relayed my thwarted efforts to reach her. 'She will.'

My mother wasn't worried, even if I was. There were other, bigger concerns on her mind now. And they all had to do with the gala reception.

It had started with Rathka quitting, but that was only the beginning. In the six days since, it seemed like everything that could go wrong had done just that. When the landscapers came to work on the yard, one of their riding mowers went haywire, ripping up huge clumps of grass and taking out a few shrubs in the process. They did their best to fix it, but the topography remained uneven. Just crossing from the garage to the steps felt like walking over little mountains and valleys. Half of the invitations we'd mailed came back due to some postal error, which meant I had to drive around one hot afternoon, hand delivering them to mailbox after mailbox. The next day, the string quartet cancelled, as three of the four had come down with food poisoning at an outdoor wedding.

The night before the party, however, my mother's luck seemed to be changing. The guys from the party rental place arrived early to assemble the tent. We stood and watched as they put it up and set up the chairs and tables beneath it, both of us braced for some sort of crisis. But everything went according to plan.

'Wonderful,' she said to the tent guy, handing him his cheque. 'I wasn't even sure we'd need a tent, but it just makes everything look that much nicer.'

'And also,' he told her, 'if it rains, you're covered.'

She just looked at him. 'It is *not*,' she said firmly, as if there was no room for negotiation, 'going to rain.'

The only other good news my mother had got was that Delia, to my surprise, had agreed to take the gala job. It wouldn't be lamb on fine china, my mother had sighed, but she'd be glad for anything at this point, even if it was chicken on a stick and meatballs.

'Everyone loves meatballs,' I'd told her, but she'd just looked at me before moving on to the next crisis at hand.

In a way, I was kind of grateful for all the various crises, if only because they kept me so busy. I didn't have time to worry about things, such as the awkwardness of seeing Wes after all this time, or handling Jason, who was now planning to drop by to say hello at some point during the evening. I'd just deal with it when it happened, I told myself, and that would be soon enough.

Now, as the tent guys drove off, I heard a car pull into the driveway. I glanced round the side of the house to see my sister getting out of a truck with a long, wide bed, which was packed with what I first assumed was metal patio furniture or some sort of construction refuse from the beach house. She parked and got out just as another car, which I recognized as belonging to one of my mother's salesmen, pulled up behind her.

'What on *earth* has she got there?' my mother asked me as we walked round the side of the house, and suddenly I realized it was Wes's stuff. Six pieces, at least, although they were stacked in such a way it was hard to tell. By the time we got up to the truck, Caroline had the tailgate down and she and the salesman were pulling a few pieces out, leaning them against the back bumper. I could see a big angel with a barbed-wire halo, as well as a whirligig that had been out at his house the last day I'd been there. It was made up of a series of bicycle wheels – from big ones to the tiny training kind – welded to a twisted piece of rebar.

'Caroline,' my mother called out, her voice forced and cheery. 'Hello.'

Caroline didn't reply at first, but the salesman waved as they continued pulling pieces out and putting them in the driveway: a smaller angel with a stained-glass halo, another whirligig fashioned out of hubcaps and interlocking gears.

'We can just set them up on the grass,' she said to the salesman. 'Anywhere's fine, really.'

'Caroline?' my mother said, as he began pulling the angel onto the lawn, dragging it over the bumpy terrain. I could tell she was concerned, but also trying to be careful to avoid another snit. In fact, she didn't say anything else, even as the angel dug up more grass in a path behind itself.

'Don't worry,' Caroline said finally, wiping a hand across her face. She was in shorts and a T-shirt, her hair pulled back in a ponytail. 'I'm only stopping for a second. I need to take some shots of these and email them to Wally so we can decide which to take to the mountain house, and which I should just bring home with me.'

'Well,' my mother said, as Caroline and the salesman began to pull the larger angel onto the front lawn, positioning it for a second before going back to grab one of the smaller ones, 'that's fine. Just fine.'

None of us said anything for a few minutes as the pieces were assembled on the lawn. People kept driving past the house, then slowing, staring. My mother kept offering up her Good Neighbour wave and smile, but I could tell she wasn't happy.

By the time Caroline and the salesman were done, there were seven pieces on the lawn: two big angels, two small, a large square piece and two sculptures, one with the hubcaps and another made out of gears and wheels of various sizes. The salesman stepped back, wiping a hand over his face. 'You sure you don't want me to stick around to help you put them back in?'

'No, it's okay,' Caroline said to him. 'I'll get one of the neighbour kids to help or something. I just wasn't sure anyone would be here. But thanks.'

'No problem,' he said cheerfully. 'Anything to help the cause. Deborah, I'll see you tomorrow.'

'Right,' my mother replied, nodding. 'See you then.'

As he left, my sister moved around the front yard, adjusting the pieces this way or that. After a second she looked down at the grass, as if just noticing the state it was in, then said, 'What's wrong with the lawn?'

I shook my head, glancing at my mother.

'Nothing,' my mother said evenly, as she walked up to the larger angel and peered at it more closely. 'Well. These are certainly interesting. Where did you get them?'

'Macy's friend Wes,' Caroline told her, wiping a smudge off one of the bicycle wheels. To me she said, 'You know, he's really something.'

'Yeah,' I said, looking at the angel with the barbed-wire halo. Away from the farmer's market, and Wes's workshop, the pieces seemed that much more impressive. Even my mother noticed. I could tell by the way she was still studying the angel's face. 'I know.'

'Wes?' my mother said. 'The boy who drove you home that night?'

'Didn't Macy tell you he was an artist?' Caroline said.

My mother glanced at me, but I looked away. Both of us knew it wouldn't have mattered at the time. 'No,' she said quietly. 'She didn't.'

'Oh, he's fantastic,' Caroline said, pushing a piece of hair out of her face. 'I've been out at his studio for hours, looking at his pieces. Do you know he learned to weld in reform school?'

My mother was still watching me. She said, 'You don't say.'

'It's just the coolest story.' Caroline squatted down, pushing one of the tiny wheels to make it spin. 'They have professors from the university do volunteer outreach at the Myers School, and one of the heads of the art department came in and taught a class. He was so impressed with Wes he's been having him take college-level art classes for the last two years. He showed at the university gallery a couple of months ago.'

'He did?' I said. 'He never told me that.'

'Oh,' Caroline said, 'he didn't tell me either. His aunt was there, I can't remember her name –'

'Delia,' I said.

'Right!' She started back towards the truck. 'So, anyway, we got to talking while he was loading up the truck. She also said he's had offers from several art schools for college, but he's not even sure he wants to go. As it is, his stuff is selling in a few galleries and garden art places so well he's on back order. And he was a winner of the Emblem Prize last year.'

'What does that mean?' I asked.

'It's a state arts award,' my mother said to me, looking down at the small angel near her feet, whose halo was decorated with small interlocking wrenches. 'The governor's committee gives them out.'

'It means,' Caroline said, 'that he's amazing.'

'Wow,' I said. I couldn't believe he hadn't told me all this, but, then again, I'd never asked. Quiet but incredible, Delia had said.

Caroline said, 'When I took those other pieces I bought and set them up in my yard, the women in my neighbourhood went nuts.' She adjusted the square piece, which, I now realized, was made up of what looked like an old bedframe. 'I told him I'd probably have offers for twice what I paid for this stuff once I get it home. Not that I'm selling, of course.'

'Really,' my mother said, looking at the square piece, her head tilted to the side. Wes had removed the legs of the frame, leaving just the boxy middle part, then put shiny chrome along the inside. It tilted backwards on two outstretched pieces of pipe, so if you stood right in front of it, it looked like a big picture frame, with whatever was behind it the image inside. The way Caroline had set it up, it framed the front of the house perfectly: the red front door, the holly bushes on either side of the steps, then a set of windows.

'I love this,' she said as we all stood looking at it. 'It's a new series he's been working on. I bought three of them. I just think it's amazing what it says, something about permanence, you know, and impermanence.'

'Really,' my mother said again.

'Absolutely,' Caroline told her, in her Art Major voice, and I felt a rush suddenly of how much I missed Wes, wishing he were there to exchange a look with me, a bemused smile, raising his eyebrows. He'd acted like he'd never heard any of it before, ever, which I knew now hadn't been true. 'An empty frame, in which the picture is always changing, makes a statement about how time is always passing. It doesn't really stop, even in a single image. It just feels that way.'

It was early evening, the sun not even down yet, but as we stood there, the streetlight behind us buzzed, then flickered on. Instantly, I saw our shadows cast across the empty space behind the frame: my mother's tall and thin; Caroline's, her hands on her hips, elbows at right angles. And then there was me, falling between them. I put a hand to my face, then let it drop back to my side, watching my shadow mimic me.

'I should go ahead and get my pictures,' Caroline said, starting towards the truck. 'Before it gets totally dark.'

As she walked to the truck, another car slowed down in front of the house, the horn beeping. The passenger side window rolled down and a woman I vaguely recognized as one of the realtors my mother did business with leaned across the front seat. 'Deborah, how brilliant!'

My mother walked a little closer to the kerb. 'I'm sorry?' she said.

'Those pieces!' the woman replied, waving towards them. She had a big clunky wooden bracelet on that kept sliding up and down her arm with every gesture. 'What a great tie-in to the finish of the construction phase, using building materials from the townhouses to make decorations! How smart of you!'

'Oh, no,' my mother said, 'it's not –'

'I'll see you tomorrow!' the woman said, not even listening. 'Just brilliant!' And then she drove off, beeping the horn again, while my mother just stood there, watching her go.

Caroline was walking across the grass with her camera now, bending down to centre the bigger angel in the shot. 'You know,' she said, looking down at her feet, 'I don't care what you say. Something is wrong with the yard. I noticed it as soon as I pulled up. It's like . . . uneven, or something.'

'We had a little problem,' I told her, as she lifted the camera to her eye. A second later, the shutter snapped. 'We've had a few, actually.'

I was waiting for my mother to deny this, or at least smooth it over, but when I turned to look at her I saw she wasn't even really listening. Instead, she was facing the street, where, as often happened at this time of night, people were starting to pass by on after-dinner walks, pushing strollers or leading dogs, and kids were circling on their bikes, racing past, then doubling back, then back again. Tonight, though, something was different: everyone was looking at our yard, at the sculptures, some people just standing on the sidewalk outright staring. My mother saw this too.

'You know,' she said to Caroline carefully, 'I'm wondering if maybe these pieces would work well at the reception. They certainly add a bit of flair to the yard, at any rate.'

Caroline took another picture, then stood up and started towards the wheel whirligig. 'I was going to leave tonight,' she said, not looking at my mother as she set up another shot. 'I have plans.'

For a second, I thought that was it. She was saying no, and there was nothing we could do about it. My mother knew this too; I could tell by the way she stepped back, nodding her head. 'Of course,' she said. 'I understand completely.'

For a second none of us said anything, and I wondered if, in the end, this is how all disputes are settled, with a shared silence as things become equal. You take something from me, I take something from you. We all want balance, one way or another.

'But,' Caroline said, 'I suppose I could stick around. It's just one night, right?'

'Yes,' my mother said, as Caroline lifted the camera to her eye. 'It's just one night.'

So Caroline stayed, first taking pictures until dark, then going inside, where she and my mother circled each other warily but politely, until we all went to bed. As usual, I couldn't sleep, and after an hour or so of tossing and turning I climbed out onto my rooftop and stared down at Wes's work on the grass before me. The sculptures looked so out of place to me there, as if they'd been dropped from the sky.

I dozed until about 3 a.m., then woke up to feel a breeze blowing through my open window. Regardless of my mother's insistence, the weather was clearly changing. Sitting up, I pushed aside my curtain, looking out over the roof to the lawn. All of the sculptures had parts that were now spinning madly, whistling, buzzing, calling. The noise was loud enough to drown out everything. I couldn't believe I'd even been able to sleep through it. I lay back down and listened for another hour or so, waiting for it to stop, for the wind to die back down, but it never did. If anything it grew louder, then louder still, and I thought I'd never get to sleep again. But, somehow, I did.

Macy. Wake up.

I sat up, fast, my father's voice still in my head. *It's a dream*, I told myself, but in those first moments of waking confusion, I wasn't sure.

The last time I'd heard those words, that way, it had been winter. Cold, the trees bare. Now, a summer breeze, strong but sweet smelling, was blowing. *A dream*, I thought, and slid back down to put my cheek against my pillow, closing my eyes. But also like the last time, about three minutes later something made me get up.

I looked out of the window, at first not believing my eyes. But after I blinked once, then twice, to make sure I was really awake, there was no denying that Wes was standing in my front yard, the truck parked at the kerb behind him. It was 7 a.m. and he was just looking at all his pieces, at their movement, and then, as I shifted, leaning in closer to my screen, at me.

For a second, we just stared at each other. Then I walked to my bureau, pulled on a T-shirt and a pair of shorts, slipped down the staircase quietly, and went outside.

The wind and the whirligigs moving made everything feel in motion. The mulch that the landscapers had laid around the beds was now scattered across the grass and the street, and small cyclones of flower petals and grass clippings were swirling here and there in smaller gusts. In the midst of all of it was Wes, and now me, standing still, with the length of the walk between us.

'What are you doing here?' I asked him. I had to raise my voice, almost yell, but the wind seemed to pick it up and carry it away almost instantly. Somehow, though, he heard me.

'I was dropping something off,' he said. 'I didn't think anyone would be up.'

'I wasn't,' I said. 'I mean, not until just now.'

'I tried to call you,' he said now, taking a step towards me. I did the same. 'After that night. Why didn't you answer?'

Another big gust blew over us. I could feel my shorts flapping around my legs. *What is going on?* I thought, glancing around.

'I don't know,' I said, pushing my hair out of my eyes. 'I just . . . it just seemed like everything had changed.'

'Changed,' he said, taking another step towards me. 'You mean, on the Fourth? With us?'

'No,' I said, and he looked surprised, hurt even, but it passed quickly, and I wondered if I'd been wrong, and it hadn't been there ever, at all. 'Not that night. The night I saw you. You were so –'

I trailed off, not knowing what word to use. I wasn't used to this, having a chance to explain a goodbye or an ending.

But Wes was waiting. For whatever word came next.

'It was weird,' I said finally, knowing this didn't do it justice, but I had to say something. 'You were weird. And I just thought that it had been too much, or something.'

'What had been too much?'

'That night. Me being so upset at the hospital,' I said. He looked confused, like I wasn't making sense. 'Us. Like we were too much. You were so strange, like you didn't want to face me –'

'It wasn't like that,' he said. 'It was just –'

'I followed you,' I told him. 'To say I was sorry. I went to the Waffle House, and I saw you. With Becky.'

'You saw me,' he repeated. 'That night, after we talked outside Milton's?'

'It just made it clear,' I told him. 'But, even before, we were so awkward, talking, and it just seemed like maybe everything on the Fourth had been too much for you, and I felt embarrassed.'

'That's why you said that about Jason,' he said. 'About getting back together. And then you saw me, and –'

I just shook my head, letting him know he didn't have to explain to me. 'It doesn't matter,' I said. 'It's fine.'

'Fine,' he repeated, and I wondered why it was I kept coming back to this, again and again, a word that you said when someone asked how you were but didn't really care to know the truth.

Something blew up behind me, hitting my leg, and I glanced down: it was a bit of white fabric, blown loose from someone's backyard or clothesline. A second later it took flight again, rising up and over the bushes beside me. 'Look,' I said, 'we knew Jason and Becky would be back, the break would end. This isn't a surprise; it's what's supposed to happen. It's what we wanted. Right?'

'Is it?' he asked. 'Is it what you want?'

Whether he intended it to be or not, this was the final question, the last Truth. If I said what I really thought, I was opening myself up for a hurt bigger than I could even imagine. I didn't have it in me. We'd changed and altered so many rules, but it was this one, the only one when we'd started, that I would break.

'Yes,' I said.

I waited for him to react, to say something, anything, wondering what would happen now that the game was over. Instead, his eyes shifted slowly, from my face to above my head. Confused, I looked up, only to see the sky was swirling with white.

It was like snow, almost, but as the pieces began falling, blowing across me, I saw they were made of the same white, stiff fabric as the piece that had blown onto me earlier. But it wasn't until I heard a yelp from behind the house that everything clicked together.

'The tent!' my mother was shrieking. 'Oh, my God!'

I turned back to look at Wes, but he was walking towards his truck. I just stood there, watching, as he got behind the wheel and started to drive away. So I'd won. But it didn't feel like it. Not at all.

We had a shredded tent. A yardful of flowers missing their petals. And now, rumbling in the distance, thunder.

'Uh-oh,' Caroline said under her breath, nudging me, and I felt myself start, coming to. I was so out of it, even as I went through the motions, doing my best to soothe my mother's frayed nerves. When the tent people said no, they didn't have another, and all their crews were booked, so we'd just have to do our best with what we had, I'd patted her hand, insisting no one would notice the tent at all. When the wind kept blowing, knocking over the chairs and tables as quickly as we could set them up, I nodded agreement to Caroline's idea of doing away with them altogether and allowing, in her words, more of a 'milling around sort of thing'. And when my mother, minutes earlier, had stepped off the driveway of the model townhouse to cut the red ribbon stretched across there and broken the heel of her shoe, I'd stepped forward instantly, offering up my own while everyone chuckled. Through it all, I felt strangely detached, as if it were all happening at a distance, far enough that whatever the outcome, it wouldn't affect me at all.

Now, my mother was smiling for the cameras and shaking hands with her superintendents with the utmost composure as mean-looking dark clouds began to scoot against the sky. She seemed just fine, until we got into the car and she shut her door behind her.

'What in the world is going on?' she shrieked. 'I started planning this weeks ago. This is not what's supposed to happen!'

Her voice filled the car, sounding loud in my ears, and as she began driving, the familiar scenery of the neighbourhood whizzing by, I had a flash of Wes and me in the yard earlier, when I'd said something so similar to him about how we would leave things: *It's what's supposed to happen.* It made sense then, but now I was wondering.

As we took a corner there was another big crash of thunder overhead, and we all jumped. My sister leaned forward, peering out through the windshield. 'You know,' she said, 'we should probably have a rain plan.'

'It's not going to rain,' my mother told her flatly.

'Can't you hear that thunder?'

'It's just thunder,' she said, pressing the accelerator down further as we exceeded, by a good twenty miles, the Wildflower Ridge Good Neighbour Speed Limit. 'That doesn't mean it's going to rain.'

Caroline just looked at her. 'Mom. Please.'

As we zoomed up the driveway, the wind was still blowing, and every once in a while a little piece of white tent sheeting would flutter past. My mother and Caroline were already going inside by the time I got out of the car, my mind still tangled with all these thoughts. By the time I caught up with them in the kitchen, they were bustling around, laying out the brochures and leaflets that would be arranged outside, getting the last of the things ready for the party. As soon as she saw me, my mother thrust a pile of folders, brochures, old newspapers and several of my sister's home-decorating magazines into my arms.

'Macy, please, take these and put them somewhere. Anywhere. And check the powder room to make sure the towels are straight and there's enough hand soap, and –' She paused for a second, glancing around wildly, her eyes finally settling on the countertop by the phone, where EZ-Key had been since I'd opened it the day before, 'do something with that, *please*, and come back here so you can help me do something with the dining room. Okay?'

I nodded, still feeling out of it, but I did as she asked. The folders I put in her office, the newspapers in recycling, the magazines outside my sister's bedroom door. When the EZ-Key was the last thing left, I went into my room, then sat down on my bed with it in my hands.

Downstairs, I could hear my sister doing last-minute vacuuming, my mother in my shoes clacking and re-clacking across the floor. I knew they needed me, but there was a part of me that just wanted to lie back in my bed, close my eyes and find myself waking up again, to this morning, to another chance. Maybe I'd still go downstairs and across the lawn to Wes, but what I'd say, I knew now, would be different. He'd always told the truth. I should have done the same.

And this was it: Wes was my friend, absolutely, but regardless of what I'd led him to believe, the night I'd seen him with Becky I'd felt more than what a friend should. It was about time I admitted it. In fact, on some level, I'd known all along, which was what had almost sent me back to Jason, back to this neat, orderly life that I hoped would protect me from getting hurt again. And here, in this world, it was entirely possible to pretend that none of my summer with Wes, and Wish, had ever happened.

But it *had* happened. I had followed Delia's van that night, I had told Wes my Truths, I had stepped into his arms, showing him my raw, broken heart. I could pretend otherwise, pushing it out of sight and hopefully out of mind. But, if something were really important, fate made sure it somehow came back to you and gave you another chance. I'd had one reaching out to grab Kristy's hand as she pulled me into the ambulance; another during the trip to the hospital that had ended with seeing Avery born. Events conspired to bring you back to where you'd been. It was what you did then that made all the difference: it was all about potential.

I stood up and pulled my chair over to the closet, then climbed up to put away the EZ box. I was about to step down when I saw the shopping bag I'd put up there all those weeks ago. This whole day I'd felt like something was different. Which was probably why I pushed the box back and finally grabbed the bag off the shelf.

'I can't believe this,' my mother muttered to herself, bemoaning the rumbling thunder as she passed my half-open door. 'It's like we're cursed or something.'

I sat down on my bed, then reached into the bag, pulling out the package. It was heavy in my hands as I shifted it into my lap, my fingers already loosening the wrapping paper.

'Honestly,' she called out, over another thunderclap, 'how are you supposed to plan for a day like this?'

The paper was coming off now, wrinkling, ripping, and even though I knew there was something familiar in the shape that was emerging I couldn't place it.

'The lawn, the catering, the tent,' my mother said, passing by again. 'What happens now?'

I just sat there, looking at my gift, feeling my heart beating loud in my chest, then lifted my hand and pressed it over the one on the sculpture in my lap. A lot of things were beginning to make sense, while others were more confusing than ever. All I knew was that this heart in hand was mine. I'd wanted a sign, and all this time it had been so close by, waiting for me to be ready to find it.

My mother's last question was still echoing in my head as outside my window there was the biggest thunderclap yet. It shook the house, the windowpanes, the very earth, it felt like. And then, just like that, it was pouring. She'd got her answer. And so had I.

Chapter TWENTY

When I came downstairs, all hell was breaking loose.

I'd put my heart in hand on my bedside table next to my angel, then stood up, sure now of what I had to do. As I came into the kitchen, though, I found my mother and sister in a frenzy of furniture rearranging, pushing chairs and couches up against walls in an attempt to somehow open up space for seventy- five people in our dining room, foyer and living room.

'Macy,' Caroline said to me, rushing past carrying an end table, 'do something about the stools.'

'Stools?' I asked.

'The island stools,' my mother shrieked as she passed going the other direction, dragging a settee. 'Put them against the wall. Or in my office. Do something with them! Just get them out of here!' Her voice was loud, wavering, crazy sounding, and for a second I just looked at her. But only for a second. Then I did exactly as I was told.

I'd seen my mother under pressure. I'd seen her grieving. But I'd never seen her look as out of control as she did just then, and it scared me. I turned and looked at Caroline, who just shook her head and went back to pushing one of the recliners against the den wall. There was no way a person could carry this much stress for much longer, I thought. Eventually, something had to give.

'Mom,' I said to her as she passed by again, reaching out my hand to touch hers. 'Are you okay?'

'Macy, not now!' she snapped. I pulled my hand back: now, even that was too much. 'Please, honey,' she said, shaking her head. 'Not now.'

For the next twenty minutes, I could see the tension building, in her neck, her features, the shaking timbre of her voice as one bad thing after another kept happening. When the phone wouldn't stop ringing. When the superintendent called to report that one of the windows in the model townhouse was leaking from all the rain. When the lights flickered, went out, then flickered back on again, still not seeming too steady. Each time, I watched my mother react, her body tensing, her voice rising, her eyes moving wildly across the room, scanning for one thing or another. Whenever she caught me watching her, I'd quickly look away.

'I'm worried about Mom,' I said to Caroline as we tried to push the huge, oak-framed couch in the living room a foot or so backwards. Even with both our weights, it wasn't even budging. 'I don't know how I can help her.'

'You can't,' she told me. 'It's not worth even trying.'

'Caroline.' I stopped pushing. 'God.'

She pushed her hair out of her face with the back of her hand. 'Macy,' she said. 'There's nothing you can do.'

Just then, I heard the front door open and someone's heels clack into the foyer.

'Good God,' Kristy said. 'What the hell is going on here?'

I let my arms go slack, grateful for an excuse to do so, and turned round. There she was, standing in the foyer, carrying a stack of foil-covered pans. Monica was beside her, holding a cooler with a couple of cutting boards balanced on top. Bringing up the rear, carrying several long loaves of French bread under each arm, was Delia.

'We're having,' I said to Kristy as the lights flickered again, 'a little bit of a crisis.'

There was a rattle, then a clank, as Bert appeared in the door, forcing Delia to step aside as he pulled one of the banged-up stainless-steel carts over the threshold. Outside, the rain was still coming down sideways.

'Crisis?' Delia asked. 'What kind?'

Then in the powder room to her right, there was shriek, a crash, and everyone fell silent, the only sound the rain pelting the windows. Then the door opened, and my mother emerged.

Her cheeks were flushed from all the exertion of moving things, her lipstick smeared in one corner. She was still wearing my shoes, which were markedly too small for her, and there was some sort of dirt stain on the hem of her skirt. She looked tired. Beaten down. Or maybe even just beaten. And in her hand was the decorative soap dish from the powder room, which was now in two pieces.

It was just a soap dish, innocuous enough that I couldn't even remember when we'd got it. But my mother, staring at it in her open palm, was for some reason close to tears. I felt something rise up in my chest, and realized I was afraid.

Terrified. I was used to seeing my mother many ways, but never weak. It made me feel small enough to disappear.

'Mom?' Caroline asked. 'Are you –'

But my mother didn't seem to hear her, or even notice that any of us were there. Instead, she started down the hallway to the kitchen, taking slow, deliberate steps. She reached up, wiping her eyes, as she turned the corner towards her office, not looking back at any of us. A second later, I heard the door shut with a click.

'Oh, my God,' I said.

'It's just a soap dish,' Kristy offered helpfully. 'I bet she can get another one.'

Beside me, I could see Caroline already turning to follow, assuming, of course, that she would be the one to handle this. But I'd been waiting for a chance to talk to my mother for too long, always finding myself thwarted in one way or another, by my fears or her own. It was time to try again.

So, as Caroline started down the hallway, I put my hand on her arm. She looked up at me, surprised. 'Let me,' I said, and then I went to my mother.

When I pushed the door open, she was standing behind her desk, her back to me. And she was crying, her shoulders shaking. The sound of it immediately brought a lump to my throat, and I wanted to turn and run. But instead I took a deep breath and stepped inside.

She didn't turn round. I wasn't even sure she knew I was there. But as I stood watching her, I realized how truly hard it was, really, to see someone you love change right before your eyes. Not only is it scary, it throws your balance off as well. This was how my mother felt, I realized, over the weeks I worked at Wish, as she began to not recognize me in small ways, day after day. It was no wonder she'd reacted by pulling me closer, forcibly narrowing my world back to fit inside her own. Even now, as I finally saw this as the truth it was, a part of me was wishing my mother would stand up straight, take command, be back in control. But all I'd wanted when she was tugging me closer was to be able to prove to her that the changes in me were good ones, ones she'd understand if she only gave them a chance. I had that chance now. And, while it was scary, I was going to take it.

I crossed the room, coming up behind her. I had so many things I wanted to tell her. I just didn't know where to begin.

Finally she turned round, one hand moving to her face, and for a second we just stood there, staring at each other. A million sentences kept starting in my head, then trailing off. This was the hard part, I thought. Whatever was said next started everything, so it had to be strong enough to carry the rest that would follow.

She took a breath. 'I'm –'

But I didn't let her finish. Instead, I took one step forward and slid my arms round her neck. She stiffened, at first, surprised, but I didn't pull back, moving in even more and burying my face in her shoulder. At first I didn't feel her own arms sliding round me, her body moving in to enclose mine. I could feel her breath in my hair, her heart against my chest. After all this time, it could have been awkward, all elbows and hipbones. But it wasn't. It was perfect.

And, as I held her, I kept thinking back to that night at the clearing, and what I'd told Wes. *For once, I'd just let her know exactly how I feel, without thinking first.* Finally, I had.

Somewhere in the midst of all this, down the hallway, I could hear Caroline's voice. She was in the kitchen, explaining our crisis to Delia, detailing every little thing that had gone wrong. As she did so, my mother and I held tight, leaning into each other. It was like that part of the roller coaster where the *click-clack-click* stops as you reach the top of the hill, and you know for sure that the uphill part is finally behind you, and any minute you'll begin that wild rush to the end.

I was ready. And I think she was too. But, if she wasn't, I could get her through. The first step is always the hardest.

'Okay,' I heard Delia say. 'Here's what we're going to do . . .'

'Ho-ly shit,' Kristy said, shaking her head. 'Now that's some rain.'

'Kristy,' Delia said in her warning voice.

Caroline sighed. 'No, she's right,' she said. 'It really is.'

'Mmm-hmm,' Monica added.

It was, indeed, still raining. Hard. So hard, in fact, that the lights had continued to flicker, although that could have been attributable to the wind, which was, yes, still blowing. Hard. A few minutes earlier, on the TV, our local weather girl, Lorna McPhail, had stood there in front of her Doppler map, eyes wide, as she explained that while a shower or two had been in the forecast, no one had expected this sort of incident.

'*Incident?*' Caroline had said as Lorna turned back to her map. 'This isn't an incident. This is the end of the world.'

'Nah,' Bert told her as he passed behind her with a trayful of wine glasses, 'the end of the world would be *much* worse than this.'

Caroline looked at him. 'You think?'

'Oh yeah,' he said. 'Absolutely.'

Now, it was seven sharp, and our first arrivals were still sitting in their cars, optimistically waiting for a break in the torrential downpour. In a minute, they'd get out, come up the walk and step inside, where everything was ready. The canapés were warming in the oven, the bar was stocked with ice and beverages, the cake that said in red icing WILDFLOWER RIDGE – A NEW PHASE BEGINS! was displayed on the table, encircled by flowers and stacks of brightly coloured napkins. Plus, the whole house smelled like meatballs. And everyone loves meatballs.

After Caroline detailed our situation, I'd listened to Delia do what she did best: move into action. Within fifteen minutes, several of the tables and chairs we'd rented had been brought inside and assembled throughout the house ('bistro-style', she'd called it), then topped with thick vanilla-scented candles she'd had stashed in the van from a bridal shower weeks ago. The lights were dimmed in case they went out entirely – while making everything feel somehow cozy – and she'd put Bert and Monica to work doubling up on baking appetizers, reasoning that if people were well fed, they'd hardly notice that they barely had room to turn round. Caroline was sent to find a soap dish, and Kristy was stationed by the door with a tray of full wine glasses to offer up the minute people stepped inside (slightly buzzed people, Delia reasoned, would notice less as well).

Meanwhile, my mother and I were sitting on the edge of her desk, the Kleenex box between us, looking out at the rain.

'I wanted this party to be perfect,' she said, dabbing at her eyes.

'No such thing,' I told her.

She smiled ruefully, tossing a tissue into the garbage can. 'It's a total disaster,' she said with a sigh.

For a second, neither of us said anything.

'Well, in a way it's good,' I said finally, remembering what Delia had said to me at that first party, all those weeks ago. 'We know where we stand. Now things can only get better. Right?'

She didn't look convinced. But that was okay. So she didn't fully get it yet. But I had a feeling she would. And, if not, there was more than enough time, now that this had finally begun, for me to explain it to her.

When we came out into the kitchen a few minutes later, Delia was laying out crab cakes. She took one look at my mother and insisted that she go upstairs and take a hot shower and a few deep breaths. To my surprise, my mother went with no argument, disappearing for a full twenty minutes. When she came back down, hair damp and wearing fresh clothes, she looked more relaxed than I'd seen her in weeks. There is a certain relief in things getting as bad as they could be. Maybe this second time round my mother was beginning to see that.

'What did you say to her?' my sister asked me, as we watched her come down the stairs.

'Nothing, really,' I said. I felt her looking at me, but this was partially true. Or true enough.

Kristy was at the front door, tray in hand, as my mother passed her. 'Wine?' she offered.

My mother paused, about to demur politely, but instead she took a deep breath. 'What is that wonderful smell?'

'Meatballs,' I said. 'You want one?'

Again, I expected a no. But, instead, she reached for a wine glass, took a sip and nodded at me. 'Yes,' she said. 'I would love one.'

Now, as she stood with all of us in the front window, there was one last thing I was wondering about. I'd held off as long as I could, hoping someone would offer an explanation, but finally there was nothing to do but ask outright. 'So,' I said, still looking out at the cars, 'where's Wes?'

I saw Monica and Kristy exchange a look. Then Kristy said, 'He had to run some pieces down to the coast this morning. But he said he'd stop by on his way back, to see if we needed him.'

'Oh,' I said. 'Right.'

An awkward silence followed this, during which I, and everyone else, just stared out at the rain. Gradually, though, I became aware of someone sighing heavily. Then clearing her throat. Repeatedly.

'Are you okay?' Bert asked Kristy.

She nodded, letting loose with another vehement *a-hem*. I glanced over at her, only to find her staring at me. 'What?' I said.

'What?' she repeated. Clearly, she was annoyed. 'What do you mean, *what*?'

'I mean,' I said, somewhat confused, 'what's the problem?'

She rolled her eyes. Beside her, Monica said, 'Donneven.'

'Kristy.' Delia shook her head. 'This isn't the time or the place, okay?'

'The time or the place for what?' Caroline asked.

'There is never,' Kristy said adamantly, 'a time or place for true love. It happens accidentally, in a heartbeat, in a single flashing, throbbing moment.'

'Throbbing?' my mother said, leaning forward and looking at me. 'Who's throbbing?'

'Macy and Wes,' Kristy told her.

'We are *not*,' I said indignantly.

'Kristy,' Delia said helplessly. 'Please God I'm begging you, not now.'

'Wait a second, wait a second.' Caroline held her hands up. 'Kristy. Explain.'

'Yes, Kristy,' my mother said, but she was looking at me. Not really mad as much as confused. *Join the club*, I thought. 'Explain.'

Bert said, 'This ought to be good.'

Kristy ignored him, tucking a piece of hair behind her ear. 'Wes wants to be with Macy. And Macy, whether she'll admit it or not, wants to be with Wes. And yet they're not together, which is not only unjust, but really, when you think about it, tragical.'

'That's not a word,' Bert pointed out.

'It is now,' she said. 'How else can you explain a situation where Wes, a truly extraordinary boy, would be sent packing in favour of some brainiac loser who severed ties with Macy because she didn't take her job at the library seriously enough and, even *worse*, because she dared to say she loved him?'

'Why,' I said, feeling as embarrassed while this was broadcast as I had been the first time she'd stated it aloud, 'do we have to keep talking about this?'

'Because it's tragical!' Kristy said.

'Jason decided on the break because you told him you loved him?' my mother asked me.

'No,' I said. 'Yes. Not exactly. It's a long story.'

'I'll tell you what it is,' Kristy said. 'It's *wrong*. You should be with Wes, Macy. The whole time you guys were hanging out, talking about how you were both with other people, it was so obvious to everyone. It was even obvious to Wes. You were the only one who couldn't see it, just like you can't see it now.'

'Mmm-hmm,' Monica said, picking some lint off her apron.

'Wes never felt that way,' I told her. I was fully aware that my mother – and Caroline, not to mention everyone else – was listening, but somehow I didn't care. Too much had happened this night already. 'He was always going back to Becky, just like I was going back to Jason.'

'That's not true,' she said.

'It is true. He's been back with her. For weeks,' I told her.

'No,' she said, shaking her head.

'But I saw them together. At the World of Waffles. They were –'

'Breaking up,' she finished for me. 'That was the night he saw you at Milton's, right, and he said he had an appointment?'

I nodded, still confused.

'He was on his way to break up with her.' She paused for a

second, as if she could see this sinking in, all finally coming together. 'He wants to be with *you*, Macy. Now if it were me, I would have told you that night, but he's not like that. He wanted to be free, totally in the clear, before he let you know how he feels. He's just been waiting for you, Macy.'

'No,' I said.

'*Yes*. Now, I've been telling him to just come over here and tell you, and ask you if you feel the same way,' she said. 'But he's not like that. He has to do it in his own way. In his own time.'

Like the final question, I thought. *He wasn't waiting to torture me, or because he didn't know it. He just wanted to get it right. Whatever that means.*

Everyone was looking at me. Once, I thought, my life was private. Now the entire world was into my business, if not my heart. But, I thought, looking across their expectant faces, this wasn't really the whole world. Just mine.

'He came over today,' I said slowly, all of this sinking in. 'This morning.'

'So what happened?' Kristy asked.

I glanced at my mother, waiting for her to realize I'd broken her rules. Instead, she was just looking at me, her head slightly cocked to the side, as if she was seeing something in me she hadn't before.

'Nothing,' I said. 'I mean, he just asked me if this, the way things are now, was what I wanted.'

'And what did you say?'

'I said it was,' I told her.

'Macy!' Kristy smacked her hand to her forehead. 'God! What were you *thinking*?'

'I didn't know,' I told her. Then, more softly, to myself, I said, 'It's so unfair.'

Kristy shook her head. 'It's tragical.'

'It's time,' Delia said, nodding at the window. The rain had let up some, finally, and people were now starting to emerge from their cars, shutting doors and unfolding umbrellas. Regardless of everything else, the show had to go on. 'Let's get to work.'

Everyone started to move away from the window, towards their various tasks: Kristy picked up her tray of wine glasses, Bert and Delia headed towards the kitchen, and my mother moved to the mirror in the foyer, taking one last look at her face. Only Monica stayed where she was, staring out of the window as I tried, hard, to comprehend everything that had just happened.

'I can't believe this,' I said softly. 'It's too late.'

'It's never too late,' she said.

For a second, I was sure I'd imagined it. After a summer of monotone, one-word answers or no answers at all, here, from Monica, was a complete sentence.

'But it is,' I told her, turning to look at her. 'I don't think I'd even know what to do if I did have another chance. I mean, what could I . . .'

She shook her head. 'It's just one of those things,' she said. Her voice was surprisingly level and clear. 'You know, that just happen. You don't think or plan. You just do it.'

There was something familiar about this, but it took me a second to realize where I'd heard it before. Then I remembered:

it was what I'd said to her that night at the party, when I'd been trying to explain why I was holding Wes's hand.

'Monica!' Kristy yelled from the living room. 'There's a tray of cheese puffs in here with your name on it. Where are you?'

Monica turned from the window, starting across the foyer with her trademark slow shuffle. 'Wait,' I said, and she looked over her shoulder, back at me. I didn't know what to say. I was still in shock that she'd spoken at all, and wondered what other surprises she might have up her sleeve. 'Thanks for that. I mean, I appreciate it.'

She nodded. 'Mmm-hmmm,' she said, and then she turned her back and walked away.

Chapter TWENTY-ONE

I'd catered enough jobs to know the signs of a good party. You had to have plenty of good food, for one. A crowd that was relaxed and laughing a lot, for another. But then there was that other thing, the indefinable buzz of people talking and eating and communing, a palpable energy that makes little things like shredded tents or pouring rain or even the end of the world hardly noticeable. An hour in, my mother's party had all of these things, in spades. There was no question it was a success.

'Great party, Deborah!'

'Love the bistro idea!'

'These meatballs are divine!'

The compliments kept coming. My mother accepted each one gratefully, nodding and smiling as she moved among her guests. For the first time, it seemed to me that she was actually enjoying herself, not focusing on getting literature to every person or talking up the next phase, but instead just mingling with people, wine glass in hand. Every once in a while she'd pass behind me and I'd feel her hand on my back or my arm, but when I turned round to see if she needed me to do something, she'd have moved on, instead just glancing back over her shoulder to smile at me as she moved through the crowd.

My mother was okay. I was okay too. Or I would be, eventually. I knew one night wouldn't change everything between us, and that there was a lot – an entire year and a half's worth, actually – for us to discuss. For now, though, I just tried to focus on the moment, as much as I could. Which was working fine, until I saw Jason.

He'd just come in and was standing in the foyer, in his rain jacket, looking around for me. 'Macy,' he called out, and then he started over to me. I didn't move, just stood there as he got closer, until he was right in front of me. 'Hi.'

'Hi,' I said. I took a second to look at him: the clean-cut haircut, the conservative polo shirt tucked into his khakis. He looked just the same as he had the day he left, and I wondered if I did too. 'How are you?'

'Good.'

There was a burst of laughter from a group of people nearby, and we both turned at the sound of it, letting it fill the silence that followed. Finally he said, 'It's really good to see you.'

'You too.'

He was just standing there, looking at me, and I felt hopelessly awkward, not sure what to say. He stepped a bit closer, lowering his head nearer to mine, and said, 'Can we talk somewhere?'

I nodded. 'Sure.'

As we walked down the hallway to the kitchen, I was dimly aware that we were being watched. Sure that it was Kristy, glaring, or Monica, staring, I turned my head and was surprised to see my mother, standing by the buffet, her eyes following me as I passed. Jason glanced over and, seeing her, lifted his hand and waved. She nodded, smiling slightly, but kept her eyes on me, steady, until I rounded the corner and couldn't see her any more.

Once in the kitchen, I saw the back door was open. In all the commotion, I hadn't even noticed the rain stopping. As we stepped outside, everything was dripping and kind of cool, but the sky had cleared. A few people were outside smoking, others clumped in groups talking, their voices rising and falling. Jason and I found a spot on the stairs, away from everyone, and I leaned back, feeling the dampness of the rail against my legs.

'So,' Jason said, glancing around. 'This is quite a party.'

'You have no idea,' I told him. 'It's been crazy.' Over his head, I could see into the kitchen, where Delia was sliding another pan of crab cakes into the oven. Monica was leaning against the island, examining a split end, with her trademark bored expression.

'Crazy?' Jason said. 'How?'

I took a breath, thinking I would try to explain, then stopped myself. *Too much to tell*, I thought. 'Just a lot of disasters,' I said finally. 'But it's all okay now.'

My sister stepped through the door to the deck. She was talking loudly, and a group of people were trailing along behind her, clutching drinks and canapés in their hands. ' . . . represents a real dichotomy of art and salvage,' she was saying in her Art Major voice as she passed us on the stairs. 'These pieces are really compelling. Now, as you'll see in this first one, the angel is symbolic of the accessibility and limits of religion.'

Jason and I stepped back as her group followed along behind her, nodding and murmuring as their lesson began. When they disappeared round the side of the house, he said, 'Did she make those or something?'

I smiled. 'No,' I said. 'She's just a big fan.'

He leaned back, peering round the house at the angel, which Caroline and her people were now encircling. 'They are interesting,' he said, 'but I don't know about symbolic. They just seem like yard art to me.'

'Well, they are,' I said. 'Sort of. But they also have meaning, in their own way. At least Caroline thinks so.'

He looked at the angel again. 'I don't think the medium works well for the message,' he said. 'It's sort of distracting, actually. I mean, regardless of the loftiness of the vision, in the end it's just junk, right?'

I just looked at him, not sure what to say to this. 'Well,' I said, 'I guess it depends on how you look at it.'

He smiled at me. 'Macy,' he said, in a tone that for some reason made something prick at the back of my neck, 'junk is junk.'

I felt myself take a breath. *He doesn't know*, I told myself. *He has no idea, he's just making conversation.* 'So,' I said, 'you wanted to talk about something?'

'Oh. Right. Yes, I did.'

I stood there, waiting. Inside, the kitchen was empty now except for Bert, who was traying up a pan of meatballs, popping the occasional one in his mouth. He looked up, saw me watching him and smiled, sort of embarrassed. I smiled back, and Jason turned his head, looking behind him.

'Sorry,' I said. 'You were saying?'

He looked down at his hands. 'I just,' he began, then stopped, as if he'd thought of another, better way to phrase this thought. 'I know I handled things badly at the beginning of the summer, suggesting that break. But I'd really like for us to begin a conversation about our relationship and what, if we do decide to continue it, each of us would like to see it evolve into in the coming year.'

I was listening. I really was. But, even so, my mind kept picking up other things: the laughter from inside, the damp coolness of the air on the back of my neck, my sister's voice still talking about form and function and contrast.

'Well,' I said. 'I don't know, really.'

'That's okay,' Jason replied, nodding, as if this conversation was going exactly how he'd expected it to. 'I'm not entirely sure either. But I think that's where this dialogue should begin, really. With how we each feel, and what limits we feel need to be put in place before we make another commitment.'

'. . . a real sense of perspective,' Caroline was saying, 'with the artist making a clear commentary on the events that happen within the frame, and how the frame affects them.'

'What I was thinking,' Jason continued, apparently not as distracted by this as I was, 'was that we could each draw up a list of what we really want in a relationship. What we expect, what's important. And then, at a predetermined time, we'll sit down and go through them, seeing what corresponds.'

'A list,' I said.

'Yes,' he said, 'a list. That way, I figure, we'll have a written record of what we've agreed upon as our goals for our relationship. So, if problems arise, we'll be able to consult the lists, see which issue it corresponds to and work out a solution from there.'

I could still hear my sister talking, but her voice was fading as she led her group round the house. I said, 'But what if that doesn't work?'

Jason blinked at me. Then he said, 'Why wouldn't it?'

'Because,' I said.

He just looked at me. 'Because . . .'

'Because,' I repeated, as a breeze blew over us, 'sometimes things just happen. That aren't expected. Or on the list.'

'Such as?' he asked.

'I don't know,' I said, frustrated. 'That's the point. It would be out of the blue, taking us by surprise. Something we might not be prepared for.'

'But we will be prepared,' he said, confused. 'We'll have the list.'

I rolled my eyes. 'Jason,' I said.

'Macy, I'm sorry.' He stepped back, looking at me. 'I just don't understand what you're trying to say.'

And then it hit me: he didn't. He had no idea. And this thought was so ludicrous, so completely unreal, that I knew it just had to be true. For Jason, there was no unexpected, no surprises. His whole life was outlined carefully, in lists and sublists, just like the ones I'd helped him go through all those weeks ago.

'It's just . . .' I said, then stopped, shaking my head.

'It's just what?' He was waiting, genuinely wanting to know. 'Explain it to me.'

But I couldn't. I'd had to learn it my own way, and so had my mother. Jason would eventually, as well. No one could tell you: you just had to go through it on your own. If you were lucky, you came out on the other side and understood. If you didn't, you kept getting thrust back, retracing those steps, until you finally got it right.

'Macy?' he said. 'Please. Explain it to me.'

I took in a breath, trying to figure out a way to say there was just no way, but then, over his head, coming into the kitchen through the side door, I saw Wes. And I let out that breath and just looked at him.

He was running a hand through his hair, glancing around at the people grouped in the living room and on the other side of the island. As I watched, Delia came bustling in, carrying a trayful of empty glasses. She put it down, kissing his cheek, and they talked for a second, both of them surveying the party. He said something, and she shrugged, gesturing towards the living room. *You sure?* I saw him ask and she nodded, then squeezed his arm and turned to the oven door, pulling it open. Then he glanced outside, and saw me. And Jason. I tried to keep my eyes on him, willing him to just stay there for another minute, but he turned round and went out the side door, and I watched it fall shut behind him.

'Macy?' Caroline came round the side of the house. 'Can you come here a second?'

'Macy,' Jason asked. 'What –'

'Hold on,' I told him. I started across the deck, dodging around groups of people, and went down the other steps, coming out right by the side door. I could see Wes at the end of the driveway.

'Do you know anything about this?' Caroline asked. For a second I thought she meant Wes, until I turned round to see her and her group standing in front of a sculpture.

'What about it?' I asked, distracted. I'd lost sight of him now.

'It's just,' she said, looking up at it, 'I've never seen it before. It's not one of mine.'

'Macy?' Jason came up behind me. 'I really think we should –'

But I wasn't listening. Not to him. Not to Caroline, who was still circling round the sculpture, making her Art Major noises. Not to the sounds of the party floating through the window. All I could hear was the slight tinkling noise of the sculpture as it moved, this new angel. She was standing with her feet apart, her hands clasped at her chest. Her eyes were sea glass, circled with washers, her mouth a key, turned upwards. Her halo was circled with tiny hearts in hands. But most striking, most different, were the things that arched up over her head, made of thin aluminum, cut with strong peaks at the top, sweeping curves at the bottom, lined with tiny bells, which made the chiming noise I was hearing. That we could all hear.

'I don't get it,' Caroline said, bemused. 'She's the only one with wings. Why is that?'

There were so many questions in life. You couldn't ever have all the answers. But I knew this one.

'It's so she can fly,' I said. And then I started to run.

• • •

I'd thought it might be like my dreams. But it wasn't. Running came back to me as easily as anything else that had once been everything to you. The first few steps were hard; it took me a second to catch my breath, but then I found my pace, and everything fell away, until there was nothing but me and what lay ahead, growing closer every second. Wes.

By the time I reached him, I was breathless. Red-faced. And my heart was thumping hard enough in my chest that, at first, it was all I could hear. He turned round just as I got to him, looking surprised, and for a second neither of us said anything as I struggled to catch my breath.

'Macy,' he said. I could tell he was shocked by my running, by the very fact that I was standing there in front of him, gasping for air. 'What –'

'I'm sorry.' I put my hand up, palm facing him, and took another deep breath. 'But there's been a change.'

He blinked at me. 'A change,' he repeated.

I nodded. 'In the rules.'

It took him a second: he had no idea what I was talking about. Then, slowly, his face relaxed. 'Ah,' he said. 'The rules.'

'Yes.'

'I wasn't notified,' he pointed out.

'Well, it was pretty recent,' I said.

'As in . . .'

'As in, effective right now.'

Wes ran a hand through his hair and I saw the heart and hand slip into view, then disappear again. I had so much to tell him, I didn't even know where to start. Or maybe I did.

'Macy,' he said softly, looking at me closely. 'You don't have to –'

I shook my head. 'The change,' I said. 'Ask me about the change.'

He leaned back on his heels, sliding his hands into his pockets. 'Okay,' he said, after a second. 'What's the change?'

'It's been decided,' I told him, taking another breath, 'that there's another step to winning the game. And that is that in order for me to really win, I have to answer the question you passed on, that night in the truck. Only then is it final.'

'The question I passed on,' he repeated.

I nodded. 'That's the rule.'

I knew, in the silence that followed, that anything could happen here. It might be too late: again, I might have missed my chance. But I would at least know I tried, that I took my heart and extended my hand, whatever the outcome.

'Okay,' he said. He took a breath. 'What would you do, if you could do anything?'

I took a step towards him, closing the space between us. 'This,' I said. And then I kissed him.

Kissed him. There, in the middle of the street, as the world went on around us. Behind me, I knew Jason was still waiting for an explanation, my sister was still lecturing and that angel still had her eyes skyward, waiting to fly. As for me, I was just trying to get it right, whatever that meant. But now I finally felt I was on my way. Everyone had a forever, but, given a choice, this would be mine. The one that began in this moment, with Wes, in a kiss that took my breath away, then gave it back – leaving me astounded, amazed and, most of all, alive.

Chapter TWENTY-TWO

'Macy. Wake up.'

I rolled over, pulling my pillow over my face. 'No,' I said, my voice muffled. 'Another hour.'

'No way.' I felt fingers flicking my bare feet. 'Hurry up. I'll be outside.'

Still half asleep, I heard him leave the room, then, a second later, the screen door slammed shut behind him. For a second I just lay there, so tempted to let sleep pull me in and under, back to dreaming. But then I pushed the pillow off my face and sat up in bed, looking out the window beside me. The sky was clear and blue, the waves crashing close in. Another nice day.

I got up, then pulled on my shorts and jog bra and my T-shirt, rolling the elastic off my wrist and using it to tie my hair up in a ponytail. I was still yawning as I crossed my bedroom and stepped out into the main part of the house, where my sister was sitting at the table, flipping through a magazine.

'You know what I've been thinking,' she said, not even looking up, as if we'd been talking and were just picking up where we'd left off, 'is that we could really use a chiminea here.'

'A what?' I said, bending down to grab my shoes off the floor.

'A chiminea.' She turned a page of her magazine, propping her chin in her hands. 'It's an outside chimney, very primal, really makes a statement. What do you think?'

I just smiled, sliding the screen door open. 'Sounds great,' I said. 'Just great.'

I stepped out onto the porch, taking in the day's first breath of cool, salty air. My mother, who was sitting in her deck chair, coffee mug on the table beside her, turned round and looked at me.

'Good morning,' she said, as I bent down and kissed her cheek. 'Such dedication.'

'Not me,' I told her. 'I wanted to sleep in.'

She smiled, then picked up her coffee mug, taking the folder from underneath it and spreading it out on her legs. 'Have fun,' she said.

'You too.'

I stretched my arms over my head as I started down the stairs to the beach, squinting in the already bright sun. Now that the house was done, we spent most weekends here. At the beginning, it had been hard to walk through the door, and I'd cried a lot the first few times, missing my dad. But it was easier now. Even with all the new fabrics and floorings, everything he loved about the beach house – the moose, the fishing poles by the door, his beloved grill – was still there, which made it feel like he was too.

There were other changes as well. My mother did come down on the weekends, but she always brought some work and her laptop, and her cell phone still rang constantly, although we were training her to let the voicemail pick up once in a while. As for me, I was running again, but now I didn't pay attention to times or distance, instead focusing on how it felt just to be in motion, knowing it wasn't about the finish line but how I got there that mattered.

And my mother and I were talking more, although it hadn't been easy at first. The trips to the beach had helped. While we sometimes had Wes with us, or Kristy, I'd come to appreciate the rides we took alone as well. During the long stretches of quiet two-lane highway, with the sun setting in the distance, it was somehow easier to say things aloud, and regardless of what was said, we just kept moving towards that horizon.

Caroline came down most weekends as well, Wally in tow, and pottered around the house examining her handiwork and musing about other changes she might make. Lately, though, she'd turned her attention to the house two lots down, which had recently gone on the market. It was a fixer-upper, just in need of a little TLC, she told us, as she spread out pictures for us to peruse, and she and Wally had been talking about buying a place at the beach. So many Befores, but I knew my sister. She could always see the After. Of all of us, she was the best at that.

Now, I walked over the dunes, the wind whipping around me. When I looked back at the house, I saw Caroline was out on the porch now, sitting on the new bench, most likely already picturing that chiminea. She and my mom waved, and I waved back, then turned my attention to the short stretch of beach I had to cover to catch up with that figure in the distance. As I started to run, feeling my feet get under me. I listened for the voice I knew so well, the one I always heard at the beginning.

Good girl, Macy! You're doing great! You know the first few steps are the hardest part!

They were. Sometimes I felt so out of sync, it was all I could do not to quit after a few strides. But I kept on, as I did now. I had to, to get to the next part, this part, where I finally caught up with Wes, my shadow aligning itself with his, and he turned to look at me, pushing his hair out of his eyes.

'Nice form,' he said.

'Likewise.'

We ran for a second in silence. Up ahead, all I could see was beach and sky.

'You ready?' he asked.

I nodded. 'Go ahead. It's your turn.'

'Okay,' he said. 'Let's see . . .'

We'd start slow, the way we always did, because the run, and the game, could go on for a while. Maybe even forever.

That was the thing. You just never knew. Forever was so many different things. It was always changing; it was what everything was really all about. It was twenty minutes, or a hundred years, or just this instant, or any instant I wished would last and last. But there was only one truth about forever that really mattered, and that was this: it was happening. Right then, as I ran with Wes into that bright sun, and every moment afterwards. Look, there. Now. Now. Now.

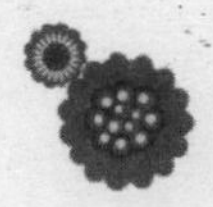

Meet Sarah Dessen

Did you always want to be a writer?
As far back as I remember, I've been writing. I've always had this wild imagination, and I love to embellish stories to make them more interesting. When I left school I wrote like crazy. At times it seemed stupid – I was broke and there was no guarantee that anything would come of it. Luckily, it did. But even if I hadn't sold a book I'd still be writing. It becomes part of you, just something you do.

Who were your favourite authors as a child and who are you into now?
I really liked Judy Blume and Lois Lowry. Currently I'm really into Anne Tyler, who wrote *The Accidental Tourist*. John Irving's *A Prayer for Owen Meany* is probably my favourite book right now.

What was your favourite subject at school?
English. Anything to do with writing and reading. I'd been writing forever, but I got frustrated in school because there were rules about what you were Supposed To Write. I wanted to be able to make everything up, even then.

Where do you get your ideas?
This is a hard question, and there's no single answer. Usually I start with something that did happen to me or to someone I know, and build on it from there. There are so many stories out there waiting to be told. You just have to keep your eyes open.

What's your best advice for aspiring writers?
I think, first of all, you have to believe in yourself and your work. Writing can be really solitary, so you have to be not only your own harshest critic but also your own biggest fan. But what really matters above all is that you are writing. When I'm working on a book I'm at the computer every day. Work out what time of day you get your best work done, and try to write at that same time, every day.